Praise for *Deal with the Devil*

"Compelling characters, white-knuckle action, and deceptively smooth world-building make this first Mercenary Librarians book a satisfying and cinematic escape."

—*Booklist* (starred review)

"Like something out of an Avengers flick, [*Deal with the Devil*] is a solid sci-fi debut with unforgettable characters."

—*BookPage* (starred review)

"Enhanced supersoldiers, hot romance, and a dangerous rescue mission make this SF series opener a postapocalyptic roller-coaster ride. . . . The chemistry and tension between the romantic leads have never been better plotted or paced."

—*Kirkus Reviews*

"This postapocalyptic tale of espionage and romance will have readers eager to know what happens next."

—*Publishers Weekly*

"A high-action, high-stakes SF romance. Intriguing characters, tragic backgrounds, and a few twists comprise a strong launch to this new series."

—*Library Journal*

TOR BOOKS BY KIT ROCHA

Deal with the Devil
The Devil You Know

THE DEVIL YOU KNOW

A MERCENARY LIBRARIANS NOVEL

KIT ROCHA

TOR

A TOM DOHERTY ASSOCIATES BOOK

NEW YORK

THE DEVIL YOU KNOW

Maps by Jon Lansberg

A Tor Book
Published by Tom Doherty Associates
120 Broadway
New York, NY 10271

www.tor-forge.com

The Library of Congress Cataloging-in-Publication Data is available upon request.

ISBN 978-1-250-20938-2 (trade paperback)
ISBN 978-1-250-78148-2 (hardcover)
ISBN 978-1-250-20937-5 (ebook)

First Edition: August 2021

Printed in the United States of America

0 9 8 7 6 5 4 3 2 1

To Claire and Sarah.
You believed we could do it.
So we did.

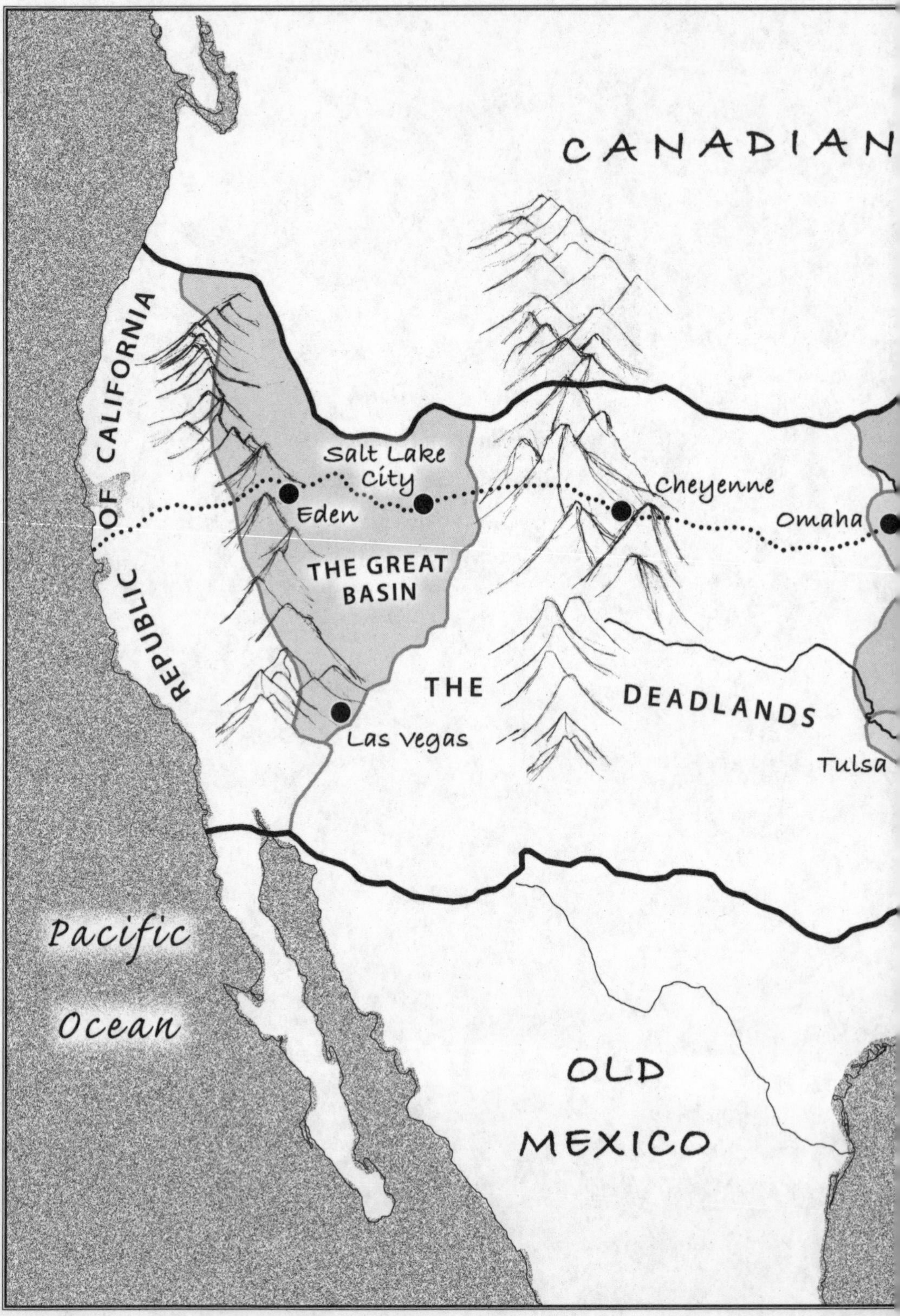
CANADIAN
REPUBLIC OF CALIFORNIA
Salt Lake City
Eden
Cheyenne
Omaha
THE GREAT BASIN
THE DEADLANDS
Las Vegas
Tulsa
Pacific Ocean
OLD MEXICO

TERRITORIES
The Twin Cities
New York
NEW ENGLAND
OUTLAW TERRITORY
Washington
MOUNTAIN COMMUNES
Franklin Center
HE HEARTLANDS
OUTLAW TERRITORY
THE EAST COAST
MISSISSIPPI
ADING FAMILY
Atlanta
TECHCORPS
Atlantic
Ocean
FISHING CLANS
Port of Baton Rouge
Gulf of Mexico

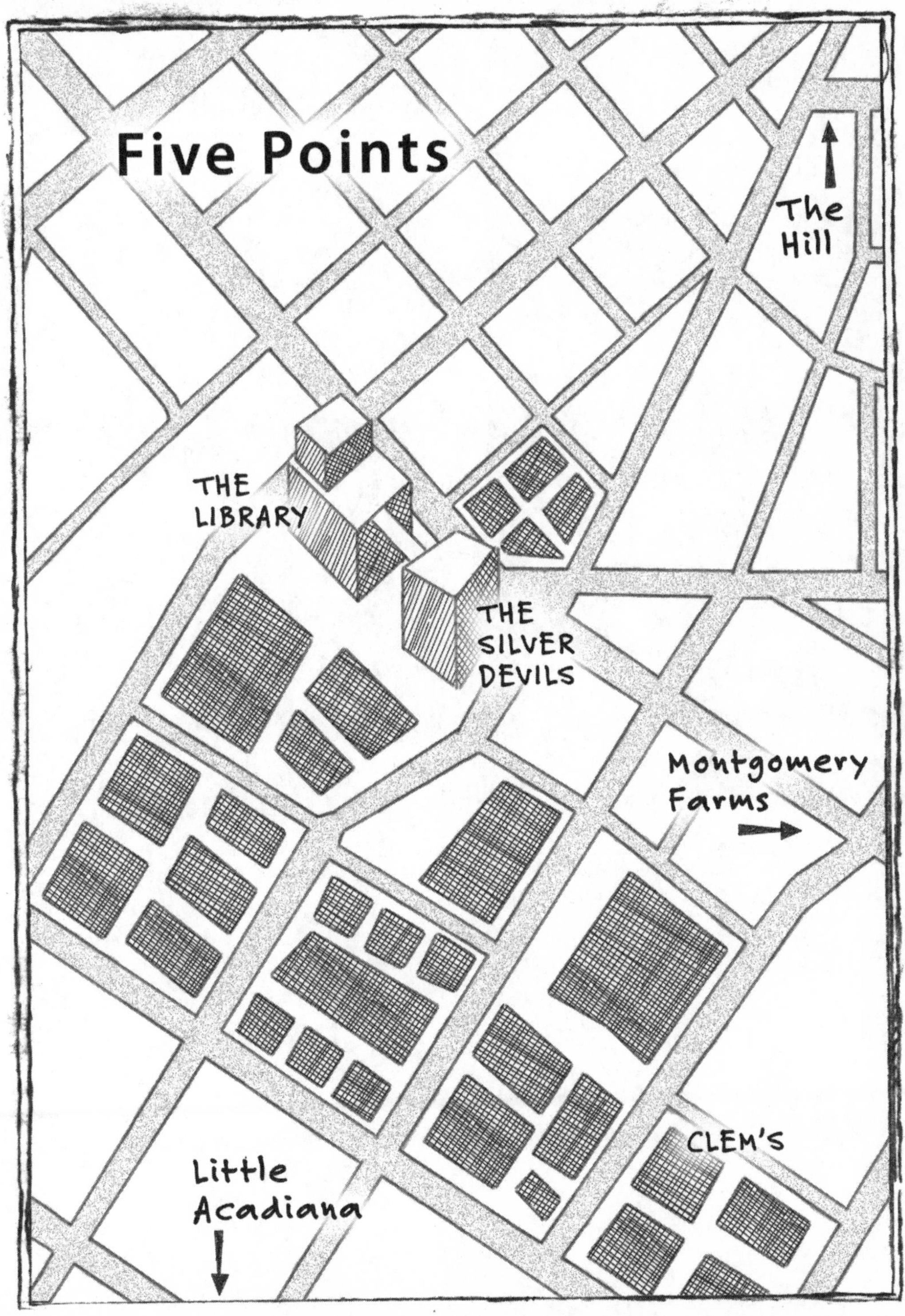
Five Points
The Hill
THE LIBRARY
THE SILVER DEVILS
Montgomery Farms
CLEM'S
Little Acadiana

THE DEVIL YOU KNOW

June 1st, 2069

I met my data courier today. If hell exists, I've surely secured my spot there for agreeing to this.

The girl is all of seven years old and already fluent in six languages. She's studying astronomy and just started integral calculus. The scientists are excited. Few of their subjects have adapted to the procedure as well as DC-031.

I'm supposed to forge an emotional bond with her over the final year of her training in order to ensure her loyalty. It would be so easy to rationalize. The child deserves a parental figure. I can almost convince myself that following protocol would be a kindness to her.

But there's no kindness in what I'm about to do. The TechCorps have already stolen her childhood. On her eighth birthday, I'll be conscripting her into a war she can't possibly comprehend, one that will very possibly kill us both.

Any warmth I could give her would be a self-indulgent lie. I am not her mother. I am not here to save her. I'm a soldier in a silent rebellion, and she's my best hope of surviving long enough to see it through.

Perhaps someday she'll forgive me for turning her into collateral damage.

The Recovered Journal of Birgitte Skovgaard

ONE

Mozart was the perfect music for a heist.

Over the years, Maya had made an in-depth study of the ideal music for every moment. Too many people considered pre-Flare orchestral music to be the sole domain of the rich assholes and their fancy ballrooms up on the Hill. To them, it was the music of tuxedos and gowns and placid recitals. Despite being raised by those rich assholes, Maya knew the truth.

Elfman was excellent for a fun, rollicking bar fight. Zimmer was the only choice for a shoot-out. Holst had all the melodrama necessary for an elaborate jailbreak. She liked Tchaikovsky on stakeouts and Williams for safecracking.

But to accompany the adrenaline of a daring heist?

Mozart. Requiem in D minor. Dies Irae.

Accept no substitutions.

"Status report."

"Hallway's clear, boss," Conall replied from beside her. "I'll have the door unlocked by the time you get there."

"Acknowledged."

Conall's fingers clacked noisily over his keyboard, echoing in the confined space of the van. He swore the sound of the antiquated tech soothed him. After a couple missions with him, Maya knew the unique *click* of most of the keys on the damn thing.

N-E-T-S-T . . .

Exhaling, Maya deliberately shifted her concentration back to the music. The choir chanted with escalating intensity, the Latin so familiar that it melted into background noise. As the sound of Conall's typing faded, her brain stopped trying to interpret either the keystrokes or the lyrics.

She resumed her survey of the security cameras, scanning the facility for any guard a few minutes ahead of his rounds or any scientist who'd decided to stay late. She'd memorized their routines during mission prep, setting their complicated schedule to music. The guard in C-block rounded the corner to the soaring sounds of the violins. Trumpets announced a distant perimeter check. She could feel the rhythm of the building, the movement of the people inside.

A complicated, dangerous dance. Her very favorite kind.

"I can't believe I still haven't talked you out of the Mozart," Conall muttered as he switched to swiping at a display tablet to his left. "I'm telling you, if you have to stick to the old, extremely dead guys, there are better options."

Maya made an amused noise as she watched the perimeter guard swipe his

ID at the farthest checkpoint. A few seconds ahead of the music, but nothing too dire yet. "You want me to switch to an even older, deader guy."

"Respect the Haydn." Conall grimaced. "I mean, if we *have* to go classical. I don't understand why you're obsessed with it. Some nice seventies techno, now . . ."

Her own lips twitched into a grimace. Techno from the 2070s was good for exactly one thing—thrashing it out in a throng of people in one of the dance clubs that lined the perimeter. Some nights after she and Dani came home, she'd lie in bed staring at the ceiling, her heart keeping time with the throbbing bass that seemed to echo inside her head.

At least the echoes drove the voices away.

On the screen in front of her, the A-block guard swiped his key at his checkpoint. She counted the seconds until the chorus lifted in the next verse.

Ingemisco, tamquam reus . . .

Her brain provided the translation out of habit. *I sigh, like the guilty one.* Latin had been the first language they'd locked into her brain, the first she'd internalized to the point of effortless comprehension. Irritating, since she'd mostly seen it in technical documents. Not even scientists sat around using conversational Latin.

Maya could, though. That was what the TechCorps had built her for. Maya could speak dozens of languages with the fluent ease of a native speaker. She'd been an expert in astronomy by nine, advanced mathematics by ten, programming languages by twelve, and cryptography by sixteen. She'd been picking away at biochemistry when . . .

When.

Culpa rubet vultus meus . . .

Maya shuddered as the translation drifted through her. *Guilt reddens my face.*

She wasn't the one who should feel guilty about the abrupt termination of her education. No, that burden lay on the shoulders of the woman who had raised her—Birgitte Skovgaard, vice president of Behavior Analysis for the TechCorps. As an executive in the sprawling corporate conglomerate that ruled most of the Southeast, Birgitte had enjoyed almost unfathomable power. She could have lived a soft life of luxury. Instead, she'd used Maya's perfect memory to organize a rebellion.

A *failed* rebellion. Biochemistry still made Maya think of blood and death and fear and pain and all the reasons she hated the fancy fuckers up on the Hill, in their expensive suits, souls empty as their eyes glittered with greed.

There was a reason she'd never gone back to studying it.

Supplicanti parce, Deus.

Maya tapped her comms. "The A-block guard is ten seconds behind schedule on his rounds. Watch the corridors up ahead."

Nina's voice whispered into her ear. "Got it. Window's narrowing."

Ten seconds might be enough to blow their whole plan, especially if the

B-block guard showed up early. Maya watched the corridor for him, her heart rate quickening with the pulse of the music. "I always do crimes to classical music," she told Conall, her foot bouncing lightly from the increased adrenaline. "It's my personal *fuck you* to all the assholes up on the Hill."

Conall snorted. "Can't argue with that. The suits would be appalled. How utterly gauche of you."

Yeah, Conall understood. Neither of them had attended the fancy parties in the elegant ballrooms frequented by the TechCorps elite, but they'd been raised by the assholes. Trained and molded into perfect tools with finely honed edges. Wielded without compassion.

Confutatis maledictis,

Flammis acribus addictis . . .

"Once the cursed have been silenced, sentenced to acrid flames . . ." Maya translated under her breath.

"Huh?"

"Nothing." God, she'd love to burn the TechCorps to the ground. In lieu of an apocalyptic rain of fire, though, she'd take the crime. Every job they pulled, every law they broke, every bit of pre-Flare data they liberated, every credit they earned and funneled back into their community . . .

Pulling heists to fund a library might not be everyone's idea of a righteous good time, but Maya lived for those middle fingers thrust firmly in the TechCorps' faces.

The B-block guard passed his checkpoint right in time with the music, and Maya started to exhale with relief. But a smudge of movement on the bottom right camera caught her attention, and she switched the image to full screen.

"Oh, *shit*."

Her tone caught Conall's attention. He leaned over, and together they watched as the perimeter guard broke from his route and headed for the parking lot.

Straight toward them.

Conall checked his watch and bit off a curse. "They're almost to the package. I need to pop the doors and manage the cameras."

Maya twisted in her seat to snatch up her shiny, new stun gun. Rafe had given her this one and trained her extensively in its use. His passion for combat training made even Nina look reasonable, but Maya couldn't fault his zeal now.

"I got this," she assured Conall, then tapped her earpiece. "B-block guard's right on time. I'm stepping out to deal with an issue, but you should have a straight shot."

"Tell the issue I said hi," Dani murmured.

"Remember the best target areas," Rafe chimed in.

Maya rolled her eyes. As if *remembering* had ever been her problem.

She reached for the door to the van, but Conall stopped her with a hand on her arm. "If you don't think you can handle this . . ."

He meant well. So had Rafe. A month together had been enough time for their blended teams to fall into a routine, but not enough for the Silver Devils to stop worrying about her.

She supposed she couldn't blame them. They were literal supersoldiers. Rogue supersoldiers, no less, former members of the fearsome Protectorate. In all of Maya's years on the Hill, she'd done her best to avoid members of the TechCorps' standing army. The biochemical implants hardwired into their brains gave them unbelievable speed, enough strength to lift a car, and the stamina to go days without rest or sleep.

Of course, they weren't the only ones with superpowers. Nina was the product of a genetic engineering project that produced soldiers with all the same perks but none of the biochemical drawbacks. And Dani was faster than all of them put together, thanks to her rewired nervous system. She'd escaped from the TechCorps, too—but not before they'd put her through their brutal Executive Security training.

The difference was that Nina and Dani never treated Maya like she couldn't handle her shit. But Maya wasn't tall and commanding and capable of lifting a car like Nina. She wasn't a ripped, back-flipping, not-so-former assassin like Dani. She was soft and squishy, something Conall and the others couldn't seem to forget.

They'd learn. She'd make sure they learned.

"I've got this," she promised him, squashing down her irritation. "No supersoldiers out there, just a nosy guard. I can handle a nosy guard."

"If you need me . . ."

"I will not be subtle about screaming for help." She patted his hand, then gave him a push. "Go on, you have a job to do. They're depending on you."

With a final worried look, Conall turned back to his work. Maya checked the camera for the guard's position one last time and then slipped from the van.

The night was warm and muggy. The start of September had brought no relief from the relentless humidity, and sweat beaded on Maya's skin almost immediately. Atlanta rarely cooled off before late October these days, though when winter hit, it would hit hard. She was almost looking forward to waking up to frost on the windows.

For now, she had to deal with the stagnant night air. She leaned back against the van. The approaching footsteps were a whisper across asphalt, the leather soles crunching across fine gravel.

She tried to focus on the *sounds*, on what they told her about the world around her and the obstacles in her path. She could tell the guard was favoring one foot by the uneven crunch of gravel. She could tell that he wasn't scared by the unhurried pace of his steps. She could tell the sound was getting louder.

She had no fucking idea how close he was.

Conall swore she should be able to tell. He'd given her shit about it just last week, swearing that anyone who could calculate trajectories in her head or crack a vault combination by the sound of the keystrokes should be able to accurately judge distance.

If her genetically enhanced brain had the ability to triangulate distances from the echoes or vibrations or whatever, no one had given her the key to unlocking that superpower.

The footsteps paused, so loud that he *had* to be near the front of the van. Probably peering in the windows. The front seat looked innocent enough, and the tinted windows hid the rolling command station in the back. The steps resumed, and Maya forced out a silent breath as she rolled her shoulders, trying to keep her limbs loose for an attack.

The second the guard rounded the van, she jumped him.

"What the—?"

She rammed her stun gun into his side and smashed the button, reducing his words to a grunt. Not exactly the shriek of pain Maya expected, and she had a half second to panic before a giant arm flailed at her. She twisted out of the way of a meaty fist, but pain exploded through her face as he clipped her with an elbow.

At least she'd been trained for this. She stumbled back a step but didn't lose her grip on her weapon. The eye he'd hit was watering, but through the tears she recognized his uniform—a thick polyester blend popular with people too cheap to equip their guards with real body armor. It wouldn't do shit to stop a gun or a knife, but it would make it harder for someone to turn his own Taser against him.

Of course he wouldn't go down easy.

The perimeter guard was still shaking off his confusion. No doubt he was staring at Maya—young, half his size, with a body that was a lot more soft curves than hard muscle—and wondering what the hell was going on. She probably didn't look like the kind of person who jumped security guards outside highly secure facilities.

In fact, she looked like what she was. A woman who spent most of her time scanning books, obsessing over metadata, freeze-drying food, teaching people how to use their tech, and sitting up half the night swearing at antiquated video file formats.

She looked harmless. That was her secret weapon.

Maya didn't give him a chance to collect his thoughts. She lunged, aiming the stun gun at the largest expanse of bare skin she could find. He moved at the last second, swatting her hand away from his neck with enough force to leave her fingers numb.

Ignoring the discomfort, Maya used the momentum of her lunge to drive her booted foot down on his toes. She had a fraction of a second to worry they'd be steel-toed, but her heel crushed down on leather, and he howled and flailed. Dancing back would save her face, but driving forward—

Instinct made the decision for her. She took the hit to the face, hissing with pain. But she was inside his guard now, too close for him to stop her.

Her stun gun hit his neck with a crackle, and it was all over. His body convulsed, and she stumbled back out of the path of destruction as he went down with all the grace of a felled tree.

"Fuck." With the guard down, Maya took a second to wipe tears from her stinging eye. She'd have a shiner tomorrow, which would only make everyone more annoying and protective. As if they didn't frequently come back riddled with bullets or bruised to hell and back.

Supersoldiers were *exhausting* hypocrites.

"Maya?" The concern in Conall's tone was palpable.

She tapped her ear. "I'm fine. Guard's down. Just gotta stash him somewhere."

"Good job." Knox's voice always managed to sound deadly serious, even at a low whisper. "We're about to secure the package. Be ready."

Shit. The fight must have taken longer than she'd realized. Maya reached down, hooked her hands under the man's armpits, and grunted with the effort it took to drag him a mere foot from the van.

"Of course no one's running out to help me now," she muttered, bracing herself to pull him again. The nearest cars were a good twenty feet away, which had seemed like nothing before she started trying to drag dead weight.

And it's your own damn fault, taunted an inner voice. *If you hadn't overruled Knox, Gray could have dropped him before he ever even knew you were here.*

During mission prep, Knox had raised the possibility of Gray finding a vantage point where he could guard the van. Maya had been the one to protest—they wouldn't have held Gray back from the main assault just to watch over Conall, and she'd be damned if she let Knox and his squad get into the habit of acting like she needed special protection.

All perfectly logical. And she *hadn't* needed protection. The unconscious security guard at her feet was proof. She didn't need a babysitter watching her through a sniper scope, ready to leap in and save her lest she break a nail—or take a stray elbow to the face. Honestly, who the hell felt *better* knowing a broody sniper was tracking their every move?

You would, whispered that traitorous inner voice.

Maya stomped on that thought with a vicious mental boot and turned her attention back to getting her assailant's limp body to cover.

The parking lot suddenly seemed a lot bigger than it had before, and it was riddled with cracks that were just begging to trip her up. She supposed even rich, evil scientist outposts didn't have the resources to keep asphalt in top repair.

Roads seemed like the last priority for most people these days, though the old-timers around Five Points insisted that the roads had been crap even before the Flares. Some swore they'd grown up watching sinkholes open up and swallow entire highways full of cars. The city had tried to keep up with maintenance, but road infrastructure had fallen by the wayside after solar flares had caused the whole damn country to collapse right in the middle of an unprecedented famine.

People who'd survived the dark days always had a certain *look* in their eyes. It had been almost fifty years since the lights had gone off and the world had changed, but some of them would still look at you like it had all happened yesterday, like time didn't mean anything when the pain cut that deep. They remembered the panic, the fear. The brutal winters without access to heat. The sweltering summers when neighbors dropped dead of heatstroke.

They remembered the hunger. The Energy Wars had shaken the country, and the second Dust Bowl had brought it to its knees. The solar flares that swept the globe in '42 might have struck the death blow to the faltering federal government, but they weren't what killed people.

The famine had done that. It lasted for a decade, right up until the TechCorps and its corporate partners had established the Heartlands irrigation program. Food started to trickle back into Atlanta after that—but only through the TechCorps. Soon, they were the only reliable source of clean water. Electricity. Communication.

The TechCorps had demonstrated how easy it was to take over a region without fighting. All you had to do was own everything people needed to survive.

Well. That, and be heartless enough to withhold it until they fell in line.

"Fuckers," Maya muttered, stepping over another fault in the asphalt before dragging the limp body after her.

"Almost there." Nina's quiet words drifted over the comms. "Couple of close calls, but we're still undetected."

Maya heaved again and imagined what was going down inside the building. The team would be slipping through the halls right now, expertly exploiting the razor-thin gaps between patrols, relying on Conall to shield their passage from the cameras and the algorithms that ran the security system. That was how Nina preferred to operate. In and out, like a ghost. Less attention meant less danger. Get the mission done and get home in one piece.

Knox would be in the lead. He would assess each tiny shift in their master plan and adjust their strategy accordingly, with Nina at his side, ready to crack any safe or lock. Rafe was the muscle, capable of ripping a door off its hinges—or a head off a body, if it came to that—while Dani ranged ahead of them like a ghost, her speed making her the perfect scout.

And, of course, Gray would be guarding their backs. He might be most comfortable with his sniper rifle, but give him a handgun and he became a protective wall. Chaos could be erupting all around him, and he'd quietly assess the situation, decide who needed to be shot, and swiftly and efficiently get it done.

Maya worried a lot less about everyone when Gray was around.

This is the one," Knox said. "427-D."

"Retinal scan paired with voice recognition. You'll have to pop it." Maya could hear the grin in Dani's voice. "Seventeen seconds."

"My record is nineteen," Nina protested.

"Don't care. I've got fifty on it. You in, Morales?"

"Any time, sugar pie. My money's on twenty-three."

"Sure," Maya muttered into her comm. "You two just keep foreplaying while I'm dragging around a body twice my size."

"Focus," came Knox's firm command. "We're almost out."

Sweat dripped down Maya's spine. Her arms were starting to ache, and her face wasn't feeling much better. The perimeter guard was actually getting heavier. She winced as his boots scraped across the gravel, even though she knew no one was close enough to hear.

Well, no one except Conall. But since he wasn't leaping out of the van to help her now, she got a better hold on the guard and continued dragging. If she made it through this, she'd start lifting weights. That would probably make Nina happy. Rafe, too. Maya wouldn't even bitch about the additional training time.

Next week. She'd start next week. For a few days, she was gonna eat ice cream and pout about her poor face.

She settled for running through a brief dissociation exercise until the ache in her muscles faded to a nagging buzz. Definitely *not* her favorite solution. Numbness was a bandage over a jagged wound—thin and temporary. Sensory input didn't go away just because she tricked her brain into not noticing it, and reconnecting with the world tended to sting twice as bad.

But sometimes you needed to get a job done and pay the price later.

She finally reached the two cars parked at the edge of the lot. Three more shoulder-punishing heaves tucked the unconscious guard neatly between them, out of sight until shift change, by which point Maya and the rest of the team would be far, far away.

Good enough.

"I'm in," Nina murmured.

"Sixteen point five two." Dani's voice vibrated with triumph. "You owe me fifty bucks, Morales."

"Add it to my tab."

A beep tickled Maya's ears, followed by the whispering slide of a metal door opening. Then silence, heavy and loud, more than the mere absence of sound.

"This isn't a vault," Gray muttered. "It's a fucking cell."

"Over here." All traces of victorious glee had bled from Dani's tone. Now, she sounded breathless, almost . . .

Stricken?

Shit. Anything that could rattle Dani was *bad*. Apocalyptically bad.

"Grab and go," Knox said tersely.

"But Cap—"

"Move."

A scuffle of boots. Heavy breaths. They were falling back to a fast retreat, which wasn't likely to be quiet *or* invisible.

Shit, shit, *shit.*

Maya bolted across the parking lot and slid open the van door. "Which exit?"

Shouts and the brash, hard sound of gunfire erupted through the earpiece. Conall swore and dove into the front seat of the van. Maya slid into his chair and cycled through the camera feeds until she caught Rafe's back disappearing around a corner as Knox and Nina laid down cover fire.

The gunfire continued over comms, their team too busy to answer her question. But they didn't need to. Knox had planned for a dizzying number of contingencies, and Maya knew which one he was enacting now.

"West side!" she shouted to Conall. "Get to the loading dock!"

"On it."

The tires squealed as Conall rocketed the van into high gear. Everything that wasn't bolted down slid across the table. Maya clutched at a handle welded to the frame as the van went up on two wheels and the speakers blared a choir chanting about the fires of hell.

She was going to have to rethink her entire musical methodology, because Mozart was entirely too stressful for a car chase.

They rounded the side of the building to the sight of the team spilling out of an open bay door in the loading area, pursued by a squad of security guards. Everyone was clustered around Rafe, who carried a blanket-wrapped bundle in his arms.

"Oh my fucking—"

Shock stole the rest of Maya's words as Conall turned so hard that the van skidded across the asphalt. Her heart jumped into her throat, but she held on as they screeched to a stop.

They'd never had to leave a site hot before, but everyone knew their places. Knox and Gray piled into the front next to Conall, with Gray riding literal shotgun. Rafe clambered through the back doors, and Nina covered them by firing off three more shots.

Dani was suddenly *there*, gripping one of the handles on the ceiling of the van as she fired past Nina's head. Their leader dove into the van as Conall hit the gas, and Maya caught the back of Nina's jacket and held her steady as they tore out of the parking lot, bullets *pinging* off the van's reinforced siding.

Rafe curled himself protectively around the bundle, and the blanket slipped to reveal shorn, dark hair, a pale face, and huge, terrified eyes.

The package was a fucking kid.

TECHCORPS PROPRIETARY
INTERNAL COMMUNICATIONS

Skovgaard: I must reiterate my concerns over clearing Dillon Walker so soon after his squad's involvement in the Ration Day Massacre. The rest of his team is exhibiting signs of considerable post-traumatic stress.

Jenkins: 66–221 is a sniper. He wasn't in the middle of it like the rest of them.

Skovgaard: Most accepted research acknowledges the paradoxical intimacy of a sniper's job. Staring through a scope can inflict trauma every bit as profound as that experienced through hand-to-hand combat. His lack of reaction concerns me.

Jenkins: It should make you grateful. We're short-staffed as it is, and the food riots aren't going to stop until the Heartlands irrigation project gets going. We need every soldier in the streets.

Skovgaard: If I clear him, it will be with my strong reservations duly noted.

Jenkins: Whatever makes you happy, Birgitte.

Department of Behavior and Analysis
Server Log, Date: 2062–04–07

TWO

Gray really, *really* wanted a cigarette.

It didn't matter that he hadn't so much as touched one in months. He still reached for his empty pocket in stressful situations. And this most certainly qualified.

They'd gone in on a retrieval mission, expecting a weapons cache or maybe some black-market research or medical supplies. Instead, they'd busted in and found a kid, no more than seven or eight years old, cowering in a dark corner of a cell.

Gray had done a lot of terrible things in his career, and kidnapping was well-established on that list. But he'd thought he and the rest of the Silver Devils had left that life behind when they bailed on the Protectorate, the private police force-slash-army that functioned as the TechCorps' enforcers.

Maybe this was some sort of cosmic lesson, a message from the universe. *Run. Hide. But the Protectorate is part of you now. It always will be.*

All the activity in the warehouse centered around the table in the middle of it—and the child seated on a high stool. In the hours since their return, she'd been bathed, changed, fed, and stared at in unrelenting horror.

Not exactly the most relaxing or reassuring situation for a kid.

Nina had slid a plate of cookies and a glass of milk in front of the girl, while Knox hovered over Conall like a storm cloud. The furrow between Conall's eyes grew deeper and deeper as he ran the girl's face through his facial recognition database.

Only Rafe seemed relaxed. He polished off a second cookie before holding one out to the girl, who studied it seriously, the way Gray might have analyzed a potential ambush point. Dani tucked a fresh blanket around the kid's shoulders, even though the room was, if anything, too warm to be comfortable. Rafe just held out the cookie, his easy smile saying he had all the time in the world.

"Sweetheart, can you tell us your name?" Knox's voice held a familiar gentleness. It was the voice he used to de-escalate a situation when it was about to spin out of control because of jumpy civilians. Calm, reassuring. It clashed with the simmering anger in his eyes, and the kid was smart enough to see it.

She hunched further in on herself. Rafe shot Knox a warning look before setting the cookie down on the plate. "Look, it's here if you want it, pumpkin. Your call."

Rafe pointedly looked away. So did Knox, bending down over Conall's tablet. After a painful moment, the girl slipped a tiny hand from the blanket and seized her prize.

Next to him, Maya exhaled sharply and looked away.

Gray just managed not to flinch. A split second later, a wave of dizziness rocked him. He locked his knees, but he still might have stumbled if he hadn't been leaning against the wall already. He clenched his teeth against the nausea that followed hard on its heels, burning up his throat like a line of accelerant that had been set aflame.

"Hey." Maya lowered her voice and leaned closer. "You okay?"

If he turned his head too fast or opened his mouth, he'd puke. He managed a slight nod.

She vanished from his peripheral vision, only to return a moment later. The cool aluminum of one of their reusable water bottles brushed his fingers. "If you need it."

He took the bottle and slowly turned to meet her gaze. She was gazing up at him, her brow furrowed with concern. He distracted himself from a fresh wave of nausea by cataloguing her features: smooth, dark skin, square jaw, full lips.

Then his gaze reached her eyes, and his body tightened with thwarted anger. A burgeoning bruise sat high on one cheekbone, courtesy of her encounter with the security patrol in the parking lot. It would turn into a full-fledged shiner soon. The rest of the team hadn't needed him, not to extract one kid. He should have been out there, watching over Maya.

Or maybe not, not with the way his hands were shaking right now.

She stared at him, her frown deepening. Even with one eye swelling, she saw too much. If he didn't say something soon, she'd start to freak out.

"Thanks," he rasped, lifting the bottle to gesture toward the little girl. "Hell of a thing, isn't it?"

"Yeah." Suspicion tinged her voice, but her frown smoothed a little.

Guilt gripped him. They were all so easy—to fool, to divert. To reassure.

Mace never would have stood for it. Their medic would have taken one look at the sweat beading on Gray's upper lip and his dilated pupils and dragged him off to an exam room—by force, if necessary.

It had never been necessary. Every one of the Silver Devils had trusted Mace absolutely. They did as he asked, when he asked, and he rewarded that trust by literally preserving their lives.

But Mace was dead now. Gone. He wasn't preserving anything, not anymore.

A strident buzz cut through Gray's reverie, and Conall looked up from his tablet. "The Professor's at the door."

Nina nodded to Dani and Rafe. "Why don't you two take our guest up to see Tia Ivonne? Go out through the front."

Rafe swept up the plate of cookies and passed it to Dani. Then he held out a hand. After another tense moment, the small girl slipped her fingers into his. Rafe gave her a big grin and led her through the door to the main loft.

When they were out of earshot, Nina turned back to Conall. "It's about time. Let him in." The command given, she propped her hands on her hips and began pacing the width of the warehouse at the back of her building. "I'm going to kill him."

"You're going to kill him," Gray's captain—*former* captain—agreed readily.

"I mean it. I don't care what we owe him, Knox. This is too much. Too far."

Nina's contact, the man they all simply called the Professor, had intervened when the TechCorps had been within days—hell, maybe even hours—of catching up to the Silver Devils and wiping them off the face of the fucking planet. That debt weighed heavy on her, so if *she* was ready to wash her hands of this guy . . .

The Professor had really screwed the pooch.

"I know, Nina." Knox touched his lover's arm, soothing rather than restraining. "*After* we find out about the girl."

The man who walked in was dressed in clothes that had been old-fashioned even back when the Flares hit. His baggy, brown pants were topped with a sweater vest and a jacket with patches on the elbows. His collar was wrinkled, as if he'd been wearing a tie but had abandoned it.

"What took you so long?" Nina hissed. It had been hours since Nina had dashed off an angry but cryptic message to the man. The sun had come up and was nearing its zenith, and he'd left them all waiting. *Stewing.*

"It took me some time to get away. Where is she?" he demanded.

"Upstairs." At least Nina had the mercy to answer the question. Gray would have made him squirm in retribution. "You should have told me, John. I won't be a party to kidnapping."

"I know," the man answered mildly. "That's exactly why I didn't tell you."

She sucked in a harsh breath and turned to Knox, who stood with his arms crossed over his chest. He'd schooled his expression into something unreadable—flat and aloof, revealing nothing of the anger seething beneath the surface.

And he *was* angry. Long association with Garrett Knox had taught Gray that the angrier he got, the more he tried to hide it. When he shut down completely like this? *Rage* wasn't a strong enough word to cover it.

Professor John Smith—the absolute fakest goddamn name Gray had ever heard—was in for a world of hurt if he couldn't answer Nina's questions to her satisfaction.

Nina took another breath, this one deep and bracing. "Who is she?"

The Professor stared back, unblinking. "She's me."

A low rumble, like muted thunder, came from Knox. "Don't be cute. Answer the fucking question."

"I did." For the first time, the man looked a little peevish. "Run a DNA comparison, if you like."

Nina's eyes widened. "She's a clone?"

"Come now, Nina. *Think.*"

Knox's hands twitched into fists, but before he had a chance to dive across the room, Maya started laughing.

"Oh my God." She jabbed a finger in the Professor's direction. "It has been driving me *crazy*, trying to figure out who the fuck you are, because I should know anyone who has access to the sort of shit you do. Except you're not just a good little TechCorps employee with access to all the sweet IP, are you? You *are* the IP."

"Intellectual property? Not quite. Not for a long time. And I am merely employed by the TechCorps." He paused. "I should start at the beginning."

"Yes," Nina whispered. "You should."

For several long moments, he just looked around the room, as if he had all the time in the world. But when his gaze lighted on Knox's still-clenched fists, he cleared his throat and focused on Nina. "You're . . . what? Sixteenth generation? Seventeenth? The Franklin Center has almost perfected its techniques."

Nina went still. "You know about me."

He went on as if she hadn't spoken. "It's not the cloning, mind you. They had that down from the start. But the engineering . . . That took them a while." He laughed, a mirthless sound that made Maya shiver beside Gray.

Gray had to stop himself from echoing the gesture.

The man pulled off his heavy-rimmed glasses and tossed them aside. Their absence seemed to change more than the look of his face. He squared his shoulders and stood a little taller, his stance shifting into a posture more suited to combat than conversation.

Then he held out his hand. "I should introduce myself properly. JH-Gen2."

Nina exploded into motion, slapping his hand away and drawing her pistol in one motion. "Designation?"

The genetic research facility where Nina and her cloned sisters had been born—made?—followed strict and efficient naming conventions for their subjects that could be broken down and decoded. Nina, for example, was HS-Gen16-A. *HS*, those were the initials of the long-dead person who'd provided the DNA material that made the Center's work possible. *Gen16* denoted that she was part of the sixteenth iteration of that particular DNA strain. And her *A* meant that Nina was a soldier, a warrior, engineered to *fight*.

Her sister Ava's designation was *B*, indicating that she was a strategist. She could analyze patterns, account for all possible outcomes, and plan operations with the deft skill of an experienced military general. And there had been a *C* once, a third clone named Zoey who had died during an op. Nina still spoke of her with sad, shining eyes, describing her vast kindness and deep empathy.

The Professor hadn't offered a letter.

"I don't have one," he explained, the words casual and conversational, as if he wasn't staring down the barrel of a pistol. "I don't have a cluster, either. Back then, the Center was still trying to make each of us . . . well. All things to everyone, I suppose."

Gray's skin crawled. "They gave you *all* the modifications."

"Yes." Slowly, the man smiled. It should have been a horrible expression, ironic and dull, but it was utterly sincere. It was only creepy because of how out of place it was. "It didn't work out as they planned."

"Made you crazy, didn't it?" Conall's tone was light, but he watched the Professor with the same wary attention he usually reserved for venomous animals. "The TechCorps tried that, too. Didn't end so hot for them."

"You'd like that explanation, wouldn't you? It's simple. Easy. Makes you feel safe." He shook his head and turned his attention back to Nina. "It worked, perhaps *too* well." His voice dropped to a conspiratorial whisper. "It made us impossible to control."

Nina sucked in a sharp breath. "So you broke out."

"We didn't have to. We'd convinced the scientists that we wanted to be there. We bided our time, and eventually we just . . . walked out." He paused. "It was beautiful, actually."

"I guess they learned from their mistakes." Her finger tightened on the trigger. "I spent my entire childhood being treated like a criminal. Locked up like an animal. Is that part *beautiful*, too?"

"Nina." Knox took a step forward, the movement putting him in position to intervene—or take down the Professor with a flying tackle. "The girl."

That wiped the smile from the Professor's face. "That was my miscalculation, leaving behind my DNA. It wasn't important enough to include in my plans. I didn't realize it would ever matter." He gestured to a chair at the end of the table. "May I?"

"This isn't a fucking tea party," Maya muttered under her breath.

But Knox was already nodding curtly. "Sit," he ordered. "And talk. No more vague rambling. Tell us what the hell you got us into."

The man took the chair, swung it around, and sat without taking his gaze from Knox's face. The movement displayed perfect awareness and somatic control, a lazy grace that could turn lethal in a heartbeat.

If Gray ever had to kill this motherfucker, he wanted to be half a mile away with his favorite rifle and clear line of sight.

"My strain was one of the first to be decommissioned," he said flatly. "You have some experience with that, don't you, Nina? They learned that early, too—if you have problems with your subjects, you discard them and start over. The fault must be in the DNA. It's bullshit, of course, but I understand the impulse. Anything to regain some measure of control."

Nina stared at him with growing horror.

"Decommissioned DNA is wasteful. Maintaining it uses up valuable resources, but they can't simply throw it away. Just in case."

"So they sell it," Nina breathed.

He nodded. "To other research centers, hospitals, biotech companies. Even private concerns."

Gray clenched his fists. "Anything to make a buck."

"You have *no* idea, Sergeant Gray." He reached inside his jacket, prompting a warning growl from Knox. The Professor raised both eyebrows and slowed his movements in a placating gesture.

Then he pulled out a cigarette case and tossed it to Gray.

He caught it reflexively, then immediately wanted to drop it. The man *knew* Gray wanted a smoke. It didn't matter if he'd found the information in a dossier, talked to an old acquaintance of his, or plucked the knowledge out of the fucking air based on nothing more than intuition or a lucky guess.

Gray didn't like it.

He threw the case back with more force than strictly necessary. "No, thanks."

"Suit yourself." The Professor tucked the case back into his jacket's inner pocket. "Emerge BioCore Systems has been buying decommissioned strains from the Center for a while now."

"Why?" Slowly, Nina holstered her weapon. "What's their game?"

"Children." The word fell into the room like a flash-bang grenade. "Full customization, with a wide range of alterations."

"For what purpose?"

"Any? All?" He shrugged. "I'm quite sure they don't ask. But they do a brisk business. The facility you hit tonight is a final handling point. They do outbound shipping. That's why I had to convince you to do it, Nina. It was my last chance to retrieve the girl."

It was good that Nina had put her gun away, because her hands were shaking. "You should have told us, John."

"You already said you wouldn't have done it."

"I wouldn't *kidnap* a child," she countered. "But this? This was a fucking rescue mission."

He blinked at her. "There's a difference?"

She turned away with an exasperated groan.

The man rose. "In that case, you should know that Emerge is shipping additional cargo through that facility—"

Gray moved. It wasn't one of those things where he didn't mean to or he was so full of righteous anger that he didn't realize he was going to until it happened. He planned it, and he meant it.

The plan, however, was to grab the man by his jacket and haul him to his feet. Instead, Gray locked a hand around his throat and lifted him.

"They're not cargo," he growled. "They're kids. And you're *just now* telling us there were more of them locked in those cells?"

John stared at him, unperturbed by the violent threat inherent in Gray's grip on his throat. "My mistake."

"How many?" Knox asked flatly.

"According to my intelligence, at least five others in this shipment."

Motherfucker.

Nina gripped the edge of the table. "Let him go, Gray."

"I don't particularly want to, Nina."

"Do it anyway."

Slowly, millimeter by millimeter, Gray relaxed his fingers. Instead of scrambling back, the Professor stood there until Gray dropped his hand.

Nina turned. "Get out, John."

His brows drew together in a stormy frown. "The girl—"

"You can't have her."

He glanced around the room, his gaze lingering on each of them with calculation so plain Gray could almost hear it echoing in his head. He was wondering if he could take them all down before they managed to get him.

"Try it," Gray murmured. "I'm begging you."

The man's jaw clenched—the first real emotion the bastard had shown since his arrival. He straightened his jacket with a sharp snap, then turned and left without another word.

Knox exhaled sharply. "Conall—"

"I'll make sure he's gone," Conall promised, clutching his tablet. "And check Emerge's feeds. They may not have locked me out yet."

"Do what you can." Conall rushed from the warehouse, and Knox drove his fingers through his hair before glancing at Nina. "Is she safe upstairs if he comes back?"

"He won't come back."

"How do you—?" Gray's words cut off as another wave of dizziness hit him. This time, it wasn't mild enough to lock his knees and grit his teeth through it. It crashed over him, nearly driving him to the floor. His muscles cramped, and hot bile rose in his throat as agony joined the nausea.

"Gray?" Maya's voice was laced with worry. "Gray!"

He slumped to the floor, and black nothingness rushed up to greet him.

CONTRACT FOR EXECUTIVE EMPLOYMENT

Page 1/371
Employee Name: DC-031
Position: Data Courier
Executive: Birgitte Skovgaard
Start Date: May 21st, 2070
Compensation: 1000/month stipend in credits, yearly executive profit sharing options to be held in trust by Birgitte Skovgaard until DC-031's 21st birthday (May 21st, 2083).
Duties: (Listed pages 2–371)

Signatures

DC-031
Employee

Birgitte Skovgaard
VP Behavior and Analysis

THREE

Maya was usually better in a crisis.

Lord knew she'd seen her share. Jobs gone wrong, Protectorate raids, bar fights, and shoot-outs—and that was *after* she'd escaped from the TechCorps.

Maya had learned to keep her cool. After all, she'd already been through the worst life could throw at her. She'd been helpless and alone, caught in the sadistic clutches of the TechCorps' VP of Security. And she'd *survived.*

Gray hitting the floor in an unexpected seizure shouldn't have rattled her brain so hard it fritzed out.

Luna arrived from the upstairs apartment she shared with her aunt at a dead run, her T-shirt inside-out and her ponytail listing on her head. She may have dressed in a hurry, but she wore an expression of utter confidence as she used her tablet to connect to Gray's implant—and for good reason. The biohacker was an expert in TechCorps implant maintenance, a literal prodigy when it came to the delicate neural interface that controlled all of the Silver Devils' artificial enhancements. She'd been keeping them all steady for months now. She *would* fix this.

Maya believed it. She just couldn't stop panicking.

This was *Gray.* Solid, implacable Gray. He was like an ancient oak tree in the middle of a raging storm. Nothing shook him. Sometimes it seemed like nothing even touched him. She'd stared at him for what felt like hours, trying to figure out what was going on behind those delightfully brooding eyes. For a while, she'd tried to attribute her attention to good old-fashioned self-preservation. An apex predator had moved in, after all, and she'd always had well-honed instincts for danger.

But the awareness that prickled over her when he entered a room wasn't fear. And Maya had never been very good at lying to herself.

The seizure had subsided, helped along by Knox administering some sort of drug up his nose. Now, Gray was dreadfully still, his forehead covered with a sick sheen of sweat.

"Got it." Luna's brows drew together as her gaze raced over the tablet's screen. "This can't be right."

Knox's voice scraped over Maya's raw nerve endings like his words were coated with gravel. "What is it? What's happening?"

Luna barely glanced up. "I can't adjust his implant. According to this diagnostic, it doesn't need maintenance. Everything is normal."

"This is *not* normal," Nina insisted.

"No, I know." Luna drove a hand through her hair, dislodging the ponytail and tangling the white streaks she'd bleached into the dark brown. "But whatever the problem is, it's not his implant."

Maya's stomach flipped. Her brain skittered in too many directions at once, words tumbling over one another—medical assessments and proprietary experimental data and all the scary Latin names for things that might be slowly killing someone with Gray's biochem implant. But she couldn't latch on to a thread and pull it free because there was *too fucking much*, and she didn't even know where to start.

What the fuck good was having what felt like half the knowledge of the known freaking universe throbbing in your head if you had to just stand there and helplessly watch someone die?

Luna was still speaking. "Without more information, I can't narrow it down. We need a proper doctor."

Nina exhaled sharply. "A neuroengineer?"

"Preferably a TechCorps-trained one."

"No," Gray croaked. "We don't."

"Gray." Knox gripped his shoulder gently. "You need help. We can find someone."

"There's nothing they can do, Captain." Gray's expression was calm, almost serene. "I'm rejecting my implant."

The words tumbling end over end through Maya's aching head zeroed in on chilling specifics. *Elevated ICP* and *inflammatory fibrosis* and *foreign body response.* The pressure was unbearable, and her lips parted before she could stop them.

Her dispassionate recitation fell into uncomfortable silence, the words crisp and clipped, a perfect re-creation of the posh British accent of the scientist who'd issued the report to Birgitte. "'In a certain percentage of recruits, implant rejection is immediate—and fatal. In a smaller subset, rejection may be delayed by a matter of months or even years. It is unknown what, exactly, triggers this belated response, but it seems to be linked to difficulties with neural interface installation.'"

Knox's expression tightened. "Delayed rejection happens, but I've never heard of it happening after twenty years."

"What can I say?" Gray struggled into a sitting position, waving Knox away when he reached for him to help. "I'm an overachiever."

Nina eyed him dubiously. "None of this was in your medical paperwork."

He didn't seem to question that *of course* Nina had reviewed his charts. "One of the techs told me while I was in recovery after my implant procedure. The surgeon had trouble, but he told them not to mark it down." Gray grinned. "Guess he didn't want me fucking up the bonus linked to his success rate."

Little flares of pain shivered up Maya's arms. She looked down and saw that she'd clenched her hands into fists so tight that her nails were cutting into her palms.

It made too much sense. It was everything Birgitte had loathed about the TechCorps, everything she'd been fighting to tear down. There were soldiers like Knox and Gray, people who lived twenty-plus years with their Protectorate implants, but even they couldn't pull the average life expectancy up over eight years.

Most soldiers were dead by year five.

Of course they'd lied on Gray's medical charts. The odds of Gray being killed in action before rejection ever became an issue had been in the surgeon's favor.

Fuck that guy.

At least the rage helped burn away her panic. "I know specialists," she told Gray. "Defectors. I can find someone to help you."

His smile vanished, and a look of remorse flitted across his features. "I'm sorry. If it was that easy, Maya, I'd do it."

There was nothing *easy* about tapping into her network of failed revolutionaries. They spanned the city and beyond, living quiet, careful lives. Scientists and analysts and administrators, people who'd once held access to the deepest, darkest corners of the TechCorps. People who knew about doctored files and acceptable losses and all the exploitative corruption that had driven Birgitte to rebellion.

Of course, Gray couldn't know about her network. The rebellion had been put down swiftly and silently. As far as most of their less seditious coworkers knew, Birgitte had been promoted to lead a satellite facility, and Maya had escaped during the transition, only to turn up dead in a ditch within the year. The TechCorps liked to keep things tidy. Dani and Nina were the only people who knew the full, ugly truth. Everyone else only knew bits and pieces of it, fractions of the whole.

But her contacts knew she was alive. And every time Maya reached out to one of them, she risked betraying her continued existence to Tobias Richter, the head of TechCorps security—and a man who featured prominently in her darkest nightmares.

For this, she would chance it.

She gathered her courage and parted her lips, ready to explain—

Conall burst into the room, trailing curses. "God fucking *damn* it, Emerge is on the move."

He tossed a tablet to Nina. She flipped through the screens, but every camera showed the same thing—empty rooms and deserted hallways.

She breathed a curse. "Damn John, anyway. If we'd known, we could have at least planted trackers on their vehicles."

Knox agreed. "Now we'll have to do this the hard way."

"We need to roll out now," Conall said. "Scour the place top to bottom. I'll check the satellite feeds."

"Tia Ivonne can look after the child." Nina turned to Maya. "Will you stay here with Gray?"

A deceptively simple question—and a terrifying one. Staying here to run their community library on her own should have been a breeze compared to strapping on armor and going out to chase mad scientists across the decaying wilds outside Atlanta. But retrieval jobs never felt that dangerous with Dani and Nina around.

Maya had never really been on her own before. She'd be the front line for any crisis that came up in the community, the person expected to show up if there was trouble and put a stop to it. She'd be the boss.

Her. In *charge*.

Nina was clearly confident that she could handle it. And Maya wasn't the sheltered, traumatized girl from the Hill anymore. "I'll hold down the fort."

"Good." Nina's next instructions were for Conall. "Round up Rafe and Dani. Tell them to be ready for anything."

"Got it."

Conall rocketed out of the room, leaving Knox to stare at Gray. "No protest from you about staying here?"

"I'm stubborn, not delusional. Besides . . ." He grimaced. "That stuff you squirted up my nose makes me woozy."

Knox squeezed Gray's shoulder. "Get some rest. I mean it."

He flexed his legs and sighed. "I don't think I have a choice, Cap."

"No, you don't." After a final back pat, Knox smiled at Maya. "Don't let him give you any shit."

"I don't let anyone give me shit," Maya retorted. "I got this, Knox. Go. Be a superhero."

Knox headed out of the room, his fingers trailing over Nina's as he passed. For all the time Maya had spent teasing Nina about those yearning stares—not to mention the couple's tendency to make out in literally every room in the building—her heart still lurched when she caught those quiet moments of affection between Knox and Nina.

Garrett Knox adored Nina with every atom of his being, and Maya adored him for it. Nina deserved to be loved.

"Come on." Nina bent and slid under one of Gray's arms, wrapping it around her shoulders. "Up you go."

She helped him to his feet easily, as if he weren't several inches taller and much bigger than her. To his credit, he didn't protest her help, though the very tops of his ears did turn a little pink.

"Thanks," he muttered.

"You're welcome." Nina raised an eyebrow, a gesture meant solely for Maya. "If he gives you that trouble Knox mentioned? You have my permission to recite something esoteric and terribly boring at him. For *hours*."

Nina left Gray standing under his own power, looking mostly steady. Maya braced her hands on her hips and ignored the urge to bundle him into bed and stroke his hair until the lines of pain etched into his face eased.

Those were ill-advised urges that would end badly. For *everyone.*

Instead, she gave him her best *try me* stare, the one she flashed at belligerent teen boys who returned tablets with cracked screens or precious books with creased or stained pages. "Are you gonna give me grief?"

"Depends." He squinted at her. "Are you gonna keep looking at me like that?"

"Not if you behave." She unbent and tilted her head. "Go hop in bed. I'll bring you something to eat later."

His squint turned into a scowl. "No, you won't."

She managed not to snap at him in reply, but those *lines* on his face were killing her. So was his unnatural pallor and the way he held himself, like everything hurt.

Her voice dropped to a whisper. "How long, Gray? How long has this been happening?"

At first, she thought he might not answer. Then he slowly turned to her, his scowl melting away, replaced by an equally grave expression. "About a month. I thought my levels were just out of whack, and Luna would tune me up during maintenance. But when she said everything looked fine . . . That's when I knew."

A month. Maya shut down the flood of research data that threatened to cascade through her brain like an avalanche, knowing she'd pay later with a worse headache than the one already starting to throb behind her eyes. She didn't need to dive into her memories to know his situation was bad.

Implant rejection was a slow death. Gray had a year if he was lucky. A couple of months if he wasn't.

Maya exhaled softly. "You should have told us."

"Why? So you could look at me like . . ." His voice trailed off, and he gestured impatiently in her direction. "Like *that*? No, thanks."

Ouch.

But he was right. Maya didn't even need a mirror to imagine the exact look in her eyes, the precise degree of concern and pity. It was the look on Nina's face every time Maya descended the stairs after a sleepless night, the shadows deep under her eyes. The *weight* of all the words Nina held back, the pulsing need to help even though they both knew there was nothing to be done.

Maya's death sentence was hopefully still years away, but she too had been handed one the day the TechCorps had messed with her brain. No fix. No cure. Just the fight to hold on to sanity and her ability to function for as long as she could.

Yeah, she *hated* that look.

It took effort, but she banished the concern from her eyes. "Fair enough. But when I put you to work chopping produce or sweeping floors, remember you could have had sweet sympathy and dinner in bed, and you're the fool who asked for tough love."

A hint of a smile curved his lips. "That's better."

It was practically a croon, his liquid-molasses voice sliding over her like an obscene promise. It was almost enough to distract her from the throb in her temples, a warning that she was headed straight for sensory overload—fast.

She jabbed her finger toward the exit. "Fine, I'll let you feed yourself. But get your ass in bed before I call Rafe back to put you there."

"Kinky." The word drifted back over his shoulder as he headed out the back door.

Maya held it together until he was gone. Then she just . . . let go.

The cement floor of the warehouse was pleasantly cool in spite of the heat outside. Maya sprawled out on it and closed her eyes. A quick shake of her wrist primed her watch for voice commands. "Play *Dance it Out*."

Her FlowMac Pop playlist rolled over her, the perky tempo and throbbing beat perversely soothing. Her new ear cuffs were unobtrusive, stylish, and the absolute cutting edge in bone-conduction sound transfer technology. Maya wouldn't have paid the black market asking price in a million years.

Turned out, there were perks to your best friend having a literal evil clone.

Nina was mildly exasperated by the fact that her sister kept trying to buy forgiveness for her past crimes with expensive gifts, but Ava was like a feral cat. She appeared sporadically, scratched anyone who tried to pet her, and vanished again without warning. But instead of dead mice, she left behind expensive technology and impossible-to-obtain weapons.

Maya was perfectly willing to be bought off.

The cuffs were better than her old earbuds. The music was a part of her, filling the inside of her skull. She breathed in time with the heavy beat and fought back the rush of memories, silencing the chaotic rush of overlapping voices one by one. Technicians, data scientists, administrators, even members of the TechCorps Board. They lived inside her, perfectly preserved, a thousand mundane moments and even more horrifying ones.

That was what it meant to be a data courier. You were the receptacle for every dark secret your VP wasn't willing to commit to paper. You were a day planner, a filing system, a living, breathing memo. Only, Maya's boss hadn't been content to advance the TechCorps' bottom line at all costs.

No, Birgitte Skovgaard had been planning a revolution. Maya had that in her head, too. Every secret. Every bit of blackmail that might put an executive in a compromising position or take down an enemy at a delicate moment. Maya knew everyone sympathetic to their cause within the TechCorps and every contact Birgitte had cultivated outside of it. All that knowledge was precisely why the TechCorps had put a two-million-credit bounty on Maya.

Some days, Maya wanted to be anywhere but in her own damn head.

The music helped. It didn't stop the chaos, but it helped her breathe through it until it was locked back away. In for three throbbing bass beats, out for three more. Steady. Deep.

Meditation. It was a gentler kind of dissociation, one with fewer consequences.

Maya could still feel the world around her—the slightly rough concrete under her fingertips, the soft fabric of her T-shirt. That had been one of the unexpected hardships about rebuilding a life off of the Hill—the clothing. For the first nineteen years of her life, she'd been able to step up to her wardrobe mirror, initiate a 3D body scan, browse through a catalog of fashion, and select exactly what she wanted, both in styling and fabric. Within twenty-four hours, a drone would deliver custom-fitted clothing tailored to her precise preferences—light and airy fabrics, no tags, no close-cut necklines, nothing that dug in or constrained or irritated.

Salvaging clothes from secondhand shops was an entirely different experience. Nina had helped her find things that worked, like denim and T-shirts washed so many times they were soft to the touch, skirts and sundresses that flowed around her body, and cozy sweatshirts she could get lost in.

It had been the first of a dozen things she'd had to relearn, bit by bit. Life down here could be so . . . *much.* Loud and rambunctious, bright and wild. She'd grown accustomed to it, bit by bit, adapting to the overwhelming scents and the tastes, the vivid colors and joyous sounds. Some part of her thrived on it, even, as if *this* was how she was supposed to be. Alive and surrounded by a whirlwind of sensation, not encased in sterile numbness.

But still, too much was too much. And she never knew when it was going to hit her—or how hard.

This time wasn't too bad. As FlowMac Pop rolled over her, she settled into the music. Her breathing steadied, and the memories stopped trying to rush up to fill the silence in her head.

She opened her eyes and stared at the ceiling. Once she had her shit together, she'd see Nina off with a confident smile. And then . . .

Then she would open for business. Prep food and package yesterday's freeze-dried haul while the new batch was processing. Organize a schedule for the last harvest rush before winter. Check the budget to see if they could afford another freeze-dryer now that demand had skyrocketed.

She would scan books, fight with file formats no one had used in fifty years, and update their catalog. She would figure out how the hell to organize the dozens of boxes of salvaged books that still lined the back wall of the warehouse. She would fix tablets, upgrade tech, and sort through a new tangle of donated tools.

And she had to do it all alone.

No, worse.

She had to do it with *Gray.*

Gray and his Gothic brooding eyes and his long, meaningful stares and his endless silences only interrupted by that smoky-smooth voice. His voice was like fine whiskey. Like sin. His voice was goddamn angels fucking.

She was pretty sure she could tip over into full sensory overload just by listening to him talk. But every time she caught him watching her, she wanted more than sound. She wanted to drag the scent of him into her lungs and feel his hands on her body. She wanted to touch him. She wanted to taste him.

She just *wanted*.

Groaning, Maya covered her face with her hands. Then she pulled them away and forced her body to move. Upright, then to her knees, then to her feet. One boot in front of the other. She'd see Nina off, then indulge in a bath to soak away the rest of her jittery nerves.

Then she'd square up and get to work. Just her and a random genetically engineered kid and Tia Ivonne with her dodgy heart and Gray with his angel-fucking voice, for who knew how long.

This was going to be a disaster.

TECHCORPS PROPRIETARY DATA,
L1 SECURITY CLEARANCE

Reminder to executives: unnecessary education for DC subjects compromises their long-term viability. Limit requests for additional course access to knowledge essential to your data courier's specific job performance.

Internal Memo, February 2074

FOUR

Gray shouldn't have worried about being served food in bed like an invalid, because Maya didn't even have time to consider it. Her luxurious soak turned into a hasty shower in between neighborhood crises.

Okay, so *crisis* was probably overstating things, but the dust had barely settled behind the team's van before Jacinth showed up, her rambunctious twins trailing in behind her. Her wavy, salt-and-pepper hair was caught up in a messy knot on her head, and she was still wearing a flour-dusted apron over her patched overalls.

Jacinth leaned all six feet of her large frame against the table and slid a tablet across to Maya. "I'm back."

Maya flipped open her own tablet and pulled up the master inventory. "Is it the industrial mixer again?"

The baker huffed. "No, I *finally* got that thing fixed, but now my oven is on the fritz! Burned two batches of loaves, and a third came out raw in the middle. I never should have upgraded from the damn brick. At least fire can't malfunction."

Sometimes Maya heard people muttering that the tech that made its way off the Hill and into the surrounding neighborhoods was designed to fall apart. She knew the evil of the TechCorps was far more banal. The failed innovations they offloaded onto the gray market hadn't been *designed* to fail. But when they did, the TechCorps had no problem selling broken shit to people who couldn't complain.

A few taps on her tablet pulled up her complete archive of appliance manuals. "It's the TL-3700 model, right?"

"Yes. I don't know how you always remember."

Because I don't have any other option. Maya forced a tight smile as she found the file. Jacinth's tablet was already set to receive, so she swiped it over. "I'm going to do the same thing I did last time," she said, popping open the GhostNet. She had a shortcut to the forum where people traded troubleshooting hacks for TechCorps hardware, and it only took a few quick searches to export all the notes on Jacinth's oven. "Start with the official manual, but if that doesn't work . . ."

"Listen to the criminals?"

Maya snorted and sent over the file. "They're all criminals. Some are just legal ones."

"Fair enou—hey!" Jacinth lunged fast enough to catch her son's hand before he could sneak one of the spare tablets off the table.

"I was just looking!" he protested immediately.

"Look with your eyes, not your fingers." Jacinth offered Maya a frazzled smile. "Sorry, their grandma usually has them now, but she's sleeping off a cold, so Nick and Tilda are making the afternoon deliveries with me."

"That's a big responsibility," Maya said solemnly to the kids as she deftly moved her stack of loaner tablets out of the way of curious little fingers. "Since you're helping your mama out with her work, maybe I have something special for you here . . ."

Two pairs of eyes lit up with anticipation as Maya lifted her tablet and flipped back over to their main inventory. She'd rescued a treasure trove of 2040s media off one of the RLOC servers a few weeks ago, and she knew exactly what would earn Jacinth—and Grandma Linda—a few hours of much-needed peace.

"Here you go," she told the twins, flicking a series of files to their mother's tablet. "Nick, I found you a series on the Second Dust Bowl and what life was like in the Deadlands back when you could grow things there. And Tilda . . ." Maya grinned. "Ready for the third season of *Teen Witch*?"

"You found it?" Tilda gasped.

"Of course I did." Maya winked at her. "I can find anything. Now you two listen to your mother and help her with the deliveries, and go easy on your grandma, okay?"

When the twins' overlapping promises of good behavior faded, Jacinth straightened. "Have I mentioned lately that you're a saint?"

"You want to say thanks, send Linda around with some of those soft pretzels once she's feeling better."

"A bucket of them." She swept up the tablet. "Thank you, Maya."

"That's why we're here," Maya replied, smiling.

She sent them off with a wave, but the door had barely swung shut before someone else showed up looking for more math books to challenge their brilliant teenager.

Math, Maya knew. She also knew Shakira would outstrip the limitations of their current collection before winter. A few weeks ago, she'd talked Conall into using his backdoor TechCorps access to pirate their entire math curriculum, so she sent Shakira's father off with a course on integral calculus and instructions to send the girl along if she got stuck.

Next in was Cheryl, who brought her client schedule for the week. Sex work in Five Points had gotten a lot safer once Cheryl implemented her check-in system. Maya had helped them improve upon it with refurbished smartwatches she'd hooked into a database hidden in an anonymous corner of the GhostNet. Failure to mark themselves safe—and fully compensated—at the end of an appointment triggered an alert . . . and a swift follow-up. Usually by Dani in full-on murder mode.

Problems had decreased rapidly after that, even for people who weren't part of the network. Maya was pretty sure the potential troublemakers of Southside told each other scary bedtime stories about Dani showing up on their doorstep like an avenging angel. Whatever the reason, everyone gave their manners a firm polish before paying for sex in Dani's territory. Just in case.

Maya *almost* got the warehouse door locked behind Cheryl, but then someone showed up needing to borrow tools for home repairs, and by the time she was shuffling them out, a familiar truck was backing up to the door, its bed loaded down with crates of shiny, red apples.

"Bryan Barnes." Maya braced both fists on her hips. "You been poaching apples from Becky?"

"Nothing so criminal." The driver swung out of the truck with a grin. Bryan was a big, burly, bald man with a red beard, scars on his hands and arms, and an air of effortless competence. He hefted three crates at once as if they weighed nothing and carried them through the door. "Becky's engine finally crapped out, so I told her I'd bring in her haul and pick up what I need to fix it."

Maya propped the door open and went to retrieve another crate. The deeply colored apples were massive—a credit to Becky's skill at coaxing her orchard to its fullest potential—and the thought of taking a bite of one set Maya's stomach to rumbling. "She still insisting on running that piece of shit on pure biofuel?"

"I'll talk her around to solar eventually." Bryan grinned. "She did agree to barter a nice bunch of apples if I can get her truck running again. You know what that means?"

"More apple cider for me?" Maya let the crate drop to the table with a *thump*. "I've been craving it since last year."

"I still owe you for the cyclepedia." Bryan carried another three crates in and set them on the sorting table. "As soon as it's ready, I'll bring it over."

Usually she would have waved off the offer—the practically ancient database of motorcycle engine and repair manuals she'd unearthed had taken her under an hour to convert to an easily searchable format—but Bryan's apple cider was even better than his mead. Sweet, tart, and just enough buzz to make her tingly without fuzzing up her brain. "You know I won't turn it down."

"I know." He placed the last box and winked at her. "I'm storing up credit for next time I need an obscure engine user manual."

Maya waved him off with a laugh. "Go fix Becky's truck."

After she'd closed the door behind him, Maya barely had time to dash upstairs, rinse off an afternoon of sweat, and grab a sandwich for dinner before Rowan arrived with their latest recordings. Maya set her plate on the table in the warehouse and offered Rowan one of the icy sodas before dragging the new files down to her computer.

Across from her, Rowan settled on a stool and took a sip from the glass bottle. Their hair was a bright teal now, shaved high up their head in the back with chunky bangs framing their face. Teal and bronze eyeshadow completed the dramatic look, complementing Rowan's green eyes and golden skin.

"I like the new style," Maya told them as she pulled up the first track. "Did you do your own hair?"

"I wish I had this skill." Rowan rolled the bottle back and forth between their hands. "There's a new place on the perimeter. They have these heat wands. No dye, no mess. Just . . . boom. Teal hair."

"Cool. I should see if we can get one of those." Maya waggled her eyebrows. "Dani would love to have instant disguises."

"Lord save us all." Rowan made a show of crossing themself, then inclined their head toward Maya's computer. "This is my first recording with the new soundproof room. Should make your job *way* easier."

A few taps, and the first strains of violin drifted from the cleverly hidden speakers Maya had installed around the warehouse. The new song started slowly, each note piercingly clear as Rowan wove them together in a melody so yearning that Maya's bones ached with it.

In past recordings, Maya had struggled to strip out the background noise. This one was close to clean, with nothing to distract from the haunting refrain as the song began to pick up speed. It built to a crescendo, and Maya's breath caught as a low bass beat erupted beneath it. The violin split off and wove itself around the new rhythm, the notes dancing higher and faster as the accompanying beat gained in complexity.

Goose bumps rose on Maya's arms, and she closed her eyes, savoring the pristine beauty of it. It was the opposite of the empty AI-generated pop she loved to listen to, overflowing with passion, with fire, with . . . *life*. Maya fell into it, bespelled by the sheer beauty the same way she sometimes felt ensnared by Gray's voice. Like a sailor on the ancient seas, steering her boat straight to the rocks because the siren sounded *just that good*.

Why not? There were worse ways to drown than slipping beneath the waves of pure bliss.

"Maya?" Rowan's voice was concerned. "You okay?"

Heart racing, Maya forced her eyes open and realized they stung with unshed tears. The warehouse had fallen silent, but the cutting beauty of Rowan's music still wound through her memory, every bit as vivid. She swiped at her eyes and pinned Rowan with a glare. "Fuck you for being this good."

Rowan's worry melted into a cocky grin. "I can't help it. Some people are just naturally talented."

Rowan was more than talented. In a different time—a *better* one—they might have been famous. Wealthy. Showered with adoration for the way they could pick up an instrument and transport you to an altered state of being. Rowan should be selling out massive auditoriums and rolling in the credits. Instead, they performed neighborhood concerts for tips and struggled to book gigs at clubs that would rather pump mindless auto-generated noise through the speakers at maximum volume.

Maya had been fighting to help change that. A few judicious leaks on the Net—and a few far more subtle lures on the GhostNet—had begun to build a following. Most people in Atlanta had minimal disposable income, but credits had trickled in through Rowan's netBusk account, enough to build the recording studio and keep food on the table.

It wasn't enough, but it was something. Maya shook off her melancholy and moved the files to her priority queue. "It may take me a few days to turn these around, since I'm handling things on my own right now, but I'll get them ready for upload. Have you thought about Conall's suggestion?"

"The music videos?" Rowan ran a nervous hand over their hair, smoothing the bright strands into place. "That's part of why I'm trying out the new style. I might be warming to the idea."

Conall had become obsessed with Rowan's music, convinced there was an untapped market there. His latest pitch had been to use his surveillance drones to film footage of Rowan playing music in various cinematic locations, complete with apocalyptic squalor and the Hill looming ominously in the background. "He knows what makes the stiffs up on the Hill spend credits," Maya acknowledged. "But don't go balancing on any collapsing overpasses for him unless *you* want to."

"Deal." Rowan slid off the stool with a wide grin. "I gotta bounce. I have an actual gig tonight. It's paying real credits and everything."

"Oooh, fancy." Maya waved them away. "Go get rich. I'll send you a message when the files are ready."

"Thanks, Maya. You're the best."

It was a refrain she heard all evening. From people who needed books, or tools, or supplies, or just help. She heard it at maximum volume after a harried waitress showed up from Clem's, begging her to fix the air-conditioning before the drunks rioted in the stifling Atlanta humidity.

That was the first thing she'd done after she realized how easy it was to listen to a product manual or mechanical guide and just . . . fix things. Maya had loaded her brain up with information on air conditioners and heaters—the two things people needed desperately when sweltering through the summer or shivering through the winter—and somehow all the disjointed data fell into her brain in neat, actionable rows. She could put down her earbuds and pick up a wrench and *fix things.*

Of course, the patrons at Clementine's bar didn't know that. They just thought she was a mechanical genius. And hell, maybe she was. The AC took twenty minutes to fix, and the first blast of cold air from the vents overhead resulted in cheers. Even guys she'd previously hustled at pool were so grateful they tried to cajole her into staying for a beer. One even offered to pay for it.

It was a tempting offer. Her home echoed with unnerving silence without Dani and Nina there. The gentle sounds of their daily routines were imprinted in her memory, and their absence grated in ways she hadn't expected.

But knowing Gray was alone in the other warehouse forced her to demur. He might be fine for the moment, but she felt better being close.

Sleep, however, was out of the question. Adrenaline still buzzed over her skin, so Maya locked all the doors and retreated back to the warehouse, to the far corner, where her prize sat.

The 3D scanner was next-next-generation. Another of Ava's guilt-assuaging gifts, it had probably cost as much as a reasonably well-off support staffer up on the Hill might clear in a couple of years. It could scan up to a thousand pages in under thirty seconds using terahertz radiation to process the interior layer by layer, and Maya had finessed the built-in optical character recognition process until the digital files it produced were nearly error-free. She'd even built a program to extract visible and extrapolate inferred metadata, an adventure that had involved learning two new computer languages during a sleepless week spent in a programming frenzy.

The results were worth it. Maya pulled up her stool and lifted a book from the box at her elbow. The cookbooks were in high demand, but she always had to baby the conversion a little to get the images right in a digital version. In the first few trials, she'd excluded them, but it turned out people really liked pretty pictures of food, so who was she to deny them?

She lined up a book titled *Twenty-Minute Bread with Clean Flour* and started the scanner. The bright green cover was distinctive of the 2030s, when the Energy Wars had been raging and the environmental cost of everything from clothes to cars to flour had become a highly politicized battleground. No one even called the artificial stuff *clean flour* anymore—thanks to the TechCorps, it had become the norm. If you wanted real flour, ground from wheat or other grains, you had to dip into the black market.

Most people didn't bother. The fake shit worked fine, which would make this book very popular.

Maya tapped her fingers as the pages began to appear on her monitor. She was skimming the images when the softest scrape of bare feet on concrete sounded behind her.

Panic jolted her, but her training under Nina had been intense and her instincts were well-honed. Also, Dani hid guns everywhere. The closest was under the table, and Maya had it in her hand a second later as she spun toward the noise.

Huge, dark eyes stared at her from a pale face under brutally short hair. The kid was frozen in the middle of the warehouse, her unblinking gaze fixed on Maya's pistol with a calm acceptance that ripped her up.

Babies shouldn't look so unsurprised to see weapons pointed at their damn faces.

"Sorry," she said, engaging the safety again and sliding the gun onto the table. "You startled me. I thought you were upstairs with Tia Ivonne."

The kid blinked again. Maya didn't even know her name. Hell, Maya didn't know if she *had* a name. Or if she spoke English.

Or spoke at all.

Moving slowly, Maya walked over to the cooler they kept stocked with bottled water. She always kept a few soft drinks tucked in the back, their carbonated sweetness one of the few guilty pleasures she'd been unable to give up from her cushy life up on the Hill. Luckily, she still had some left over after Rowan's visit, so she retrieved two chilled glass bottles and offered one to the kid. "Try this. It's sweet and bad for your teeth, but I love it anyway."

After an endless moment, the young girl reached out and took the bottle. Her brow furrowed as she stared at the top, and Maya demonstrated twisting the cap off. "If it's too tight—"

The girl twisted effortlessly, and the top came away slightly bent. Concern shadowed her eyes, but Maya just laughed. "Okay, so you're super strong. Don't worry, Nina is, too. She gets frustrated and breaks things more often than we admit."

Understanding sparked in the girl's eyes, followed swiftly by relief. So she *did* understand English. That was something. Maya tilted her head toward the scanner and nudged a second stool toward the table. "Want to help me? I'm scanning books."

Another hesitation. A nod. The kid carried the glass bottle over to the stool with painstaking gentleness, then sat the same way, as if she really was concerned she'd destroy it. A suspicion kindled in Maya's gut, but she settled onto the stool and watched the kid take her first tentative sip. "It's okay, you know. If you broke something upstairs in Tia Ivonne's apartment."

Startled green eyes met hers, and Maya knew she'd guessed right. "Hey, as long as you didn't break *her*, things are just things. We can replace things, okay? No one's going to be mad at you."

An endless pause. Then, in a voice wrapped in a dread that settled in Maya's bones, she whispered, "I pulled the handle off the faucet. I didn't mean to. Please don't punish me."

It took everything in her for Maya to keep her smile steady and easy. The rage crawling under her skin needed an outlet, but not *here*. Not with her. "No punishment, kiddo. We're not even going to get mad. You might get teased, though. I teased Nina for a week last time she twisted so hard she broke a handle off something."

"Teased?" The voice was a little louder. "Does it hurt?"

Fuck.

"No, honey." Maya didn't reach out. She didn't try to hug the kid. That would have freaked her out at this age. "Teasing's just . . . being silly with someone you care about. *No one* is going to hurt you. I promise."

After a moment, the girl nodded and took another sip of her drink. "Do you need to know my designation?"

The ghost floated up through her memory, Birgitte's cool voice. *She'll need a name.*

Her designation is DC-031.

A name, Ms. Linwood. Every person deserves a name.

I know you're supposed to bond with her, but . . . Well, this might be easier if you don't think of her as a person, Ms. Skovgaard.

It might also be easier if you were unemployed.

My apologies. Would you like us to provide a name?

No. She'll take care of it.

The kid's intense gaze was still fixed on her face, so Maya shoved back the memory of a conversation she wasn't supposed to have heard and answered the question carefully. "Only if you want to share your designation with me."

That earned her a considering look, as if the kid wasn't sure what to do with having a choice. When she finally answered, it was with dull acceptance. "I'm JHX-7."

In the Franklin Center, where Nina had grown up, designations had indicated genetic lineage. The Professor had also given them the initials *JH*, an indication that they actually might share the same DNA. The *seven* could mean there were seven of her or she'd been the seventh try. Either possibility churned horror through Maya.

But at least she knew how to handle this. "That's not who you are, you know. Mine was DC-031, but it's not who I am."

"You have a designation?"

"*Had.*" Maya said it firmly. "A designation is something they give us to define our place in their world. A name is something we take to define ourselves."

After a moment of fidgeting with the glass bottle, the girl peeked up at Maya. "I can pick a name?"

"Hell yeah." Maya smiled around the ache in her throat. "We'll call you anything you want."

"What if I choose wrong?"

"There is no wrong. If you try a name and decide it doesn't work . . ." Maya shrugged. "You pick a new one. And then we call you that."

The girl's mouth formed a silent O of wonder. Her brow furrowed a moment later. "How did you decide?"

"Wait here." Maya hopped off the stool and crossed to the bookshelf where she'd been hoarding her special finds. The Rogue Library of Congress bounty had created something of a logistical nightmare in the best possible way, leaving Maya hip deep in a barely organized tangle of ancient treasures. But she knew exactly where the box filled with dozens of brightly colored children's books was, and right there at the top . . .

The cover was still surprisingly vivid, showing a young girl in a spacesuit against a background of stars. Maya had stared at a digitized version of this book a thousand times, imagining that this girl with her glowing, brown skin and determined eyes and softly curving face and world-saving brilliance could be *her*.

It almost had been. Unfortunately, taking down the bad guys was easier in stories.

Maya carried the book back to where the girl sat watching her with wary eyes. "Put the drink down first. No spilling on this."

Obediently, she set the bottle aside. Maya extended the precious book, feeling like she was exposing a vulnerability. "It's a story I loved when I was your age. It's about a girl named Marjorie. She lives on the moon, and she uncovers a conspiracy where evil grown-ups are doing terrible things. She and her friends figure out how to stop them, even though they're just kids."

Maya watched as the girl turned the book over, her gaze skimming the text on the back in a way that made it clear she knew how to read, at least. Maya didn't need to read it. She could close her eyes and recite the book cover to cover from memory. She'd read about Marjorie and her misfit gang of friends compulsively, even though books about space travel were spurned by the TechCorps, whose company policy was that reaching for the stars had been a barbaric selfishness when there was so much suffering that needed alleviating on Earth.

As a moral stand, it sounded good on paper. Unfortunately, barbaric selfishness was alive and well on Earth, and the TechCorps had refined it to an art form.

But as a child, she'd *believed*. When Birgitte had recruited her into the simmering internal rebellion, it had seemed like the most natural thing in the world. Of course it was Maya's responsibility to help Birgitte carry the burden of dismantling a broken system of greed and exploitation. She had been determined to live up to the example of her namesake. Marjorie Starborn, genius rebel, defender of the moon.

It had taken Maya a long time to get mad at Birgitte for putting that on a child.

It would take a lot longer for Maya to forgive herself for failing.

"Did this really happen?" the kid asked with wide eyes, back to staring at the cover.

"No, it's a story. Fiction." At the unblinking gaze, Maya frowned. "They taught you to read, right?"

"We read tactical manuals," she replied. "Military history. Combat strategy. Physiology. PsyOps."

"Sounds like what Knox reads to relax." Maya retrieved one of the loaner tablets and started loading age-appropriate books off the server. Not that she was the best judge of age-appropriate—*she'd* been reading books on physiology and psychological warfare at eight, too. But she knew which types of stories the kids in the neighborhood devoured.

"I'm going to give you some books," she said. "These are just about fun. You read them so you can imagine having adventures or falling in love or all sorts of things. If there's any you like, I'll get you more like it, okay?"

"And I can find my name like you did?" the kid asked, perking up.

"If you want. We should come up with a nickname, though, just for now. Something we can call you until you pick a name."

After another solemn moment of considerable thought, the girl braced her entire body as if for a blow. "Rainbow."

It was almost defiant. She was clearly prepared for laughter or derision. Summoning a warm smile was the easiest thing Maya had ever done. "I think Rainbow is a great name."

"I saw one once," Rainbow said excitedly as the tension fled her tiny body. Her words came faster, as if Maya had passed a silent test. "They brought us out for endurance training during a thunderstorm. But there was a break in the rain and the sky . . ." She trailed off in awe. "Everything in our rooms was always just . . . *gray*. But the sky was painted in so many colors. It was the most amazing thing I've ever seen."

The torrent of words faded, and Maya held her smile even with her heart twisted in knots. "I bet. Next time it rains, I'll take you up on the roof. Sometimes we don't just get rainbows in the sky, but the light reflects off the big buildings up on the Hill like they're prisms. Rainbows everywhere."

"Wow," Rainbow whispered.

"Wow is right. Come on, grab that drink." Maya rose and held the tablet in one hand. "This is yours for now, until we get you one of your own. I put some movies on there, too. Let's get you back upstairs before Tia Ivonne realizes you snuck out."

Rainbow accepted the tablet, cradling it oh-so-gently against her chest. "Can you show me how to fix her faucet? I want to make it better."

"Sure." Maya gave Rainbow's shoulder a gentle squeeze of encouragement and unlocked the warehouse door. Her tool bag sat near the exit, and she scooped it up and led Rainbow upstairs. Ivonne's niece Luna answered Maya's knock with a look of confusion but stepped aside without comment.

The faucet proved to be an easy fix. Maya let Rainbow hold the wrench and showed her how much force to use. Once it was repaired, Maya tucked her into the bed Ivonne had made up for her and left her exploring the books on her new tablet.

The partly open window over the bed answered the question of how the girl had gotten *out* at least. The thought of her scrambling down the side of the building was enough to make Maya's stomach lurch, but Dani probably scaled their building sometimes for fun. When the team got back, Maya would put *her* in charge of all cat burglary–adjacent childcare.

Ivonne was standing in the entryway when Maya returned, her silvering black hair in a long braid and one hand pressed to her chest over her long nightgown. "I'm sorry, Maya. I don't know how she got past me."

"She's apparently a tiny Dani," Maya replied, shaking her head. "Or a tiny Nina. Either way, I think the easiest way to keep her somewhere is to convince her she wants to be there."

"The poor thing. Did she finally talk to you?"

"A little." Maya dug in her back pocket and surfaced with an emergency card loaded with untraceable credits. "Her name is Rainbow. If you have time tomorrow, it would be a huge help if you could help her pick up some clothes."

"Of course." Ivonne folded her fingers over the card before leaning in to kiss Maya's cheek. "You're a good girl, Maya."

"I try." Maya returned the kiss. "Get some sleep."

Maya waited on the stoop until she heard the older woman engage all the locks, then hurried back down the stairs. Ivonne had come into their lives only a few months ago, but she'd adopted Maya, Dani, and Nina within moments of settling into the upstairs apartment. For the first time in her life, Maya now knew what it was like to be smothered in vaguely parental affection.

She actually didn't hate it.

Ivonne and Luna were a nice addition to their growing family. They mostly didn't talk about the fact that they'd met when Nina's crazy, evil clone sister had kidnapped Luna in an attempt to blackmail Knox and his team, just like they didn't talk about the fact that Knox and his team had basically lured Nina, Maya, and Dani into a trap in response to that blackmail.

Lies, betrayal, backstabbing—not the *best* way to kick-start a relationship. But everything had come out okay in the end. They had all bonded over the fact that they hated the TechCorps the most. And all families had drama, didn't they?

Once she was inside and had the warehouse locked up again, Maya paused by the scanner. The stack of cookbooks waited for her but so did her precious paperback. The main character stared up at her from the top of the pile with those wise, determined brown eyes.

Marjorie Chevalier was officially dead. Nina had arranged for the TechCorps to find skeletal remains with bone marrow that matched her DNA, the My First Fake Murder version of the way she'd helped Knox and his men stage their own deaths a few months ago. After Marjorie's remains had been verified, the two-million-credit reward on her head had been canceled. The TechCorps wasn't looking for her anymore.

Maya had picked a new name. It didn't have the power or magic of that first one she'd chosen for herself, but it didn't have the danger and pain, either. Maya had never watched a bullet tear through the face of the woman who had raised her. Maya hadn't sat for weeks, strapped to a chair, watching the VP of Security carve pieces off the man she loved in an attempt to force her to reveal the names of Birgitte's coconspirators.

That pain was Marjorie's. That *life* was Marjorie's. Maya was trying to build a new one. Yet here she was, obsessing over Gray, another man about to die because of the TechCorps.

She might actually be an emotional masochist.

Maya grabbed the book and carried it up to her room, where she curled up in her bed. She turned the real paper pages with reverent fingers and tried to remember what it had felt like to know she could fix anything. Save anyone.

Maybe she could save him.

TECHCORPS PROPRIETARY DATA,
L1 SECURITY CLEARANCE

It was a barracks fight, Birgitte. If we ordered additional observation for every Protectorate soldier who punched a squadmate, you wouldn't have time to do anything else.

Your obsession with 66–221 is damaging your objectivity. Stop harassing my men, or I'll have you stopped.

Internal Memo, June 2064

FIVE

Gray managed to sleep through what was left of the day and night, but not even sheer physical exhaustion could keep him there after six the next morning. His internal alarm clock had been set by years of disciplined training, and his body wasn't about to let little things like being drugged or slowly dying screw it up.

It had absolutely nothing—not a thing—to do with how his dreams were filled with warm lips, soft sighs, and the lingering peach scent of Maya's hair.

He rose and stripped his bed, folding the bedclothes neatly at the foot of his cot. It was another habit he'd picked up over the years of breaking camp. If he was still there when night fell, he'd remake the bed and start all over.

The warehouse that Nina's sister, Ava, had helped them acquire through a shell corporation had a deep, narrow footprint and had been fully divided into two floors. They'd barely touched the top so far, except to clear out the animal skeletons and old mattresses, detritus left behind by squatters, both human and otherwise. On the ground floor, they were still sleeping in barracks-style cots while they put up walls.

Gray dressed and headed toward the front of the building. They were nearly finished framing up a dividing wall to separate Knox's clinic from the rest of the warehouse. It would provide a safe space for the neighborhood doctor to see patients. Later, when the remaining Silver Devils had finished renovating the second floor into their living space, the rooms downstairs could be repurposed to expand the clinic.

It felt good to have a goal for once instead of a mission.

He picked up a hammer and got to work, letting the repetitive physical labor lull him into that narrow space between single-minded focus and zoning out. He'd spent many hours in that place, set up and waiting for the perfect moment to take a shot. It wasn't a circumstance that allowed for distraction *or* active engagement, so Gray turned inward, letting his mind drift between the two in a soothingly hypnotic rhythm.

He finished the framing quickly, then frowned at the skeletal wall in front of him. Conall had special wiring to do for the security system he wanted to set up, and any further work Gray did might interfere with that.

Time to find another piece of busywork.

He headed to clean up. They might not have bedrooms yet, but the Silver Devils had spent enough years out in the field that they had all agreed on the first thing they wanted: a bathroom with proper showers. That was already finished, a beautiful tiled set of rooms with three separate showers and enough space to accommodate four men living under the same roof.

Gray lingered longer under the steaming water than he normally would have, but when he finished and dressed again, the digital clock Conall had set up to project high on one wall still only read 9:38.

With a sigh, he brewed two cups of coffee and headed across the street.

"Morning, Sam," he greeted the old man sitting on his front stoop.

"Gray." Sam had weathered dark skin, snow-white hair, and observant brown eyes framed by smile lines. His gaze sparked with humor, even as he faked a scowl and jerked his chin toward the Devils' building. "Lot of hammering over there with the sun barely up. Some of us like to sleep."

"Liar. You were out here before I started." He handed over one of the mugs. "Extra strong, no sugar."

Sam grumbled, but he took the coffee and savored a slow sip. "Someday you kids'll tell me how you've always got the real shit."

"Hell, that's easy. We grow it out back," Gray lied, then sat one step down from Sam and stretched out his legs. "Anything interesting happening this morning?"

"My knee's aching something fierce." He lifted the cup. "A bad storm's blowing our way."

"It's September in Atlanta, Sam. Tell me something I *don't* know."

"You weren't the only one up early." This time he tilted his head toward the building where Nina and her crew lived. "Couple of folk from Little Acadiana were waiting when Maya opened the door this morning. Don't see them outside their neighborhood that often."

He didn't ask how Sam had identified the visitors as displaced Cajuns. If the man had bothered to mention it, it was because he was certain, and Gray wasn't about to waste his time asking. "Looking for help or trouble?"

"Help, I reckon. The young one, she looked scared. But the older one was plenty pissed off, so . . ."

"I'll check in on her," he promised. "Anything else?"

"Nothing important." Sam cradled the coffee cup in two gnarled hands. "Tell Maya I wouldn't mind her taking a look at that air conditioner she rigged up for me, if she gets a chance. It's rattling."

"You got it." Gray rose. "Watch your six, old man."

"I always do, kid. I always do."

Dead bolts and other assorted locks edged the front door of the ladies' warehouse. Only one was engaged at the moment: a state-of-the-art magnetic lock secured by a code. Conall had wanted to beef it up, but Nina had drawn the line at biometrics.

Her paranoia seemed justified to Gray. He barely trusted anything that gathered his identifying biological data. If he'd been grown in a lab full of clones, as Nina had?

No fucking way.

He punched in the eight-digit code, waited for the lock to disengage, and slipped inside.

The ladies' warehouse was the same size as the one the Devils had taken over, but that was where the similarities ended. Instead of two full floors, this one had been sectioned off. The back third of the building served as their storage and general work area, while the front part had been renovated into their home.

As he walked through the living area toward the kitchen, the ceiling opened up above him. He craned his neck, trying to catch a glimpse of Maya up in the loft area where the bedrooms and gym were located, but the place was still. Quiet.

He headed for the back, then paused by the open door when he heard another language—Louisiana French. People displaced by the flooding in southern Louisiana had mostly moved west, into Texas territory or Old Mexico, but a handful had settled in a section of Atlanta known as Little Acadiana.

Although Gray recognized the dialect, he couldn't speak the language. Maya, it seemed, was fluent. Her voice rolled over him, both drawling and rapid-fire, all at once. He caught words here and there—*trouble* and *doctor* . . .

And then *pregnant.*

He peered into the workroom. Maya was talking to an older, grandmotherly type, and the woman was *pissed.* She glowered as Maya scribbled something on a piece of paper, and then sighed when she put it in her hand.

Beyond them, a young woman—a girl, really—with red-rimmed, shadowed eyes sat on a stool. She caught sight of Gray with an obvious jolt of shock. He tried to smile, but it felt more like a grimace, so he stopped immediately, and she looked away.

Maya turned to her, her words bringing a spark of hope to the girl's face. "You'll be okay, Emeline. I promise."

"*Ouais.*" The girl nodded jerkily. "I just feel so stupid."

"Hey, no. Don't. You did your best." Maya gave the girl's shoulder a gentle pat. "Your grandmother has the address. I trust this doctor, okay? He'll take care of the abortion *and* replace that shit implant with the real deal. It's fast and easy, I promise. And no more side effects."

Emeline swallowed hard. "We can't afford—"

"It's taken care of," Maya interrupted. "Like I told your grandmother. And don't think this is charity. I'm trusting you to come back when the harvest is in and put in a day or two doing food prep for the freeze-dryers. I *hate* chopping vegetables."

That prompted a small, shaky smile. "It's not so bad. I don't mind doing it."

"Don't tell me that, or I'll have you back here all the time." Maya smiled back, her brown eyes sparking with warmth. "Go on. The doctor will be waiting. *T'inquiète.* You'll be fine."

The girl hurried to where the older woman waited by the back door. Maya said something else in that rolling dialect and waved cheerfully. Her expression held until the door closed behind the pair.

By the time she'd turned to face Gray, there was murder in her eyes. "Wanna help me kill someone?"

"Why not?" He shrugged. "I don't have any other plans for the day."

Maya scowled and snatched up a tablet, her fingers flying over the screen. "Apparently, there's a new quack preying on the more insular communities south of us."

"I gathered. What does Nina usually do about that shit?"

"Ask them to stop. Then tell them to stop." She finished her message and tossed the tablet onto the table. "If they don't listen, she makes them stop."

There was a bushel of peaches on the long, low table, waiting to be peeled and sliced and readied for the big steel freeze-dryers in the corner. Gray picked up one of the peaches and ran his thumb over the fuzzy surface.

It reminded him of his dream.

He took a big bite, then licked the juice off his hand. "Sounds fair enough."

She was silent for a beat too long, then jerked her gaze away from his face. "I'm not feeling fair. I'm feeling murdery. All of the snake-oil shit is bad, but the faulty birth control implants . . ." She hissed in a breath between her teeth.

"Want me to handle it?"

Maya traced one finger along the edge of the peach basket, looking seriously tempted—by the fruit or by the prospect of murder, he couldn't be sure. Then she sighed. "I don't know. Neighborhood policing is Nina's deal. Besides, you're supposed to be resting, not doing crimes. Even righteous ones."

"Hmm." He held out his half-eaten peach. "Want the rest of this?"

She reached out, her fingers brushing his as she accepted the offer. She lifted the peach to her lips and took a small bite, and her eyes fluttered shut. She savored the fruit, chewing slowly as bliss transformed her expression to something almost ecstatic.

"Like Eve in the Garden of Eden," he murmured.

"What?"

It was a dangerous path—for the conversation *and* his thoughts. "Nothing. So." He turned away. "Do you always do what you're supposed to do?"

"Depends," she replied. "Mainly on who's going to get hurt if I don't. If I drag you out to beat down some punk-ass fake doctor and you have another seizure, Knox will tear my head off. And I'll deserve it."

"That's fair." Gray tilted his head to one side, then the other. "But, then again . . . who's going to get hurt if we wait?"

Maya tossed the peach into the garbage can hard enough to rock it on its base. "Too many people. Are you *sure* you're feeling up to it?"

"What, beating down some punk-ass fake doctor?" He snorted. "I could do that in my sleep. Relax, Maya. I'm fine."

"Okay. Let me check in with Tai real quick and make sure Rainbow is still settled in upstairs with Ivonne." She waved a hand at him vaguely. "Do you need to . . . I don't know, weapon up or something?"

As if he'd leave the confines of these warehouses empty-handed. "I'm already armed."

Her gaze broke from his to skim down his body in a slow assessment. "If you say so. Don't move, I'll be right back."

She hurried out of the warehouse, leaving Gray to wonder what words, what circumstances could induce Maya's warm gaze to linger on his body for more than a few seconds.

Maya could always tell when she crossed over the invisible boundary at the edge of their unofficial territory.

When she'd first come to live with Nina, their relative influence had been small. Neighbors for a few blocks in any direction might come to Nina to ask for help or to access her impressive digital library. When you lived on the fringes and couldn't afford the strings—and surveillance—that came with TechCorps-approved net access, it was *hard* to find information. People traded battered how-to manuals and books on home remedies like they were black-market contraband—which they would be, if the TechCorps had their way.

The TechCorps *really* liked being people's only option for survival.

By the time Dani had joined them, Nina and Maya's reputation had spread across Five Points. Year by year, they'd added to their offerings, helping people grow their own food, fix their own tech. Giving people the skills and knowledge they needed to step back from the exhausting ledge of struggling just to survive.

Then they'd added the sweetest part. Books about deathless romance and daring adventures. Movies to show you a world you could barely imagine or keep the kids entertained while you stole a moment to yourself. Music to fill the silence, whether it was real or just in your head.

Survival had bought the community's trust, but joy had bought their devotion.

These days, damn near everyone in Five Points recognized Maya on sight. They smiled at her, or tossed her a wave as she passed. Some called out, asking about a book they wanted or promising to come in to help with the harvest prep.

The little kids were always the hardest to deal with. They bounced up to her with a lack of fear that twisted protective anxiety in her gut, and babbled nonsense at her like they didn't have a care in the world. The contrast between these cheerful, confident kids and Rainbow's wary caution couldn't have been starker.

Maya could handle the neighborhood kids during movie nights, where all she had to do was throw a vid up onto the wall to be their hero, but the rest of the time . . .

She didn't know how to cope with normal kids. She hadn't exactly been one. At least she *understood* Rainbow.

Still, even the way the kids freaked her out was preferable to the vibe when you left Five Points. On the other side of that invisible line, the sense of community faded. Desperation showed in a thousand ways—broken bottles and trash strewn in the streets, damaged storefronts. Apartments with the windows boarded over.

People leaned against crumbling brick walls, their hardened, considering gazes crawling over anyone who passed. Maya never left Five Points without being visibly, *aggressively* armed. Sometimes that was enough to deter trouble. When it wasn't . . . well, she never left Five Points without being ready to shoot someone in the face if she had to.

It quickly became clear that today, she would not have to.

Even though he'd said otherwise, Gray didn't look armed. He was dressed the way he usually was, in jeans and boots and a T-shirt that hugged him in loving ways Maya was pretending not to notice. He was just a man, striding next to her in companionable silence.

Predators took one look at Gray and all but combat rolled back into the grungy alleys they'd come from.

"That is seriously annoying," she grumbled, the third time a tight-faced would-be mugger melted back into the shadows after his gaze skimmed over Gray. "Does this always happen?"

"What?"

"You and the lowlifes." She waved a hand toward the darkened alley. "I could come out here with a rocket launcher and they'd still try me. You're over there in your sexy T-shirt with no visible weapons, and they're pissing themselves as they flee."

The corner of his mouth ticked up. "My *sexy* T-shirt?"

Fuck. Her cheeks burned, but she scowled at him. "Whatever. Don't act like y'all don't do it on purpose. Hell, Rafe has basically weaponized his biceps. Nuclear-grade muscle flexing."

"Now, that is true," he allowed, "but that's Rafe, not me. Besides, I don't think my clothes have much to do with why we're not getting jumped out here."

No, probably not. Tight shirts and Gray's entrancing shoulders might inspire unwanted thoughts of a different sort of jumping, but that wasn't what scared off the street toughs. "You've got the same thing Nina and Dani have. People just look at you, and they *know*."

"Probably," he agreed. "Speaking of, any updates from the team?"

"Just one. They hit the building we raided, and it was scoured clean, of course. But Conall caught them leaving on one of his pop-up cameras." Maya sighed and rubbed a hand over her shoulder. The bruise she'd gotten when the guard had slammed her into the truck was deep purple today, and a reminder of why people saw her as less dangerous. She *was*. "They're following the trail as fast as they can."

Gray exhaled and squinted up at the sky. "Wonder how long they'll stay out there, looking. Could be days, knowing Knox. Hell, Nina, too."

"Nina won't come back until she's exhausted every possible lead. And when she does come back, it'll be to regroup." Remembering the look in Nina's eyes brought a gentle ache to Maya's chest. "This is personal."

"For all of us, I think." His hand grazed her shoulder, then fell away. "In one way or another."

That warm, seductive voice wrapped around her. The ghost of his fingers lingered on her shoulder, a quiet promise. *We'll take care of this together.* And he was such a solid presence next to her. Strong, effortlessly competent. The criminals watching with fear from the shadows couldn't tell that he'd collapsed on the floor last night, seizing. That his weeks were numbered.

She kept forgetting. It would be so, so easy to forget.

The TechCorps had taken him and experimented on him, just like they had with her. And Dani. And Rafe and Conall and Knox. The people who'd hurt Nina and the ones who had created the scared young girl huddled in the upstairs apartment with Tia Ivonne might have been different monsters, but they were all part of the same evil.

Every last one of them had a score to settle.

"We'll find them," Maya said, forcing herself to sound confident. "I mean, we're a bunch of badass superheroes, right?"

"Who are you trying to convince, Maya?"

She wasn't sure. And she *really* didn't want to dig deeper and figure it out. She cleared her throat. "This is the place."

The building, like everything else in this area of downtown Atlanta, had once been nice. It was square and squat, with large picture windows framed by classic brown brick and terracotta accents. Sure, the brick was chipped and pocked, the terracotta crumbling, and every window smashed, but the building's bones were solid. That was a big ask in a place like this.

It was also utterly deserted. Through the broken windows, Maya could see a few boxes and broken pieces of furniture, but everything else had either been hastily packed or scavenged. Beside her, Gray cursed and sent a shard of glass skittering across the uneven sidewalk with a single harsh kick.

A familiar, helpless rage kindled in her chest. The cockroach had scurried away, no doubt spooked by the threats Emeline's grandmother had shouted at him. Spooked, but not deterred. He'd resurface somewhere else, peddling his false hope to people who couldn't afford the strings that came with a visit to a TechCorps "free" clinic. And Maya would only find him again after he'd wrecked more lives.

Next time, it might be something she couldn't fix.

"Stay here," Gray muttered.

Glass crunching under his boots jerked her around, her mouth opening to call Gray back. The words froze on her tongue.

The lethal predator who'd strolled casually into the dangerous side of town was gone. Gray shuffled toward a pair of shifty-looking loiterers, his face twisted with pain, his gait unsteady. His hands trembled, and he looked pale and desperate and about five seconds from face-planting right there on the dirty street and then dying in the gutter.

Even knowing it was an act, Maya's heart tried to climb into her throat.

God, it had *better* be an act.

Gray approached the men, who seemed wary but didn't scatter. They were too far away for Maya to hear their conversation, but as she watched from the corner of the building, the locals almost seemed to *relax*, as if they were speaking with an old friend instead of a stranger.

Slowly, Gray made his way back. By the time he reached her, he was standing tall, his expression clear of pain, with only the frustration lingering. Relief twisted through her, followed swiftly by unease. The act had been superb. He was a damn chameleon.

The only way she'd ever know if Gray was hurting was if he let her know.

"No dice," he told her. "They don't know where the hell he went." The corner of Gray's mouth tipped up. "They did tell me about some new clinic someone's putting together in Five Points, but they warned me to be careful. No one knows what to make of it yet."

Unsurprising. Knox's clinic would seem too good to be true to the people who scraped by on the edges of survival. It would take time to build trust.

Well, it would take *most* of them time. "How did you do that?" she asked as they turned back toward Five Points. "I thought Rafe was the team's resident grifter."

"What, that?" Gray shrugged. "That's not grift, that's just—"

The peaceful quiet of the street exploded into the unmistakable cacophony of a firefight—rapid gunfire, shouts, bullets ricocheting off buildings and pavement. Training kicked in, her hand going for her holster before the first crack echoed through the alley.

In the same moment, Gray slammed into her.

Her back hit solid brick. Her head snapped back, smacking into the hand he'd slid behind her neck to protect her. He was *everywhere*, holding her against the wall, his body curved to shield hers. Her face ended up pressed to his throat, her shocked inhalation filling her lungs with the scent of him—gun oil and coffee and soap and sawdust.

Adrenaline surged through her, making everything worse. The press of his body. His scent. The sound he made, some sort of subvocal rumble that was probably supposed to soothe her, but his chest rumbled against hers and her brain blanked.

If she parted her lips, she'd be able to taste him.

Sweet merciful fuck, if he didn't get the hell off her, she might actually do it.

Frantic, running footsteps echoed down the street, followed by the safety of silence. But Gray didn't move.

Maya braced a hand against his chest, even though the contact burned. "Hey. It's okay." She pushed a little. It was like shoving granite. Or Nina. "I'm okay."

He finally stepped back but left one hand flat against the brick. It left him leaning over her, a posture more oddly intimate than his body pinning hers to the wall. Something electric shivered through her, and she spread her fingers wide, intending to give him another gentle push.

His eyes met hers. Held. His chest tensed under her fingertips. She parted her lips, but no sound came out. For once in her life, she couldn't remember a single damn word.

Then his gaze dropped to her mouth. His fingers pressed into the wall next to her head. He wasn't touching her anywhere except where her hands were splayed against his chest, but she felt him from the top of her head to the tips of her toes, which were doing their best to curl inside her boots.

The hand next to her head shifted. His thumb stroked one of her braids. Her scalp tingled, and a whimper lodged in her throat then emerged as his name. "Gray?"

His gaze snapped back to hers. The wild look faded, and he pushed abruptly away from the wall, leaving her slapping her palms against the brick to keep from swaying after him.

"Sorry about that," he rasped.

She hadn't realized the sheer heat of him until he was gone. Even in the muggy morning air, she felt suddenly chilled. Her fingers tingled as she flexed them. "It's fine," she managed, forcing herself to speak lightly. "Dani tends to jump on me when guns go off, too. But I can take care of myself, I promise."

"I know you can. It's just . . ." Gray dragged a hand through his hair. "Never mind. You want to get out of here?"

Her heart stuttered. She couldn't tear her gaze from his disheveled hair. It was just long enough for pieces to stand up, little spikes she wanted to smooth down. Because that was what she should be thinking about, standing in the midst of broken glass in a gutted-out alley thirty seconds after a shoot-out. Touching his hair.

Fuck, he'd broken her brain.

"Yeah." She forced herself to straighten and fell in beside him as he started to walk. Totally casual. Very normal. Nothing weird or awkward at all. If she avoided him for the next fifty years, maybe she could convince herself it was true.

Hard on the heels of the thought came guilt. It twisted through her, a sick reminder.

Gray didn't have fifty years. Gray likely didn't have one.

For a heartbeat, it *hurt*. It hurt as badly as knowing the quack doctor had fled to do more harm. It hurt like knowing Nina was out there, tracking down bad guys who would probably slip through their fingers and keep on hurting children. One more thing she couldn't do a damn thing to fix, and if she let herself feel all of them at once, she'd sink under the weight of them and never resurface.

So she didn't. With her rigid TechCorps dissociation training, she enforced discipline on her unruly thoughts. She just . . . stopped feeling. She'd pay for it later, like she always did, but she'd made an art form of it by now. She crushed every hurt and distraction into a tiny ball and shoved them into the box deep in her mind. They settled, a tangible weight across her shoulders, a tension in her body that never entirely left.

But her mind was blissfully, beautifully blank.

As she and Gray walked back to Five Points, Maya filled that blank space with a list of things she could control, each one spawning a list of things she could *do.* She whispered each task to herself, locking it into memory.

When she got home, she'd work until she collapsed. She'd check off every damn thing on that list and make new ones if she had to.

Maybe, this time, it would be enough.

August 4th, 2072

DC-025 has enrolled in the same assembly language class as Marjorie. I'm sure Tobias Richter's data courier already knows such basic material.

I can't see this as a harmless coincidence.

The Recovered Journal of Birgitte Skovgaard

SIX

Maya was avoiding him.

As soon as they'd made it back home, she'd murmured an excuse about being busy and ducked into the work area of the ladies' warehouse.

Oh, who was he kidding? She'd *fled*, and he honestly didn't even blame her. Not only had he talked her into going on what amounted to a wild-goose chase, but he'd shoved her against a wall and drooled on her.

Smooth, Gray. Real fucking smooth.

He snagged a couple of beers and went across the street in search of Sam. The old man was bound to get tired of seeing his face sooner or later, so Gray planned to make the most of his taciturn acquaintance while he could.

Sam was out, but his neighbor, a pretty, young widow who'd been flirting with Rafe nonstop, flagged him down. Gray spent nearly twenty precious minutes trying to extricate himself from her interrogation—what was Rafe's favorite food, did he like redheads, was he dating anyone?

The poor woman didn't stand a chance, so Gray handed her the beers and bluntly told her that the butcher who lived downstairs was a better bet.

His potential distractions exhausted, he headed back to the warehouse where Maya was, undoubtedly, still hiding. He punched in the code for the back door this time, and stopped short when Maya spared him a single distracted glance before returning her attention to the massive 3D scanner in front of her.

Okay, then.

The back wall of the warehouse had been set up with a desk and several tables, the surfaces covered with a computer, two scanners smaller than the one Maya was using, and boxes and boxes of books. Gray wandered over to one of the tables, where he straightened a slightly crooked pile of books before turning back to Maya. "Want some help?"

Without looking up, she swept up a box cutter and tossed it toward him. "Grab a box."

A frisson of warning flickered up his spine, like someone had a bead on him and a laser dot was about to show up dead center on his chest. "I'm sorry, Maya. Truly, I am."

"You don't need to apologize." Her gaze stayed fixed on the screen as the scanned pages flickered across it. "Like I said, Dani likes to tackle me in firefights, too. I get instinct. I just wish y'all's instincts weren't convinced I'm helpless."

He sliced open the nearest box, grimacing at the slightly musty scent that spilled out of it when he pried open the flaps. "I don't think you're helpless."

She made an amused noise. "Really?"

"Really. Look, I understand that you could probably tell exactly where those shots were coming from in an instant, but it took me a second, all right? I thought someone was shooting at us. And bullets hit capable people just as hard as they do helpless ones."

Another amused snort. "I've got a good memory, not psychic powers."

An entirely different sort of alarm jolted through him. "Maya? Don't you train?"

"Uh, all the damn time. Cardio, hand-to-hand. Rafe's making me wrestle him with the stun gun now."

"How about ranged weapons?"

"I'm proficient with small- and large-caliber semiautomatic pistols," she recited obediently. "I've even trained with Mark series rifles, but that's more Dani's speed than mine. I like my Ovechkin 9mm. Not too light *or* too heavy, decent capacity, manageable recoil. Oh, and I have a crossbow. Half points for efficiency but double points for style."

She'd mentioned nothing beyond regular target practice. Gray clapped his hands together. "Okay, then. Who else can do this here? What about that lady who helps out around here sometimes, the one Luna has a crush on?"

"Who, Tai? She already helps with this." Maya shot him a sidelong look. "But it's not like scanning is beneath me or something. I'm the one who set up the digital catalog and figured out how to automate metadata importation from the scanner."

"Uh-huh."

The scanner *beeped* softly, and Maya removed the book and checked the listing on her computer. After a second, she pursed her lips. "I admit, it is slightly less exciting now that I have it working reliably."

"I'm already about to fall asleep." He plucked the scanned book from her hands and set it aside. "You should be training."

Maya groaned. "I *know* how to shoot—"

"We're gonna do something different," he corrected. "Question: how does ear protection work for you?"

Maya shrugged. "I use it sometimes, but I'm not sure I really need it. Loud noises don't bother me on their own."

Whatever the TechCorps had done to her, they'd been smart about it. A data courier who could be disabled with one good sonic boom would be useless to them. "No ringing in the ears, muffled hearing, nothing like that?"

"Nah." Her teeth sank into her lower lip, and she gave him another quick, sidelong look. "Sometimes I get overwhelmed, but that's not really about volume but duration. And you saw me at those underground fights. I have a couple of triggers."

"I remember." Her reaction that night had been as familiar to him as his own name. He'd seen it often enough while serving in the Protectorate, though brass always denied post-traumatic stress was an issue for their soldiers.

Like hell it wasn't.

Gray dusted off his hands on his jeans. "Tomorrow. You're gonna show me what kinds of tricks you can do with that brain and those ears of yours."

Maya groaned and spun around on the stool. "Not this again. Conall has been giving me shit all month. I mean, I'm good at math, sure. I can calculate trajectory or hustle you at pool. But it's not like I have superpowers."

"Sure you do. You *remember everything you hear*."

She stared back at him in exasperation. "And?"

"And what?"

"Exactly." She threw up her hands. "So what? I tried listening to that guard the other night, and I couldn't figure out how far away he was. If remembering everything helped, maybe I wouldn't have a shiner today."

"Maya, it's not magic. Perfect auditory recall won't help you judge how far away a sound is on its own." He took her hands in his, stilling their fluttering movements. "You still have to *learn*. But once you know what it sounds like when a ninety-kilogram man in tactical boots walks on gravel one meter away, or three, or ten? Your brain won't forget it like everyone else's does. And you'll be able to use it."

She stared at him, her brow adorably furrowed. Her hands trembled slightly in his. A moment later, one of her boots began to thud softly against the rung of the stool in a steady rhythm, as if the nervous energy had passed to her feet. "Huh," she said finally. "So . . . like a key."

"Yeah, sure. A legend on a map."

"I guess that makes sense." She tilted her head. "It's weird. The TechCorps had a million selfish reasons to convince me I was only good for one thing. I *know* that. But sometimes it's still hard to think outside that little box they put me in."

Remorse struck him like a blow to the sternum. "Sorry, I didn't—"

"No. *No*. I don't want to live in the box." Her full lips curved in a tentative, almost shy smile. "Just let me get my head around it, okay? It's kind of always been the thing, you know? Dani and Nina have superpowers, and I win trivia night."

Here it was, right in front of him. A way he could help, something he could do that would make a real difference for Maya. "I need the rest of the day to put something together, but we can start tomorrow morning."

She hesitated a moment, then nodded. "I can do that. Tai can cover walk-ins for a while."

"It won't be quick or easy," he added as a belated warning. "Training like this will take a lot of time and effort, even for someone like you."

"You know you're not really selling this, right?" She shook her head and spun back around on her stool. "Don't worry. I let Dani toss me around the training room and Rafe growl at me about Tasers. I think I can handle you."

"Famous last words, darling. Famous last words."

She snorted. "Now you're just asking to get forked."

"Maybe." He started pulling books from the box and stacking them on the table in a careful pile. "I thought you were avoiding me."

"Avoiding you?" She glanced at him, her expression contrite. "No. I'm sorry if I was—"

"No, I was—"

They both stopped abruptly, and a heartbeat later Maya smiled nervously. "I swear I wasn't avoiding you. Sometimes when I'm focused on something, I just get so in my head that the building could be on fire and I wouldn't notice. I've had entire conversations with Nina without realizing it."

He couldn't tell if it was the truth or if she was trying to make him feel better. "I'm not like Rafe," he told her haltingly. "Hell, I'm not even like *Knox*. I make people uncomfortable."

She seemed to absorb the words as she set the next book in place and hit the button to start the scanner. Then she turned on her stool to face him fully. "You don't make me uncomfortable," she said seriously. "You never have. You're . . ." She hesitated. Licked her lips. "Conall is fun, but he can be exhausting. The *energy* around him. Rafe can be just as bad, and sometimes Knox is so intense he gives me a headache. But you're . . . careful. Peaceful. You're *safe*."

He didn't feel very peaceful, but careful and safe? He'd take it. "Is that why we had that . . . *moment* today?"

Her nervous energy returned abruptly as her gaze skittered from his. "I don't know," she said with forced lightness, twisting to pick up another book. "I mean *I* was having a moment because you and your sexy T-shirt and your muscles you swear you don't weaponize were leaning over me."

He took the book from her hand and set it aside. "I don't know how to flirt. I only know how I feel."

Her throat worked as she swallowed. "How do you feel?"

He'd pressed her against that wall and covered her body with his out of instinct, a drive to shield and protect. But once he was there . . . "I liked being close to you. I want to do it again." He couldn't help smiling a little. "Maybe with fewer bullets involved."

Her gaze snapped back to his. Her breathing seemed a little unsteady, but her nerves seemed less like anxiety and more like anticipation. "Fewer bullets is good," she agreed.

"Good." He passed her another book and watched as she placed it on the scanner.

It was slow, steady work, the mindless kind where you could let your mind wander. At first, Gray thought Maya would need to talk to fill the silence, but she seemed content to just enjoy his company.

A tension lingered in the air between them, but it wasn't a bad sort of feeling. It was more like an awareness, one that prickled over Gray's skin and spiked when his fingers touched Maya's to pass books back and forth.

She blushed, and Gray stifled a sigh. It felt good just being near her. Even better when he saw how her eyes lit up and her mouth tilted up at the corners in a persistent smile.

In that moment, he resolved to make that happen more. As much as possible.

TECHCORPS PROPRIETARY DATA,
L1 SECURITY CLEARANCE

66–221: Heard you finally got slapped down for riding my ass.

Skovgaard: I'm simply concerned about your well-being, Sergeant Walker.

66–221: And I think you're a nagging bitch who gets to live a soft life because I'm out there bleeding for you.

Skovgaard: Do you resent the work you do?

66–221: Fuck off, lady.

Recruit Analysis Session Log, July 2064

SEVEN

Even after his quasi-confession in the warehouse, Maya had been confident she could deal with Gray.

Her confidence took a drastic nosedive when she saw the blindfold. "I don't know what sort of kinky shit you're into, but if you wanna put that on me, you're gonna have to buy me dinner first."

His head fell back on a groan she could hear all the way across the mostly empty expanse of the Devils' warehouse. "Will you please be serious?"

Irritating him was good. Irritating him would hopefully distract him from the fact that he'd said he liked touching her and she was forgetting all the reasons she definitely couldn't let him. Bravado was her only escape, and she embraced it. "Uh, have you met me? I mock evil clones to their faces and stab bad guys with forks. I don't do serious."

"How could I forget?" He motioned to the low stool near her. "Have a seat."

Maya scanned the room again as she moved to obey. It didn't *look* like a training course. It was mostly just taped marks on the floor, evenly spaced in concentric circles surrounding the stool, and a bunch of freestanding targets off to one side.

Confused and still a little unnerved, she sank onto the stool. "So what exactly is this serious training going to involve?"

"Like I said yesterday—listening." Gray approached only to kneel in front of her. "That's it. Maybe, if you feel up to it, some target shooting later. But first, I want to talk about the blindfold."

"Okay," she told him, holding herself very still. He was close enough that her leg might brush him if she swung it. "Tell me about the blindfold."

"This kind of training can be a real trip," he rasped. "If the blindfold starts to fuck with your head, you tap out. There's no shame in it, you hear me?"

His *voice* was fucking with her head. That was how all of this bullshit had started. Maya had always had a comfortable understanding with her subdued libido. She appreciated pretty people, but she appreciated them *from a distance*, without the messy complications of trust and touch or having strangers invade her personal space and the inevitable sensory meltdown that followed.

Gray wasn't even the prettiest of the Devils. Rafe was *gorgeous*, unmistakably one of the most objectively attractive people who existed in Atlanta or potentially the world. Having a crush on him would have made sense.

But no. Gray had opened his mouth, and his voice had stroked its way under her skin. Her libido had roared to uncontrollable life. And now she was sitting in an empty warehouse with him, about to let him blindfold her and whisper things in her ear that would echo there tonight like a taunting fantasy.

And he *liked touching her.*

This was a fucking fabulous idea.

"I'll be okay," she told him, forcing a grin. At least this was likely to be a useless exercise. Gray would grow bored and go torture someone else with his sin-inducing voice. "Let's do this."

He rose with a nod, then slid the blindfold into his jacket pocket.

Maya opened her mouth to protest, but he was already moving to one of the taped marks on the floor. He had a tiny device in one hand, and when he pressed a button on the top, it emitted a melodious *beep.*

Without a word, he moved to the next mark and repeated the process.

"Uhm . . ." Maya twisted to watch him. "Is this the training part?"

"Let me guess." The corner of his mouth quirked up. "You expected something from an action movie."

"I mean, at least some lasers or something." She watched him traverse two more of the taped markers, the *beep* at each one short and cheerful. "Should I be doing something besides watching you?"

"Yeah. Listening." He shook his head with a laugh. "Don't worry, the lasers come later."

"Oh boy."

Fifteen minutes later, Maya thought the lasers couldn't come fast enough. She'd heard beeps in front of her. To each side. Behind her. Backward and forward and everything but upside down. Upside down might at least be interesting. The blood rushing to her head would have livened things up.

And Gray wasn't talking. Even her libido was getting bored. Thank God.

"Ready?" His hand brushed her shoulder, his fingers blazing hot against the skin bared by her tank top, and when she turned . . .

He was holding the blindfold, one eyebrow arched.

Oh, *shit.*

She swallowed hard. Managed to sound almost casual. "Go for it."

He stepped behind her, and the fabric slid over her eyes, blotting out everything but the steady sound of his breathing and the prickling feel of him so close to her back, he might as well be touching her all over. Gray smoothed the back of the blindfold into place over her braids, then dropped his hands to her arms. "Steady?"

Depended on his definition of *steady.* His hands blazed on her arms. Skin on skin. She had fucking *tingles.* "I think so."

"Good. When you hear the sound, turn toward it and tell me how far away it is."

Soft, almost noiseless footsteps whispered across the bare concrete, and the first *beep* came from off to her left. It seemed like a ridiculous request until her body started to move, and an image formed in her head that matched the sound—Gray, standing on the fifth ring of the circles.

Fifth ring. Evenly spaced. She pointed at where she knew he'd be. "Ten meters."

"Nice." He sounded pleased. "Most people can judge immediately if something is maybe one or two meters away, but the longer distances trip them up."

"I *have* practiced hearing subtle differences in tone." She wiggled her fingers at him. "That's how I opened that vault in Dalton. I only have to hear the keypad sequence once to duplicate it. I got to a hundred and twenty-seven digits once before Dani got tired of quizzing me."

"Then you're going to be really damn good at this. Now *focus*."

The first few times, it was fun. Her brain had always been quick to pick up on new skills, and she loved the challenge of it. But the more she turned to point to the sounds, the quicker the answers came, until she didn't need to stop to match a tone to a particular image in her head.

Beep. "Two meters."

Her brain just *knew*.

Beep. "Twelve meters."

And when her brain knew things . . .

Beep. "Two." *Beep*. "Four and a half." *Beep*. "Two, again."

. . . her brain got so damn bored.

She started to fidget on the stool. She struggled to hide her irritation. Surely they should have progressed to something challenging by now. Unless this was just more bullshit with the supersoldiers underestimating her.

Beep. Beep. Beep.

If she looked like a badass like Nina or a literal femme fatale like Dani, Gray wouldn't have her sitting here doing baby training exercises.

Beep.

She wanted guns. She wanted lasers.

Beep. Beep.

Hell, if she was going to make irrational choices, she wanted sexy sparring, goddammit.

"Maya." Gray was so close she started. Not only did his voice tickle over her skin, but she could *feel* his presence as he leaned over her. "It's time."

Oh God, could he read her thoughts? "Time for what?" she choked out.

"For this." He pressed a pistol into her hand.

Maya sat up straighter, her fingers curling tight. "You're not going to let me shoot you, right? That would be *super* awkward to explain to Knox when he gets back."

Gray laughed. "Don't worry. It's simulated fire. Sounds real, but there are no bullets, so you won't have to explain my untimely demise to the captain." He pulled her to her feet, and the stool scraped over the floor. "Each of the targets is equipped with one of the devices I was using. When you hear the *beep*, you'll have three seconds to tag it with the pistol's laser sight and fire. It starts off slow, but it gets faster. You ready?"

She had tingles again, but these were different. It always felt like this when she found an engaging challenge, as if the noise inside her head settled for a blissful moment, every neuron poised to fire in glorious harmony.

Maya found her balance as Nina had taught her and lifted the gun. "Bring it on."

Silence. And then . . .

Beep.

Behind her. Six o'clock. Fifteen meters.

Maya whirled in the direction of the sound and remembered the shape of the targets. They'd been constructed so that a bull's-eye would hit a person just under two meters center mass. She knew the way that felt, the angle of her arms, the exact posture required.

The rest was just . . . math. Math was easy. The TechCorps hadn't planned to teach her more than the basics, but when they'd denied her access to the higher-level classes, Birgitte had overruled them. She'd made it clear that she wanted Maya to be capable of contextualizing complicated scientific data for her, and a vice president's requests about the education of their personal data courier were final.

So Maya had filled her head with math until she ran out of classes to take.

It was all still there. She used it to model algorithms and balance the books, to calculate the potential blast radius of explosives, and to pull off pool shots so impossible, Dani had more than once rescued her from impending fistfights over her alleged pool hustling.

Maya was good at math, so she used it to lift her arms in the third second after the *beep* filled the warehouse and fire on the spot she knew the target would be.

Not thought. *Knew.*

Gray had been right. This was easy. She'd just needed someone to give her the reference points.

The next beep sounded, and she spun again. Three meters. Much closer. She adjusted the angle of her arms slightly and fired faster this time.

Next time was faster again. Heady exhilaration filled her as her brain sparked, the challenge only increasing as the chimes accelerated. Soon, they were coming one right after the other, almost overlapping. Conscious thought turned into effortless confidence, and she smiled as she squeezed the trigger again and again and again.

This was more like it.

Finally, a burst of three sounds came from her left, so close together that it took her a moment to figure them out. But she took her shots without overthinking them, then poised on her toes, waiting for the next beep. When that didn't come, she waited for Gray to say something.

He didn't.

Seconds ticked by in agonizing quiet. Some of her confidence fizzled, and she reached for the blindfold. "What, did I miss them all or something?"

Gray was standing in front of her, four and a half meters away, surrounded by targets. He stared at her, his eyes wide and unblinking. Then he exhaled sharply and shook his head.

When he spoke, his voice was low, as always, but not smooth. In fact, it held just the slightest hint of a tremor. "Twenty-one shots. Twenty-one hits."

The words sounded good, but his body language screamed tension. Maya turned in a slow circle, checking off the targets one by one. Only a handful were solid bull's-eyes. Most of her shots had hit in the outer circles, and a few had just barely winged them.

"Well," she said finally. "I mean, my shooting was a little sloppy. I was kind of extrapolating based on comparable experiences. I could probably do better if I knew what a bull's-eye felt like at different distances."

Gray scrubbed both hands over his face, muffling a slightly hysterical laugh.

"What?" she demanded, dragging the blindfold off her head. "Hey, I may not be a supersoldier or whatever, but I think I did pretty fucking good for my first try."

"You don't get it." Gray hooked his thumb at a target, one that displayed a bull's-eye hit. "Hitting six targets—winging them, not even solid shots, mind you—is considered decent enough for the field. The Protectorate considers you for in-depth training if you hit nine. The record? Is seventeen hits."

"Well, I didn't get *that* many more—"

Gray interrupted her. "That was Hwang. Not only is he really fucking good at it, but he'd been training for *three years* by that point. Like I said . . ." His eyes gleamed. "You don't get it. You're not just okay or good, Maya. You're a goddamned savant."

Maya stared at him, unsure what to say—or think. For perhaps the first time in her life, silence echoed inside her head. The compliment, gleeful and sincere, didn't provoke an avalanche of memories.

No one at the TechCorps had spent their time telling her she was amazing. At *anything.*

Unable to contain the warmth bubbling up in her, she thrust out her hand and waved the blindfold at him. "I want to do it again."

"Whatever you want." He fixed the blindfold into place, plunging her into darkness once again. Then he spun her around a few times, his hands warm on her arms. "Ready?"

She steadied herself with a hand against the solid wall of his chest, then nodded. "Ready."

Gray vanished. Maya lifted the pistol, her grip easy. She didn't try to think. She didn't try *not* to think. It was like relaxing a muscle she kept painfully tense even in her sleep, and the sudden relief of it made her giddy.

It was dangerous to let go of her hard-won control. In moments, the memories might surge and sweep her under. But she floated on the bliss and waited for the first *beep*.

When it came, she moved.

Maya closed her eyes behind the blindfold and *imagined* the room. She conjured it out of the darkness with her too-vivid memory and flowed from one shot to the next. Every kick of the pistol came with a thrill of success. She might not be able to see the targets, but she knew she was hitting them.

Maybe she was a supersoldier after all.

Maybe she was something better.

The crack of her final shot echoed through the space. The *beeps* fell silent. Maya stood with her feet parted, the pistol out at one side, her breathing a little too fast. Not from exertion. From excitement. "I hit them all, didn't I?"

"Do you even have to ask?"

She didn't. Maya stripped off the blindfold and tossed it onto the stool. The pistol followed. Then she made a slow circle, studying the targets.

Twenty-one hits. Twelve bull's-eyes.

Her slow circuit stopped when she was facing Gray again. Unable to contain her excitement, she bounced on her toes. "I'm a fucking rock star."

He grinned. "Yes, you are."

Two steps closer, and her cheeks hurt from how wide she was smiling. "I have actual, literal superpowers."

"Yes, you do."

Excitement overflowed. She felt like she was floating. Like her feet were barely touching the ground. She forgot all the reasons touching him was dangerous. Another step, and Maya crashed into Gray, flinging her arms around his neck. "Thank you."

"You're welcome." After a moment, he folded his arms around her waist, lifting her against his body. *That* penetrated the giddy bubbles in her brain. She slammed back into her body as her awareness of him roared to life.

They were touching. So much touching. All-over touching, and the muscles of his chest were as solid as she remembered. His arms were warm steel.

He still smelled like soap and sawdust.

Math. Math was a distraction. She'd do more math. If Gray was 185 cm tall and she was only 162 cm, the surface area of their bodies crushed together was—

Numbers disintegrated into stardust when she made the mistake of meeting his eyes. No dark and brooding Gothic terror today. No, Gray's eyes were warm. Gentle.

Aware.

The only thing more terrifying than having an inexplicable, uncontrollable crush on a dying man was her increasing certainty that it wasn't unrequited.

Trying to fuck him would break her brain. Loving him would shatter her heart.

He licked his lips. "Maya—"

The crash of a door slamming cut him off, and he raised his head with a frown. "Was that over at y'all's place?"

"I think so." She braced a hand against his shoulder, barely holding back a shiver as he let her slide back down his body. Even with her boots solidly on the floor again, she felt unsteady—which was a problem. "If they're back this soon and slamming doors, that isn't good."

"We'd better go hear the news."

"The trail must have stayed cold." That was chilling enough to sober Maya up. Not that the tingles were entirely gone, but by the time they made it out the back door she was at least steady enough to fake it.

Conall was standing next to the open van doors, his face tight with exhaustion. He shook his head in answer to their silent question and jerked a thumb toward the warehouse door. "Nina needs a hug. She's in rough shape."

"Shit." Maya picked up her pace, racing through the warehouse with a perfunctory wave for Tai and crashing through the door to their main living quarters.

Nina was at the kitchen table, her face buried in her hands and her entire body stiff in a way that provoked an ache of sympathy in Maya's chest. She caught a glimpse of Dani disappearing up the stairs while Rafe hovered uncertainly at the base, his dark eyes worried.

Knox was already in the kitchen, pulling down their stash of soothing tea. His worried gaze eased somewhat when he caught sight of Maya, and he tipped his head silently toward the table.

Maya hooked a chair and pulled it close enough to touch Nina's shoulder. "Hey. What happened?"

Nina looked up and tried—*tried*—to smile. "Not much. We gave it our best shot, but . . ."

But chasing down a few trucks that had disappeared into the vast wilderness between here and the Mississippi River was a nearly impossible task. "No buts," Maya said firmly, wrapping her arm around Nina and pulling her close. "You couldn't find the trucks. That doesn't mean it's over."

"No. We'll regroup and go from there, but we're *not* giving up." Nina took a deep breath. "How were things here?"

Warmth flooded her face. She almost opened her mouth, but the clink of mugs on the kitchen counter reminded her that Knox was right there, and Gray with him. Her confused hormones would have to wait. "Fine. Tai's scanning the cookbooks now. I put out word that we have new home-improvement guides, and people have been showing up with their tablets."

"Rest," Knox said firmly. He brought a mug of tea to Nina and placed it on the table in front of her. "You haven't slept since we left."

"You're one to talk." She wrapped her fingers around the mug and studied Gray. "What about you? Any more issues with your implant?"

"Nope. Things here have been uneventful." Though he still leaned against the wall, his arms crossed over his chest in classic Gray posture, he glanced at Maya.

And *winked.*

The bastard was *teasing* her now.

Knox set a second mug of tea down in front of Maya. It was her favorite kind, a peach blossom blend that Ma Kendrick made for Maya in exchange for the occasional tune-up on the solar generator that powered her rooftop greenhouse. Knox had even prepared it exactly the way Maya liked it, with a precious splash of real milk and too much honey.

Knox was like that. Meticulously observant and relentlessly thoughtful. It would be churlish to reward his gesture by flinging the tea at Gray's head in an attempt to discourage his dangerous interest. But even that was probably a better life choice than giving in to the temptation to jump into his arms again.

Yeah, her hormones were *seriously* out of control. After years of lying dormant, they'd roared to life at the worst time and focused on the most hopeless person. She shouldn't even be surprised, considering her romantic track record. Falling in big, horny lust with a man whose impending death would shatter her heart was *exactly* her flavor of self-destruction.

She wished that knowing that would change something. *Anything.* But when she peeked at him over the rim of her cup, his gaze was fixed on her lips in a way that practically *screamed* that he was imagining that almost-kiss.

Now she was, too. The heat of his body. The iron of his arms as he held her pinned to his chest, her boots dangling above the floor. His mouth—his *mouth*—

Full-body tingles raised the hair on her arms, and she fought to hide a shudder as she scalded her tongue with her too-sweet tea. It was a miracle she hadn't skated into full sensory overload already today. Tingles were nice, but they always became *too much.* Which was what she had to remember.

Fantasies were fine. And if she didn't want to hasten the expiration date on her own increasingly overwhelmed brain, fantasies had to be enough. It was safer that way. For her *and* for Gray. Because the last time she'd let things progress past fantasy . . .

One name, Marjorie. Give me a name, or I break the next bone. And then another, and another. . . . How much pain can Simon endure, do you think? Shall we find out?

It was like being dropped into an icy mountain lake. Sweet tingles turned to a chilled shudder, and Maya locked down the memory before it could bloom into a full sensory flashback.

Loving her had already been the death of one man. She wouldn't repeat the mistake.

RAFE

Dani was going to hurt herself.

His chest tight with sympathy, Rafe hovered in the doorway of the women's workout room. He'd been impressed the first time he set foot across the threshold. Everything in the room was state of the art, even for the TechCorps. Automatically calibrating weight and resistance training, treadmills that folded out of the wall, a beautiful array of practice weapons, and a padded floor perfect for sparring.

Nina was a woman who took training seriously.

Of course, today Dani was ignoring all of that. She'd stripped off her shirt and shoes by the door and lowered one of the heavily reinforced punching bags. Her body was a blur as she drove her unwrapped fists into it over and over. Too fast. Too hard.

Her knuckles were already raw. They'd be bleeding soon. If it had been Knox or even Nina, Rafe might think that was the whole point—drowning frustration and failure in the distraction of physical pain. Rafe could even understand it. He'd heaped his share of abuse on his body, just trying to escape the demons in his nightmares.

But Dani would never have that escape. Because she literally couldn't feel the pain.

Rafe stepped across the threshold, his bare feet silent on the mat.

Dani stopped and stilled the bag's movement, her fingers digging into the canvas. "Not now, Morales."

"If you want me to just shut up and stand here, fine. But I'm not leaving until you're done pulverizing your hands."

"My hands are fine." She turned and flexed all her fingers in a show of dexterity. "See? It's the rest of me that's not doing so hot right now."

"I can imagine." He took another step forward and braced his hands on his hips. "Instead of punching the skin off your knuckles, we could talk about it."

A short, harsh laugh tore out of her throat.

"What's wrong, cupcake?" Rafe hid his concern beneath his laziest drawl. "Don't think I can talk?"

"Oh, I know you can." Dani glared at him. "You're *all* talk, aren't you?"

"As opposed to what?" He knew he shouldn't say it. He *knew* he shouldn't. Rafe had never thought he had anything to prove before, but when that hot challenge sparked in Dani's eyes, it was like his brains melted out his ears. "You want something? *Ask* for it."

Her chest heaved, something between a sigh and a shudder. They stood staring at each other in charged silence, his challenge thrown down like a gauntlet between them. If she asked him to touch her, he would. He wouldn't know how to stop.

Lock it down, Morales.

Dani didn't need to be provoked into a fight. Or a fuck. She needed someone to take care of her, though God knew she'd combat roll out a third-story window before admitting it. "Come here," he said softly, holding out his hands. "Just let me check your knuckles, okay? It's either me or Maya."

Her jaw clenched, but she relented, holding out both hands with a short nod. "They're fine, but knock yourself out."

Dani's hands were deceptively delicate compared to Rafe's. Her pale skin showed the abuse from the bag all too readily, her knuckles an angry red and scraped nearly raw. Rafe bent her fingers gently and rubbed his thumb across the backs of her fingers. "We're going to find those kids, Dani. Knox knows how to get the job done."

"You're so sure," she whispered. "Always. How can you be that sure of everything?"

"Because the only mission Knox has ever botched was betraying Nina." Rafe stroked her fingers again and tried not to wonder at the nightmares lurking in her eyes or why the idea of children trapped like experiments shook her so hard. "We're not leaving kids behind. It's just not an option."

"It's not just this. It's . . ." She shook her head and repeated the word. "Everything."

A dozen possible replies came to his lips. Easy, reassuring. But not honest. The honest truth was darker. "Because I have to be, Dani. I can't entertain the alternative. Too many people are depending on me getting my shit done, and when I don't . . ."

When he didn't, people got kidnapped. Hurt. People got dead.

"Like your family."

He'd almost forgotten he'd told Dani about his sister—yet another time his good sense had taken flight. Rafe didn't talk about his family with *anyone*. Not even Knox. "Yeah. My family."

Her fingers closed around his for a split second, then relaxed. "How are they?"

"I don't know. Fine, I guess." He exhaled softly. "I gave my mother my cut from the RLOC bunker. That should hold them over until my youngest sister is grown."

"You won't be able to see them."

It wasn't a question. Because Dani understood. "Conall's been keeping an eye on the TechCorps with that backdoor into their server, and he swears they're convinced we're dead . . . But all it takes is one fuckup. One careless moment. I won't lead them back to my family."

Dani stared up at him, her soft, blue gaze full of sympathy and commiseration and something else, something suspiciously like longing.

Or maybe that was just what he wanted to see.

Then she blinked, and the moment dissolved. She turned away, tearing her hands from his. "If you really want to help me, give me something to hit besides this bag."

She didn't need to fight. She needed *sleep.* And if Rafe told her to get some, she'd stay awake until she collapsed just to spite him. "I was going to go hit the showers and then fall into a bed. Just because I *can* stay awake for three days in a row doesn't make it fun."

"Suit yourself." She squared up to the bag and took another swing at it, shaking the bag so hard that the chain securing it rattled.

He watched her for another agonizing moment, his own knuckles stinging with the pain she couldn't feel. He could stay and give her a better target. God knew she'd be an exciting sparring partner. He was twice her size and easily five times as strong, but her *speed*—he'd never seen anyone move like Dani. Fast and fearless.

And if he got his hands on her now, it wouldn't end with fighting. He was just strung out enough to make a lot of *very* bad decisions. And as satisfying as a hard fuck on the training room floor might be . . .

Rafe had Dani's number. That would be it for him. She'd ride him hard and kick him out of her bed. Probably slam the door behind him for good measure. Dani didn't let the men she fucked into her life, and that wouldn't be enough for him. The fractures would damage their fragile new shared family and hurt the people they loved.

Rafe had decided the first time Dani stabbed him that he was playing the long game with her. All or nothing.

Turning silently, he retreated back along the hallway and down the stairs. Maya was still at the kitchen table, sipping from a mug of tea, but she offered him a smile over the rim. "Headed to take a nap?"

"At least a few hours." He stopped next to the table. "Dani's up there scraping her hands raw against the bag. I can't get her to stop."

"I can." She set the mug down and rose from her chair. "Let's trade. I'll take care of Dani, you make sure Gray's okay. He didn't want to rest the whole time you were gone." She wrinkled her nose in an adorable display of irritation. "He made me do training."

The low-level dread in his gut jumped at the reminder. He'd tried to compartmentalize Gray's deteriorating condition, but Rafe had never been good at that. "You got it," he replied, struggling to hide the hoarseness in his voice.

Apparently, he didn't hide it well.

Rafe had learned early to respect Maya's personal space—she was skittish as hell about physical affection and rarely offered it to anyone other than Nina and Dani. But now she paused long enough to wrap him in a tight, reassuring hug. She even let him hug her back, and for a soul-healing moment it was like having one of his sisters leaning trustingly against him. *God.* Maybe two years before he saw them again. They'd be grown. They'd be strangers.

He'd miss all of it.

No wonder he looked miserable enough for Maya to offer him a hug.

After another tight squeeze, Maya pulled back and flicked her fingers at him. "Go. Gray's probably over there building a new addition on your warehouse or something by now."

Knowing how true that might be, Rafe hid his seething worry and tossed her a cheerful salute before heading out the back. He let the false smile fade as he crossed the short distance to their new home and was ready to find a heavy bag and beat out some temper of his own by the time he walked inside.

Instead he found Gray hauling around huge targets. Of *course* he was.

Rafe hovered in the doorway again, silently taking in Gray's brand of self-destructive behavior. It wasn't nearly as overt as Dani's, but Gray could be a sneaky bastard. Unlike Dani, he *could* feel pain. No doubt he'd been feeling a wide and wonderful array of it over the past few weeks. He just ignored it so smoothly and skillfully that he'd started falling apart right in front of them, and none of them had noticed.

Rafe couldn't help but feel the sting of that. He *always* noticed.

Blowing out a frustrated breath, he crossed the threshold to do battle for the second time. "You should let me do that."

Gray frowned but continued with his task. "Why?"

Rafe stalked to the nearest one and hefted it with one hand. It probably weighed no more than thirty or forty pounds—nothing for someone with Gray's enhancements. But Gray's enhancements were on the damn fritz. "You need to be taking care of yourself, man, not pushing yourself into a damn seizure."

He rolled his eyes. "I'm dying, not an invalid."

Rafe dropped the target in the corner and went back to retrieve another. "What the hell were you even doing with these? Maya said you were making her train."

Gray shrugged. "With her memory, I figured she could take Hwang's blind-shooting trick and crank it up to eleven."

"And?"

"And I was right, of course." He paused and arched an eyebrow at Rafe. "Perfect score on her first attempt."

Rafe froze. "Are you sure you're not hallucinating now, too?"

"That, so far, has not been one of my symptoms. And I *never* joke about bullets."

Rafe considered the careful spots marked on the floor and how close together they were. It had taken Hwang months to be able to precisely pinpoint direction and even longer to be able to distinguish five meters from ten. Then again, Rafe had never seen anyone listen to the sound a security panel made over comms and then punch in the code until he'd watched Maya pull the trick.

Of course, Gray had seen the potential in that.

Rafe carried the target to the corner. "That's pretty wild. I've heard Dani tease her about hustling pool before. She must be like Conall. A superbrain on top of the auditory recall."

"Must be." Gray nudged him with one shoulder. "How's Knox?"

"Tense." It took an effort not to let his fingers curl into fists. There was nothing here to fight. "Nina's taking this hard, and he wants to fix it for her."

Gray shook his head. "Did you ever think you'd see the day?"

"Honestly?" Rafe snorted. "Knox taking care of someone is nothing new. He's always had it in him. But he lets her take care of him, too. And *that*? That is something I never thought I'd see."

"No." Gray stowed the last target with a sigh. "Mace was the only one who ever got to do that."

Compartmentalization. Rafe tried to ball up his grief for Mace and put it in its place, but there was more of it than there should be. The months since they'd been forced to watch Mace die hadn't blunted the pain. The memories were still crystal clear. The see-through walls of their cells, the acrid stink of recycled air, the dispassionate faces of the biochem techs who'd refused to rebalance Mace's implant once it started to go haywire.

Every seizure, every pained groan—Rafe could even remember the way Knox's bones had sounded, shattering on the polycarbonate wall as he tried to beat his way into Mace's cell to hold his dying friend.

Losing Mace had broken something in Knox that might never be fixed. Rafe could only pray Nina was strong enough to hold him together while they all watched Gray fall apart.

Compartmentalization was a fucking joke. But Rafe tried, slapping Gray on the shoulder as he summoned his biggest smile. "Come on. Let's figure out where you can make Maya practice next."

But Gray shook his head again. "Not right now, man. I think I'm gonna rest a while."

"Even better. Go on. I'm gonna hit the shower."

Rafe held his smile until Gray was gone, then blew out a rough breath and turned. Instead of heading for the showers, he descended to the basement. Only one corner of the vast space was finished, with bare light fixtures affixed to the naked cement columns and a thin mat laid out on the floor.

Prioritizing a workout room seemed silly with so much else to build, not to mention virtually unlimited access to the state-of-the-art training room next door. But sometimes Rafe needed solitude and physical release.

The heavy bag was a special design, meant to withstand the punishment dealt by someone with biochemical enhancements. Rafe took his time taping his hands, trying not to think of how raw Dani's knuckles would be by now. Maya would stop her. He had to believe that.

All he could do was work off the tension and find his center. Knox was going to need him in the days ahead, and Rafe would be ready.

He always was.

July 7th, 2073

Marjorie is truly remarkable, and I am terrified for her.

No one understands how unprecedented her cognitive processing abilities are. Most data couriers are mimics, retrieving the things they've heard by rote. Marjorie breathes in knowledge and makes it part of her. It's likely she would have been an extraordinary mind without the genetic enhancement. With it . . .

I've done my best to shield her from the curiosity of the scientists by administering her ten- and eleven-year benchmark aptitude tests myself and logging false results. It's within my purview as the VP of Behavior to oversee testing, but it's an oddity that will draw attention eventually.

To keep her safe, I must clip her wings. If they realize how swiftly she's outstripped their expectations, they'll take her apart to find out why.

I have to teach her fear.

The Recovered Journal of Birgitte Skovgaard

EIGHT

Six hours after her tense moment with Gray in the warehouse, Maya was still jacked up on adrenaline. The world seemed too bright and her skin felt tight, and it was a miracle neither Nina nor Dani had called her on it yet.

Maya was pretty sure her reprieve was almost up.

Dani probably wouldn't be the one to notice. Maya had talked her out of beating her hands to a pulp against the heavy bag, but Dani hadn't stopped trying to vent her feelings through movement. Instead of her usual spot sprawled across the foot of Nina's bed, she was on the floor doing fluid, effortless push-ups.

Maya stopped counting after two hundred.

Nina had fallen into bed for a far-too-brief nap only at Knox's firm urging, but as soon as he'd gotten up to check on his men, so had she. The tension lingering in her eyes hurt Maya's heart, all the more because Nina *had* taken up her usual position: cross-legged on the edge of the bed, her elbows braced on her knees, her whole body leaning forward in active engagement.

When Nina *listened* to someone, she did it with her whole being.

That was why Maya was screwed. She'd broken open a new bottle of nail polish to give her something to do with her restless hands, but staring at her thumb as she painstakingly applied the shimmery chromatic silver would only let her avoid Nina's gaze for so long. "So I sent the girl to Dr. Wells. He already left a message. He took care of the abortion and got her a real contraceptive implant."

"Good." Nina tilted her head.

Maya kept her gaze firmly on her fingernails. "It feels like for every one of these assholes we chase out of the neighborhood, two more are popping up."

"When Knox finishes the clinic, it'll help a lot." Nina touched her shoulder lightly. "People only visit these places because they have no other options. That's going to change very soon."

Nina could sense something was off. Maya charged ahead anyway, even knowing her voice was too bright. Too fast. "I told the girl she could pay me back by chopping vegetables, but I might see how she does with the scanner. That'd free Tai up to get back to helping with people who come in. And maybe if Emeline is good at it, we could hire her. Digitizing that catalog—"

"Maya."

She swallowed back the frantic babble of words. "I'm fine. I swear I'm fine. It's just . . . It's been a weird day. I'm in a weird headspace."

Dani paused mid-push-up. "That's one word for it."

"Excuse me?"

"You. Gray." Dani flipped over and landed on her back with a grunt. Then she grinned. "That's what's up, right?"

So much for Dani not noticing.

"Dani," Nina murmured.

"What? Tell me I'm wrong, because I know I'm not."

Her grin was so open. So easy. To Dani, attraction *was* easy. If she found someone hot, she went for it. Sex was like a sport for Dani—athletic, occasionally competitive, and probably a little dangerous. Her flings lasted for a night or a week but rarely longer. And nothing about the activity required her vulnerability.

"It's hard for me," Maya whispered, carefully twisting the top back onto the nail polish bottle to hide her nerves. "You guys know that. Touch is hard."

"You don't have to do anything you don't want to do." Nina held up both hands to cut off Maya's automatic protest. "No, I know Gray wouldn't. But the pressure we exert on ourselves can be difficult, too."

"It's not even about what I want. It's about what I can have." Maya swallowed hard against the sudden knot in her throat. "I never know what's going to be too much. And last time—"

Her voice broke on the word. If she closed her eyes, she'd be back there. On the Hill. In Birgitte's posh, coldly elegant penthouse, the hardwood floors stained with blood. Too much blood. She hadn't known a person could bleed that much and live for weeks.

That had been her first mistake.

If she closed her eyes, she'd see his face. Simon had looked nothing like Gray. His blond good looks had still held a boyish softness. He'd had freckles and a mischievous smile utterly unsuited to the gravity of his position. Simon had been far too young to be a bodyguard to a TechCorps VP, but he'd had other qualities to recommend him. Loyalty. Morality. A dedication to Birgitte's revolution.

He'd smiled at Maya through all that blood, his lip split and his face bruised, and whispered the only words he'd say for those final, nightmarish weeks.

It's okay. I love you. Don't talk.

"Maya," Dani whispered softly.

She clung to Dani's voice, following it back to the present. Her friend's face came into focus. Her serious eyes. Her blond hair.

Maya was safe. Safe, like Simon would never be. "I watched him die," she said softly. "It was slow. So damn *slow*."

Dani breathed a curse, but Nina just leaned closer, her gaze solemn.

Maya had never talked about it before. She hadn't needed to—Dani and Nina had lived with her nightmares. They'd coaxed her back every time she woke screaming, trapped in a bloody past that would never fade from memory because it *couldn't*, not for her. It only ever took one stray thought to put her back there, in the moment, so real it was like she was living it all over again.

At least the bad dreams *had* faded, coming less and less frequently. It had been over a year since the last one. Sometimes whole weeks went by where nothing reminded her of those terrible twenty-three days that had started with Birgitte's death and ended with a shaken and traumatized Maya waking up under Nina's protection.

But Simon had been more to her than just the terrible way he died. Maya took a steady breath and eased past the darkest memories, like walking a tightrope over a pit of spikes. Her first teenage love was on the other side, all of the nervous flutters and gentle warmth. One of the few sweet things from her life up on the Hill.

"He was part of Birgitte's security team," she said, holding on to Nina's gaze like a lifeline. "Only a few years older than me. I didn't notice him at first, but he was our bodyguard in the evenings and at night. The one who slept in our penthouse. I'd eat dinner with him, and we'd talk . . . I knew him for a year before I kissed him the first time."

"Simon," Nina murmured. "You've called out for him before."

"Simon," Maya agreed. "We didn't have long together. Only a few months, really." But when you were nineteen, a few months felt like half a lifetime. Simon had been so gentle with her, never pushing when she felt overwhelmed, all too aware that one wrong move would put them both in peril.

No, they'd been in peril from the beginning. But Simon had let her forget that for a few brief, stolen moments.

And then he'd died for her.

Nina's hand was so close. Maya reached out, grasping it to ground her in the present. "He was sweet. It was nice. But he's the only person I've ever kissed. He was the only person I'd ever wanted to until . . ."

"Until now?" Dani smiled a little, the expression half encouragement and half understanding. "Until Gray?"

Maya groaned and flung herself back on the bed, covering her face with her hands. "Remember when I had that panic attack at the underground fight?"

"Uh-huh?"

"He came outside with me. Talked me through it." The words had been ridiculously mundane. About a hurricane he'd gotten trapped in down on the Gulf. But that voice had been like the best liquor, smooth and warm and blurring all the sharpest edges off the memories clawing her up inside. "I think I imprinted on his voice."

"Uh, no, it's just hot." Dani sighed. "Not everything is some kind of mystical, cerebral experience, Maya. Some things are just . . . visceral, you know?"

"Yeah. Visceral is right." Maya propped herself up on one elbow and leveled a look at Dani. "Now imagine you couldn't forget it. That any time you thought about it, or him, you heard it again. Crystal clear, and just as . . . visceral."

"Sounds like a one-way trip to hornytown," Dani observed gravely.

Nina covered her face and groaned.

"She's not wrong," Maya said darkly. "What if I kiss him, and it's *good*? What if I can't forget *that*? Up on the Hill, we were drilled constantly—no nonessential sensory input. I was half-numb the last time I made out with someone. What if I try to kiss him, and my brain just fucking *explodes*?"

Nina dropped her hands and shook her head. "Your brain's not going to explode, I promise you that."

"Something else might, though."

"Dani."

"What?"

Maya dragged a pillow from behind her back and flung it directly at Dani, who snatched it effortlessly out of the air.

Nina grabbed it and set it aside. "I think what she's trying to say is that if you take things slow, and you communicate, then whatever happens will have a much better chance of being—"

"Orgasmic?"

"—pleasant," Nina finished, as if she hadn't been interrupted.

Maya sat up again, her heart fluttering with nerves. They made it sound . . . possible. "But what if I can't—" She swallowed and tried again. "I'm not *easy*. Who the hell would want to put up with kissing someone who might kiss them back or might decide she can't be touched for the rest of the day? Sometimes I'm a fucking mess."

"So what?" Dani demanded. "You're also awesome, and if anyone gives you any shit, I'll stab them."

That simple. To Dani, it always had been. Nina's smile of encouragement wasn't quite as murderous, but it was no less real. Maya let their support wash away her doubts—the support that had been the only constant in Maya's life from the day she'd crawled out of the darkest depths of the TechCorps, shattered and hopeless.

Nina had been the one to sit with her, night after endless night, when she screamed herself awake from all those vivid memories masquerading as nightmares. Nina had secured Maya's future by faking her death, then patiently taught a sheltered girl from the Hill how to survive in the world.

Dani had crashed into their lives a year later. Impossible, outrageous Dani, who would stab anyone who looked at Maya funny and murder anyone who hurt her. It was impossible to be afraid when Dani was with her. Dani had introduced Maya to the pressure valve of a dark club with a heavy bass beat, and dancing until her body was tired enough to chase the oblivion of sleep no matter how restless her mind got.

Dani was teaching her how to live.

Maya might as well tell Dani the rest of it, then. "Something else happened while y'all were gone."

Nina straightened in alarm.

"No, nothing bad." Maya took a breath. Blew it out. "Gray blindfolded me and had me shoot at targets."

Dani shook her head with a laugh. "Snipers have weird hobbies."

"Maybe." That tiny thrill of success shivered up Maya's spine again, a blissful momentary distraction. "But I hit every fucking one. On my first try."

"Sweet," Dani proclaimed.

Nina studied her. "I didn't know you were interested in that sort of training."

Warmth flooded her cheeks, because she *hadn't* been. If Knox or Rafe had pulled a blindfold out of their pocket, she would have politely invited them to fuck themselves and gone back to her comfortable corner to scan more books.

Gray made her judgement suspect.

But Gray wasn't the reason she wanted to do it again. And even her out-of-control hormones couldn't entirely drown out the remembered freedom of that moment when she'd really let her brain off the leash. The reckless joy of it. Like she'd flexed a muscle she hadn't known was there, one that had been stiff and aching from neglect.

She'd been waiting for the crash all afternoon, but the usual ache at the base of her skull was gone. So was the restless itch under her skin, the pressure that came from everywhere and nowhere. And the jittery energy setting her leg to bouncing didn't feel like impending sensory overload.

It felt like . . . anticipation. Excitement.

Like maybe she could kiss Gray, and her brain might not explode after all.

Nina was still watching her with those serious, concerned eyes. Maya forced herself to stop thinking about Gray's lips. "I didn't know I was interested in training like that, either," Maya promised her. "It's not how they taught me to think about myself. Other people have the superpowers. I'm just . . . trivia girl."

"Bullshit," Dani protested.

But Nina's expression had darkened, and she spoke haltingly. "Have we made you feel that way, too?"

"No." Maya reached out to grip Nina's wrist. "Nina, *no*. You've always been the opposite. Hell, remember when you first took me in? I was scared to leave the damn house. You two taught me how to take care of myself."

"Sure," Nina agreed. "But I should have seen that you needed more."

"How? *I* didn't know I needed more." Maya leaned forward, bracing her elbows on her knees. "But it felt good to use those parts of my brain. It felt like I've been pulling my punches my whole life, and I finally just got to *swing*."

"Then keep swinging." Dani dropped across the bed. "What other kind of magic tricks can you do?"

"Fuck if I know." She grinned at Dani. "Got any ideas?"

"Hmm." The look Dani gave her was pure innocence. "Maybe we should ask Gray."

Maya lunged toward Nina. "Give me the pillow back. I'm going to hit her this time."

"Try it, baby," Dani taunted.

"No." Nina held Maya back and pinned Dani with a mock severe look. "You two want to duel, we do it properly."

"Fuck that," Maya muttered. "If she wants to duel, I'm gonna tell Rafe she doodled his name in her diary with hearts around it."

Dani gasped. *"Lies."*

"Yeah, I took that too far," Maya admitted. "You would never keep a diary. You'd probably just carve his initials into trees with one of the five thousand knives you had on you."

"He wishes."

"Yeah. He *really* does." Maya leaned into Nina's side, relieved that the tactile contact didn't overwhelm her. Sometimes she just needed a damn hug. "Okay, I will consider the possibility of kissing."

"Don't worry," Dani said immediately. "I won't tease you."

"Yes, you will. And you're the only one who gets to." Maya wrapped her arm around Nina's waist, leaning into her embrace. Tears stung her eyes. "Have I mentioned lately that I love you both, even when you make me do cardio?"

"It's always nice to hear it again."

"Yes, yes, love all around." Dani rested her chin on her hands. "I want to hear more about this superpower Maya has. Spare absolutely no ballistic detail, please."

Maya laughed. And then she obeyed, because she had never been able to deny Dani or Nina anything.

They were the only family she'd ever had.

TECHCORPS PROPRIETARY DATA,
L1 SECURITY CLEARANCE

Our current aptitude and assessment criteria for recruitment to Protectorate sniper training overwhelmingly selects for candidates who show significant antisocial behavior. Attached, please find my full analysis, which is based on data compiled over the last two decades.

I believe that continuing to overlook these warning signs will result in tragedy.

Internal Memo, June 2065

NINE

Gray was a light sleeper.

Some people assumed that was a habit all soldiers shared. And it was true that years of military life and fieldwork had shaped Gray's sleep patterns. But some Protectorate recruits in his class had slept like logs, and not even the harshest punishments levied by the drill instructors had been able to break them of it.

It had always baffled Gray. How could anyone lie there, snoring and drooling, insensate to the activity around them, much less blaring alarms? If he'd ever slept like that in the group home, he'd have had all his belongings stolen—or worse.

He'd gotten a little better over the years. He no longer jerked awake at distant noises, his heart thudding painfully, but the barest whisper of footsteps would still rouse him. He'd open his eyes, lying still and alert as he assessed the potential danger of the situation.

He didn't get the chance this time. There was no noise, no warning, only steely fingers that locked around his throat. They pressed in on either side of his neck, cutting off the blood flow to his brain.

Most people assumed that effective strangulation was about being unable to breathe. But it took over thirty pounds of pressure to completely occlude the trachea—you really had to use an arm or a knee, and fucking *commit*. But a fraction of that pressure applied precisely to the major blood vessels of the neck?

Your target would lose consciousness in as few as ten short, easy seconds.

Instinct kicked in. Gray bucked, attempting to break free of his assailant's grip, but whoever it was held tight. A heavy weight dropped onto Gray, pressing him into the cot, quelling his struggles.

But not trapping his hands. He lashed out at the shadowy figure on top of him, a flurry of blows that should have landed. But his attacker ducked and bobbed his head, somehow managing to avoid Gray's fists.

A gentle rasp cut through the pounding of the blood in Gray's ears, the sound as familiar as it was deadly—a knife clearing a ballistic nylon sheath.

Shit.

Gray twisted his body as the blade slammed down, tearing through his pillow. The second blow sliced across the top of Gray's shoulder, and he gritted his teeth against the searing pain. His assailant was already adapting to Gray's evasive maneuvers, which meant the next thrust wouldn't miss.

With a mighty heave, Gray shoved hard at his attacker, spilling them both from the bed to the floor. His slashed shoulder hit the concrete with an agonizing jolt that made his vision go white. A roar filled his ears, so loud he almost missed the sound of the knife skidding across the floor. He pushed through the pain and rolled, struggling to pin his attacker.

He couldn't make it stick. Their murderous intruder was well-trained, maybe even as well as Gray himself. They struggled, crashing about his little area of the makeshift barracks, slamming into boxes and knocking them over. Once, the would-be killer—because that's what this was, no doubt, an attempted assassination—managed to grab hold of Gray's hair and smack his head against the floor.

The world imploded. An inky blackness darker than the room began to dance before Gray's eyes, and he kicked out. His foot grazed the heavy metal footlocker at the end of his cot, and Gray almost laughed.

He might not be at full fighting trim, but he'd grown up *hard*, and he wasn't afraid to fight dirty.

He clutched the front of his attacker's jacket and rolled again, using their joint momentum to pick up speed. He calculated the distance automatically, adding force at just the right time to whack his uninvited guest's head against the footlocker.

The resulting grunt of pain startled Gray. Before he could pause to figure out *why*, the man surged up, and Gray hit him with a hard right to the jaw. The force of the blow reverberated up Gray's arm, and he drew back for a second, harder swing. Rule of twos—one to stun, and one to end the fight for good.

"Go on, kid. Do it."

The low words scraped at Gray's brain, and he froze, his fist upraised, his heart in his throat. The roar of blood in his ears was back, filling his head until there was no room for anything else. No action, no thought, just still, icy horror.

Vaguely, he heard yelling. Heavy, running footsteps. Then the overheads switched on, flooding the barracks with feverish, blinding light.

Conall's voice. Rafe's. The sounds flowed over Gray, past him, without penetrating his consciousness. Every single cell of his being was focused on the impossible, bleeding man beneath him.

Gray's stomach lurched, and his lips formed the name in a barely audible whisper, one that ricocheted through his chest like a low-velocity bullet tumbling around inside his rib cage.

"Mace."

KNOX

The cool edge of metal biting into Knox's fingers was the only thing that felt real.

He tightened his grip on the dog tag, holding it until he swore he could feel the raised text on it burning its way into his palm.

James Mason. MD-701. Silver Devils.

A memento of a dead man. A dead man who was currently zip-tied to a chair on the far side of the room, enduring Rafe's patient interrogation with a blank expression. Dani hovered nearby, her body coiled with readiness. At Mace's slightest twitch she'd pounce, protecting Rafe from attack.

Mace didn't look like a man planning on twitching.

Hell, Mace didn't look like a man planning on *surviving*.

"I don't get it," Conall whispered fiercely. He had a tablet gripped in one hand, his fingers a blur as they danced across its surface. "We have a back door into Security. I have read *everything* that mentions us. There's nothing about Mace still being alive. Or even some plan to impersonate him."

"Richter has a shit ton of latitude inside the TechCorps," Maya replied, her gaze fixed on Mace. "Sometimes he runs projects off the books. They don't care as long as he gets results and doesn't exceed his budget."

In an uncharacteristic explosion of temper, Conall pitched his tablet into the wall. The screen cracked as it crashed to the floor. "Then what the fuck good is it?"

"Hey." Maya squeezed Conall's shoulder. "You knew this was a possibility. That's why people like me exist, to keep track of the secrets they won't even put in their own systems. This isn't your fault."

Knox stared at the spiderwebbed cracks on the tablet's face, his thoughts every bit as fractured. He should be the one comforting Conall. The pain in the younger man's voice cut deep, but not as deep as the guilt.

Mace was alive. Mace was *alive*.

And while the rest of the Silver Devils—his *brothers*—had been settling into their soft life of freedom, tiling bathrooms and building a clinic in Mace's honor, he'd been locked in some dank, forgotten hole in the depths of the TechCorps, tortured and alone.

Tortured and *abandoned*. Knox had left a man behind.

Nina wrapped her fingers around his hand and squeezed firmly, forcing him to meet her gaze. "Don't. If Richter's behind this, this is part of his plan. You, blaming yourself. So don't."

She was right. Knox *knew* she was right. But the only thing worse than the guilt gnawing him from the inside out was how easily his brain still clicked over into clear-eyed assessment of the situation.

It shouldn't be so easy to view a friend as a security threat.

"Conall." He used his captain voice, and it worked its subconscious magic on Conall. He straightened, ready for orders, and Knox provided them. "Get your equipment so you can scan him again for tracking devices. Make *sure* we didn't miss anything. And see if you can connect to his implant and verify the serial number."

"Got it." Conall picked up his shattered tablet and stalked from the room.

"Let's run it down," Nina said quietly once he was gone. "Number one question is obvious: is it even really him?"

"It's Mace," Gray countered. No hesitation, no doubt.

Nina eyed him with gentle sympathy that almost hurt to look at. "I know you want it to be. We all do. But everyone in this room has been bioengineered, Gray. You know what the TechCorps can do with cosmetic surgery—"

"It's him." Gray turned to Knox. "When we were fighting, even before I realized it was Mace, it felt . . . familiar. He was using moves *you* taught him, Knox. Stuff I watched you teach him."

Like Conall, Mace hadn't come to the Silver Devils with the same basic combat training Gray and Rafe had received. As a medic whose augmentations tilted toward the mental over the physical, he'd needed a different style. Devious. Abrupt. Brutal. So Knox had taught him how to end a fight fast and dirty.

"Assume it's him, Maya," Knox said. "He showed up trying real hard to kill Gray. What would you guess?"

Maya tilted her head, her gaze growing distant. "I don't know. Brainwashing, maybe?"

"Brainwashing?"

"Reprogramming." Her voice had taken on that slightly detached tone, sliding from her usual warm drawl to clipped enunciation. "Even with the advances in neural reconditioning, success rates have been limited. Anyone can be broken with sufficient application of pain, but the results are unpredictable and the process is time-consuming."

"So why bother? It's a gamble, at best. If Richter suspects you're all still alive . . ." Nina shook her head. "There are easier ways to remedy the situation."

"Because it's not just about killing us anymore," Gray rasped. "He wants it to hurt like hell. It's personal now."

It always had been. Knox's knuckles ached with phantom pain, a reminder of those brutal days when Richter had kept them locked up in a forgotten TechCorps basement.

How carefully he'd designed that prison and its five cells. Unbreakable polycarbonate walls. They'd all watched in horror as the kill-switch hidden in every Protectorate implant kicked into gear and Mace began to decline. Without biochemical adjustment, his death had been too fast, and still so agonizingly slow.

Knox had shattered his hands against the wall between them, unable to tolerate the agony of watching his soldier—his *friend*—die alone.

"It's more than that," Knox said quietly. "He's the only weapon Richter knows I would never destroy."

Maya's eyes tightened, her body tensed as if in remembered pain. "Fucking with your head would definitely be a bonus. Richter's the kind of sadist who goes all in. Especially if he feels like you made him look stupid."

"Psychological warfare," Nina whispered.

"You have no idea." Her voice trembled, just a little, and Knox didn't want to know what Richter had done to put that dread in her usually warm gaze.

Knox didn't have to know. He could imagine. Richter's reputation for brutality was unparalleled, even in the relatively coldhearted ranks of TechCorps executives.

And Mace had been in his hands for months.

A chair scraped across concrete on the far side of the room. Rafe rose, his expression too relaxed, too easy. He strode toward Knox with Dani stalking at his side, a perfect foil of barely contained agitation.

"Well?" Knox asked when they reached the group.

Rafe exhaled roughly. Up close, Knox could see the stress lines creasing his forehead. "It *sounds* like him, but he's not really talking."

Dani snorted. "And when he does, he's not making any damn sense."

Rafe winced but didn't disagree. "You'd think if someone was impersonating him, they'd have shown up armed with enough knowledge to answer basic questions. But he's not even trying."

Plans of action unfolded before Knox, a dozen possibilities, each hampered by the lack of solid intelligence. "Stay here," he murmured to Rafe and Gray. "Keep an eye on Conall when he gets back."

Gray nodded. "Don't worry. We won't let him spin out."

Knox pivoted and started toward Mace, assessing him physically as he came closer. He was leaner than he'd been before. His dark hair was longer than usual and unkempt, and though Mace had always been pale, there was an unhealthy pallor to his skin.

Like Knox, Mace was in his early forties. Unlike Knox, he no longer looked a decade younger. Pain had left its mark on his face. His nose had been broken at least once and left to heal crooked.

The harshest change was his eyes. The warm, blue gaze that had set the injured and sick at ease was gone. Mace watched him approach with dead eyes carved from ice.

Pain sliced through Knox's palm. He eased his grip on the dog tag, but when he opened his fingers, blood stained its silver edge.

That seemed appropriate.

Knox stopped a few feet away from the chair. Mace could break free of the zip ties with one good heave of muscle—but they'd slow him down enough for Knox to have time to react. "Mace."

The answer was automatic, chilling, with the flat affect of recitation. "Mason, James. Medic. Designation MD-701."

Knox's heart seized. "Mace—"

"Knox, Garrett. Captain. Designation 66–615."

Knox crouched down to be at eye level with Mace. "Yes. I'm Garrett Knox."

"Gray, Matthew. Sniper. Designation 66–793."

Reciting his own designation was the standard training in this sort of situation. Reciting the rest of them . . . It was as off as the tone of his voice. Wrong. Terrifying.

"Morales, Rafael." A hint of desperation crept into Mace's eyes. "Intelligence. Designation 66–942."

"Quinn, Conall," Knox finished for him softly. "Tech. Designation TE-815."

Mace turned his head, his gaze darting wildly as he strained against the plastic ties binding his wrists.

If he tugged much harder, he'd snap them, and the situation could easily escalate into violence. Knox lowered his voice, but the words still rasped out around the lump in his throat. "C'mon, old man. You and me are the only things standing between these puppies and certain death."

Mace froze, then dragged in a rough, uneven breath. "Or pissing all over the furniture."

Uncertainty vanished. How many times had they exchanged those wry words in the first months after Knox had formed the Silver Devils? Rafe had been all of twenty-three years old, and Conall just twenty-one. Their exuberance at being freed from the rigid confines of training had been *exhausting* sometimes.

Moving slowly, Knox settled cross-legged in front of Mace, his hands resting carefully on his legs. No weapons. No sudden movements. "They still piss on the furniture sometimes, but they grew up okay."

Mace looked at him. *Studied* him, his gaze flickering from Knox's relaxed hands up to his face, then back again. "You've changed."

"We all have." Knox didn't hide the pain from his voice. "Losing you changed us."

Mace didn't react to Knox's words or his pain. His stare remained flat, dead. "My captain never turned away from hard truths."

Knox exhaled softly. "You're a trap."

"Yes. So what are you waiting for?"

"Were you released, or did you escape?"

"Does it matter?"

"Maybe. How did you find us? Richter?"

"No. I know you better than Richter ever did." A simple answer, one that Mace followed with a soft noise of impatient disgust so familiar that it ached. "You're stalling."

"No," Knox corrected him. "I'm doing what I've always done when presented with a trap. Studying it to understand my enemy. What kind of tracker did you have?"

"Trackers," Mace corrected. "Standard subcutaneous and IM installations. Several satellite-enabled, and a backup radio frequency model." He paused. "I cut them out, but there might be more."

"Conall will look. He has this whole building signal-blocked, so no one's getting anything off them right now, even if they are there." Knox focused on keeping his hands relaxed as he asked the question he didn't want to know the answer to. "Why were you attacking Gray?"

Mace shuddered. His eyes glazed over, and he whistled a few discordant notes before shaking himself and focusing on Knox once more. "Richter is hoping you'll be too sentimental to do what needs to be done." His voice dropped. "Prove him wrong, Garrett. Now, before it's too late."

"No." The word cracked out of him too harshly. Knox couldn't claw it back. Wouldn't. He turned over his right hand and uncurled his fingers, one by one.

Mace's dog tag sat there, edged with Knox's blood.

"I will *not* kill you," Knox told him softly. "Don't ask me to go through this again."

A hint of sympathy and something like regret flashed through Mace's eyes, gone in the literal blink of an eye. "I warned you. Remember that."

"I don't need warnings, Mace. I need *intel*."

"And I don't have it to give, Captain." He exhaled roughly. "All I have is a mission. And the Devils don't know how to fail . . . even when they want to."

"I won't let it come to that." Knox rose and curled his fingers around the dog tag once more. "Conall's going to scan you, and then we'll make a plan. Okay?"

Mace turned his head, his wrists straining against his plastic bonds again as he resumed whistling.

His heart shredded, Knox returned to the tense knot of people on the far side of the room. Conall had returned with a bag of equipment, his expression haunted. Rafe looked shaken, and even Gray's eyes were tight with concern.

Nina's sympathetic gaze was Knox's only relief as the potential pitfalls of their situation spun out in front of him, every plan he considered prohibitively dangerous.

Nina touched his arm. "Is it what we thought?"

"Yes. A targeted weapon, sent to eliminate us." Knox looped the dog tag back over his head and tucked it under his shirt. The metal burned over his heart. "He asked me to kill him."

Conall made an incoherent noise of grief, and Maya wrapped an arm around him with a soothing noise. "That's not an option," she stated firmly. "Obviously."

Knox couldn't look away from Nina. Reality loomed between them, vast and unspoken.

Tobias Richter knew they were alive. Maybe the rest of the TechCorps didn't believe him. Or maybe they did and they were keeping that knowledge off the record for reasons of their own.

It didn't matter. Only one thing did. "He's a threat," Knox said softly. "To all of us, but to you, too. Especially Maya. If Richter tracks him here . . ."

"Then we'll deal with it," Nina said firmly. "Mace is your family, Knox. His place is here."

"If Richter shows up, I will murder the shit out of him," Maya said, her cheerful confidence a thin layer of bluster over the fear lingering in her eyes. Knox opened his mouth, and she glared at him. "Or I'll let one of you bastards do it. I don't care. Dead's dead, and between all of us, we can make the guy real dead."

"Hell yeah, we can," Rafe said.

Knox turned to Dani, who shrugged one shoulder. "I'm always up for a little murder. It's my favorite pastime, right?"

That easy. Knox supposed he shouldn't be surprised. They'd reached out a hand to save him when he hadn't deserved it. Of course they'd extend a hand to Mace, a man who had never done anything but try to help people. Healing was a bone-deep instinct in Mace, the truth that had defined his life.

And Tobias Richter had broken him into pieces small enough to reassemble him as a killer.

"He's still dangerous," he warned.

"He's fighting it," Gray insisted. "He had the element of surprise *and* a sleeping target. I should have been dead before the first drop of my blood hit the floor, but I'm not. He's trying."

"Of course he is." Nina slid her hand down to Knox's and gripped it tightly. "We'll take precautions. We'll be careful, and we'll help him through this. I promise."

The tightness in Knox's chest eased. He took a full breath and let it out as he squeezed Nina's hand in return. "That means I'll have to stay with him tonight instead of chasing down leads at this club of Maya's."

Maya choked on a laugh. "Wait, you thought you were coming? To *Convergence*? You're gonna have to loosen up a lot more before visiting any criminal nightclubs."

She could have been trying to give him a guilt-free out. Then again, solid tactics required an awareness of his own limitations, and setting criminals at ease was *not* part of his skill set. "Fine, Rafe and Conall can go—"

"Nope." Conall shook his head. "Sorry, I can't go to Convergence. I . . . might have had a run-in with the owner."

Maya spun on him. "You had a run-in with *Savitri*?"

"Kind of. I tried to hack her, and her chief of security humiliated the shit out of me before booting my ass." He winced. "So yes. Big run-in. Anyway, I scored myself a lifetime ban without ever setting foot inside, so I should probably stay here. Besides, I need to do these scans."

"All right." Knox turned to study Gray. His shoulder was already bandaged, and he had a bruise rising on his face, but otherwise there was no indication of any pain he might be experiencing from his implant rejection. Gray always hid his discomfort, major or minor. Knox would never know how close he was to dropping until he hit the ground.

Every instinct screamed for him to hold Gray back. But the man met his eyes, calm and determined, and Knox knew he couldn't. Gray had sacrificed so much for the right to decide how he lived his life.

He had the right to decide how he died, too.

Knox swallowed pain. "Gray? You up to it?"

The answer came, steady and certain. "Always."

It would have to be enough.

October 15th, 2075

I told her the truth about her brain. The cruelest parts, the ones that will make her hold back. The parts that will make her cautious, and small, and scared. I'm doing it to save her. Does that make it better?

She'll never know how amazing she could be. But neither will the TechCorps.

The Recovered Journal of Birgitte Skovgaard

TEN

The entrance to Convergence was an unassuming steel door decorated with faded recruitment posters promising exciting job opportunities up on the Hill. The door itself was tucked in between a tattoo and body-mod shop on the left and a secondhand tech parts peddler on the right. At first glance, it didn't look much like a door at all. There was no handle, no keypad, and clearly just enough space between the neighboring businesses to house a tiny closet.

Or a staircase.

"Doesn't look like much," Gray observed.

"Looks can be deceiving," Dani shot back. "But you know that, don't you?" She gestured to the scant space between the tattoo shop and the parts store. "If you guys had come to us for help instead of kidnapping us—"

"Excuse me," Rafe interrupted. "You mean invited you on a delightful road trip under false pretenses."

"Whatever. This would have been our first stop. I've never met her personally, but Savitri has the best black-market shit around—and she knows how to use it. Rumor is, she's some sort of tech savant."

"Oh, it's more than rumor." Maya eased the copper chain over her head, and the light reflected off the old-fashioned circuit board embedded in her pendant. "Brace yourselves."

Regulars to Convergence had tiny, embedded RF chips that opened the door. Maya, unwilling to let *anyone* embed trackable tech in her body, had scored a highly coveted permanent visitor's pass from the contact they were about to meet. As she swung the pendant close to the door, the invisible RF chip triggered the lock.

A soft *click* sounded in response, and a crack of neon-blue light spilled into the shadowed street.

"Anyone else miss the days of secret passwords?" Dani muttered.

"They were sexier," Rafe agreed.

Maya huffed and pushed the door wider. Stairs lined in glowing LED lights led down to a tunnel. "Trust me, you'll get all the sexy you could ever want inside."

"Don't spoil the surprise now, Maya." Dani went first, striding in like she owned the place, Rafe hard on her heels.

Gray rolled his eyes. "At least they're predictable."

Looking at his eyes was a mistake. Looking at him at *all* was a mistake. Considering the way Gray made a T-shirt and jeans look like combat fatigues, he should have looked ridiculous rolling out dressed like a techno punk kid. But he wore the shredded jeans and strategically ripped retro shirt as easily as he did the chain-wrapped boots and heavy belt buckle. The big silver rings only emphasized the sheer size of his fingers, and the liner smudged around his eyes gave him a sleepy, sexy look that shivered straight through to her toes.

His eyes were blue. She'd spent so much time angsting over their dark Gothic quality that she'd never really noticed their color. They were the ocean at midday, deep enough to drown in.

And observant. Too damn observant. She could *not* get caught gawking at him.

Planting a hand on his shoulder, she gave him a push that felt as effective as shoving a brick wall. "Come on. If we leave them unsupervised down there, who the fuck knows what'll happen?"

Inside the entryway, the graffitied walls seemed to pulse with the force of the dull, throbbing music, an effect that only intensified as they descended deep into the tunnel. More strident lights cast its narrow length in stark glows and deep shadows, alternately revealing and hiding the clubgoers leaning against the walls.

If hell were full of neon, it would probably look like this.

Then they reached the end of the tunnel, and everything opened up. *Everything.*

The club was enormous. Buried three stories underground, the main dance floor was at least the size of a city block, with a high ceiling strung with enough flashing LEDs to light half a neighborhood. They pulsed with the music, shifting color with the mood of the song and the energy in the room.

On the far end of the room, dual staircases blocked off by silver chains and guarded by hulking muscle swept up to the second-floor balcony that ringed the main dance floor.

The VIP floor was the kind of exclusive reserved for serious debauchery or the highest class of criminal hacker—neither exactly Maya's area of expertise. She probably could have bought her way up to see the club's elusive owner with a few of the TechCorps secrets buried in her brain but not without exposing herself in ways that would end her life as she knew it.

Opposite the staircase was the centerpiece of Convergence. A sleek, six-meter-long bar was crowded three deep with people jostling to reach the embedded ordering tablets. Behind the bar itself, dozens of glowing backlit tubes climbed the wall, a dizzying array of liquor and mixers and wildly colored liquid alchemy that, according to rumor, could do anything from give you a pleasant buzz to open your mind to the mysteries of the universe.

All of the tubes fed into a trio of elegant machines that whirred and hummed and produced perfectly mixed drinks as fast as the pair of bartenders could provide the glasses. Blended, straight, on the rocks, glowing, *smoking*—the only thing the drinks had in common was that you could feed a family of six for a week on the credits you had to fork over to enjoy one.

That was Convergence in a nutshell. Big. Flashy. Expensive.

Too much.

Maya had only been here a handful of times. No place in Atlanta beat it if you wanted black-market tech or hacks—be they software, hardware, or biological. But the sound of it alone was enough to set her bones to humming. The flash of lights, the press of half-naked bodies, the smell of those expensive drinks and aftershave and sweat, the *taste* in the air, like high-scale crime and lush sin had been converted to oxygen.

Sensory overload wasn't just a danger after a trip to Convergence, it was an honest-to-God certainty.

But it was the only place where she could meet her most dangerous contact.

"Are you going to be okay in here?" Gray spoke close to her ear, the only way to be heard. His breath tickled her skin, the warmth of it too intimate combined with that honey drawl.

She was not going to be okay if he kept doing that.

"I can handle it," she replied, turning so he could hear her soft words. "I can almost always keep it together when I have something to focus on. A mission. I'll just crash a lot harder tonight when we get home."

"All right," he relented, but his gaze held hers, intense and searching.

Dani broke in, bouncing a little to the beat of the music. "Who are we meeting here, exactly?"

Maya checked her watch, but no new messages had come through. "She's not here yet."

Rafe grinned and tilted his head toward the dance floor. "Then I'm doing recon."

"Knock yourself out, Morales." Dani headed in the other direction, slipping into the masses of people moving together.

Maya swayed, instinct almost driving her after Dani. Dani was the perfect clubbing partner for someone who needed to exhaust her body without dealing with the constant physical contact that came with a mass of thrashing dancers. Dani's entire vibe screamed *fuck off* loudly enough that Maya usually danced it out in a blissful circle of personal space. The few idiots who crossed the boundary and actually touched one of them were lucky to leave with all of their fingers.

As the crowd closed around Dani, Maya took a step back. Her arm pressed into Gray's. His entire body was scalding heat against her, but for all that her awareness of him was an ever-present prickle against her skin, his presence didn't bother her the same way.

Gray was like Nina and Dani. Gray was safe.

"Can I ask a favor?" She had to stretch up on her toes to be easily heard.

He touched her elbow, so lightly she almost wondered if she'd imagined the contact. "You know you don't even have to ask. Just tell me what you need."

"Turn on your scary predator vibe." Someone bumped into her from behind, and she edged closer to Gray, close enough to curl an arm around his neck. "Just don't let them all dance into me."

He nodded, one arm sliding around her. His palm pressed against the middle of her back, right between her shoulder blades, and his other hand landed on her hip. Then something *changed*—his expression hardened, and waves of sheer possession crashed outward from him.

The crowd writhed around them. Nothing obvious, nothing *overt*, but within a minute it was like an invisible force field had edged the dancers back. Some eyed them with curiosity, some with appraisal . . . but no one accepted his silent challenge and encroached on Gray's starkly declared space.

Survival instincts were one thing everyone in Convergence had in abundance.

The music booming over the speakers shifted to something slow and deep and grinding, and the rhythm of the crowd shifted with it. The bright neon lights flashed across the dance floor and faded, replaced with a sultry red that turned the twisting bodies into some puritanical preacher's nightmare vision of a hell populated by lustful sinners.

The large hand splayed between her shoulder blades flexed, and Maya curled her other arm around Gray's neck. Their bodies were already moving to that rolling bass beat, and she wasn't sure which of them had started it. "You're really good at that."

He didn't bother asking what she meant. "You learn early on the streets, or you don't last."

Sympathy tightened in her chest. "Is that where you grew up? Was it here in Atlanta?"

He nodded. "Bankhead. Spent most of my time in a church-run orphanage."

She fought an instinctive twist of her lips. Some of the churches had clung to a message of hope and healing after the Flares, but too many had gone in the opposite way—fire and brimstone and shouting that the collapse of the world they had known had been fitting punishment for society's sins.

Maya didn't want to imagine how those orphanages treated their charges. She curled her fingers protectively around the back of his neck, the short hair there tickling her palm. "Did your parents . . . ?" She trailed off. "I'm sorry. You don't have to answer if it's too personal."

He did anyway. "Dead. I barely remember them." His hand tightened on her hip. "Not sure if that's better or worse, but it's how things are."

"I understand." He was still giving off scary monster vibes that cleared a path for them as they rolled with the music, but the low, tense rumble of his voice and those fingers clutching her hip . . . She stroked her thumb up and down the strong column of his throat, softly comforting. "I never knew my parents. Most of the time I think it's easier. Nothing to miss except the idea of what parents are supposed to be."

"You can still miss something you've never known."

The words slid over her, low and oddly intense. She couldn't tell if they were supposed to be suggestive or if everything sounded suggestive when you were practically riding a guy's thigh to a bass beat that promised the kind of sex she'd never had and was pretty sure she wouldn't survive.

Her limbs felt loose. Her whole body felt loose, except the parts that were wound too tight. Her heart pounded, and she waited for him to ruin it. To take the silent invitation in her flushed cheeks and parted lips, to slip his fingers under the thin cotton of her layered tank tops, for the hand at her hip to slide down to cup her ass. To drive this fluttery feeling inside her from warm and melting to the sharp edge of *too much*.

His hands stayed fixed where they were, one splayed wide between her shoulder blades, the other gently gripping her hip. His gaze roamed her face, his focus so total that his brow furrowed when an uncontrollable shiver shook through her. His fingers flexed, gentling their movements, putting careful space between their bodies before she had to ask.

Gray would never take advantage of an unspoken invitation. He'd never push. He'd always give her exactly what she asked for.

Anything she asked for.

Just tell me what you need.

Maya had no fucking idea what she needed right now, short of finding an improbable Atlanta snowbank and flinging herself into it.

Her whole body was buzzing. No, her *wrist* was buzzing. It was buzzing the impatient staccato of someone trying to get her attention. Tearing her gaze from Gray's felt like trying to defy gravity, but she managed to lift her wrist and squint at the gentle glow from her watch.

The flex of her wrist displayed the message. Just one word.

Boo.

Maya raised her voice to be heard over the music, fighting the urge to jump back as if she'd gotten caught doing something wrong. "She's here. Let's find Rafe and Dani."

Dani was at the bar, a line of smoking, rainbow-colored shots lined up in front of her. The crowds had stepped back, clearing a space around her as the bartender counted off each drink as she downed them. One right after another, until she finished the last shot with a flourish amidst cheers—and a loud groan.

A young man in a sleek, bespoke suit stood to one side, a dismayed expression on his baby face. Dani plucked a credit stick out of his hand, then leaned in with a wicked grin. "Remember this," she purred, "the next time you think about challenging a lady."

Maya choked back a groan and caught Dani by the only part of her dress that looked sturdy enough not to snap in two—the waistband. "You are so gonna feel those shots later."

"Are you kidding me? They're 150 proof, max. *And* I got the arrogant rich boy's money." She flipped the credit stick over her knuckles. "Is it go time?"

"As soon as we find Rafe."

Rafe was leaning against the wall not far beyond Dani, engaged in easy conversation with a tall figure clad in jeans and a T-shirt. Dark-pink hair cascaded over one shoulder, with the other side of their head shaved. Big, brown eyes stared up at Rafe with surprising familiarity, considering this was one of the names on Maya's mental dossier of former TechCorps revolutionaries.

Nat had been one of the leading experts in food synthesis, their breakthroughs of a magnitude that could have helped eliminate hunger throughout Atlanta—except the TechCorps did not particularly want hunger eliminated. It was too effective as a lever of control. Only Birgitte's direct intervention had saved Nat from the kind of "promotion" that ended with your body turning to ash in an incinerator while all of your colleagues muttered jealously—and obliviously—about the posh, new private lab you'd supposedly taken over.

The kind of promotion Birgitte had gotten, in the end.

Rafe grinned as they approached. "Hey, this is—"

"Maya!" Nat reached out as if to hug her but checked themself at the last second and offered a hand for a high five instead. "You look good. I didn't know you and Rafe were tight."

"We recently became acquainted," Maya replied dryly. "I'm more surprised you two know each other."

"What can I say?" Rafe held up both hands. "I'm just that loveable."

Maya rolled her eyes and jerked her thumb. "Sorry to bounce, but we have a meeting with someone you don't keep waiting."

"No worries." Nat gave Rafe a swift hug and offered Maya a wave as they started off. "Thank Nina for those books she sent me, would you? And tell her I think I finally have a prototype for y'all to test . . ."

The music swallowed the rest, but Maya shot back two enthusiastic thumbs up. No need to fake the excitement—a potential prototype food synthesizer from Nat would definitely perk Nina up. Something like that could push back the threat of hunger in Southside this winter, and when people weren't struggling to feed themselves, they could turn that extra energy toward building a little more security.

That was the hope Maya carried with her as she used Rafe's size and Gray's menace to carve a path across the dance floor, straight to a single booth set directly beneath the VIP section, a table that rested in a relative oasis of peace.

Nobody would fuck with the woman sitting there. No one would even get close without an invitation. She lounged on one of the leather-padded benches, her no-nonsense black tank top showing off tattooed brown skin a shade darker than Maya's. Her dark braids were studded with silver rings, and she wore dark denim jeans, knee-high motorcycle boots, and high-end tinted smart glasses that obscured half of her face.

Persephone. Queen of the criminal underworld. She *owned* the GhostNet's black market—and hackers rose to prominence or tumbled to oblivion at her whim.

What few except for Maya knew was that Persephone had created the GhostNet.

Persephone turned to study them as they approached. No doubt those glasses were already running facial recognition scans on the three she hadn't met before. By the time they sat, she'd know that both the TechCorps database and the GhostNet had been scrubbed clean of any trace of them, thanks to Conall's industrious work.

Maya had hoped the mystery would intrigue her. But Persephone's brow furrowed, and when they were still a few paces from the table, she pushed her glasses up to the top of her head and quirked one eyebrow in silent challenge—and *not* at Maya.

Gray stopped short and sighed. "Well, *shit*."

"Fuck me," Rafe groaned.

Maya froze, looking from Persephone's furrowed brow to Rafe's dismayed expression. Hell, even *Gray* looked vaguely agitated. For an endless, torturous moment, no one moved. Even the music seemed far away, as if the tension between Persephone and the men had formed an impenetrable bubble.

It popped with Persephone's sudden wry laugh. "You know I went a month without a decent night's sleep because of you assholes? Every tight-ass on the Board wanted their security tripled until they managed to kill y'all."

Gray turned to Maya. "*Charlie* is your contact? Conall's nemesis?"

"I don't—" Her brain buzzed, the sudden spike of adrenaline unleashing a hurricane of remembered conversations. Conall's voice first, in an overlapping litany of grievances against Charlie, his chief competition for the top spot in the elite tech training program. Charlie . . . Charlie . . .

Charlotte Young. Birgitte's cool voice drifted through her memory, bringing with it the full sensory memory of being seated next to Birgitte in their penthouse. A rare January snowstorm swirled outside the windows, and the fireplace crackled. *A nonentity, for our purposes. She's settled in to do security for the Board. Disappointing, really. She had so much potential.*

Maya's head still throbbed painfully with other people's voices when Persephone—*Charlie*—laughed again. "Nemesis? He wishes."

"He made a pretty compelling case," Rafe drawled. "Wouldn't shut up about how you two were always fighting for the number one spot."

"If I had wanted it, I'd have it. I mean, how did that number one spot turn out for him?" It was clearly a rhetorical question. Both Gray and Rafe seemed to vanish from her world as she stared at Maya, humor and tension in her eyes. "So."

"So," Maya echoed. That same tension burned in her gut, and she knew Charlie was doing the same thing she was—reassessing a relationship built on fragile strands of slowly growing trust wrapped around ropes of mutually assured destruction. The punishment facing the founder of the GhostNet balanced against the reward coming to whoever turned in Maya. Knowing Persephone was Charlotte Young balanced against the knowledge that the Silver Devils hadn't died in a warehouse a few months ago.

So many secrets and lies. So much potential destruction. Maya had just accidentally exposed the Silver Devils . . . but the Silver Devils had, in turn, exposed Charlotte Young.

Those fragile strands of trust stretched. The potential for violence throbbed more loudly than the music.

Dani giggled.

Maya couldn't tear her gaze from Charlie's. "You okay, Dani?"

"I'm sorry, but you were right. That was too many shots." She laughed even harder. "Because this is *hilarious*."

Charlie's full lips twitched. In that moment, her brown eyes softened, and Maya knew they wouldn't be killing each other today. Charlie slid from the booth and rose to face them, her hands braced on her hips. "I trust Maya. So I'll trust the two of you. As long as we all agree there's no reason to go spilling secrets that'll only do more harm than good."

That was meant for Maya as much as the two men—a warning that Charlie didn't want her identity as the founder of the GhostNet betrayed. Maya answered her the same way. "I trust her, guys. She has as much to lose as any of us. Maybe even more."

After a beat, Rafe held out a hand. "If Maya trusts you . . ."

"Just like that?" Charlie asked, clasping his hand. "Conall will be devastated."

"Conall will understand," Gray retorted. "He has faith in Maya's judgment. Besides, what's going on is more important than a little workplace rivalry."

"All right." Charlie waved a hand to the booth before resuming her seat. "So tell me."

Rafe and Dani slid into one side. Maya ended up next to Charlie, with Gray's body a solid, protective wall between her and the dance floor. A quirk of the building's acoustics made the music vibrating up through her shoes feel farther away, and they sat in a relative circle of quiet while Maya outlined the bare bones of the story.

She knew before she finished that she was looking at a dead end, even before Charlie shook her head regretfully. "The underground market in Atlanta doesn't trade in people," she said flatly. "At least no part of it I control."

"We assumed that much, based on what Maya told us," Gray assured her. "But if you've seen or heard *anything* suspicious, it might give us a solid starting point."

"I didn't make myself clear." Charlie leaned forward, elbows braced against the table, and the intensity in her eyes burned. "The last thing anyone with a truck full of kids would do is get within a hundred miles of me. I have a temper and a reputation."

Gray subsided with a nod and a resigned sigh. "Fair enough."

"However . . ." Charlie leaned back, her fingertips tapping the table thoughtfully. "You said this started with independent labs selling genetic data?"

“And other labs buying it,” Rafe confirmed. “Or at least some sort of mobile lab unit. They cleared out of that place too fast and too clean for it to have been the first time.”

Charlie nodded. “Then y’all need to go upstairs.”

Maya’s stomach sank. “Upstairs, like to the VIP section?”

“Not just that.” Charlie flashed a grin. “Upstairs like straight to Savitri herself. If you want to know who’s trading genetic IP, that’s who you have to ask.”

“Okay, then.” Dani pushed up from her seat with both palms on the table. “Let’s do it.”

“Wait,” Maya protested. “It’s not that easy. Unless Charlie can get us up there . . .”

“I could get you into the VIP section,” Charlie acknowledged. “But I can’t promise you face time. The only way to get that with Savitri is to intrigue her so much she wants to see your face. Or more than your face.”

“Mm-hmm.” Dani held out her hand. “Rafe? Care to show these nonbelievers how it’s done?”

“It would be my pleasure.” He clasped Dani’s hand and rolled to his feet. Then, after a moment’s thought, he peeled his shirt over his head with an effortless grace any stripper would have envied.

The shirt hit Gray in the chest before falling to the table in a heap. Rafe’s full arsenal of weaponized muscles flexed under the neon lights, and he winked at Dani. “Ready, cupcake?”

She rolled her eyes and pulled him toward the dance floor.

“Well.” Charlie propped her chin on her hand. “This should be interesting.”

She sounded amused—and more than a little doubtful. That would change. Rafe’s resting state was smoldering, and he threw sparks whenever Dani entered the same room. The question wasn’t whether Savitri would notice them.

It was whether Savitri would notice them before they burned the whole place down.

DANI

Dani didn't do self-denial.

The reasons were few and vital. For starters, it wasn't fun. Beyond that, it wasn't even effective. Oh, people pretended it was, that their sacrifice and discipline would allow them to reap multitudes of rewards at some nebulous point in the future.

What bullshit. Fortune favored the bold.

And she was feeling very, *very* bold.

The music filling the cavernous space throbbed through her, repetitive and heavy with bass. It sounded a little like that procedurally generated FlowMac shit that Maya loved so much, only deeper. More primal.

It had an edge to it, one she felt keenly as Rafe spun her in a tight circle before catching her against his body, her back pressed tight to the blazing heat of his bare chest. His hand slid down her side before settling over her navel, fingers splayed wide. He rolled his hips, taking her with him in a slow, deliberate circle, and warm breath tickled her ear.

"You sure you're up to this?"

"Says the walking hard-on." She slipped around to face him again and slid up his thigh. "Check your four."

Rafe's fingers found the bare skin at the small of her back, flexing as he urged her higher. He moved with the pulse of the music, making it look natural as he turned them. "The blonde by the bar?"

"Mmm, she's armed. Heavily. And the guy under the sign for the bathrooms?"

"Corporate mercenary." Rafe made an amused noise as he dipped her back over his arm, giving her an upside-down view of the hulking soldier lurking beneath the sign. It lasted for only the space of a heartbeat before he pulled her back up. Her hair flew around them as their upper bodies collided, the space between their faces millimeters at most. "Knox couldn't scrub the soldier off, either," he rasped, his voice too intimate for such pragmatic shop talk, "but at least he ditched that damn haircut."

Dani couldn't help it—her gaze dropped to Rafe's mouth. It was unstoppable, a chemical reaction. This pull had always been there between them, but lately it was getting more intense. It drew her in faster, deeper—and she had a harder time swimming free of the undertow.

"Uh-huh." She broke away, raising her arms to dance in a circle before facing him again. "So . . . tell me about Charlie."

The flashing neon lights intensified the play of muscle. Rafe's bare chest was drawing covetous glances as more space opened up around them. Onlookers swayed to the music and watched as Rafe dragged his hands up her sides before twining their fingers together above her head. "Charlie's trouble," he rumbled, rolling his hips toward hers. "She and Conall were the top of their class during training. Probably means she's the smartest hacker left on the Hill."

"Maybe. But she's obviously not much of a company gal, if she's down here, slumming it at a place like Convergence."

"Interesting, isn't it?" He used their joined hands to spin her, dragging her back against his chest as he ground against her ass to the rhythm of the throbbing bass beat. His lips brushed her ear this time. "Nobody's ever who they seem."

It was the very definition of *preaching to the choir*, but Dani found herself strangely reluctant to remind him of that fact. Instead, she bit her lip, and a jolt of something suspiciously like longing streaked through her when he reacted with a low groan from so deep in his chest she felt the vibrations against her back.

Then he was gone, leaving a trail of hot kisses down her spine as his fingers molded to the curve of her hips.

Startled, Dani turned. "Rafe—"

Then her eyes met his, and the words vanished. Her protest, her question, whatever the fuck she'd been about to say—just *gone*, like he had the power to crawl inside her head and take up so much space there wasn't room for anything else.

His fingertips ghosted over her calves and trailed up her legs. His brown eyes glinted with heat as he passed her knees and finally encountered the hem of her dress—then inched higher.

Rafe's thumb found the strap of her thigh sheath. He stroked along the edge until he reached one of her knives, and his lips quirked up.

"Hot," he mouthed to her silently.

Dani sucked in a breath.

Rafe curled his fingers along the back of her thigh, and then they were moving, exploding upward as he rocked to his feet with inhuman grace and hoisted her up against him. She wrapped her legs around his waist instinctively, then celebrated and regretted the action in equal measure when his abs clenched.

She stared into his eyes, captivated by the desire reflected back at her. At moments like this, she could almost believe that his attraction to her was more than physical. That he didn't just *want* her, he wanted *her*, and he knew the difference.

They froze that way, his fingers hot on her bare thighs, their lips so close she could taste his shuddering sigh of regret.

Then she realized she could *hear* it, too.

The music had stopped. There was none of the chatter and ambient noise that Dani would have expected to rise in its place, either. The whole club was silent, barely breathing. Waiting.

Breaking away from Rafe's gaze almost hurt, so she did it gladly, deliberately.

She followed other people's riveted stares to the balcony, where Savitri stood, looking like a queen about to address her subjects.

Instead, she met Dani's eyes, smiled, and crooked one finger.

Rafe sighed again as he slid her body down the length of his.

More regret. So Dani released him quickly—*gladly*—and stepped back with a breezy smile. "Great game, Morales."

Heat flashed in his eyes, and Dani turned away. It was just another thing nobody had time for right now. Especially them.

TECHCORPS PROPRIETARY DATA,
L3 SECURITY CLEARANCE

Birgitte Skovgaard has been demoted from her position as senior analyst and placed on administrative suspension pending disciplinary action.

Internal Memo, July 2065

ELEVEN

There was an actual orgy happening on Savitri's balcony.

Naked bodies writhed under the pulsing lights, flashing in and out of shadow. Moans and cries drifted to Gray's ears, sounds that had previously been drowned out by the music but were clear as fucking day—pun intended—once he got this close.

Maya walked straight past the scene, her eyes carefully fixed on the dais at the far end of the room, while Rafe studied the sweaty, enthusiastic participants with an appreciative grin. Dani was the one who lingered, eyeing the various tangles of limbs like she was deliberating over a dessert cart.

Gray elbowed her. "Put your tongue back in your mouth."

She huffed. "Boring. So many other places to put it up here."

"I have a few suggest—" Rafe cut off with a grunt as Maya stomped one boot down onto his foot.

"Focus," she murmured, still staring at the dais. "This is one of the most dangerous rooms in Atlanta."

It was definitely in Gray's top three, and he'd been in some goddamn dangerous places—including Protectorate headquarters. On the surface, it might have seemed like nothing more than hedonistic fun. But if you really thought about it, every single person literally fucking around on that balcony was ready and willing to make themselves *vulnerable.*

They'd only do that with full, absolute confidence in Savitri's ability to keep them safe.

The woman in question sat on a large, velvet-upholstered chair at the back of the dais. The image was undoubtedly meant to evoke royalty, a benevolent but powerful queen looking down at her subjects from her lofty throne. She even managed to *look* regal, even though her clothes were just like Dani's—half cyberpunk club kid, half high fashion. The black leather she wore made her already dark hair look even darker, and her skin glowed like the burnished gold that accented her outfit.

A stone-faced man stood beside and a little in front of her. He was *huge*, taller and wider than Rafe, his stature as intimidating as his impassive stare. His skin was paler than Savitri's, and his hair, though just as dark, was shot through with gray at the temples. It also peppered his short, neatly trimmed beard.

A guard. Not surprising, except for the fact that Gray only saw the one. It wasn't unusual for people in positions of power to have undercover protective detail—not being surrounded by bodyguards made them seem more approachable, plus it was easier for those guards to thwart an attack if they had a little of the element of surprise on their side, too. But Gray could typically spot a guard at a hundred paces, no matter how good they were at blending into a crowd, and he saw . . . nothing.

The fine hairs on the back of his neck rose in warning. Savitri only had this one guy standing between her and the rest of the world. Was she naive? Reckless? Or was this inscrutable bastard just that lethal?

No wonder Charlie had declined to accompany them upstairs.

Savitri crossed her legs as they approached, baring one leg to the thigh as she lazily bounced her foot. Her gaze slid over each of them in turn, sharp and intelligent, and when she tilted her head, Gray caught the telltale reflection of light off one of her eyes. Smart lenses.

Maya stopped a few feet from the dais. Rafe continued another few paces, stopping just out of arm's reach of the imposing guard. He swept an elaborate bow that should have seemed ridiculous, but the mischievous twinkle in his eyes as he peeked up at Savitri was concentrated charisma. "You summoned us, your majesty?"

Savitri tapped her fingers on the arm of her chair and studied Rafe. "Isn't he pretty, Adam?"

The man at her side grunted.

"Can't fault your taste, but you should know . . ." Dani's flirtatious grin grew downright wolfish. "He's all talk. If you want someone who comes through, you want *me*."

Maya made a strangled noise.

"What? She's fucking *hot*."

"I am," Savitri agreed with a lazy smile. "That was quite a show you two put on. You must have wanted to catch my attention a great deal. I'm intrigued. For the moment."

It was a dance, just like the one Rafe and Dani had been doing downstairs. They'd spend the next few minutes prowling around each other, trying to size up so many things about the situation—motivation, intent, interest—without giving any real intel of their own away.

Gray knew the steps to this dance. He could do it when it was necessary. He was even pretty good at it. But Christ, sometimes he just wanted to ask a straight fucking question and get a straight fucking answer.

"Can we cut the shit?" he asked bluntly. "We're not here to cause trouble or be a problem for you. All we need is some information."

"Oh, is that all?" Savitri raised one perfectly shaped eyebrow. "I guess they're not here to play after all, Adam. How disappointing."

"We play," Dani corrected. "We play *hard*. Gotta get the work done first, though. You know how it is."

"I do." Savitri inclined her head slightly, then returned her attention to Gray. "So. You want information. It so happens that I have a great deal of it, but it's not always cheap."

Nothing ever was. He'd learned about the transactional nature of life early, and he'd never forgotten those brutal lessons. "You get what you pay for," he agreed. "Emerge BioCore Systems."

Her brow furrowed slightly, and she glanced at Adam.

"Formerly Paradigm BioTech," he supplied immediately. "Also PolyMax Bioengineering, ParaMax BioCore, ParaMax Bioengineering, ApiGen—"

"Ahhh, *those* assholes." Her gaze developed a distinct chill as she surveyed them all again. "And how did you get tangled up with ApiGen?"

"We broke into one of their facilities," Dani answered blithely. "We'd like to do it again."

"You *do* play hard, don't you?" Savitri tapped her fingers on the arm of her chair. "Let me guess. You went back only to discover they'd vanished. No trace. As if they'd never even been there, even though it should have been impossible for a lab of that magnitude to pack up and leave without warning."

"They have it down to a science, don't they?" Adam murmured. "The bastards."

Maya took a step forward, speaking up for the first time. "So you've run into them before?"

"Them, and a dozen more like them." Savitri sighed. "That's why they're so good at disappearing. Their survival is about hiding. Hiding their IP and scientists from the TechCorps. Hiding from Charlie . . ."

Adam growled. "Hiding from us."

Gray dragged his hands through his hair. "So they're just gone? That's it?"

"They're *somewhere*. But the one place they're not is in Atlanta. If they were, I would know. You need to talk to the guy who knows everything that's happening outside of Atlanta."

Gray studied her, looking for the silent, subtle signs of deceit. But there was nothing sneaky or dishonest in her demeanor. Her eyes were clear and bright, and she gazed back at him easily, without avoiding *or* holding eye contact too forcefully.

Finally, he nodded. "Who is that, and where do we find him?"

"Jaden Montgomery," Savitri began. "And you can—"

Dani snorted out a laugh, then clapped her hand over her mouth. Maya dropped her face into both hands with a groan.

Rafe frowned, looking back and forth between them. "Uh, is that a problem?"

"Not exactly." Maya dropped her hands. "We know Jaden."

"Well . . ." Dani tilted her head to one side, then the other. "We know Dakota."

"One of Jaden's drivers," Maya supplied. Then she winced. "Also our boss Nina's ex-girlfriend."

"Emphasis on the *girlfriend* part, not the *ex*." Dani started toward Savitri's chair. "See, the problem with Jaden is—"

In a flash, Adam moved, blocking Dani's path to the dais. He reached for her wrist, but she twisted away faster than Gray could blink. Adam's eyes widened in momentary shock, and he reached for the weapon in his shoulder holster, only to stop short as Dani backed away.

"You're fast," Dani observed.

"You're faster," Adam retorted, his brows drawn together. It didn't sound like a compliment. "Don't get near her."

"Sure." A wink followed Dani's breezy assurance. "But I've got to warn you—if she asks nicely, all bets are off."

"Adam."

That was all Savitri said, but the man stood down. When he moved aside, Savitri propped her chin in her hand, her expression amused. "Do continue. What is Jaden Montgomery's problem?"

"He has a jealousy issue, not to mention a little bit of denial. And the two intersect wherever Dakota happens to be standing." Dani paused. "Anyway, Nina's not his favorite person."

"Nina sounds fascinating," Savitri murmured, before straightening. "Well, I'm sorry I can't be of more help. Consider this one on the house."

"No, thanks," Gray told her. "We pay our debts up front." The only thing worse than owing someone was owing a stranger.

"I've got this one." Dani smiled, the expression tinged with playfulness. "I don't mind Savitri having my marker. I trust her."

"I like people who recklessly trust me." Savitri laughed and slipped a silver ring off her thumb. She tossed it to Dani, who caught it easily, one eyebrow upraised. "For you," Savitri purred. "A VIP pass. Come back when you want to play hard. Bring the pretty boy."

"You hear that, cupcake?" Rafe grinned at Dani. "No leaving me at home."

"We'll see."

"Oh, you wanna go now?"

Maya drove her boot down onto Rafe's foot again. "We should *all* go now. We have shit to do."

"And I have people to do." Savitri flicked her fingers at them. "Run along. If you *do* find them and need help crushing them, though . . . Well, that really *would* be on the house. Some practices are simply too abhorrent to allow."

Dismissed, they made their way downstairs. By unspoken agreement—and with their mission completed—they headed straight for the exit. Gray found himself holding his breath as they wove wordlessly through the smoke and the neon glare and the jostling bodies.

Outside in the alley, he could finally breathe, though the night air was still muggy and thick. "That could have gone worse."

Dani rolled the VIP pass Savitri had given her between her fingers. "Not as productive as I'd hoped, but at least we have a standing invitation from the owner."

Gray snorted. "You and Rafe do, anyway." Savitri had made her priorities—and her motivations—crystal clear.

"Next time, maybe at least *try* turning on the charm," Dani advised. "It might work, even though you suck at it. You never know."

"Hey." Instead of putting it back on, Rafe slung his shirt over one shoulder and wagged a finger at her. "Gray has his strengths. We can't *all* be smoldering sex bombs."

She rolled her eyes in response, but her smile quickly faded. Her seemingly perpetual expression of flirtatious amusement vanished, replaced by pensive concentration. "One thing's bothering me, though."

That sent prickles of warning skittering up Gray's spine. "What is it?"

"Her guard—I've seen him somewhere before."

Fucking hell. "TechCorps?"

"Maybe. I don't know." She shook her head. "Can't place him yet, but I'll figure it out."

Maya remained silent, and Gray sidled closer to her as Rafe and Dani began to bicker and bargain over the VIP ring. She'd been bizarrely quiet during their interaction with Savitri, but he couldn't tell if it was by design or because she'd had nothing to say.

"You okay?" he asked softly.

"Yeah." She drew in a slow breath and held it for a few seconds before letting it out in a soft sigh. "Savitri makes me nervous. All that sexy vampire queen shit doesn't fool me. I'm pretty sure she could figure out who I really am if I made her curious enough . . . and I'd be worth a *lot* to someone who trades in TechCorps secrets."

Gray was more than *pretty* sure about that. "Luckily, she doesn't seem to be hurting for credits."

"No." Maya's lips quirked in an almost smile. "And Rafe and Dani are next-level good at keeping everyone's attention on them."

"Yep, I've gotten used to being invisible next to Rafe." When she didn't laugh at his joke, he touched her arm—lightly. Carefully. "Are you sure you're all right? You seem . . ."

"Overwhelmed?" She twisted one of the half dozen rings she'd donned nervously around one finger, her gaze unfocused. "I should be. I haven't had time to do my meditation exercises in days. But it's not actually that bad? I just feel a little . . ." She choked on a laugh. "No. Not a little. I just feel. A *lot*."

"Is that bad?"

"Probably." She stole a quick glance at him but looked away before he could meet her eyes. "Nah, ignore me. It's been a weird couple days, hasn't it? Are *you* okay? I mean, you're the one who had a friend come back from the dead."

Gray almost stumbled.

He hadn't thought about Mace at all during their outing—which wasn't unusual. His Protectorate training had included harsh lessons on compartmentalization. It was a necessary part of life as a soldier, being able to temporarily quiet your racing thoughts. You couldn't very well charge across a battlefield, with rounds zipping past your head and grenades exploding around you, if you couldn't lock away basic things like fear and horror and self-preservation.

In truth, the Protectorate hadn't had much to teach him that the streets hadn't already taken care of. Gray had already mastered the art of shoving things into little boxes in his head by the time he'd joined up.

But he was always, *always* aware of it. And he hadn't made a conscious choice not to think about Mace's return.

How *did* he feel about it? The question was almost too huge to answer, and trying to break it down into smaller issues didn't do a damn bit of good.

Mace was alive. And he had come after them, which meant someone at the TechCorps likely knew the rest of the Silver Devils weren't dead, either. Worse, his friend was barely clinging to sanity.

Somehow, the fact that Mace had tried to stab Gray in the face was low on the list of things about this situation that were 100 percent fucked up.

Maya was still looking at him, so Gray shrugged, even though the muscles in his neck and shoulders were so tense the action literally *hurt*. "I'm worried about Mace, and about Knox. And about what this means."

"That Richter thinks you're alive." Her low rasp couldn't hide the way her voice hitched on his name. "He's probably not sure. If he had proof, there'd be some trace of it in the official record. Doesn't make him less dangerous, though. He didn't have proof about Birgitte at first, either."

Nothing made Richter less dangerous.

Gray opened his mouth to remind her of that fact, but the words wouldn't come, and he wasn't sure why. It wasn't as though it were new information; if anything, Maya knew it better than the rest of them. The official TechCorps story that Birgitte had been transferred to some far-flung satellite office was a fucking joke.

No, the woman who had raised Maya had been murdered, and Gray wouldn't have been surprised if someone told him that Richter had pulled the trigger himself. The man was a lot of things, but *hypocrite* didn't number among his many flaws. He wasn't afraid to get his hands dirty. Maybe the bastard even liked it.

Then again, bad memories were one thing—inescapable, perhaps, especially when the burden of your memory was as cumbersome as Maya's. But they were still in the *past*, and that mattered. Gray didn't want to be the one to shove merciless reality in her face for no damn good reason, to turn the specter of Richter into cold, murderous flesh.

Instead, he shrugged. "Whatever happens, we'll deal with it. I'm glad Mace is alive, and he's someplace now where we can look after him. Everything else is tangential."

"Agreed." She hesitated. "How do you think he found y'all?"

That much, Gray knew. "Mace is a good tracker. He's patient, you know? Plus, he thinks just like Knox sometimes."

"Takes a Devil to find a Devil?"

"Something like that."

"We'll take care of him," Maya promised softly. "That's what Nina does. And she's a fucking rock star at it."

"I have no doubts," he assured her. Rafe and Dani were still arguing, though they'd moved past combativeness into laughter and now were working their way around again. "Come on, let's hurry back. It's gonna be one hell of a debriefing tonight."

March 30th, 2077

Richter's data courier has continued to cultivate Marjorie as a friend. No creature raised by Tobias Richter could be anything but broken inside. He taints everything he touches. I have no doubts he's using the girl to spy on me.

I need to find a way to separate Marjorie from DC-025.

The Recovered Journal of Birgitte Skovgaard

TWELVE

Maya couldn't get the music out of her head.

Hours after everyone else had gone to bed, she climbed toward the roof and stepped out onto the walkway that connected their building to the one the Silver Devils had purchased. Kudzu had climbed the side of the warehouse to twine around the metal bars of the waist-length railing, but Maya always kept a space clear right in the center of the catwalk.

The view was perfect from here. She settled down, sitting cross-legged with her back braced against the warm metal. The night had begun to cool, but it was still humid enough that sweat dotted her temples, even though she'd stripped to a tank top and her pajama shorts before realizing sleep was impossible.

The Hill stretched out in the distance, a perfect, shining beacon. Towers of glass and steel pierced the night, climbing two hundred stories or more at their tallest. Tiny, blinking lights zipped between them in spite of the late hour. Even before the Flares, the people on the Hill had given up such barbaric notions as *cars*. Automated AirLifts carried the rich and privileged of Atlanta from rooftop to rooftop in elegant luxury. Their feet never had to touch the ground upon which the peasants strode unless they found walking among the less privileged charmingly retro.

It was a stomach-churning indulgence when babies in Five Points went to bed hungry and parents tried to make a handful of credits stretch for a week. Sometimes Maya stared at the flickering lights and felt sick with the memory of how often she'd lounged on cooled leather seats as Birgitte traveled between meetings. A VP of the TechCorps lived well, on the Hill, and so did her data courier.

Until they didn't.

Maya stared at the glowing lights until her eyes burned, but memories of the Hill didn't overtake her. Convergence still throbbed inside her skull. The low beat of the music. The scents: sweat, cologne, liquor, dry ice. Gray's hand at the small of her back, a burning warmth she couldn't stop feeling.

That was new. Her memory had always been focused primarily on auditory retention, and she'd been trained ruthlessly to ignore her other senses and focus on her duty. There were exceptions, of course. Moments she relived with such piercing clarity she couldn't always tell memory from reality. But that was usually the *bad* shit. Trauma etched into her neurons with blood and tears and fear.

Gray's touch was different. Gentle and sweet. Warm.

Good.

Closing her eyes, Maya thudded her head lightly back against the iron railing. It didn't help. Too much had happened in the past forty-eight hours. In the past, she would have stretched out somewhere quiet and ruthlessly forced her mind back into disciplined order using one of the dozens of meditation tricks Birgitte had drilled into her.

It's survival, Marjorie. You must stay in control at all times. They watch data couriers for signs of instability. Showing weakness could be fatal.

For years, Maya had struggled against what felt like the inevitable, terrified that if she slipped for even a second, she'd hasten her own downfall. Because that was the secret Birgitte had told her, the one data couriers weren't supposed to know. Eventually, the stress on her brain would break her. Her only strategy to prolong sanity was rigid training, the cultivation of absolute control, and to avoid using the full extent of her gifts any more than absolutely necessary.

Maya had never questioned her. She'd never had a *reason* to question her. For all of Birgitte's flaws, the last thing she would have done was endanger Maya in any way. Not out of affection but practicality—Maya had been the heart of Birgitte's rebellion. The only reason the organization had even been possible. Maya's stability and functionality had been her primary goal.

At least, Maya had *thought* it was.

With her eyes closed, Maya re-created that moment in the warehouse. The feel of the gun in her hands. The darkness behind the mask. The giddy feeling of her mind *stretching*, as if she'd kept it locked in a too-small box for years and it was finally getting the chance to move. An ever-present ache had vanished in those few precious moments when she'd just . . . let go. She hadn't realized how much she was holding in until she stopped. And now she didn't know how to go back.

She didn't know if she *wanted* to go back.

A trip to Convergence should have put her flat on her back, especially after the stress and chaos of Mace's unexpected arrival on top of two days of handling everything on her own. But as jumbled as her mind felt, it didn't *hurt*. Maybe because she wasn't fighting it.

Or maybe the hurt was coming, and it would prove Birgitte right. Maybe she'd fall the fuck apart.

Nina's boots echoed on the walkway as she approached. "Okay, I left a message with Jaden's people. He and Dakota are out on a run, so it could be a few days before we hear back."

Maya opened her eyes slowly, half expecting the world to swim the way it sometimes did when she felt overwhelmed. But she just saw Nina, still dressed in jeans and a sleeveless T-shirt, looking ready to face down the world.

Everything was always a little less scary with Nina around. "That's good," Maya said, tilting her head in invitation to sit. "You think Jaden's gonna be an ass about it?"

"I doubt it." The corner of Nina's mouth ticked up as she slid down next to

Maya. "He may not like that Dakota and I had a thing, but he's a stand-up guy. He doesn't want a place like Emerge BioCore operating any more than we do."

"No, definitely not." Maya grinned. "Maybe he'll try to poach me again to run his books. His last offer wasn't bad."

Nina laughed. "Apparently it wasn't very good, either."

"I like the benefits package here." Maya's smile faded as she tilted her head to rest on Nina's shoulder. "Can I ask you something?"

"Always."

"How do you know when they lied to you? The Franklin Center? How do you even start to untangle it?"

Nina didn't answer right away. Instead, she looked up at the night sky, which was strangely light—and blank. There were never many stars this close to the Hill; the lights and skyscrapers tended to drown and blot them out. But a few remained, too bright and insistent to be ignored.

Finally, she spoke. "Honestly? I have no idea. Memory's a tricky thing anyway, and when you throw in lies on top of that, shit gets muddled *fast*." She turned her head and met Maya's gaze. "Most of the time, I rely on things I know to be true now. Not just about the Center, but about myself."

"That's the part I'm not sure about." Maya rubbed a hand over her chest, as if she could soothe away the tightness there. "I never even considered that Birgitte might lie about what they did to me. She was brutally honest, especially about herself and our situation. She was there to get a job done and to use me however she could."

Nina waited.

"She told me so many hard truths." Maya swallowed hard. "But that doesn't mean she never lied, does it?"

"No." Nina sighed. "Not all lies are as pretty as you'd think."

Maya closed her eyes. "The first thing I remember them telling me is that the outside would be dangerous for me. That the sensory input would be overwhelming. They even discouraged us from learning any more than we had to for our jobs. It was basically, 'don't worry your pretty little heads,' but they always made it sound like a perk. We didn't have to do the boring schoolwork everyone else did. We got to watch movies and shop instead."

How many times had the TechCorps blocked one of Maya's requests for advanced courses of study as unnecessary to her core function? How many times had Maya gone to Birgitte, pleading, every part of her *itching* with the need to learn more? Birgitte had always found a way to justify the additional education, but she'd never let Maya forget—she could have her education, but she had to be unremarkable. Silent, efficient, and, as far as anyone else knew, placidly content with her place in the hierarchy.

A happy, cosseted pet, just like the others.

Maya shivered. "After Birgitte told me that most data couriers break under the strain eventually, I always figured everything they told us was true, more or less. They wanted to preserve our usefulness for as long as possible, and what's the point of teaching us things that will just clutter up our brain and use it up that much faster?"

Exhaling shakily, she admitted the thing Nina knew, the thing that lurked in silence between them every time Maya came downstairs with shadows beneath her eyes from another sleepless night. "I've been holding on so tight. Walking this damn tightrope . . . Trying not to burn out, trying to stay in control. But I want to *live,* Nina. And sometimes it feels like holding it all in hurts more than the world ever could."

"Ah. You know, there's something Knox told me—about when we met." Nina shifted position, crossing her legs and taking Maya's hand in hers. "I don't know if you've noticed, but he's a terrible liar. Just *abysmal.*"

Maya fought a smile. "I think we've *all* noticed."

"Exactly. But he still had to convince us to walk into a trap. He said Rafe coached him, and his biggest piece of advice was to lie with the truth." Nina squeezed her hand. "Misrepresentation, Maya. For you, control likely *is* super important. But there's more than one way to have control over yourself and over your abilities."

Maya gripped Nina's hand like a lifeline. *Rely on the things you know to be true.*

She knew Birgitte was a skilled, efficient liar.

She knew Birgitte would have done anything to protect her rebellion. Not needlessly or cruelly. She had been neither of those things. But ruthless? Willing to sacrifice her own happiness and well-being, and Maya's, if it advanced her goal?

In a heartbeat.

Maya knew some nights she climbed into bed and dug furrows into her palms with her fingernails as the ghosts of other people's words chased themselves around the inside of her skull in an incoherent Möbius strip of overlapping voices.

She knew some nights a listless nervousness drove her from bed in search of anything that would soothe that intangible itch inside her head. She'd pick up tasks and discard them, unable to focus long enough to find a cure for her restlessness.

She knew that it wasn't getting better. But it wasn't getting worse, either. And if being out in the Big Bad World was going to crack her head like an egg, wouldn't it have happened by now?

That, she didn't know.

"I have to throw it all out, don't I?" She glanced at Nina. "Everything the TechCorps told me. Everything Birgitte told me. All of it."

"Not all of what they told you is false," Nina answered matter-of-factly. "But it's all unreliable. Every goddamn word."

It was almost as freeing as the moment in the warehouse. Maya tilted her head back and closed her eyes. "So . . . I guess I just start flexing my brain and see what happens, huh?"

"And remember—" Nina's hand closed around hers again. "We're all here for you, no matter what."

"You always are." Maya smiled gently. "And speaking of no matter what . . . How's Knox doing? Did y'all get Mace settled in?"

"He's next door, in a secure place. Knox is staying over there with him tonight."

Maya trusted that Conall had blocked any potential signals from trackers, but she couldn't stop from shifting nervously as her gaze drifted back to the Hill. In one of those shining buildings, Tobias Richter was sitting at his desk, no doubt gleeful at the knowledge he'd unleashed the cruelest weapon imaginable on the man who had escaped his grasp.

"Just answer the question, Marjorie, and this will all stop."

Ice trickled down her spine as Maya scrambled to fill her mind with the music from Convergence. Or some nice, vacant FlowMac Pop. Anything but *his* voice.

When that didn't work, she grasped for a distraction. "Does he seem . . . okay? Mace, I mean. Because he was their medic, right? A TechCorps-trained doctor. And if anyone can help Gray . . ."

"Honestly?" Nina exhaled sharply. "I don't know yet. We have no idea what he's been through, but he was almost certainly tortured. He may never be *okay* again. But I have to hope. For Knox's sake."

Wrong distraction. The memory surged like a rogue wave threatening to sweep her under. Rope bit into the already-raw skin at her wrists. Crueler than the plastic zip ties somehow as the rough abrasion pushed her toward sensory overload. She tasted blood. Just a little—Richter hadn't dared do more than backhand her once, barely hard enough to split her lip. But the metallic scent of it overwhelmed her. Not her blood.

His.

Maya stumbled to her feet, locking her hands around the metal railing on the walkway. It bit into her palms, grounding her. She dragged in a breath, as deep as she could, and there was no blood, no sterile air cooled by the air-conditioning. Just a muggy Atlanta night, the air perfumed by the honeysuckle climbing up alongside the kudzu.

Nina didn't touch her, but Maya could feel the hand hovering just shy of her back. "Maya?"

Another breath. A third. Maya managed to form words. "Are you up for some late-night training?"

A hesitation, then Nina relented. "Sure. Pick your poison."

Maya pushed upright and managed a smile. "Hand-to-hand. Rafe's taught me some new tricks. I might surprise you."

Nina's smile was readier, brighter. "I welcome the challenge."

She needed to move. Sweat. She needed to feel strong enough to face any ghosts that showed up. After all, Tobias Richter was the monster from her nightmares . . .

But he was just a man. A human. No special abilities, no inherent strength. Take him off the Hill, where he had power, and he was just another bully.

And she wasn't a scared little girl anymore.

TECHCORPS INTERNAL
EXECUTIVE COMMUNICATION

From: JOHNSON, J
To: RICHTER, T
Date: 2066–07–03

Why the hell did you let Skovgaard lay four fucking years of paper trail on this guy? Your tamed killer snapped, and now we have an entire Protectorate squad that was massacred by one of their own, two dozen civilian bodies to explain, and the VP of R&D is burying her favorite grandson tomorrow.

Someone is going down for this. You'd best decide quickly who it's going to be.

From: RICHTER, T
To: JOHNSON, J
Date: 2066–07–03

It's being taken care of.

THIRTEEN

Mace was in the kitchen.

More precisely, he was sitting at the ladies' dining table, a steaming mug in front of him. Gray paused in the back doorway, struck by how fucking *normal* a picture he presented.

Nothing had been normal about Mace since his miraculous return from the dead. He wouldn't sleep in the warehouse, barracks-style, with the rest of the Devils. He'd insisted on being separated, so Knox had given him the one private room they'd already finished. It had been meant for Knox, but seeing as how he spent most of his nights in Nina's bed, he'd been more than willing to give it up.

He'd drawn the line at locking Mace in, however. And no amount of argument from their recently resurrected medic had been able to change his mind on that subject.

So Mace had locked *himself* in. He'd asked Rafe to find him a giant mag bolt, the quick-deploying kind you used when you were running out of a job hot and you needed to put a few precious seconds of space between you and your pursuers. Then he'd slapped that thing on his brand-new bedroom door and disappeared behind the wood.

The metallic rasp of such a lock engaging had always been a nothing sound to Gray—muted, inoffensive, easily ignored—but now it was seared into his brain. It had haunted his dreams the previous night, displacing more welcome things, like images of flashing neon lights reflected off Maya's full lips.

Gray shook himself. He couldn't stand there forever, with uncertainty pinning him in the open doorway. So he took a careful step forward—slow, deliberate. Loud enough to be heard.

Mace's fingers tightened around the earthenware mug. Then the tension spread throughout his body, as if he was poised to spring from his chair and flee.

"Stay," Gray urged quietly. "Please. We haven't had a chance to talk since . . . Since . . ." He couldn't bring himself to finish the sentence.

So Mace did it for him, with a wry twist to his lips that almost looked like a smile. *Almost.* "Since I tried to stab you in the head?"

Gray managed not to flinch. He tried to think of a reply, but nothing about the subject seemed safe enough to broach with his stilted, awkward words. Mace had been *tortured*, for fuck's sake, then sent out into the city to find and eliminate the Silver Devils. Discussing it in such a mundane, domestic setting—at the kitchen table over morning coffee—seemed too bizarre, almost surreal.

So he took the coward's way out—he changed the subject. "How did you sleep?"

"Fine."

Gray snagged a mug from the rack near the sink. "Do you like your room?"

"It's fine."

Fine. Suddenly, the thought of coffee made Gray's stomach roil. He abandoned the mug on the counter, sat down across from Mace, and just *looked* at him.

Mostly, he looked the same—blue eyes, sharp features, dark, spiky hair. Sure, he bore a pallor over his already-light skin, and his eyes were rimmed with red, but his face was the same one Gray had always known.

There were deeper differences, though, like his voice. Gone was its steady, calm timbre and cadence, the one that would always tell them the truth, even if it hurt, but in the gentlest way possible. It was scratchy now, wavering from one note to the next. And Mace's body language was all fucked up, tense and twitchy and—

And Mace was staring at him, too. Studying him intently—and with a tinge of decidedly professional curiosity.

Gray sighed. "Knox told you about my implant."

"He didn't have to. I fought you, remember? You weren't at a hundred percent."

How embarrassing. Gray felt his cheeks heat, and he cleared his throat. "I managed to hold you off, old man."

"Because I—" Mace's voice cut off abruptly. "Because I wasn't—" It happened again. This time, his jaw clenched, and the cords of muscle in his neck strained. Then Mace relaxed, shook his head, and sipped his coffee. "I'm not at a hundred percent, either."

"Fair enough." Gray hesitated, but he had to ask. He *had* to. "Do you know anything we don't? Has there been some sort of medical advance?"

"To treat implant rejection? No. It's always been possible." The more Mace spoke, the more comfortable he seemed, and the words flowed. "The surgery itself is simple, in theory."

"In theory?"

"Sure. Remove the old implant, debride the site, install the new one. The trickiest aspect of the surgery itself is rewiring the implant interface." He looked away. "What comes after, that's the rough part."

"The healing. I remember." After the initial surgery to place and wire his implant, he'd spent two solid weeks in a veritable bubble.

"Fuck what you remember," Mace countered.

It sounded so much like *him* that Gray had to dig his fingernails into his thighs to keep his expression neutral and even. Maybe this was the secret, the thing Knox had been wracking his brain trying to figure out—how to bring Mace back to them.

So he nodded and gestured for Mace to continue. "Go on."

He hesitated, then pushed his mug aside. "The problem is that you're not starting with a clean slate or a healthy patient. With a replacement surgery, you're operating at a dangerous disadvantage, on someone who's already suffering complications."

"But it *can* be done," Gray pressed. He had to find out—for Maya's sake. Because of the way she'd looked at him the night he'd collapsed. "You know the procedure."

"There is no procedure," Mace told him flatly. "It's too risky. The probable mortality rates kept the TechCorps from ever bothering to develop a protocol, much less perfect it."

So that was it. End of the line, no more possibilities. It was strangely freeing, like he'd had the weight of uncertainty hanging over him, and now it was gone. Sure, it meant the pronouncement of his death sentence was complete and final, utterly certain . . . but at least *something* was.

Still, that look on Maya's face haunted Gray. "Feel like giving it a shot anyway?"

Mace's answer was immediate, blunt—and Maya would have slapped him for it. "You may as well have let me stab you in the head the other night."

Gray couldn't help it. He barked out a laugh, one that almost drowned out the soft click of a door opening upstairs. In moments, Knox and Nina began to descend the stairs, both obviously fresh from the shower, their hands not twined but brushing as they moved.

When Nina caught sight of them, she smiled, a brilliant, bright expression. But when she spoke, her voice was soft. Careful. "Good morning."

Mace grunted, and Gray suppressed his flinch. Mace being *okay* was so goddamn important to Knox that she'd make it happen—by sheer, indomitable will, if necessary. She'd drag Mace into the warmth and cheer of the life she'd built here, and she'd sit on him to keep him from fleeing like his ass was on fire.

Mace had always been the most determined and stubborn of the Silver Devils, maybe the most obstinate person he'd ever known. But Gray wasn't sure who would win this battle of wills, this steel-cage matchup between Mace's trauma and Nina's unwavering smiles.

With Knox's heart on the line, smart money was on Nina.

"Mace." Knox's fingers touched Nina's one last time before they broke apart. He circled the table and slid into the seat at the end of the table. "Sit rep?"

Mace didn't answer. He was busy casting nervous, sidelong glances at the kitchen, where Nina was peering into the refrigerator. Knox followed his gaze, his jaw tightening, but a moment later he'd locked down the expression.

Knox was in Captain Mode.

He leaned forward slightly, bracing his elbows on the table. "James."

Mace's gaze snapped to his, and he frowned as he raised his mug. "You want a situation report? The coffee's good. I made it extra strong."

Knox smiled. "Just how we like it."

But falling into old, familiar rhythms couldn't be so easy, not with a stranger in their midst. The focus and ease Mace had displayed only moments earlier vanished. His mug dropped to the table with a thud, and he began to count under his breath, the rapid words barely audible.

Gray's chest ached.

Knox's voice stayed soft and even. "What do you need, James?"

Mace's hand jerked, upsetting his mug. Gray reacted out of instinct, reaching for a kitchen towel as the steaming liquid spread across the table.

But the quick action made things worse. Mace sprang from the table, his chair scraping loudly over the floor as he dove blindly for the exit.

Knox bolted out of his chair, but Nina intercepted him. He stopped, chest heaving, eyes fixed on the door Mace had disappeared through. "I'm going to tear Tobias Richter apart one piece at a time."

"Yeah." And Gray could only hope he lived long enough to see it.

"We'll get through to him, Garrett." Nina rubbed Knox's shoulder. "I know it's hard, and it'll take some time, but you *will* have your friend back."

"He won't be the same." Knox flexed his hands—the hands he'd shattered trying to beat his way through indestructible polycarbonate to get to Mace. "None of us are the same after they break us. At least I had a mission to live for. I don't know what to give him."

"Something Richter can't fathom—your love." She touched Knox's face next, made him look at her. "I don't think they broke him at all. Not if there's enough of him left to fight like this."

"Nina's right." Gray tossed the soaked, smelly towel in the sink and leaned against the counter. "Before you came down, we were talking about my implant. He seemed . . . almost steady. So that's the purpose we can give him. The mission. We let him take care of us."

"He always has." Knox turned his head enough to kiss Nina's palm, then stepped into the kitchen and grabbed his own mug. "Any news on your implant?"

"I knew it!" Dani's voice echoing down the stairs saved him from having to answer. "I fucking *knew* it!"

The room seemed to fill at once. Dani swept downstairs, a sheaf of papers clutched in one hand, with Maya right behind her. Rafe and Conall came in through the back door, their brows knit in confusion.

"I knew it," Dani repeated, enunciating each word triumphantly. She slammed the papers down on the table, then recoiled in disgust. "Ew, why is the table sticky?"

"Long story," Nina told her. "What's up? Did you find something?"

"You bet your ass I did." She shuffled through the stack of papers, then stabbed her finger down on one. "This."

Curiosity drew them all closer to the table, and Gray flicked the stack of papers. "What are these—dossiers?"

"Employee files for TechCorps Executive Security. I printed these out when I worked there. I thought they might prove useful someday."

"You did *what*?" Conall stormed to the table on a wave of outrage. "You *printed* them? Jesus, what is this, the 1900s?"

"I like hard copies," Dani shot back. "Hard copies can't be scrubbed out of existence. Anyway, shut up, you're ruining my moment."

"Wait a fucking minute." Rafe had drifted up behind Conall, looking amused, but his expression sharpened as he lunged at the table and snatched up the piece of paper. "Are you kidding me?"

Dani's eyes gleamed as she grabbed Rafe's shoulder and leaned over his arm to peer down at the paper he held. "I told you, didn't I? It's *him*."

Rafe squinted. "I mean, it's his face, for sure. Younger. But definitely him."

Conall snapped a picture of the paper, then flipped open his tablet and propped it facing the whitewashed brick. The image filled the wall. Most of it was black-and-white text, but the image—a simple, serviceable shot of a man's head and shoulders—was in color.

Gray inhaled sharply in recognition.

"It's Savitri's bodyguard," Dani explained. "I thought I knew him from somewhere, and I was right. Ryan Lemieux—former Ex-Sec grunt and current dead person."

Nina crossed her arms over her chest and frowned. "Real dead or fake dead?"

"*Dead* dead. Or so I thought. Killed in the line of duty." Dani pointed at the projection. "I remember when this happened. Someone tried to kidnap the scientist he was assigned to, and he got shot in the head protecting her."

She said it casually, as if it were to be expected—but Gray supposed it was. Protectorate soldiers may have had tragically short life expectancies, but executive bodyguards?

To the TechCorps, they were downright disposable.

"Ryan Lemieux. On it." Conall drew a second tablet out of a pocket on his cargo pants and started tapping at the screen.

"You won't find anything," Dani told him. "Like I said—scrubbed."

"Watch me," Conall muttered, his fingers flying. But his brows had drawn together, and his glare deepened as he started to jab at the screen. "Where the fuck are you?"

"The TechCorps doesn't like bad outcomes, remember?" Gray muttered. His own pristine medical record was proof enough of that. "You're chasing your tail, Con."

"Nikita Novak," Nina read aloud. "This scientist—do we know anything about her? What was she working on?"

"Hold on." Another round of furious typing against the screen, and Conall's scowl deepened. "What the fuck? She's gone, too."

Maya wandered over to the table, cradling her mug of coffee. She peered at the projection, her brow creasing. "Nikita Novak . . ." she murmured. She reached out for the back of the chair next to Gray but froze, her fingers resting against it. "Nikita Novak. Got her."

Gray pulled out the chair, then guided her into it when she didn't move. She didn't seem to notice. "Nikita Novak," she said again. Her voice had fallen into its rhythmic cadence. "Father, Dimitri Novak. L2 scientist, Bioengineering. Mother, Jaya Novak. L1 specialist, Neural Networks. Nikita Novak was promoted to L1 specialist in 2075, at age twenty-seven. Lead Scientist, Guardian Project."

Maya blinked, then frowned. Her voice returned to normal. "Birgitte could never figure out exactly what the Guardian Project was, just that it was something military. But if Nikita was promoted to L1 specialist status at twenty-seven, she was a *scary* kind of smart."

"The scary kind of smart who could disappear, change her name to Savitri, and build an infamous criminal nightclub?" Rafe drawled.

"Probably." Maya squinted past him. "I don't think I ever saw a picture of her, so I can't say for sure. And whatever she did, she didn't pop up on Birgitte's radar very often. With parents like hers, she was basically TechCorps royalty. Birgitte wasn't exactly recruiting for the rebellion from the ranks of people with everything to lose."

"Legacy's a tricky thing," Gray agreed. "You never know what you're gonna get—a kid disillusioned with the whole thing, ready to tear it down? Or a true believer?"

Nina's watch beeped. "We'll have to handle this later. That's Dakota. Her boss is ready to meet with me."

Maya hopped up. "It's Market Day, isn't it? I want to come."

"Knock yourself out. Knox and I will meet with Montgomery, and the rest of you can do some shopping."

Dani gathered her papers. "I'll go get Rainbow."

Rafe started for the door. "I'll let Mace know. See if he needs anything."

As they scattered, Maya hovered next to Gray. "Are you gonna come, too?"

After his conversation with Mace—and his friend's subsequent meltdown—the last thing he wanted was to be in a crowd, surrounded by people. But as Maya stared up at him with big eyes and a shy smile, he found himself unwilling—unable, even—to disappoint her.

He was going to be hurting her enough already by dying.

"I wouldn't miss it," he assured her. "But I've never been before. You'll have to show me around."

Her smile grew. "It's a deal."

NINA

On Market Day, Jaden Montgomery held court on a raised platform overlooking the bustling maze of stalls and tables that spread out to fill his little corner of Atlanta. The half walls of the gazebo-like structure dampened some of the noise—voices and laughter, crates slamming together, even chickens clucking—but didn't block it out completely. So while vendors and shoppers went about their business below, Jaden sat up here, tending to his own.

And there was plenty of it. People came to Oakland from all over Atlanta to speak with him. Some needed favors, and others wanted him to invest in their ventures. Still others had disputes for him to settle, interventions that both parties had agreed for him to mediate.

It was easy to see why people considered him an authority figure. His practical and financial influence was readily displayed by the market he oversaw. In addition to vendors who flocked to the site to take advantage of the foot traffic, the market was filled with goods his band of smugglers had attained at great personal risk. Plus, he was a big man, powerful in every sense of the word. His stern countenance made it seem like he was always glowering, even when he smiled.

Or maybe it only seemed that way to Nina because *he loathed her.*

It wasn't fair, but she understood. Fair didn't usually come into play when matters of the heart—especially jealousy—were involved. And Jaden Montgomery was one jealous son of a bitch.

The reason for that jealousy stepped forward to greet Nina and Knox when they approached the platform. "Nina!" Dakota grasped her upper arms and pressed a fond kiss to her cheek. "It's good to see you."

"You, too." Nina returned the gesture and studied her friend and former lover. Dakota's dark, curly hair was pulled back from her face, and dark circles shadowed her brown eyes. "You look exhausted."

"Long run. And by the time we made it back, it was a hustle to get ready for this morning." She glanced over at Knox, tilted her head, and smiled. "Who's this?"

At least Knox didn't seem jealous. He smiled, warm and easy, and held out a hand. "Garrett Knox. Nina rescued me."

"Yeah, she's good at that." Dakota shook his hand then raised both eyebrows at Nina. "He's cute."

"And he knows it."

Dakota burst out laughing. At the back of the gazebo, where he sat in his big chair that might as well have been a throne, Jaden's glower deepened.

Nina tilted her head toward him. "Your boss is looking stormy today. He hasn't forgiven me for romancing you."

"Ignore him. He's naturally cranky." She rolled her eyes, then gestured for them to follow and led them through the small crowd. "Jay, you remember Nina."

Jaden leaned back in his chair, one elbow resting on the arm, his eyes filled with lazy arrogance. The sun burnished his deep-brown skin, and even dressed in denim and flannel and his hair cut with military precision, he managed to look like a king already bored by an interloper.

His gaze skimmed dismissively over Nina before jumping to Knox. His brow furrowed. Next to her, Knox tensed. The two assessed each other in increasingly fraught silence as the promise of violence filled the space between them.

Dakota sighed, perched on the other arm of Jaden's chair, and leaned in close to his ear. "It's customary to greet guests, asshole."

The tension broke with his abrupt, booming laugh. "Even when it's your ex-girlfriend dragging some fucking TechCorps muscle behind her?"

"Former TechCorps muscle," Knox corrected mildly.

"I assume former if you're running with Nina," Jaden shot back. "She's a pain in the ass, but she's no traitor."

Coming from him, it was a definite compliment. Well, as close as Nina was going to get. "Thank you, Jaden."

Dakota shook her head. "They're here about that thing I told you about."

"The children." Jaden's eyes froze over, and Nina realized that every glare of irritation had been just that—mild, casual. Because this?

This was anger.

He lifted one hand and crooked a finger. A massive bear of a man with pale skin, a buzz cut, and a spattering of silver in his reddish-brown beard straightened from where he'd been watching them and ambled over, his stern face breaking into a smile.

"Nina!"

"Lucas." She grasped his outstretched hand and returned his half hug, half pat on the back.

"Been too long, girl." He pulled back. "Tell me you brought Dani. I found a couple toys for her on my last run."

Dani and Lucas enjoyed a casual, occasional sexual relationship that Rafe would no doubt despise. "She's shopping."

"I'll find her." Lucas pivoted to face Jaden. "What do you need, boss?"

"Nina has intel on another group trying to run cloned kids through our territory. I want them found."

Nina handed over the data stick that Conall had prepared. "This is everything we have—surveillance footage, satellite imagery, every bit of information we were able to scrape together."

Jaden rose from his chair. "I'm going to put out a call now, just in case. But if no one's spotted them, I want you to run the whole network for her."

"Got it." Lucas tucked the data stick into his pocket and stepped aside to let Jaden pass. Jaden gathered Nina and Knox with a tilt of his head and led them away from the gazebo and around the back of the largest warehouse.

The well-worn path ran a few hundred yards through a field of wildflowers to the top of a small hill. At the end was a two-story log building that looked like someone's rustic getaway cottage tucked between a few massive pine trees.

Knox tilted his head back, studying the tallest tree—and the way the sun reflected off something metallic high in its branches.

A radio tower.

Knox whistled softly. "How far can you broadcast with that?"

"Far enough." Jaden flipped open a wooden box near the entrance and pressed his hand to a biometric scanner. The lock popped, and he hauled open the door. "It's not about distance so much as coverage."

"Multiple towers, you mean." Nina studied the tower. It was well-camouflaged—expertly, even—but that didn't mean jack shit when you were sitting in the TechCorps' backyard. "They monitor your communications. They must. There's no way they would just let you . . . have this."

"Oh, someone records every goddamn thing we say." Jaden gestured to the open doorway in silent invitation. "Why do you think they haven't firebombed my market yet? Gotta keep me complacent so I'll keep transmitting."

Inside the cabin was a mess of tech. Tables lined one wall, covered in boxes with dozens of dials, displays in a half dozen different colors, and display monitors every few feet. A tanned young woman with blond hair in a high ponytail sat in a chair in front of one of them, a headset around her neck and her feet propped up on the desk. One of Maya's favorite dramas played on the largest monitor, showing a group of astronauts fighting to contain some crisis on Mars.

As soon as Jaden stepped through the door, the girl bolted upright and paused her show. "Delta team just radioed in. They made the pickup okay and are on their way back."

"Good." Jaden crossed his arms over his chest and leaned back against the table. "Laura, I need you to put out a roll call to everyone in the field. Looking for any of those genetics companies either on the move with kids or setting up shop."

The blonde hesitated, glancing at Nina and Knox. Jaden waved a hand. "They're fine. Show Nina how we put all the TechCorps' little snoopers straight the fuck to sleep."

"Got it."

She unplugged her headset from the speaker and pulled the microphone toward her. "CQ, CQ, Alpha Romeo Tango calling CQ. Alpha Romeo Tango. Listening."

After two more repetitions, static crackled through the speaker. "Alpha Romeo Tango, I hear you. This is Bravo Whiskey Victor. Go ahead."

"We've got a nine-one-one request from a neighboring farm. Looking for kale seeds. Gotta get them in the ground before the first frost. Over."

So that was his game, hiding potentially valuable intelligence by using the most boring, commonplace-sounding code they could muster. Nina had to admire the simple elegance of it. Still, the fact that the situation was common enough to warrant an established code made her sick to her stomach. She nudged Knox, who tilted his head, his brow furrowing.

After a moment, the radio crackled. "Sorry, no love here. Try Echo Foxtrot Sierra?"

A new voice popped up, higher pitched with a deep Southern twang. "Echo Foxtrot Sierra here. No kale seeds, but I'll keep my eyes peeled."

"Understood," Laura said into the microphone. "Delta Charlie Lima, do you copy? Alpha Romeo Tango calling Delta Charlie Lima."

This time a booming baritone with an even more extreme drawl answered. "Delta Charlie Lima, checking in. No kale. I repeat, no sign of kale. Want us to check with the neighbors?"

"Please. The planting window is closing. Thanks, y'all. Hope the harvest is going well."

Perfectly mundane reports about corn and apples followed until Laura cut off the flow by plugging her headset back in and slipping it over her ears.

Jaden's face was serious. "Some shit we just don't fuck around about," he said softly. "I have a deal with Savitri. I find them, she shuts them down."

Nina glanced at Knox, who met her gaze and nodded once. "We want in."

"Silent communication already?" Dakota said from behind them. "That's fucking *adorable*. I love both of you."

Jaden grunted and opened his mouth. "I should—"

"Uh-uh." She cut him off with a grin and a shrug. "Duty calls. You have to get back to work."

He snapped his mouth shut, then sighed. "She's right. Lucas will work up the details into our more complex code and get it on the network tonight. My contacts stretch from the Mississippi to the Atlantic, and from the Gulf to the Heartlands. We *will* find them, eventually."

Nina wanted to argue. Those kids might be anywhere by then, passed around to the highest bidders for Christ knew what purposes. They might not have *eventually.*

But Jaden knew that. This was the hard reality of the situation: as much as they wanted it, as hard as they tried, they might not succeed.

Nina clenched her eyes shut, and Knox wrapped an arm around her shoulder. His lips found her temple. Soft, barely there . . . but a promise.

"I'll get in touch when we have news," Dakota murmured. "Until then . . ."

Until then, they just had to wait.

TECHCORPS PROPRIETARY DATA, L2 SECURITY CLEARANCE

Of course DC-035 has my permission to attend advanced cryptography classes. Do you think I have time to take them myself?

Internal Memo, September 2077

FOURTEEN

Montgomery Market Day was Maya's favorite Atlanta ritual.

It was the opposite of Convergence in almost every way. Instead of being buried deep underground, the market sprawled across a wide dirt expanse framed on the north and south by warehouses with their huge bay doors flung open and on the east and west by an apple and peach orchard, respectively. The open air dispersed the noise of the chattering crowd, and instead of industrial tech and flashing lights, the aesthetic was rustic farm chic and bright afternoon sunlight.

Sometimes the wind even shifted enough to carry the scent of honest-to-God *manure*, which was a bit *too* much farming realism for Maya's personal tastes, but she supposed nothing was perfect.

The jumble of tables and stands held everything from fresh produce to gray-market goods to pre-Flare antiques. She'd made some of her favorite finds browsing dusty stacks of books pillaged from someone's great-great-grandmother's library. And there was usually a ton of broken or ill-repaired tech that just needed a little love. Most of the loaner tablets she sent home with families had come from stacks of electronics on her favorite scavenger's table.

Today, she had a more immediate mission. With Rainbow's tiny hand clasped in hers, she navigated the stalls until she found one that looked promising. Racks of bright and cheerful clothes in children's sizes fanned out from the main table, which held a chaotic jumble of tiny folded T-shirts, scuffed but decent footwear, and a wealth of tacky but sparkly jewelry that would delight any kid.

Well, maybe not any kid. But hopefully *this* kid.

Ivonne's best efforts at coaxing Rainbow into a shopping spree had resulted in two pairs of practical black pants, two gray T-shirts, and a pair of boots. She'd dug in her heels as if suspecting a trap—or more likely a test she might fail—and Ivonne hadn't pushed.

Maya wasn't going to push, either. But she could . . . reframe. Crouching down next to Rainbow, she met the girl's serious gaze. "You said you studied tactics, right?"

A solemn nod.

"What about infiltration? Going undercover?"

"A little bit." Rainbow's gaze skipped from Maya's face to survey the booth briefly, then swung back. "Am I not dressed right?"

"You're dressed *fine*," Maya reassured her. "There's no right or wrong. If that's what you want to wear, you can wear it. But when I came down off the Hill, the first thing I did was buy new clothes. Because people dress different down here, and I didn't want them noticing me. Plus?" She leaned closer and lowered her voice, like she was sharing a forbidden secret. "I found out I really like pretty colors."

Rainbow studied Maya's outfit. Today she'd dressed for the heat, in a pair of cutoff denim shorts, her favorite boots with their neon-blue laces, and a matching bright-blue tank top. She'd accessorized with a wrist full of silver bangles, a blue stone wrapped in wire for a necklace, and her favorite pair of facial-recognition-algorithm-busting sunglasses, which were currently propped on top of her head.

Not exactly full club glam, but a far cry from the business professional that had been her default as a data courier on the Hill.

Rainbow's attention drifted back to the table of brightly colored clothing. The yearning was there now, subtle but visible. When she spoke, it was a whisper. "I don't have any money."

And presents always came with strings. Lord, did Maya know the truth of that. "How about we barter? You can help me in the warehouse some this week, unpacking boxes and putting the books on the scanner. And I'll buy you any five outfits you want today."

A tilt of the head. "Anything I want?"

"Sky's the limit, kiddo."

After another moment, Rainbow thrust out her hand. Maya shook it with due ceremony, and that was it. Her too-mature seriousness broke, and Rainbow almost vibrated in excitement as she bounded over to the stand.

"Oooh, kid shopping." Rafe stopped next to Maya, a fond smile curving his lips. "I used to take my little sister shopping. I would beg Tessa to buy some nice jeans or fancy boots or *something* . . ."

"But she always wanted art supplies," Dani finished.

Rafe's eyebrows went up. "So you *do* listen to me sometimes."

She stuck a melting, red Popsicle in her mouth and shrugged, then waved a second plastic-wrapped frozen treat. "I got one for Rainbow, too."

"Well, you better go give it to her," Rafe drawled.

Dani rolled her eyes and stalked away. Maya bit her lip, struggling to hold in a laugh. Her fight was doomed when Rafe shot her a mournful look. Giggles escaped, and she slapped a hand over her mouth.

"I'm wounded, Maya."

"Sorry." She scrunched up her nose at him. "If it makes you feel better, I've never seen Dani work this hard to ignore *anyone*. Usually it comes naturally to her."

"Actually, that does make me feel better." He flicked his fingers at her in a shooing motion. "Go. I know you wanted to check out the tech tables. Uncle Rafe and Aunt Dani are all over this."

Maya glanced at Rainbow, who was happily accepting the Popsicle from Dani. God knew the two of them could defend her against any improbable threats more efficiently than anyone else on the planet. "Fine. But I'm expecting you to make sure she gets *something* to wear before Dani takes her off for rappelling gear or her first throwing knife set or whatever."

Rafe saluted her with a wink and moved toward Rainbow and Dani. That left Maya to turn on her heel and yelp when she almost slammed into Gray. "Shit, you're quiet."

He steadied her with a hand on her elbow. "Occupational hazard. Where are you off to?"

She was going to have to start wearing shirts with sleeves, and fuck the heat. The brush of his fingertips raised goose bumps on her arm. She covered it with a torrent of distracting words. "There's a few vendors who move broken tech. I usually pick up what I know I can fix so we can lend it out to people. And I always check out the books. Sometimes I find some gems."

"Mind if I tag along?"

"Of course. I mean not." She barely avoided a cringe. God, having a crush was agonizing. No wonder Dani was ignoring Rafe so diligently. It seemed like the only sane survival move. "I mean I don't mind. I'd like the company."

If Gray noticed her awkwardness, he didn't let on. He just fell into step beside her—close, but not too close—as if it were the most natural thing in the world.

And suddenly it *did* feel natural. The nervous flutters in her chest eased as she led him across the open lot, toward the southern warehouse. He'd shortened his strides to match hers, and that tangible force field was still active, even when he wasn't trying. They sliced through a crowd that seemed to part before them like magic.

She could definitely get used to that.

It felt so natural, she said the same thing to him that she would have to Nina. "So. Dani and Rafe."

He made a low noise that sounded suspiciously like exasperation and amusement tinged with dread. "I know. I *know*."

"He knows he's playing with fire, right?"

Gray shrugged and stuck his hands in his pockets. "Usually, I'd say that's the point. Rafe likes living dangerously, and he skates through most things okay."

Most things weren't Dani. Maya had watched a string of men with egos far larger than Rafe's break their self-confidence and occasionally their hearts against the brick wall of Dani's disinterest. "I hope so. Weaponized biceps aside, I'm kinda fond of him."

She felt Gray's gaze on her, but when she glanced his way, he looked away. "What about her?" he asked softly. "Aren't you worried about Dani's heart?"

"Not usually," she replied just as quietly. "Not many people get close enough to break it. Rafe might be the first one."

"Hey." Gray came to a stop, pulling her to a halt with him. "Why are we so down, huh? Who knows what's going to happen?"

The look in his eyes lodged in her chest, and she knew they weren't talking about Rafe and Dani anymore. Maybe they never had been. The tension between them tightened another notch, until she wasn't sure she could draw a full breath.

She'd thought her nerves would settle. That this *wanting* would mellow enough that she could kiss Gray and it wouldn't be a big deal. But every day only deepened her craving and heightened the sweet agony of anticipation.

There was no safe way to do this. No way to protect her mind *or* her heart. And Gray didn't have *time* for her to work up her courage. Either he was worth the risk, or he wasn't.

She had to choose. Soon.

Swallowing hard, she curled her fingers around his, ignoring the tiny frisson of electricity that jolted up her spine. She made her voice cheerful, casual, as if she hadn't just stepped off her safe ship and onto a plank stretched out over a dangerous ocean. "Have I told you my theory about you?"

"No." His fingers closed around hers, warm and careful. "It's not anything like your old boss's theory, is it?"

Birgitte had been convinced that Gray was some sort of stone-cold killer. That his rigid self-control and emotional reticence masked some sort of psychosis—or, at the very least, deep instability.

She'd turned out to be wrong about plenty of things, but in nothing more so than her assessment of Gray. He so obviously *cared* about people. Every slow, deliberate movement practically screamed it. "Nah, Birgitte had baggage. You're not a crazy serial killer. You are clearly a Gothic hero in desperate need of a castle or some misty moors to perfect your tortured brooding."

He smiled. No, he *grinned*, a wide, amused expression so generous it might as well have been a laugh. "You watch too many old movies."

"Someone's got to categorize them," she retorted, tugging at his hand to get him moving again. "But let me warn you now. If you've got any wives or anything locked in an attic somewhere, I am *definitely* rescuing them."

"I don't have any family, remember?"

The words sounded easy, but his fingers tightened around hers. When she glanced up at him, there was a tension around his eyes. A forced casualness to his expression. She gripped his hand harder. "Of course you do. Knox, Conall, Rafe. Mace, too. They're your family in every way that counts."

"You're right." He stopped again, this time by a booth laden with seedlings. He thumbed idly through the paper envelopes of seeds in a lopsided spinning rack, but his gaze was on her face. "How did you meet Nina?"

The skin on her wrists itched, her clearest warning sign that memories were trying to surface. She locked them down ruthlessly and drew in a deep breath. The air smelled fresh, with hay and spices and the tart smell of apple cider drifting from a nearby booth.

It steadied her enough to get the words out. "Birgitte had a contingency plan, I guess. If something happened to her, one of her coconspirators was supposed to smuggle me out of the TechCorps. They hired Nina to hide me for a few weeks. She was the one who came up with the idea of faking my death."

He chuckled.

Maya felt her lips twitch. Humor chased away the rest of the ghosts. "Yeah, it's a bad habit she has. Rescuing people, faking their deaths, taking them in, and convincing them to help her build community resources. Real dastardly criminal shit."

"It's not that, it's just . . . secrets." He seemed to be searching for the right words. "Nina's had to hide the fact that she'd rather save someone's life than claim a two-million-credit bounty. And every time Knox saved a handful of lives on a mission, he had to act like it was just the most expedient way to get the job done." He sighed. "Not everything about ourselves that we hide from the world is ugly. Sometimes it just makes us too vulnerable."

She knew the truth of that in her bones. Her memory held a litany of plausibly deniable heroics, every tiny victory of Birgitte's quiet revolution. Compassion was the ultimate weakness according to the TechCorps. The enemy of progress and pure scientific advancement.

That was a lie, of course. In the years Maya had lived on the outside, she'd seen that compassion might actually be the ultimate driver of innovation. Rogue scientists solved problems every day, and they did it with a fraction of the TechCorps' massive resources. Not out of some sterile intellectual curiosity or selfish need for glory.

They did it because they cared.

But it was still seen as a weakness. The rot and greed and suspicion had seeped down from the Hill and poisoned the earth around Atlanta. No one trusted altruism anymore. Every generous offer from the TechCorps came with enough strings to strangle you and everyone you loved for a generation. It was the brick wall Nina had run up against again and again as they expanded their little library.

They thought you were scamming them until they thought you were a pushover. And then they usually tried to rob you. Or kill you.

"You don't know how hard it was to earn even a little bit of trust in the neighborhood," she told Gray, pulling him deeper into the warehouse. "No one knew what to make of Nina. I'm sure you can relate."

"I can." Then Gray grinned again. "Imagine if Knox *had* known, though. He'd have been standing outside her bedroom window every night with flowers and a proposal scribbled on a piece of cardboard."

Maya huffed and shot him a sidelong look. "That would have been *mildly* preferable to the whole long-con-betrayal thing we've generously forgiven him for, on account of the extenuating circumstances."

"That road trip was fun. Admit it."

The thing was, it *had* been fun. Knox and his team might have lured them on the trip under false pretenses, but the enjoyment had been real. Breaking into pre-Flare movie theaters to see space battles play out against a massive, tattered screen. Camping in the woods with the crackle of fire and the scent of roasting turkey in the air. Even the torturous, sweltering night in the abandoned gas station when Maya had used the knowledge gleaned from dozens of mechanics texts to fix the industrial-strength fans.

For two decades, Maya had lived a sheltered life on the Hill. She'd been ferried between penthouse floors in AirLifts and helicopters. She'd sunbathed on terrace gardens a thousand feet into the air. Her feet had quite literally never touched solid earth, because people who traveled in executive circles at the TechCorps rarely lowered themselves to walk among the rank and file.

She could still number the times she'd been outside Atlanta on her fingers. Every memory was sharp and precious . . . *especially* the ones with the Silver Devils. Because their arrival had changed everything.

Gray was watching her with that small, warm little smile. She couldn't call his eyes Gothic *or* brooding today. They were blue and bright and glinting with an emotion so subtle she kept thinking she was imagining it.

Mischief. She'd always known he had a sense of humor under those blank stares.

"Don't get cocky," she advised him, stopping in a sheltered little niche. Two towering shelves overflowing with spare parts shielded them from the rest of the market. When she turned to face him, the breadth of his shoulders blocked out the rest of the world. Her voice came out breathless. "You don't know how many forks I'm packing."

His reply came in a whisper. "I always assume that answer is *enough to get the job done.*"

God*damn*. His normal voice was intoxicating. Having him whispering practically against her ear was enough to lay her out. Tingles prickled over her scalp and down her spine.

"So," he went on. "What are you after?"

He wasn't really talking about her shopping list. The plank beneath her feet wobbled. That vast ocean stretched out beneath her, the waves churning. Maya wet her lips nervously and took another step. "That's what I'm trying to figure out."

There was that *grin* again. "No rush."

He'd say that. He'd keep saying it, even as the time he had left slipped away one minute at a time. Gray would sit there, as patient and unmoving as a stone, waiting for her to come to him.

She couldn't sit here, waiting for someone to give her a push. She had to close her eyes and leap.

Her heart beating faster, Maya reached up to touch his cheek. His skin was as warm as she remembered, his jawline rough with the first hint of stubble. The contact shivered through her, too intense for something so innocent, but not bad. No, the warmth unspooling deep in her belly was the literal opposite of bad.

"I'm complicated," she whispered. "I don't know how to do this. I don't know how much touch is too much."

"We're not so different, Maya." He closed his eyes and turned his face to her palm. "It can be complicated for me, too. There's no right or wrong answer, there's only . . . finding out."

She let her thumb sweep out to touch his mouth. *Wanting* pulsed in her, reckless and wild, the strength of it terrifying her. Control had always been central to her being. Toying with letting go in bits and pieces was one thing, but this . . .

Oh, the fall would be so sweet. The crash might break her. The fact that she didn't care scared her most of all.

"Are you sure you want this?" she asked softly. "Are you sure you want me?"

Gray's eyes flashed, and he moved closer. He stopped carefully, *painfully* shy of touching her, then slowly pulled her hand from his face. Holding her wrist lightly, he dragged her hand down until it rested on his hard chest, just over his heart.

It thumped beneath her palm, strong and reassuring. She licked her lips again, and the steady beat stuttered and picked up speed.

His gaze was locked on her mouth. Her own heart skipped a beat.

"I want you," he rasped, "but I can wait. I *will* wait."

Nina's voice drifted up from memory. *For you, control likely is super important. But there's more than one way to have control over yourself, and over your abilities.*

The only way to find out what she could handle was to try.

So she leapt.

Maya went up on her toes, bracing herself against his chest. His mouth was tempting, but bravery only went so far. She brushed her lips along his jaw, inhaling the now-familiar scent of soap and sawdust. Just a glancing kiss, before she let her heels *thump* back to the ground and hid her face against his neck.

Their joined hands were trapped between them, and she could feel both of their hearts racing. She shivered and leaned into the solid strength of him. "I know you'll catch me when I fall."

"No matter what."

Maya closed her eyes and let him hold her as the implacable wall of his body blocked out the chaos of the world. Maybe this could be its own sort of meditation . . . lulled by protective warmth, utterly safe as she matched her breathing to the steady beat of his heart. Her breaths slowed as it slowed, until she felt steady enough to straighten.

His hand still gripped hers. She stepped back but kept their fingers twined together. "Want to help me find some tablets I can rescue?"

"You're in charge." He lifted their joined hands to his mouth but barely grazed her knuckles with his lips. "I'm just along for the ride."

Her heart did a funny flip in her chest at the gentle promise in the words.

And as she tugged Gray toward a shelf of cracked tablets, she decided Nina had been wrong.

Kissing Gray would *definitely* make her brain explode.

She might do it anyway.

TECHCORPS INTERNAL
EXECUTIVE COMMUNICATION

From: RICHTER, T
To: SKOVGAARD, B
Date: 2077–012–11

Given your obsession with personal security, may I inquire about your choice to appoint Simon to your Ex-Sec team? He is a literal child. I have hundreds of far more qualified candidates.

From: SKOVGAARD, B
To: RICHTER, T

You may inquire. I'm under no obligation to answer.

FIFTEEN

"Put this one down at the other end, would you?"

"Do we need knives or just forks?"

"How many chairs?"

"Eight." Gray grunted softly as he and Nina set the butcher's block island from the kitchen down at the end of the dining table. It was just the right height to extend the surface, but *damn*, it was heavy. "Luna and Ivonne went out, so it's just us tonight."

"I count nine, then."

Everyone froze and stared at Mace, who was standing in the back hall.

"If that's all right," he added belatedly.

"Of course it is," Knox called from his place in front of the stove. "You're just in time."

"A little late if you like bread, though." Maya slid a basket with only a few slices remaining down the table until it rested near the butcher's block. "Don't tell Knox, but we've all been eating it warm before dinner and ruining our appetites."

"Speak for yourself," Gray muttered. "I can still eat. It smells *good*."

"Tastes good, too," Conall said, snatching up one of the final pieces. He ignored Maya's chiding look and shoved half of it into his mouth.

Rafe carried in a massive platter of Knox's handmade spaghetti and settled it on the table. "It should smell good. That marinara has been simmering since we got back from the market. And there are meatballs, made from *actual* beef from *actual* cows. We are living the high life right now."

Gray hid a smile as he took a stack of plates from Dani. "Nina must really like them, if he went to all that trouble."

"Oh yeah, she does. Here, Rainbow." Maya handed her a fistful of silverware. "Do you know how to set the table? Just put the knives and forks next to the plates when Gray puts them down."

Rainbow accepted the forks with the solemn nod of a soldier on a mission. She followed Gray around the table, dutifully placing a fork on the table precisely one second after he placed each dish.

He set the next plate on the table upside down. When she looked up at him, startled, he made a face.

The giggle that escaped her was bright, cheerful, and over too quickly. "You're very silly," she proclaimed.

"Gray?" Dani asked dubiously.

"Sometimes," he allowed. "When I'm happy. That's the best time to be silly, isn't it?"

After some serious consideration, Rainbow set a fork down next to the plate. Upside down. Her small face broke into a smile.

Maya carried a full pitcher of sweet tea to the table and set it next to the icy pitcher of lemonade. Her gaze found his, and her smile was sweeter. Warmer. "I could get used to silly Gray. We'll save a *ton* of money on the windswept moors and the haunted castle."

He rolled his eyes at her, but it was no use. Her smile only deepened, and his stomach gave a strange little fluttering flip.

Rainbow poked him, and he realized he'd stopped setting the table. "Right. Priorities, kid. Got to get this done so we can eat."

Moving slowly, Mace slid into the same chair he'd occupied that morning—and Gray finally realized why he favored it.

It was the chair closest to the door.

Rafe came back to the table and started setting out glasses. Maya ducked under his arm to deliver a cutting board with a fresh loaf of bread still steaming from the oven. Nina appeared behind her with a wooden trivet, which settled in place in time for Knox to set down his huge pot of marinara and meatballs.

It was a careful, coordinated dance, no different in some ways than a firefight or a building infiltration. Even Rainbow slid into it like an errant card into a shuffling deck. Only Mace sat outside of it, stone-still, his face a neutral, exact mask.

It hurt to look at him.

But not as much as it hurt to look at Knox. He watched Mace carefully as he circled the table, settled into the seat next to him, and unfolded his napkin. "You'll have to tell me what you think of the sauce—"

An ear-splitting noise rocked the room, something between the sharp crack of a pistol and a small-yield explosion. Gray ducked instinctively, curling his body over Maya's. A moment later, his brain categorized the sound.

"Just a car backfiring," Nina said calmly. "I swear, these ancient combustion engines—"

With a roar, Mace snatched up a dinner knife from his place setting and dove at Knox.

The room exploded into motion.

It all happened so *fast*. Rafe's chair toppled over backward as he swept a wide-eyed Rainbow out of her seat. Knox rose to meet Mace, angling his body to take the knife in the shoulder instead of the throat.

His grunt of pain galvanized Nina. She dragged him back, out of Mace's reach, as a blur of red and white shot across the room. Dani vaulted over the table, slammed Mace against the wall, and followed him down to the floor.

He roared again, rolling over to pin her to the hardwood. But she kept the momentum going, bashing into the scattered chairs as she flipped him onto his back again. Mace lay there beneath her, his chest heaving, his eyes slowly drifting shut.

That's when Gray saw the syringe sticking out of the side of his neck.

Dani pulled the blue needle cap from between her teeth and blew out a breath. "Nighty night, Doc."

"Fucking hell." Maya's elbow poked him in the ribs, and Gray realized he was still curled around her. Her entire body was shaking, her breathing coming too fast, but she elbowed him again. As soon as he gave her a few inches, she scrambled out of her chair and surveyed the wrecked dining room.

"Fucking *hell*," she repeated. No sign of her trembling showed in her voice or the slightly outraged look she pinned on Dani. "Since when do you come to dinner packing goddamn *tranquilizers*?"

Dani frowned, looking affronted. "Since we started needing them, obviously."

Maya threw up her hands. "Oh, *obviously*."

Nina looked up from Knox's shoulder. She knew better than to remove the knife, but she'd packed a clean dish towel around it. "He went down like a rock. How much did you give him?"

"Just enough to make it count." Dani rolled her eyes. "Don't worry, it was a carefully calculated dose based on his body weight."

Conall knelt beside a now-snoring Mace. He winced as he gingerly removed the syringe, then checked his carotid artery. "You've been carrying around a Mace-calibrated sedative? I honestly don't know if that's hot or terrifying." The joke sounded forced, and worry lines bracketed Conall's eyes. "Pulse is steady. He's just out. That's a less pressing concern than the knife in Knox's shoulder."

"It's fine," Knox said, still watching Mace, his brow furrowed with concern. "Rafe can deal with it."

"Uh, no." Rafe still had Rainbow balanced on his hip, one protective arm curled around her. "When we're in a Florida jungle and there's no help for three days, I pull knives out of you. When we're in Atlanta, you shut your fool mouth and let Nina take you to an actual doctor."

Knox clenched his jaw and glared at Rafe. Rafe stared back impassively. After a moment, he opened his mouth.

The bastard was actually about to ask Gray if he could handle this. With a *piece of cutlery* hanging out of his shoulder.

Gray just managed not to slap his palm to his forehead. "We've got this. Now please go see the doctor."

Knox let Nina lead him away. Maya moved by rote, righting chairs and pushing them back under the table, as Rafe crouched to whisper something to Rainbow.

Working together, Gray and Conall lifted Mace from the floor and, hooking an arm around each of their shoulders, carried him next door. He stirred a little, lifting his head to mumble something unintelligible.

"Yeah, I don't think so, pal," Gray said soothingly. "It's gonna take you a while to sleep this one off."

They maneuvered him into his small, stark room that still felt like a cell to Gray, stripped off his boots, and got him settled into his bunk.

Gray hesitated, torn. "He shouldn't be alone right now."

But Conall had already pulled up a chair outside the tiny room. "I'll sit with him."

Back in the kitchen, things were back to something almost surreally *normal.* Rafe and Dani sat at the table with Rainbow. They'd resumed their dinner, undoubtedly for the girl's benefit—someone had to make her feel safe, and *fuck,* she still had to eat.

Maya was nowhere to be found.

Gray kept walking, his feet taking him slowly but unerringly through to the warehouse space at the back of the building, where the ladies scanned books and processed food for freeze-drying.

Maya was lying on the concrete floor, stretched out with one arm flung above her head and the other resting on her forehead.

"Maya?" he said gently, even though he knew she'd be listening to music and couldn't hear him. There wasn't enough give in concrete for her to feel his approaching footsteps, either, and her eyes were closed.

He reached out, froze with his hand just shy of her leg, then wrapped his fingers loosely around her ankle. She yelped and kicked out with her other foot. He ducked to the side, narrowly avoiding a thick heel to the nose.

He released her, holding up both hands instead in placating surrender.

"Shit!" Maya scrambled to her knees and tapped at her watch. She stared at him, wide-eyed for several fraught heartbeats, then let out a laugh that verged on hysterical. "Oh fuck, I'm sorry. You startled me."

"No kidding." He nudged her foot. "You okay?"

She twisted until she was sitting with her back against a pile of boxes filled with books. "Will you believe me if I say I'm fine?"

"Probably not." He shrugged. "*I'm* not."

Another tense pause. Then she patted the concrete beside her. "Wanna sit?"

He very much did, so he lowered himself to the floor at her side. "You're not freaking out?"

She rubbed at her bare wrist absently, her gaze slightly unfocused. "I feel like a rubber band someone stretched as far as it can go. I keep thinking I can just . . . keep ahead of this. Outrun the memories. But you can't, can you? You can't outrun something that's inside you."

"No. We all try, I think, but in the end . . ." They carried all of their scars, all their traumas with them, like battered, scuffed luggage patched with duct tape.

Maya shuddered next to him and closed her eyes. "Twenty-three days," she whispered. "That's how long Tobias Richter had me. And I remember every second of it so clearly, sometimes I think it's still happening."

She was still rubbing her wrist, harder with each passing moment, until she was nearly abrading the delicate skin. Maybe she wasn't hyperventilating like before or lashing out like Mace, but she was still caught up in a nightmare of memory, a prison in her own head.

He could help her. He *needed* to help her.

"Have you ever seen the ocean?" He pulled her hand away from her wrist before she could hurt herself and kept talking. "It's a hell of a thing. Different everywhere you go. Down in Florida, the beaches are all soft sand, and the water is blue and green. But when you travel up the coast, everything turns to rock. And the water gets dark."

Her fingers flexed in his. She took a shuddering breath in and closed her eyes, tilting her head back against the boxes. "How far north have you been?"

"I drove all the way up to the Canadian Territories once." He kept his voice even and low. "I would have kept going, but they turned me back at the border."

"What was it like?"

"Cold."

She nudged him with her elbow. "Tell me more. About other places."

So he did. He told her about flying through the Heartlands, looking down on the perfect, irrigated circles of the big agriculture co-ops as well as the tiny family farms. About the Mississippi River, how it was a whole mile wide in some places, which didn't sound like a lot but sure as hell looked like an uncrossable chasm when you were staring out at the swift, turbulent currents. He told her about the mountains and valleys of east Tennessee, where some of the more insular communities had given up completely on modern technology. Being there was like stepping back in time, all simple wood cabins and oil lamps and livestock, and if the world ended again, Gray wasn't sure they'd even notice.

As he spoke, the tension slowly bled out of her. The line of her clenched jaw relaxed, and her hand closed around his. And it wasn't a desperate bid to ground herself but a point of contact, of *communion*.

Eventually, her eyes fluttered open. "Thank you."

"Anytime." It sounded like a deflection, a casual, meaningless platitude, so he tried again. "Whenever you need anything, I'm here, okay?"

Her lips quirked. "Watch out. I might take you up on that, and then you'll have to tell me stories until I fall asleep every night."

She said it as if it were a ridiculous request, but if it gave her good things to hear as she drifted off, a way to stave off the nightmares, he'd do it. "Deal."

That won him a real smile before she rested her head against his shoulder, her hand still clutching his. "Is Mace okay?"

The easy answer, the *calming* one, was right there on his tongue, But what tripped out instead was, "He stabbed Knox. Dani had to hop a table and sedate him for everyone's safety, including his." Gray sighed. "I don't know what Richter did to him, but no. He's not okay. Not yet."

"Dani probably has an idea what Richter did to him." Maya's voice dropped to a whisper. "So do I."

It explained a lot. "He's the reason this happens to you?"

She leaned into him, as if grounding herself against him. "There's a thing about data couriers. We know all these secrets, right? Corporate espionage–level experimental tech, and all the skeletons in the Board's closet. We'd be a massive liability if you could strap us to a chair and torture it all out of us."

"How do they keep that from happening?"

"Too much sensory overload and I just . . ." She flicked the fingers of her free hand. "My brain goes offline. Full system reboot. It has to be pretty extreme to trigger a complete shutdown, but getting tortured is pretty extreme."

He managed to suppress a wince, but nothing could stop his shiver of revulsion. "They did it to you on purpose. Altered your brain so it's harder for you to deal with stress."

"They did a lot of bad things to a lot of people on purpose. Including you." She sighed and closed her eyes. "I know all of the horrible things they did. That's one of the reasons Richter needed to break me. So many people were working with Birgitte. Passing her all the dirty secrets, undermining leadership from the inside. He had to make me talk."

"He would have done it anyway." Even if Maya had known nothing about Birgitte's rebellion, Tobias Richter would have broken her down into pieces so small and so scattered that putting them back together was a question of *if*, not *when*. It was what he did. "How?"

Maya didn't answer for a long time. When she did, her voice was a sad whisper. "His name was Simon. He was too young to be in Executive Security, but his dad was loyal to Birgitte, so she trusted him. And she was a VP. Nobody could tell her no when it came to staffing her own office."

She swallowed hard. "My only friend was another data courier a few years older than me. Cara. But she was Richter's courier, and Birgitte hated that. She encouraged me to spend time with Simon instead. It was just the three of us most of the time, and Birgitte was so much older than us. And Simon was . . ." She sighed. "Young. Like me."

The truth, the part she wasn't saying, trembled between her words. "You loved him."

"Maybe?" Her tiny laugh broke his heart. "I was nineteen. Maybe everything feels like love when you're nineteen and it's the first time. But he mattered. And I mattered to him. After Richter shot Birgitte, he pointed a gun at my head. Simon went with him without a fight. And spent the next three weeks getting tortured in my place."

Cold fury prickled over Gray. "What a dumbass move."

Maya went still against him. "What?"

"You heard me." Gray eased her away just enough to peer down into her confused eyes. "He blew it. If Richter needed intel that he couldn't torture out of you, and he'd already killed Birgitte, then Simon was all he had left. That situation was only headed in one direction, and it wasn't a good one. The kid should have taken a stand. At least he would've gone down fighting."

"But—"

"And you wouldn't have these memories." He traced his thumb over her lower lip, stilling its fine tremor. "He was always going to die. But he could have saved you from this."

Tears filled her eyes. "I could have stopped it. I could have just told Richter what he wanted to know."

"You know better. It wouldn't have saved him, just doomed dozens of other people, too." Gray cupped her jaw, his fingers sliding under her ear, under the warm fall of her braids. "I will never let myself be used as a weapon against you, Maya. I swear it."

"I can't think about it like that. I can't—" The tears spilled over. She squeezed her eyes shut and turned her face into his hand. "How can I be mad at them when they're dead and I'm *fine*?"

"Being angry doesn't mean you're not sad or that you don't love them anymore. Your feelings don't have to be *fair*." He pulled her closer again. "Hell, I'm mad at Mace right now. How fucked up is that? But I still love him, and I'm glad he's here, and I'm going to do everything I fucking can to help him. If I can hold all that inside me, you've got room for a little resentment."

Maya buried her face against his chest, her arms going around him. Her shoulders trembled. "I hate being helpless when people are hurting."

He couldn't do a damn thing about her past except comfort her when the memories grew claws and teeth and threatened to rip her apart. But the future was a different story, a clean slate yet to have any tragedy scribbled on it.

"Okay." He put on his most commanding voice, the one that made Knox roll his eyes and Rafe chuckle and everyone else in the world jump to follow his orders. "So we won't let you be helpless, then."

She pulled back, wiping her eyes with shaking fingers. "Do I get to shoot things again?"

"Even better." He pointed at his face. "You get to punch me."

KNOX

Knox couldn't sleep.

It wasn't the fact that he'd been stabbed. The wound in his shoulder was inconsequential, all things considered. Instinct and experience had helped him there—Knox knew all the least harmful places to take a blade or a bullet, and Mace hadn't exactly been aiming for maximum damage.

Regeneration tech had already taken care of the issue. His shoulder itched, but Knox had long ago learned how to block out the singular discomfort of artificially healed wounds.

Nina wasn't keeping him awake, either. She was a warmth at his side, her chin pillowed on his uninjured arm, one of her long legs tossed absently over his. He liked the reassuring weight of her, the tickle of her hair over his skin when she shifted, her slow, even breaths.

He'd never imagined that sharing a bed with someone could be peaceful, not after a lifetime of light sleep and combat awareness. But it was hard not to feel safe snuggled up next to a woman who could fight anyone into the ground. Including him.

No, it wasn't the stab wound, and it wasn't Nina. Knox couldn't sleep because Tobias Richter was winning.

Mace was a perfectly honed weapon aimed at Knox's most vulnerable spots. He didn't even have to stab Knox to make him bleed. All he had to do was *hurt*, and he was doing plenty of that.

Knox flexed his fingers. Most days, he forgot they were flesh over alloy and polymer. But he'd shattered his own bones trying to claw his way to Mace's side as the medic lay dying. Knox's dedication to his team was well-known, but after that performance, he'd given Richter a road map to his heart.

Mace was in pain again. There wasn't even a wall between them this time, but Knox still couldn't fix it.

And he couldn't *end* it. Richter had known that, too. Mace could stick a dozen knives in him, and Knox would still hesitate to act.

He'd already watched Mace die once. He'd die himself before *killing* him.

Nina stirred, rubbing her cheek against his shoulder. "Do you want to talk about it?"

Knox lifted a hand to stroke her hair. "Am I keeping you awake?"

"No." She propped herself up on her elbow and leaned over him. "I just want to make sure you're okay."

She wasn't asking about his shoulder. Nina knew him too well. "This is what Richter counted on. Whether Mace escaped or was released doesn't matter. *This* was the whole point—to turn him into a threat I can't bring myself to neutralize."

"Well, then." Nina hummed softly and placed her hand on his cheek. "It's a good thing we have experience with those."

He turned his face into her palm and closed his eyes. "Am I doing the right thing?" he asked softly. "Mace is our family. We can take the risk. But you, and Dani, and *Maya*. If he hurt Maya—"

"We're practicing risk mitigation, Garrett. So far, he's stayed far away from Luna, Ivonne, and Rainbow. Maya is never alone with him, and the rest of us are on our guard." She brushed her lips over his forehead. "He's your family, which makes him mine, too."

Knox slipped his fingers through her hair and tugged her down for a lingering kiss. "Thank you," he whispered against her lips. "Thank you for saving us."

"You were worth it," she said simply. "So is Mace."

To her, it would always be that simple. Nina believed in giving people a chance to be their best selves, even if they stumbled along the way. She was everything the TechCorps wasn't. Open, generous, compassionate. Strong enough to give people a chance to disappoint her.

All the instincts Richter had counted on when he'd unleashed an assassin on them. "How?" he asked, settling her against his side once more. "How do we fight someone who weaponizes all of our best impulses against us?"

She was silent for a moment, then sighed. "You just answered your own question—you fight them. Literally."

"Can we? They control most of the food, the electricity, the fresh water. They have the tech. The weapons. Between the Protectorate and Executive Security, that's *two* private armies, and God only knows how many classified experiments." Knox closed his eyes. "How do you fight something like that?"

"We don't have the manpower or resources for a frontal assault, no. It would have to be a guerrilla campaign—quick, dirty strikes at carefully chosen targets. With the proper strategy and enough time, we could wear them down."

He let himself consider it. Not even the practicality of it, but the tactical possibilities. For all their shiny public relations, the TechCorps was hardly a happy family. Internal political wrangling for status and power could be brutal. More than one Protectorate squad had been swept up in those power struggles, only to be sacrificed in the name of someone's next promotion.

Knox's skills as a captain had insulated the Silver Devils from the worst of it. But he'd seen the fractures. The Board sat so far above the daily grind of the rest of humanity that they'd practically evolved into a new species, incapable of comprehending the needs and desires of the rabble. The executive-level staff fought one another bitterly to ascend to that final pinnacle. And every person beneath them was just waiting for an opening.

It seemed rife for exploitation, but that only went so far. Because as much as they craved power, as much as they laid traps and scrabbled for status or stabbed each other in the back, they all had one thing in common.

They were terrified of the vice president of Security.

"Richter's the key," Knox said finally. "If you could take him out, it would leave them vulnerable on at least a dozen fronts. But he's the one person I can't imagine getting to. You'd have to lure him off the Hill somehow."

"Don't even think it," she whispered. "You will not use yourself as bait. That's one chance I'm *not* willing to take."

He stroked her hair soothingly again but didn't deny the accusation. She *did* know him too well. "Even if I were tempted, I wouldn't. We have too many people to protect. I can't do that if I'm dead."

Nina sat up again, the scant light limning the bare curve of her back. "Ava would throw in with us, but it wouldn't be enough. If we had more help—locals, people motivated to fight the TechCorps. Savitri, maybe, and Jaden Montgomery. That's resources *and* manpower, right there. But we'd still need one more person."

She didn't want to say it. He didn't, either. But one of them had to. "Maya."

"I can't ask her to do it, Garrett." Nina's voice held a rare note of pleading. "It'd be like you locking Mace away. I can't, and I won't."

"Hey." Knox sat up and wrapped an arm around her shoulders, pulling her into his embrace. "I would never risk Maya. *Never.* She's my family, too, now. Right?"

"Right." She shuddered and pressed closer. "We'll bide our time. Make our plans and wait for our moment."

"There's plenty we can do in the meantime," he reminded her. "Get the clinic open. Prepare the shelters for winter. The TechCorps only win if people are hopeless, right? We can take that from them."

She tipped her face up to his. "It's a start."

May 21st, 2078

I thought limiting her would protect her and my hope for this revolution. What if I was wrong all along? What if she *is* the hope for this revolution, and I've stripped her of the tools she would need to win?

The Recovered Journal of Birgitte Skovgaard

SIXTEEN

This time, Maya was ready for the blindfold.

Still, she waited while Gray went through his recitation again—if it bothered her, if she started to freak out, it would all stop. Every single thing, immediately.

Maya loved him a little for it.

She held her breath as Gray gently tied the black silk in place. Pleasure tingled over her scalp as his hands smoothed her braids back over her shoulders, and she didn't fight it this time. So few things felt *good* in this world. This? This she wanted to keep.

She tucked it safely into her memory, along with the protective warmth of him at her back and the kiss of his breath against her temple. Next to the memory of his thumb grazing her lower lip and how safe she felt when he wrapped his arms around her and promised to protect her heart.

That memory she held closest of all.

Gray had already put her through the boring part of training. Ten minutes of watching him circle her on the padded sparring mats, fixing every sound into her memory with a visual to match. Except now that she understood what he was doing, she didn't have to try. Her whole life had been a desperate struggle to absorb as little as possible of the world around her, to stave off sensory overload by disconnecting. No wonder she'd never realized the potential of her perfect memory.

Noticing things really was a superpower.

By the fifth minute, Maya could have closed her eyes and reconstructed the space so perfectly she could have found a pin dropped at ten meters. But she let Gray go for another five because she liked watching him move. He was graceful and deadly, every flex of muscle perfectly controlled, every movement planned with calm deliberation and executed with precision.

She couldn't see him now, but she could feel him.

"The hardest part of fighting in the dark is finding your opponents," he told her—conversationally, as if discussing the weather. "The faster you can locate them, the more of an advantage you'll have."

Her instinct was to turn toward his voice. She could visualize him easily . . . a fraction of a meter behind her, slightly to the left. She could also remember how fast the Silver Devils moved. Maybe not quite Dani's speed, but they could give Nina a challenge in a footrace, and Maya was never going to be on that level.

But she could be sneaky. She tilted her head to the right, as if listening. "What do I do when I find them?"

"What do you—?"

She moved like Nina had taught her. No winding up, no tells. She lunged as fast as she could to where she *knew* Gray would be, using the momentum of her body's turn to launch a punch from the hip.

She hit air as Gray danced around her. "Good. Answering your own question."

His voice was close, but she didn't swing again. A moment later she heard it—the whisper of his feet against the mat. Soft, barely audible . . . but she'd fought a hundred battles across this room. She knew the sounds of it in her beating heart, in her bones. She tracked him on instinct, keeping her hands up as she turned her body. "You know, it's not fair for me to have to chase you around when you're not blindfolded."

"It's not going to be fair to your opponent when you track him, sight unseen, through a pitch-black room and lay him out flat, either," he retorted. "*Focus*, honey."

Maya danced a few feet forward, twisting toward the sound of him again. "Well, yeah. But it's fair when the unfairness is good for *me*."

She didn't wait for him to answer but lunged in another attack. This time, he stepped into it, pressing his body against hers. Her swing connected, but without her weight behind it, she didn't have enough leverage to make it count.

Gray spun her around by the shoulder and wrapped his long arms around her, trapping her fists at her sides. His breath warmed her ear as he leaned in and rasped, "Oh, this will be *very* good for you, Maya. Trust me."

She stopped breathing.

She stopped *everything.*

For a heartbeat—or what would have been a heartbeat, if she weren't definitely *actually* in cardiac arrest—her brain simply couldn't process anything. Then her heart gave a shuddering thump and she felt everything.

She felt *him*.

His chest against her back felt like safety. His arms pinning hers was a thrill of danger. She could fight him, the way Dani and Rafe seemed to fight in a way that was clearly totally sex even if they pretended it wasn't.

Or she could melt into this bliss and find out what *very good* felt like.

She let her head fall back against his shoulder, shivering as it bared her throat to the heat of his soft exhale. Her skin tingled everywhere he was touching her and everywhere she wanted him to be. "Gray."

His voice rasped over her nerve endings, low and lazy. "Again?"

No. Yes. Hell, how was she supposed to *think*? But his arms dropped away, freeing her, so she reacted the way Dani had trained her to react—swift and vicious and definitely cheating.

Even as she drove her elbow back toward his ribs she knew it was a mistake. Her back was still pressed to Gray's chest and the flex of muscle gave her away. He caught her elbow and spun her around for a dizzying, disorientating second. Then her feet left the mat.

She only had seconds to brace. But Gray didn't let her crash into the mat. Her back thudded softly against the padded surface. Her breath left her in a *woosh* anyway as he stretched out above her, almost-touching her everywhere. "Cheater," she accused hoarsely.

"Completely legal move," he countered. "You're the one dropping the ball here." He rolled, and she found herself on top of him, straddling his stomach. "The fight's not over until it's over. If they take you down, don't give up. Use it."

She braced herself with her hands on his chest, savoring the feel of him even through his shirt. But just for a moment. The world was bright even behind her blindfold, as piercingly *real* as she could ever remember it being. She rolled smoothly to her feet and stepped back, confident in the placement of her feet because she knew exactly where she was.

Perfect recall really was a damn superpower.

Two more steps put her in the center of the mat. She bounced on her toes, smiling in the direction Gray was, and listened to him as he rose almost silently. Almost. She'd spent so much time pretending she wasn't watching him, and it was all there in her memory. A perfect road map to his slightest gesture, to the way he moved, to the way he fought.

Her awareness of him wasn't a distraction. It was her secret weapon. So she smiled and crooked a finger at him. "Come get me."

He dove for her. It was fast, the creak of the mat and the whisper of his clothing the only real warning. But Dani had lunged at her a thousand times on this mat. Her brain knew the sounds of it, and her body knew the response.

She pivoted at the last moment, turning in to him and grasping his arm. He was bigger than Dani, but she'd practiced this with Rafe, too, and Rafe was like Gray—a mountain of muscle. The adjustment was instinct and his height made it easier. Maya used Gray's momentum to execute a flawless shoulder throw.

The thud of Gray hitting the floor was sweet victory. Maya laughed and danced backward, bouncing in her glee. "Try again."

So he did. Again and again, they clashed. More often than not, she ended up on her back with Gray's body pressing hers into the floor, but she held her own. Each time they lingered a little longer, the tension prickling as his breath tickled her ear or her hands pinned his wrists.

The urge to kiss him was overpowering. But she denied herself, breaking away to grapple again. The moment she kissed him, everything would change. There'd be no pulling back, no slowing down. She craved it with an intensity that should have made her dizzy but instead sharpened her focus.

Tracking him got easier, as if his presence prickled along her skin. Maybe she had an entire sixth sense that was attuned to Gray. If so, she was drunk on him by the time she narrowly avoided a grapple and tripped him in a desperate move. They went down in a tangle of limbs, and Maya ended up straddling his stomach, breathless as she hastily pinned his arms with her knees.

"Okay, I give." Gray's smile was audible through his light panting.

Maya dragged the blindfold off, and the sight of him slammed into her. Mussed hair, lazy smile, blue eyes that burned with a heat that should have singed her from the inside out instead of warming her all over.

She'd pushed too far. She had to pull back, had to put *some* barriers between her sensation-drunk brain and the intensity of the world. But the temptation was too much. She reached down and traced his lower lip with one trembling fingertip. "You're beautiful."

His smile didn't fade so much as it melted into something warmer. More intimate. "So are you."

God, she loved that smile. She traced his upper lip, unguarded enough to admit the truth. "I don't know what I'm doing. Touch takes so much trust for me, and the last time I got to know someone well enough to want it . . ." Her breathing hitched, but the dark memories couldn't intrude. Not with Gray so warm beneath her. "I've never tried again. I never wanted to."

"And now?"

She let her fingertip trace up his nose, lingering over the little bump, then higher to caress his brow. His face was stern and serious, all the easy humor and warmth subdued and locked away. But not for her. Never for her. She knew where to find it—in the subtle quirk of a brow or the way his eyes crinkled just a little whenever laughter sparked in their Gothic, brooding depths.

Knowing him made the craving so much fiercer. "Now I just . . . *want*. All the time."

Gray sat up, heedless of her knees pinning his arms to the mat, and caught her easily when she slid down his body. "But you're not ready. It's okay, neither am I."

A shiver claimed her, followed by a warning throb in her temples. Would pleasure overwhelm her the same way pain could? She'd never had to worry about it before. Her inexperienced explorations with Simon had been joyous and exhilarating but not exactly intense. And the pleasure she gave herself was gentle and easy.

Straddling Gray's thighs with their bodies pressed together so tight she could feel the pounding of his heart might feel joyous and exhilarating, but the hunger it sparked sure as hell wasn't gentle *or* easy.

She dropped her forehead to his shoulder and closed her eyes, but her deep, steady breath only dragged the scent of him into her lungs. Sweat and coffee and just a hint of pine, because he must have washed his hands with the soap in the kitchen. She inhaled again and let it go on a shaky laugh that sounded intoxicated. "You smell good."

His hands clenched on her hips, then immediately relaxed. "Yeah?"

"Mmm." The urge to squirm closer was nearly overwhelming. Maya locked her body with effort, her fingers twisted in his shirt. "I think I'm drunk on you."

"I know the feeling." His lips brushed her jaw, featherlight, a caress so fleeting she might have imagined it—except for the desire that rocketed straight to her core.

Then she was moving, Gray's hands lifting her as if she weighed nothing. "Time to knock off for the day."

I'm sorry. She bit her lips before the reflexive apology could escape. Instead she relaxed into his arms and whispered what she really meant. "Thank you."

He murmured something against her hair, his voice vibrating in her bones, but she couldn't turn the sounds to words. Sensory overload had never hit her like this before. It wasn't the familiar painful drip of sensation wearing down her stubbornly reinforced mental protections but a distracting cacophony sweeping her away on a wave of scent and touch and sound.

Gray's footsteps on the hardwood floor crashed like meteors plummeting to earth. She could taste him even with her lips pressed firmly shut—the tang of salt on her tongue as if she'd given in to temptation and kissed his throat. The scent of pine grew forests in her imagination, so vivid she cracked open her eyes to make sure they were still inside.

The light hurt. She flinched, and Gray's arms tightened protectively. The brush of fabric across her skin was overwhelming. She tried to block it out, but the heat of his body remained, burning her everywhere he was touching her.

It vanished abruptly. She gasped—in relief. In loss. Her fingers curled and found the familiar soft weight of her heavy quilt, and she realized he'd carried her to her room. She swayed, then stiffened her spine, desperate to not fall over.

"Maya."

Oh, that voice. Low and smooth, but with a rasping undertone that could have been tension or worry. He didn't touch her—he knew better, he *always* knew better, but she could imagine him standing just in front of her, his hands hovering on either side of her shoulders, ready to catch her if something happened.

"I'm okay," she lied. "I just need a second."

"Should I get Nina or Dani?"

"No. No—" She forced her eyes open, and the sight of him hit her low in the gut. Oh God, she wanted to touch him. She wanted to cling to him, drown in him. If her brain had to shatter apart, this was how she'd want to go. Falling into him and riding the pleasure down into oblivion.

Maya gripped her quilt and managed a shaky smile. "I'll be okay. I promise."

His fingers grazed one of her braids. The gentlest touch. His smile warmed her to her toes. Then he was gone, and she collapsed back to her bed, arms splayed wide, too raw to even put on her music.

Shit was seriously dire when even the empty, safe rhythms of FlowMac Pop might push her over the edge.

It was hard, gathering her thoughts back into coherence. Usually the discomfort was its own motivation, but she didn't *hurt* this time. Her thoughts were like a litter of enthusiastic puppies, and chasing down one to corral it into order gave the others free rein to scatter in every direction.

She'd been waiting for the drop. The inevitable punishment for using her brain to its full capacity, for letting go of that precious control. That was what she'd been promised—an inevitable, painful crash.

This was the opposite. A high, every bit as incapacitating but anything but painful. She could feel the warning flashes at the edge of her senses. It would hurt, if she didn't pull back. But right now she felt wild. Invincible. And oh, she could see the lethal danger in that. How easy would it be to make reckless decisions right now?

Her senses were razor-sharp. Her mind encompassed whole universes. She could traverse Southside blindfolded and never falter. Her fingertips itched for a tablet. She wanted to *do* something. Reorganize their metadata system. Figure out a new automation system for scanning their backlog. Hell, she had some manuals on robotics, maybe she could build a system . . .

"Stop," she whispered. She forced her eyes open and stared at the ceiling of her bedroom. Nina had helped her paint it black in her first months here, a project that had given her a sense of ownership over the space. Maya had reconstructed the stars that she'd never been able to see from the roof of their penthouse across the inky-black canvas, constellations hidden by the light pollution of Atlanta.

Polaris. Ursa Minor. Cassiopeia. Perseus. Ursa Major.

She listed them in order, spiraling out from Polaris, then listed them backward as she spiraled back in. Her breathing slowed to match, inhaling as she expanded into the universe, exhaling as she contracted back down to the center.

To the North Star. The way home.

This was it, the truth Nina had told her to find. The truth about her brain. Birgitte had lied with the truth after all.

Maya didn't have to hold it all in. She didn't have to make herself small. But she couldn't let it all go, either. Not all the time. Not recklessly. She had to find the balance, how to use enough of her mind to soothe that restless itch without overextending herself.

Unless it was important. Sometimes, the high would be worth it. The crash, too. She'd have to learn where her lines were, and decide when to cross them.

She rubbed her fingertip against her thumb, remembering the firm softness of Gray's mouth, the warmth of his skin, the tenderness in his eyes.

Even if she drowned in him, Gray would be worth it.

TECHCORPS PROPRIETARY DATA,
L2 SECURITY CLEARANCE

It's time to harvest a certain asset. Send recruiters to the orphanage.

Internal Memo, August 2066

SEVENTEEN

The moment the door closed with Maya on the other side of it, Gray sagged against the wood. He whispered silent thanks that he'd managed to hold on *that* long and lifted his left hand. It was shaking—not trembling or wavering, but jerking unsteadily—and his knees felt weak, wobbly.

Somehow, he needed to get down the stairs.

Gray moved slowly, inch by hard-won inch, one hand braced against the wall until he reached the open stairway. There was no one in the living area or kitchen downstairs, no one to watch as he painstakingly navigated the stairs, locking his knees so that he wouldn't tumble down them.

With only four steps to go, his legs gave without warning. He clenched both hands on the railing to hold himself up as he waited for the rolling waves of weakness to crash over him and subside.

He was certain Maya had been confused when he'd pulled away, maybe even thought she'd done something wrong, but it was better than her seeing him like this. For a moment, he imagined it—pictured her horrified reaction to him now, frozen on the stairs, barely able to stand—and panic knifed through him.

That got him moving again.

Finally, he slipped through the door separating Nina's warehouse from the one belonging to the Devils. He gritted his teeth, steeling himself for the seemingly endless journey to his bunk.

"What the hell?" Mace stood in the newly framed and still-empty doorway between their makeshift living area and the emerging clinic, his brows drawn together in a stormy frown.

Gray couldn't quite quell his dismayed groan, but busted was busted. He might as well avail himself of the medic's presence. "A little help here?" He reached out, and the sudden shift in his center of gravity almost sent him crashing to the floor.

Mace threw aside the half-crushed box of gauze pads and dove, catching him as he stumbled. He looped Gray's arm around his neck and started back toward the examination room. "When did this start?"

Somewhere between sparring with Maya and holding her on his lap. It had been a delicate moment, full of warmth and openness and *trust*, and he felt just as betrayed as she must to have lost it. "About ten minutes ago."

"What were you doing?"

"Training."

Mace's jaw tightened as he lowered Gray to a folding chair—the exam tables and other specialized equipment were in place but covered with plastic to protect them from the sawdust that hung in the air. All the consumable goods they'd procured were still packed away in sealed boxes, protected from the construction—bandages and med-gel and basic medications.

Several of those boxes were open now, their contents laid out in neat, orderly rows. Mace must have been inventorying the supplies. He dug through one of the boxes and resurfaced with a pen light.

He flicked the tight, focused beam into Gray's left eye, then his right. "Were you alone? Why didn't you call for someone?"

"I was with Maya," Gray confessed, bracing himself for a lecture.

It didn't come. Mace eyed him knowingly, sighed, and tore open another box. After several moments of searching, he retrieved a bottle and shook out two small, beige tablets. "Here, try these. Under the tongue."

Gray shoved away his outstretched hand. "Uh-uh. I hate that shit. It makes me loopy."

"You hate the benzos," Mace countered. "This is a fast-acting dopamine agonist."

As if Gray knew what the fuck that meant. "English, please."

"It'll help with the tremors, but it won't knock you on your ass."

Grudgingly, Gray took the tablets. By the time he slipped them under his tongue, Mace was checking his pulse with two fingers laid along the side of his neck.

What a difference a few days could make. "Last time you had your hands this close to my throat, you were trying to strangle me," he observed mildly.

"I feel better," Mace admitted. "Since Knox refuses to lock me up, I had no choice. Had to get myself under control."

"Don't forget Dani and her Mace sedatives."

He snorted, then gestured around at the tiny clinic space. "Being here helps. I think it grounds me."

Gray agreed. Moreover, he *understood.* When he had his rifle set up, waiting for a shot, he slipped into this liminal space between thinking and just . . . being. It was meditative in a way, more familiar to him than his own name. That was Mace when he was in the zone. He got this look on his face, like the whole world just made sense.

"Good," Gray managed finally. "Because if you haul off and stab Knox again, I'm pretty sure Nina's gonna fucking kill you."

The corner of his mouth twitched. "She may have already sworn an oath to that effect, yes."

"Word to the wise, man—she means it."

"I know." Mace pulled up a stool and sat, facing him. "So. If you were sparring with Maya, why didn't you get her to help you down here?"

Gray stifled a groan. "*No.* I mean, I never want her to see me like this, but now? She'd assume that I pushed too hard with her training and that it was all her fault."

Mace snorted. "Well, it's not. It's yours."

Gray scoffed, taken aback by the blunt words. "I forgot what an assface you can be sometimes, man."

Mace waved that off, his face screwed up into a grimace of disgust. "Shut up. I can't do my job if I have to tiptoe around your feelings, and this job? It's the one thing I'm good at." He paused, then dropped his gaze. "The only thing I have left."

Feeling properly chastened, Gray inclined his head. "Fine. I'm sorry, I overdid it. But it was just a little training, nothing major."

"Nothing major," Mace echoed, then sighed again. This time, when he spoke, it wasn't tough love that filled his gruff voice but something gentler, scarier—quiet compassion. "Your condition is progressive. You'll have good and bad days, but on the whole, time isn't your friend. You're deteriorating. It's a process, and it isn't going to stop."

The room was so cold that Gray shivered, and he rubbed at his bare arms. He wasn't stupid. He knew he was dying—but that was just it. He *knew* it, the way he knew the universe was infinite or that the world was billions of years old. It was a formless thing, an unfathomable fact he recognized to be true without truly comprehending it.

Because it was fucking incomprehensible. How was he supposed to feel this impossible truth in his gut, where it counted? Death had to remain distant, a nebulous thing that Would Happen Someday but didn't bear closer scrutiny. Anything else was paralyzing. If he faced it, he couldn't move, couldn't *breathe*, because every breath he drew was one fewer left in his life.

He wasn't just going to die; he was dying, hour by hour, bit by bit. It was happening to him every day, this slow slide that he still couldn't manage to comprehend.

And, despite his determination not to add to Maya's collection of perfect, incandescently terrible memories, she was going to watch it happen.

So he did what any cornered animal would do—he fought. "I feel fine most of the time."

"Yes."

The sheer lack of argument drained some of his anger, his frustration. His panic. "I feel fine most of the time," he said again, then went on. "But I'm still dying."

"But you're still dying." Mace smiled, commiseration in the truest sense of the word. "It's the great irony of the human condition. We all die, but none of us know how to do it."

"So . . . what do I do?"

Mace arched an eyebrow. "Didn't I *just say* no one fucking knows?"

"Jesus Christ, Mace."

"All right, all right." He eased his chair closer and laid his hand on Gray's shoulder. "You take the time you have left, and you live it. I'll get Conall to go in hard on the Protectorate medical archives, see if we can find *anything* that might help. Even if we can't save you, we can probably give you more time."

There was that panic again. "I don't want to be helpless. I don't want to be lying in a bed, hooked up to a bunch of shit, not knowing what the hell is going on. I don't want to be gone but still breathing."

"I wouldn't let that happen to you," Mace soothed. "To any of you."

No false hope. No maybes. Perversely, it helped. "Okay. I guess I just have to . . ." He trailed off.

"Gray?"

He couldn't hold back his slightly morbid grin. "I was gonna say *learn to live with it*, but shit. I guess not."

"That's it." Mace rose. "Get out. Get out of my clinic."

Gray had been through things that would have broken most people—being orphaned, growing up alone and terrified—and he'd faced it head-on. He'd never turned away from a hard truth in his life, and he wasn't going to start with his death.

He just hoped he didn't bring Maya down with him when he finally fell.

AVA

There was a man brooding on the roof of her sister's building.

No, best to be precise.

There was a dead man brooding on the roof of her sister's building.

Ava perched in the shadows, balanced effortlessly on the edge of the building in spite of the three-inch heels on her boots and the heavy bag slung across her body. Her favorite point of entry into the warehouse was on the opposite side of the roof, and she'd expected a clean shot at it.

Instead, it was being guarded by a ghost.

Several months ago, Ava had made a tactically questionable decision. After undergoing years of torture and captivity, she'd escaped only to discover that her beloved sister, far from being dead, was alive and well and living a comfortable life with a new family in Atlanta.

She had not taken Nina's apparent abandonment well. In retrospect, she could acknowledge her emotional response to this discovery had been . . . less than ideal. Ava did not like admitting to having acted irrationally, but the string of increasingly reckless decisions she'd made while in the grip of rage and grief had been unfortunately extreme.

A rational person might have approached Nina. Ava had decided to have her retrieved. Of course, most of the people you could hire to kidnap someone with Nina's unique capabilities were hardly the sort of people she'd have wanted manhandling her sister, no matter their current degree of estrangement. But Captain Garrett Knox had presented such an intriguing prospect. So irrationally noble. So nauseatingly idealistic. So conveniently on the run from the TechCorps.

So emotionally compromised.

Security on the TechCorps intranet wasn't the hardest she'd ever cracked, though she gave Tobias Richter full credit for being the nastiest. The traps he'd laid were elegant, devious, and vicious. She'd learned a thing or two by narrowly avoiding them.

During her deep dive into exploring Captain Knox's pressure points, she'd learned of his ultimate weakness. Being forced to witness the slow and brutal death of his team's medic had left Knox with an almost compulsive need to protect the remaining members of his squad. Ava had leveraged that against him.

Which made the fact that said medic was standing ten meters away problematic.

It also made him a threat to Nina.

Moving silently, she eased the strap over her head and set her bag and its precious cargo down on the roof. The shadows were deep this late at night, with the moon's silvery glow falling at a sharp angle, but it shone on the medic.

Whatever the TechCorps had done to him had been brutal—and recent. Time would ease some of the deep lines of pain carved into his face and the way he stood as if everything hurt. She'd been an emaciated wraith with dead eyes for those first six months after escaping, too.

The outside would heal. The inside? Well, some things not even time could fix.

A piece of gravel scraped under the heel of her boot, only a whisper of sound, but he stiffened, his head turning.

His gaze locked on her, pale and flashing in the scant moonlight. Ava drew her gun in one smooth movement and aimed for his head, her finger already caressing the trigger. It was a struggle *not* to shoot. Her instincts screamed for it. Every muscle trembled, her body eager to eliminate the danger before his presumed risk could become a tactical certainty.

It was the logical thing to do. But Nina would be disappointed if Ava shot Knox's unarmed friend in cold blood just because he was clearly here to hurt them.

Trying to avoid disappointing Nina was exhausting.

The medic was still watching her. Ava eased her finger off the trigger enough that she wouldn't shoot him by mistake and tilted her head. "You're supposed to be dead."

"Likewise." His voice hovered somewhere between interest and boredom. The one thing it lacked completely was *concern*—for his own welfare, or for her sudden appearance.

Ava knew that numbness well. Worse, she knew how lethal it could be. "So, James Mason. I know why I'm still alive. Why are you?"

The corner of his mouth ticked up, and he turned back toward the distant lights of the Hill. "I thought you were supposed to be the smart one."

"And I thought you were supposed to be a decent man. And yet, here you are. Clearly a danger to your friends. And my sister." Anger flattened her voice. "I assume you at least dealt with active trackers. Do you know how to scan for passive ones?"

He didn't answer right away. Instead, he turned his entire, surprisingly big body toward hers. He was slender but quite tall, and those attributes combined gave him an air of slim, wiry strength. Of course, his center of balance was too high. If she had to take him down, she'd go in low, knock him off his feet and over her shoulder.

She was halfway through analyzing the best places to kick him while he was down when he arched one eyebrow at her, a look of wry disbelief, as if he couldn't believe she was still calculating the most efficient way to murder him.

Odd. He'd seemed rather intelligent in his file.

Ava had no intention of letting his amusement distract her from risk assessment. "I'll assume even Knox is smart enough to have dealt with the passive trackers. What about radioactive isotopes? The military bases out west inject those to track their genetic experiments."

He made a quiet, mildly disgusted noise and gestured behind her. "What's in the bag?"

She didn't take her eyes off him. "A debt I owe. Stop dodging my questions. I understand Knox is too soft to eliminate a threat to his family, but I'm not. Tell me why I shouldn't shoot you now and get it over with."

For the span of several heartbeats, he merely stared out at the patchy lights of the city. "Do they ask you that?" he said finally. "Every time you show up, unannounced, to be creepy all over their idyllic existence?"

She couldn't argue with his characterization of her activities. It felt like a profoundly accurate assessment. "Only the smart ones. Mostly Dani. That's why I like Dani."

"Fair." He nodded decisively. "I make it a point never to lie, so I'm not going to answer your question—if that even qualified as a question. You do whatever you have to do."

It would have been nice if he'd given her an excuse. Or at least a plausible explanation for Nina. If she shot him now, while he was just brooding on the roof . . .

Her finger drifted toward the trigger anyway.

And he *moved.*

His speed was uncanny. He had the gun out of her hand before she realized he'd lunged. Ava didn't fight to keep hold of it. She slammed the heel of her hand toward his nose, assessing his response even as he swung up an arm to block. She used his distraction to kick her gun out of his hand and barely escaped large fingers closing around her ankle.

He fought dirty. No testing feints or honor, and he knew where to jab to make it hurt. She barely avoided a blow that would have numbed her arm to the elbow and jammed the hard heel of her boot down where his instep had been a fraction of a second earlier. There was no style to assess here, no thought or strategy behind his movements.

This was pure feral instinct. Cunning and ruthless. So damn *fast.* Survival in its purest form.

Nothing was deadlier. She should know.

It was over in seconds. His massive hand closed around her throat and she let it, absorbing the impact as he slammed her back against the wall. Her boot knife was already in her fingers, and she let the lethally honed edge kiss the skin beneath his Adam's apple. When he swallowed, a tiny, red line appeared.

"So," she said, studying him curiously. "You do care if you live."

"Do I?" Casual words, devoid of anger or fear or even exertion. "I thought I was proving a point."

"I'm sure you did." His grip at her throat was precise. A casual, efficient warning. She likely wouldn't even have bruises. She supposed a medic knew exactly how much pressure was required as a threat and how hard to squeeze to incapacitate. "Not everyone cares, you know. Not right away. Richter must have had you, what? Eight months, at least? Plenty of time to carve the will to survive right out of you."

"Ah, the voice of experience."

"Not particularly. It wasn't the pain that broke me. It was what I did to make it stop." She raised one challenging eyebrow at him. "What did you do to make it stop, James Mason?"

For the first time, he eyed her with something that almost looked like . . . sympathy? "*The point* is that I'm in control now. If that changes, I'll reassess. Either that satisfies you, or . . ."

Her pulse beat a little faster against his palm. Not because of the physical threat, but the damnable *pity* in his eyes. Choking her out was fine, but if he thought he could feel sorry for her . . .

She locked her elbow to keep her arm steady, mostly to keep from slicing his throat to escape that look. "Or what?"

"Or we resolve this now." The arm not raised to her throat flexed, and the dull edge of a blade pressed against her left flank, just over her kidney.

She glanced down. The knife had a familiar hilt, twin to the one she was holding to his throat. He'd gotten her second boot knife at some point, and turned it against her.

Impressive.

Not impressive enough, granted. No matter how surgical his strike, she had a better chance of living long enough to get treatment for a kidney laceration than he did of surviving a slit throat. She had the tactical advantage and, at this point, all the rationalization she needed to follow through on the kill. Surely Nina couldn't argue that a knife jabbed in her kidney wasn't provocation enough for self-defense.

Except . . . Nina might. Because Nina would never believe Ava had been helpless. Nina wouldn't make the so-often-fatal mistake of underestimating her. Nina would know Ava could have resolved this without killing Mace and would expect her to do so unless vulnerable lives were on the line.

Not disappointing Nina really *was* exhausting.

She eased the blade from his throat and let her arm fall away. "I'm going to scan you for radioactive isotopes. And passive trackers. And everything else I can think of."

"Not even planning on buying me dinner first? Shameful."

She couldn't tell if he was mocking her or hitting on her. The latter would be continued evidence of self-destructive tendencies, which made it plausible. She used the flat of her blade to shove away the hand still holding a knife pointed at her kidney. "I'm not the sister who feeds strays."

"Duly noted." He flipped her boot knife and offered it to her, hilt-first. "Welcome home."

She could still feel the ghost of his fingers at her throat. That would be a good reminder not to forget he was dangerous. She accepted her knife and sheathed both of them, using the familiar movement to ground her. "It's not home," she started, but when she turned she realized she was addressing an empty roof.

Mace had vanished. Whether silently through the door or just by vaulting over the side she couldn't be sure.

But for the first time she understood how irritating that was.

Ava shook off her annoyance and retrieved the bag. Her usual point of entry beckoned, but breaking into the place felt childishly performative now that Mace had already seen her. Especially when Nina had pressed the access codes on her in spite of her protests.

The keypad beeped softly in the night—proof that Mace couldn't have used it to escape. Ava frowned as she slipped into the shadowy hallway and silently descended the back staircase. *She* could have vaulted off the roof and compensated effortlessly for the several-story drop upon landing, but she was in peak physical condition. The medic certainly hadn't appeared to be.

Perhaps she should have stabbed him after all.

The second floor in Nina's apartment was silent. No lights shone from underneath Maya's or Dani's doors. Ava paused before Nina's and rapped her knuckles gently against the door—three soft knocks, repeated three times. Their childhood signal.

The knob turned, and Nina peered through the crack in the door. "When did you get here?"

"Fifteen minutes ago." Ava tilted her head. "Knox is sleeping?"

"Hello, Ava." Knox's long-suffering voice drifted out of the darkness. "It's the middle of the night. Lots of us sleep at night."

Ava didn't sleep much, especially when she was in Atlanta. But antagonizing Knox only made Nina sad, so she bit back her instinctive response. "Should I come back tomorrow?"

"Not at all." Nina murmured something to Knox, then donned a robe over her T-shirt and shorts and slipped out into the hallway. "Let's go down to the kitchen. I'll make tea."

Ava followed her sister down the staircase that led into their open first floor. Someone had extended their table with a butcher's block, and an unusual number of chairs were scattered around it. Ava counted them absently as Nina went to put the kettle on. "I found James Mason on your roof."

"Ah. And you'd like to register your objections."

"He's clearly a trap. An effective one, considering his continued presence."

Nina leaned a hip against the counter and shrugged. "Some traps are worth it."

Ava set her bag on the kitchen island and tried a different tactic. "The Tech-Corps could be tracking him to your front door right now. If you're not worried about Knox and his men, consider the risk to Maya."

A mug clattered to the island in front of Ava, accompanied by a pointed stare.

"Don't try to manipulate me, and don't insult me. I know you think I'm soft, but I'm not stupid."

No, Nina was never that. Ava accepted the rebuke as a result of her own tactical failure. Combative strategies rarely succeeded with Nina. She needed to be collaborative. "There are some tracking methods the TechCorps might have utilized that you're not familiar with. I'd like to scan him to be sure."

"I'm not familiar with them, hmm?" Now Nina almost seemed to be suppressing a smile. "If you'd like to scan Mace, that's his decision."

Fine. Ava would find a way to make it clear to him that allowing it was in everyone's best interests. "I still don't think you should let him wander around. There's nothing wrong with his biochemical enhancements, and he's clearly emotionally compromised. He could hurt someone."

Nina's almost-smile vanished. "Would you like to know our reasoning or just continue to tell me what I'm doing wrong?"

"I'd like to know your reasoning."

"Mace has been incarcerated for months. *Tortured* for months. If we lock him up again, it could trigger a post-traumatic stress response. He's not well, no. But he's better now than he was when he got here." The kettle began to whistle, so Nina pulled it off the eye and shut off the burner. "We are *handling* this, Ava. Our way, not yours."

"I was incarcerated for months," Ava replied softly. "I was tortured for months. I thought I was getting better, too. But I was still capable of doing terrible things to the person I loved most." Ava swallowed back the bitter memory of seeing Nina for the first time—happy, laughing with friends, blithely living her life in a world that had no place for Ava. "I don't want him to hurt you. That's the only thing I care about."

"I know, and I appreciate it." Nina poured hot water into their mugs, then braced her elbows on the island and tilted her head toward the bag Ava had brought. "What's that?"

Ava rested a hand on the heavy fabric. "Last time I was here, I heard Rafael Morales say he was struggling to find effective medications for the young biohacker's aunt."

"Yes, Ivonne has a heart condition . . ." Nina trailed off. "Ava, you didn't."

"Transplants aren't nearly as risky with a DNA-customized biomechanical organ. And I know a talented surgeon who owes me a significant favor."

Nina dropped her head to the counter with a groan. "Oh, honey. No. This is not a thing people *do*. You can't just show up with a heart in a bag."

"Most people wouldn't have the capacity or resources to do this. I do." Ava frowned, earnestly perplexed by Nina's unexpected response. "Why should she continue to suffer if I can fix the situation? And I owe the girl a debt."

"Luna?" Nina scoffed. "You didn't borrow fifty credits and forget to pay her back. You *kidnapped* her."

"I caused her emotional suffering. This is the only way I could think of to alleviate emotional suffering." Ava shrugged and adjusted the strap on the bag, a nervous gesture unworthy of her. But Nina was the only one who could make her nervous. "She doesn't have to forgive me. I don't *care* if she forgives me. But she should have her family. Healthy."

"Desperately needed hearts are nice." Nina met her gaze. "But so is sticking around."

The silent challenge lay there between them. A DNA-customized biomechanical organ was simple, easily paid for in credits. Credits meant little to Ava. She had taken plenty from the man who'd thought to cage and use her.

Sticking around? That, she would have to pay for with her precious time and emotional vulnerability.

Slowly, Ava straightened. She looped the strap of the bag over her head and squared her shoulders.

This would be incredibly difficult. "Do you still have those cots in the basement?"

"We do."

Ava exhaled. "Then I guess we'll have plenty of time to catch up tomorrow."

"Ava?"

"Yes?"

Nina smiled and held out one of the mugs. "Don't forget your tea."

Ava accepted it with a faint smile and watched Nina retreat back up the stairs, to where Knox was undoubtedly waiting for her. Knox would probably be pleased to find Ava here in the morning—not because he particularly enjoyed her company, but because he had zero patience with her absences hurting Nina.

Pleasing Knox was almost reason enough to sneak back out the door. But Ava cradled the mug and stubbornly passed her final potential exit, turning instead to the staircase that led down into the basement.

It was a far cry from her tastefully appointed penthouse on the Hill. Just a clean, carefully swept room, a few worn rugs trying to warm the place up, and a row of cheap but sturdy cots adorned with colorful, heavily patched quilts.

Ava supposed she had slept in worse places.

One of the cots had a lopsided little side table next to it. Ava set down her tea and placed her precious bag beside the bed. The soft whir from the box inside was barely audible. The heart would beat with artificial life until a surgeon lifted it from its housing and placed it into a human body. It was a miracle of science. And a damned *fortune* worth of credits.

And Nina valued it less than Ava's presence. Utterly irrational.

Honestly, Ava couldn't imagine that her mere presence could possibly live up to such lofty expectations. She'd likely disappoint Nina before the end. But tomorrow, one way or another, she'd fully assess the threat James Mason presented.

Disappointment or not, Ava *would* protect her sister.

TECHCORPS INTERNAL COMMUNICATION

From: RICHTER, T
To: SKOVGAARD, B
Date: 2078–07–01

Is there a pressing reason DC-035 hasn't completed her Year 16 benchmark tests? I can understand a certain degree of preferential treatment, but you, of all people, should understand how important regular testing is.

EIGHTEEN

Ava would not stop staring at her.

Maya tried to ignore her as she sliced another lemon and handed half to Rainbow. The girl's face was fixed in an expression torn between fierce concentration and outright wonder as she gently pushed down the lever on the citrus press. The tart smell of lemon juice filled the room, and Rainbow solemnly removed the rind and deposited it in a bowl slowly filling with them.

"You know, there are machines that do that," Ava pointed out as Maya passed over the next lemon half. "There have been for at least a century."

Rainbow froze, gaze darting from Maya to Ava and back. Maya barely bit back an exasperated sigh. No one other than Nina ever responded *well* to Ava's sudden appearances, but Rainbow was reacting with heartbreaking awe to the sudden tangible proof that Nina and Ava were like her—clones, genetically enhanced and ruthlessly trained. Maya supposed she might feel the same confronted with a data courier in their sixties who'd somehow mastered the seemingly impossible task of thriving in a world that would never understand you.

Nina knew how to handle the girl's hero worship. Ava, on the other hand . . .

Maya wasn't sure Ava knew how to handle anyone she wasn't planning to kill.

"We don't need a machine," Maya said firmly, giving Rainbow's shoulder an encouraging squeeze. "We make lemonade for ourselves, for fun. If we decide to go into business, we'll discuss streamlining the system for mass production."

Ava lifted one shoulder in a barely visible shrug, and Maya knew that she was already trying to decide where to obtain a top-of-the-line citrus juicer. She'd leave it behind, the same way she'd left Maya's fancy ear cuffs, or the 3D scanner, or the set of perfectly balanced prototype throwing knives that wouldn't set off metal detectors. Because she couldn't seem to help herself.

"We *don't* need a machine," she repeated, a little more firmly.

"Don't bother, Maya," Rafe drawled, flipping around the chair at the head of the table so he could straddle it. "Ava doesn't know how to express herself with words, so she's just going to keep buying us presents until we like her."

Ava turned her cool gaze on Rafe. Her face might have been identical to Nina's, but Nina had *never* managed to pack that much absolute disdain into a single look. "Don't flatter yourself. I neither need nor desire your approval."

"Yeah, you say that. You say it all the time." Rafe leaned closer to Maya and stage-whispered, "Do you know what she had in that huge-ass bag she hauled in here?"

"I don't know, gold bars?"

"A heart."

Maya blinked at him, her imagination immediately supplying the grisly visual. "What, like ripped with her bare hands from the chest of a man who'd wronged her?"

"Don't be stupid," Ava retorted, her voice bland. "Why would I get my hands dirty for such an inefficient kill? There are much better ways to kill someone."

"See, now she's just trying to look like an asshole." Rafe propped his chin on his hand and grinned. "She *grew* the heart. From Ivonne's DNA. And paid a surgeon to be on standby."

Maya's own heart skipped a beat. Ivonne couldn't afford the artificial organs created by the TechCorps, and even the best treatment Luna and Rafe could buy had only been a stopgap measure. "Ivonne is getting her transplant?"

"Don't make something of this that it's not," Ava snapped. "I inconvenienced Luna—"

"Kidnapped," Maya interjected. "You *kidnapped* Luna."

"—and she deserves compensation for her trouble. That's all it is."

"Uh-huh." Rafe dragged the cutting board away from Maya and started slicing the lemons in half with effortless strokes. "You will work harder than anyone on this whole damned planet to avoid apologizing. It's honestly impressive. I have deep respect for your dedication to never saying you're sorry."

Deprived of anything to do with her hands now that Rafe had taken over slicing the lemons, Maya nudged Conall. "Don't you have anything to say?"

"Nope," he replied without looking up from his tablet. "I don't poke bears or psychotic evil genius clones."

Rafe snorted. "You *literally* poked a bear on that mission in the Carolinas. As I recall, it tried to eat your face."

"Exactly. That's why I don't poke bears." Conall tapped his fingers rapidly over the screen of his tablet. "Besides, this whole conversation is irrational. Who wants *I'm sorry* when you could get latest-gen smart lenses instead?"

He flashed a grin at Ava, and the light caught his eyes just right, reflecting off his new contacts. Maya's one attempt to try the things back on the Hill had put her flat on her back for a day with vertigo she couldn't shake. The last thing she wanted was *more* shit trying to get her attention. But Conall had clearly missed looking at the world through his customized heads-up display, so she wouldn't begrudge him the gift.

Rafe clearly did, though. He exhaled and shook his head. "It's the principle of the damn thing, y'all. She can't just kidnap and blackmail everyone and then buy them presents."

"Obviously I can," she told Rafe, baring her teeth at him. Maybe she thought it was a smile. Maya found it mildly terrifying.

"Ava."

Ava's fearsome smile-grimace disappeared. Her expression went utterly flat as Knox leaned past her to set a stack of salad plates in the center of the table.

His voice hadn't been particularly chiding or serious. It hadn't been *anything.* But Knox and Ava circled each other like two scary monsters with one shared vulnerability—Nina.

Maya was pretty sure they hated each other. And equally sure neither would ever act upon it. Neither of them would risk Nina's heart.

It was the main reason Maya had grown fond of Knox and even softened toward Ava. No one who loved Nina as fiercely as Knox and Ava did could be beyond redemption. The urge to make Nina happy made them better people. Maya could see it with Ava already. Her jaw was clenched around whatever undoubtedly caustic thing she wanted to say to Knox . . .

But she wasn't saying it. That was something, anyway.

Knox eased the large jar from beneath the juice press and held out a hand to Rainbow. "Do you want to see how we turn this into lemonade?"

After another covert glance at Ava, Rainbow silently slipped her tiny hand into Knox's huge one and followed him back to the kitchen area.

"That was a good move," Rafe said. "We should probably talk less about murder in front of the baby."

"She's not a baby." Ava narrowed her eyes as she considered Rainbow where she stood at the far side of the room next to Knox. "Depending on what her training protocols were, it's possible she's already made her first kill. I doubt it, though. They have a certain look, after that."

"I imagine they do." Rafe's knife sliced through a lemon and sank into the wooden cutting board. "You sound like you know a lot about this."

"Not really." Ava's cool gaze swung back to Rafe. "There are groups who help people like her, though, and one in particular that operates in the Southeast. Given my background, our interests often intersect."

The words tugged at a memory. Maya braced herself for it, but the swell wasn't as overwhelming as usual. Maybe relieving the pressure had helped, even if she'd been counting constellations for half the night. She closed her eyes and let the thought she wanted drift gently to the top. "Sydney Winters," she murmured.

The scrape of a chair across the floor popped her eyes open. Ava was leaning forward, her brown eyes terrifyingly intent. "How do you know that name?" she demanded.

"Hey." Rafe drew the knife out of the cutting board with one swift movement and jabbed it in Ava's direction. "You don't talk to her like that."

Ava ignored him. "What else does the TechCorps know about Syd?"

Maya laid a soothing hand on Rafe's arm—and thanked God that Gray hadn't shown up yet. "She's a friend of yours, I take it?"

"I don't have friends." Her voice was icy and calm, but the tension in her eyes told the truth. Ava might not have *friends*, but she had people she'd protect. "Like I said, our interests intersect."

"Mmm." Maya let her eyelids droop again, and this time she didn't try to control the flow of memories. They rose in swift succession, overlapping in an absolute anarchy of sensory recall. For a heartbeat, she thought she'd made a terrible mistake. Instinct screamed for her to exert control, to thumb through the memories in order until she found the necessary one.

She ignored her rigid training and exhaled, trusting her brain to know what was needed.

And it did.

It was just like the mechanic manuals. Like all the other things she'd ever learned for herself, instead of having them shoved into her brain against her will. A few overwhelming moments of uncertainty, and then patterns emerging from the chaos. Everything she knew about Sydney Winters, gathered from a dozen memos and scraps of conversations, fell into neat rows, and she felt like she was reading them from the air in front of her.

"Sydney Winters," she recited. No, not recited. This was her own voice, not an echo of a memory. "Exact age unknown, but likely born before the Flares. Suspected product of one of the privatized military initiatives in Virginia. Likely an offshoot of the original Makhai Project, which aimed to produce supersoldiers for the military."

"Is that all?"

"She doesn't leave much of a trail, and the TechCorps doesn't know what to make of her. She's suspected of shutting down at least five illegal operations that the TechCorps had targeted, which they're fine with. But she killed the scientists, too, which they're not."

"Yes, I imagine so." Now Ava sounded amused. It figured that mass slaughter would amuse her. "Brilliant scientists with nonexistent morals and a high tolerance for the suffering of children must be a precious commodity for the TechCorps."

"Pretty much." Maya raised an eyebrow. "So what does she do? Run some sort of clone liberation underground?"

"Something along those lines." Ava nodded to where Rainbow stood on a stool next to Knox, mixing the lemonade with heartbreaking care. "If nothing else, you should let me reach out to her about the child. There are safe houses. They know how to deal with children who could kill an adult by mistake."

Something unexpected twinged in Maya's chest. She'd never explicitly thought about keeping Rainbow around. She wasn't exactly an expert on parenting, and she was pretty sure raising a child in between crime sprees and dangerous heists was all sorts of not cool. Not to mention they were pretty much *all* wanted by the TechCorps.

But the idea of letting her go to strangers didn't feel good, either.

Dani walked in, a vague smile playing at the corners of her lips. It vanished when she saw Ava. Instead, her head fell back with a groan. "*Ugh*, you again."

Maya picked up the stack of plates and started setting the table, mostly to get out of the line of fire.

But Ava took Dani's open disgust with remarkable calm. "You're as eloquent as always, Dani."

"Okay, how do I say this nicely—wait, fuck it, I don't care." Dani stopped in front of Ava, bent at the waist to rest her hands on her own knees, and said slowly and loudly, *"You—do not—live here."*

Ava rested her elbow on the table and propped her chin in her hand. "Of course I don't. I have a penthouse. With a cleaning service. And actual modern amenities."

"As if that's something to be proud of."

"Give it up, cupcake." Rafe sliced through the last lemon and stacked them on his cutting board. "She likes it when you insult her. You want her to run for the hills, give her a big hug."

Ava furrowed her brow. "Please don't."

"Wouldn't dream of it." She breezed past them to where Rainbow stood and ruffled the child's brutally short hair. "Whatcha doing, bug?"

"Mixing lemonade," came the serious answer, as Rainbow continued her careful work with the wooden spoon. Maya hid a smile and slid a plate in front of Rafe.

"She's ignoring me again," he muttered.

"Dani does that." Maya patted his shoulder and slid the last plate into its spot. "Chin up, soldier."

Rafe winked at her as he gathered the cutting board and sauntered over to where Dani and Rainbow stood. Maya shook her head and retrieved the jumble of silverware as Nina delivered a stack of bowls to go along with the plates.

"Stew's almost ready," she announced. "Who's handling the salad?"

"I'm on it," Knox replied, and Maya hid another smile. She supposed Knox's domestic streak shouldn't have been a surprise. A meal plan wasn't that different from a battle plan, and Knox was almost as bad as Nina when it came to fussing over people. He'd been downloading the cookbooks as fast as she could digitize them and strategizing ways to feed their sprawling—and growing—little family.

The smell of sourdough bread in the oven was a reminder that he wasn't half bad at baking, either.

Maya tried to ignore Ava's renewed scrutiny as she distributed the silverware and bowls. She paused at Conall's elbow and nudged him. "Is Gray coming to dinner?"

"Not sure," Conall replied absently. "He was with Mace when I left."

"I'm surprised you let James Mason roam freely," Ava noted. "Especially with the child here. He's clearly a threat."

Conall shot Ava a chilly look over the edge of his tablet. "Don't go there, lady. We've all agreed to have a case of amnesia about the bullshit you pulled, but Mace is off-limits. Talk shit about him again, and my memory's gonna get real good."

Maya froze. It was an outright threat, and from *Conall* of all people, whom she'd never heard say an actual angry word to anyone. The kitchen had fallen silent, too, everyone caught in the tense breath before violence exploded. Another heartbeat and Dani would be across the table again, probably packing an Ava-calibrated sedative this time.

The corner of Ava's lip quirked. That might actually be a real smile. God, she really *did* like it when people threatened her. "Acknowledged."

"What the fuck ever." Conall pointedly returned his attention to his tablet. Ava watched him for several moments in earnest curiosity as the gentle rhythms of the dinner prep resumed around them. After a straight minute of Conall intently pretending she didn't exist, however, her attention drifted back to assessing the activity in the kitchen.

Maya placed the final fork and slid into her usual seat next to Conall. His slightly unfocused eyes darted back and forth like he was reading words in the air in front of him—which he likely was. One glimpse at the surface of his tablet confirmed he'd synced it with his smart lenses, feeding most of the data straight to his virtual display.

But there was enough on the tablet screen to twist her gut into anxious knots. "Is that what I think it is?" she whispered.

"Do you think it's Tobias Richter's inbox?" Conall's voice had resumed its usual good humor. "Because yeah. I'm doing my daily check-in, thanks to our evil genius murder-friend over there."

Maya's gaze stole to Ava again, who seemed utterly oblivious as she watched Knox navigate the kitchen with the predatory gaze of someone assessing vulnerabilities.

Several months ago, when Nina had coordinated a little mass fraud against the TechCorps by faking the deaths of the Silver Devils, Ava had provided a twist of her own—malware encoded directly into the faux corpses' DNA. The TechCorps had taken the 3D-printed fake bodies back to their labs for analysis and introduced the nastiest bit of code Maya had ever seen directly into their high-security systems.

Of course, Maya was living proof that not every damning thing made it to their servers. She existed solely to hide the secrets too volatile, too dangerous, or simply too potentially damaging to commit to a digital paper trail. Richter's plans with Mace hadn't been anywhere in the TechCorps system.

Plenty of other horrifying things were. Maya propped her chin on her hand and leaned closer, scanning the list of subject lines from his incoming messages.

Re: Termination of Labor Organizers in East Atlanta
MEMO: Reduction in benefits to L5 Employees
Prisoner conscription for Project Cerberus
Re: Expanded Ex-Sec Recruitment
Security Evaluation & Background Check: Cerys (Surname Unknown)

Protectorate candidates at St. Mary's
Executions scheduled for: 2086/10/17

"If this is the sort of shit he wants a digital trail for," Conall murmured, "I'd hate to see the inside of *his* data courier's head."

The memory sideswiped Maya. She was ten, so young and already feeling ancient, huddled alone in the back of a class on assembly language. The entire back row had cleared out when she sat down, students scrambling to distance themselves from a data courier who could remember their slightest transgression—and presumably report it straight to a VP. Even the teacher wouldn't look directly at her, probably hoping she'd give up and switch to taking the course virtually.

Maya almost had . . . and then *she'd* walked in. Fifteen to Maya's ten, already tall and long-limbed, looking glamorous in a sequined sundress in vivid green that complemented her long, red hair and pale skin. Cara Kennedy had flashed the teacher a challenging smile that dared the woman to comment on her tardiness—or her flagrant violation of the dress code—then glided between the desks as if the other students were simply beneath her notice.

She'd claimed the seat next to Maya with a mischievous wink and her first murmured bit of advice. "Don't ever let them run you off. *They* should fear *us*."

"Maya?" Conall's low whisper was edged with worry. "Are you okay?"

Maya squeezed her eyes shut and gently shook her head, physically shaking free of the memory. "Sorry," she said, drawing in a deep breath. When she opened her eyes, she saw the dining room table again.

"Hey, don't." Conall flipped the tablet shut. "Was it something I said?"

"No. Well, kind of." Maya exhaled roughly. "It's just . . . I know her. Richter's data courier, I mean. We were kind of friends. For a while, anyway."

"No shit. What's she like?"

Brilliant. Confident. Generous. Relentless. Cara had been all of those things—sweet on the surface but capable of pivoting on a dime to swift and ruthless vengeance. Cara had known the leverage she held as Richter's data courier—not of her official position, but the reflected power of the fear Richter inspired. And she'd used it. Constantly.

"Complicated," Maya said finally. "She's complicated."

"I bet." Conall shoved the tablet away and raised his voice. "Hey, are we eating soon?"

"Absolutely," Dani declared. "Gray and Mace will just have to hope there are leftovers."

"We made plenty." Knox smiled reassuringly at Maya as he carried the huge stew pot over to the table, and that was when she really thought about what Conall had said before.

Gray . . . was with Mace.

Gray was with the medic.

Worry knotted in her gut so tight that not even the scent of Knox's fresh bread could revive her hunger. She glanced at the empty chair where Gray normally sat and tried to pretend everything was fine as dishes were passed around the table.

But she couldn't relax.

Finally, Gray and Mace stepped through the back door, deep in hushed conversation. Then Gray looked up, and his eyes locked with hers.

And he smiled.

The biggest knot unraveled. But Maya studied Gray's face as he crossed to the table, and pinpricks of worry remained. Most people probably wouldn't notice. His expression was unremarkable. Maybe even unusually relaxed. But his stride was a little off, his usual grace and precision replaced by the forced casualness of someone who couldn't entirely trust his body would do what he told it to. There were shadows beneath his eyes, and the lines around them were deeper than they should have been.

He slid into the chair next to her, and Maya snuck her hand under the table to find his. "You okay?"

He squeezed her hand. "I'm good."

She wanted to tell him that he didn't have to be. That he could show her his weakness, and she'd take care of him, the way he had taken care of her. But Conall jabbed her with an elbow to get her attention, and she had to release Gray's hand to take the basket of bread and tear off a hunk.

The last time they'd tried a family dinner, Knox had ended up with a knife in his shoulder. But no one said anything as Mace slid into what was now his customary seat—the one with the quickest path to the exit. He didn't exactly look *comfortable* as he ladled stew into his bowl, but at least he was less jumpy.

Knox surveyed them all, looking happy enough to burst. So did Nina, for that matter. Just a proud mom and dad overseeing their misfit band of rogue supersoldiers, fugitive criminals, evil clones, and one random superkid.

It was ridiculous. And kind of perfect. Maya snuck her hand under the table to find Gray's again, and this time she didn't let go.

TECHCORPS PROPRIETARY DATA,
L1 SECURITY CLEARANCE

DC-035's Year 16 benchmark tests have been flagged as abnormal. Her inconsistent performance is likely related to her unorthodox level of extraneous studies.

Recommend immediate cessation of unnecessary education, along with a four-month course of remedial dissociation and meditative training.

Internal Memo, July 2078

NINETEEN

Gray stuck around after dinner to help clean up. Knox and Nina kept feeding them all, so the least he could do was pitch in without complaint.

Then he got caught between Dani, who was washing the dishes, and Rafe, who was drying and putting them away. Normally, their customary bickering would amuse or at least entertain Gray. But Dani was in a mood, and she seemed hell-bent on sharpening her claws on Rafe.

Rafe, of course, responded to every swipe with increasingly outrageous flirtation. His lazy drawl and teasing come-ons only pissed her off even more. Eventually, Gray made his excuses and practically fled the kitchen, leaving them to handle the dishes on their own.

They barely noticed.

Gray headed upstairs to see Maya, then stood outside her bedroom door without knocking for so long that Nina wandered by. She smiled and told him to check the catwalk that connected their buildings.

The night air was surprisingly cool as he climbed the steel stairs past the kudzu and swung out onto the catwalk. Maya was sitting cross-legged in the middle of the expanse, her back resting against the railing, her gaze fixed on the distant lights of the Hill.

He cleared his throat. "Mind some company?"

Maya started, her gaze swinging to him. A smile lit her face as she patted the spot next to her. "Not at all."

He sat next to her and stretched his legs out in front of him. The catwalk wasn't quite wide enough to accommodate their length, so his boots dangled between the railings. "That's what the Hill looks like from here?"

"Yeah. Almost pretty, huh?" She shook her head. "It's not that far away. Not even twenty kilometers. But it's like a different world up there."

Curiosity assailed him. The key to understanding Maya lay somewhere between them and the distant, twinkling lights. "Which building did you grow up in? Can you see it from here?"

"The tallest one." She pointed to the central TechCorps headquarters, which thrust skyward in the midst of a cluster of massive skyscrapers. Bright lights on the roof shone straight up into the air, giving the impression that the building itself extended into the starless sky. "Everything above the two hundredth floor is considered a penthouse. Each floor belonged to a different executive. Birgitte's was 217."

The TechCorps treated its data couriers well—materially speaking, anyway. They had innumerable creature comforts, their glittering cages stuffed with baubles and trinkets. To a lesser extent, they did the same thing with their Protectorate techies. Conall often spoke wistfully of having every wish fulfilled, every whim indulged. Maya's situation would have been even more luxurious.

But false. Everything about that excess was meant as a distraction, to make the DCs forget that they were glorified copy machines, walking, talking memory banks with no independence, no free will.

No life outside those shining walls.

Gray may have grown up in a grubby orphanage, but at least his childhood had been honest in its deprivation. No one would have looked on and envied it for short-sighted, misguided reasons.

He reached out and clasped Maya's hand. Her fingers were warm, soft except for where the blunt edges of her nails pressed against his skin. "I did *not* grow up on the Hill." He pointed off to their left, where heavy darkness obscured the roads and buildings. "St. Jude's was right over there, on North Avenue. Not far away at all."

"The orphanage?" she asked softly.

"It's gone now. Burned to the ground close to ten years ago." He tried to smile. "Someone saved me the trouble."

Maya tugged their joined hands over to rest on her knee. She ran her fingertips lightly over the backs of his knuckles, a sweetly soothing caress. "Do you want to tell me about it?"'

"You don't really want to hear it, do you?"

"It's you," she whispered. "I want to hear anything you want to share with me."

It wasn't pretty, his life. He'd sketched a vague picture for her before, a rough outline that left out most of the depth and the shadows. Filling all that in by talking would mean she could never forget even the slightest, silliest detail.

But when she said she wanted to know him, Gray *believed her.*

"We had visitors," he began haltingly. He wasn't sure how to describe the strange mix of hopeful parents and shrewd businesspeople that had flowed in and out of the home. "Some were people looking to adopt. But there were also folks from local businesses—tradesmen who were looking for cheap apprentices. Shopping for labor, essentially."

He glanced over at her, braced for her horrified expression. But she only gazed at him, waiting.

So he continued.

"The nuns only bothered to show the really little kids to the prospective parents. That's all they wanted, anyway. Babies. But depending on who you went to work for, apprenticing wasn't half bad. They'd feed you and clothe you, but mostly they'd teach you, so at least you'd come out of it knowing how to do a job. And some of them were decent people, maybe even most."

She stroked his palm, the caress gentle and soothing. "But you ended up somewhere else."

Not because he hadn't wanted it. For years, he'd done his best to distinguish himself in the eyes of the local tradesmen—he'd demonstrated his strength, his stamina, his cleverness. But he'd been passed over every single time, left to rot in the orphanage and be turned out the moment the clock ticked over on his childhood.

"The Protectorate recruiters were the only ones who wanted to take me on," he admitted. "I don't know why I'm not blowing glass or laying brick. A trick of the Fates, I guess."

"Oh, Gray." She shifted to her knees so she could face him, her eyes soft with echoed pain. "I'm sorry."

"It could have been worse. But you can't help but wonder . . ." He took a deep breath and plunged ahead. "What was wrong with me? What did they see that was so unbearable?"

"*Nothing* is wrong with you." Her voice was fierce. "If they couldn't see what you are, something was wrong with them."

He smiled—at her insistence, her sincerity, and the sheer lack of logic in the assertion. "You're biased."

"What, because of the time you lured me into a trap? Or my boss thinking you were a random serial killer?" She huffed and smoothed his hair back from his forehead. "Gray, I had every fucking reason in the world to look at you and see someone bad. But do you know what I see?"

He suspected he did, and he longed for and dreaded the answer in equal measure. "What?"

"You're careful. You're guarded. How could you not be?" She leaned closer, her voice a whisper. "But you're loyal. And patient. And protective. You think through everything and don't make a move until you know what it will cost. And you're so, so gentle with me."

If only those last two things were true. He hadn't seen this coming, hadn't known she would care *this much*—

And he was dying.

The fair thing, the *right* thing, would be to walk away. To back off and give her a little distance while it was still possible. Right now, she would mourn him, but that pain would be a mere drop compared to the ocean of grief she would feel if they grew closer. If they fell in love.

She stared down at him, her dark eyes gleaming in the moonlight. Tension twisted between them, smoldering like a banked fire. Gray's heart throbbed in his ears, and he felt himself reaching out to draw her near.

He should pull away.

He *needed* to pull away.

Instead, he tugged her closer. "May I?"

Her hand dropped to his shoulder to steady herself, but her body closed the space between them willingly. "I trust you."

The words almost did what his own internal struggle hadn't, but the tension curled around them like ink in water, blotting out everything but *Maya*.

He wasn't strong enough to let her go. Not yet. She gasped as he pulled her into his lap, her knees on either side of his hips, and his body tightened, as much from the sound as from the contact.

Maya's free hand landed on the railing to the side of his head. Her grip crushed some of the honeysuckle twined with the kudzu, scenting the air as she stared at him from two inches away, her breathing quick, her eyes liquid with desire. "Gray."

The dull ache in his belly sharpened. "Kiss me, Maya."

Her eyes drifted shut. The first brush of her lips was hesitant, soft warmth feathering across his lips before she swayed away. But she came back again, and again, a quiet hum of yearning leaving her as her fingers dug into his shoulder.

His calm shattered. He took her head in his hands and tilted it, fitting his mouth more closely to hers. Her lips parted, and he pressed the advantage, gliding his tongue between them.

She shook against him, whimpering into his mouth. She squirmed in his lap, hips grinding down against his erection, and he had to lock his hands around her hips to freeze her in place before his control snapped.

Her whimper was of protest this time. Her nails pricked the back of his neck, in demand. In warning. A heartbeat later she tore her lips from his. She hid her face against his shoulder, panting for breath. "Oh . . . Oh *fuck*."

Too much. "Are you all right?"

"I think so?" After another moment, she lifted her head. Her hands trembled slightly as she cupped his face. "I keep thinking I can manage this. That if I'm calm, or I'm ready, I can touch you and it won't just sweep me under." Her gaze dropped to his mouth, and she swept out her thumb to touch his lower lip. "It's not getting easier. It's getting harder. Because every time I touch you, I want you more."

"Does that mean you want to stop?"

Instead of answering, she kissed him again. Slow and sweet, her lips parting this time in silent but certain invitation. When his tongue met hers she groaned, sliding her fingers up to tangle in his hair. The kiss flashed from warm to hot, her body pressed tight to his, her hips fighting his grip in an attempt to roll against him.

This time when she broke away, she pressed her forehead to his temple, her panting breaths hot against his ear. "It's scary as hell," she whispered. "And it's still the best thing I've ever felt in my life."

It didn't have to be one or the other. It never did. "As long as it's worth it."

"It's worth it to me." Her voice trembled. "Is it to you?"

For years, Knox had trusted Gray as his second-in-command, as a guiding force when he wasn't sure what path to take. Even though the other Silver Devils outranked him, it was his judgment that their captain sought and trusted. Because Gray always knew the right thing to do, even when they couldn't do it.

Just like he knew the right thing now. He needed to let Maya down easy, to push her away so gradually and gently that she thought the distance was *her* idea.

He needed to disconnect.

Instead, he chose the hard truth. "Yes. You're worth it."

The tension in her body eased. She turned her head, her cheek coming to rest trustingly on his shoulder as she relaxed in his arms. "Is this okay?" she asked softly. "If we just . . . sit for a bit?"

"It's more than okay," he told her.

It was perfect.

MACE

Ava didn't look much like her sister.

Mace knew they were clones. He recognized that their features were identical in appearance and arrangement—same nose, same eyes, same long limbs and lean torsos contributing to the same height.

The devil was, as always, in the details. Sure, they had the same general build, but Nina had dedicated more of her time in the gym to developing strength and stamina. Ava was leaner, with muscles conditioned more for flexibility and speed. Stealth.

No wonder she was so good at sneaking around.

She watched him dispassionately as he levered himself up onto the exam bed and peeled off his shirt. That was another difference—even when she wasn't actively smiling, Nina's eyes often danced with warmth. Ava's resting state was more of an icy glare.

He smiled at her, and her brow furrowed, clearly discouraging any friendly overtures. "I assume there were trackers you removed yourself? Where were they located?"

"There were four—three sub-Q and one submuscular. Which would you like to know about?"

That little crease between her brows deepened. "You cut out a submuscular tracker on your own?"

She sounded so shocked that if his ego had been a little more fragile, he'd have been hurt. "I *am* a medic. Though, technically, it was installed between the rectus femoris and the vastus lateralis." He arched an eyebrow at her. "Wanna see my scar?"

"Not at the moment."

"Keep the pants on. Got it."

There was that icy glare again. In frigid silence, she sat on one of the rolling stools, crossed her legs, and unfolded a tablet to balance on her knee. "Nina tells me you escaped from Tobias Richter. That must be an interesting story."

More like a frantic, desperate one. His wrists itched from phantom restraints, and he had to carefully moderate his breathing. Flashes of bloody memories began to play behind his closed lids every time he blinked, threatening to overwhelm him.

So he held his eyes steadfastly open as he answered her. "A small convoy was tasked with transporting me from TechCorps HQ to another location. I'm not sure where or even why. I took advantage of the opportunity."

Ava reached into her bag and withdrew what looked like a handheld radioisotope identification device and clipped it onto the front of her tablet. "Do you remember when they embedded your trackers?"

"I wish I didn't. But they weren't big fans of anesthesia in the torture chambers."

"No, it rather defeats the purpose, doesn't it?" She paused, and for the first time she seemed to actually notice his bare chest. Starting at his belt and traveling up, she visually cataloged every scar they'd left on his body, her gaze meticulous but, sadly, completely lacking in carnal appreciation. "Did they forgo regeneration therapy entirely, or are the scars . . . aesthetic?"

Mace couldn't answer. Not because he didn't remember, but because everything blurred together in a patchwork of misery. Not pain, *misery*. Because the physical torture, while sufficiently horrifying at the outset of his secret captivity, was the least of it. He'd learned quickly enough that Richter had even more harrowing torments in store for him.

"Couldn't tell you," he said finally. "They may have wanted to hurt Knox as much as possible, or they could have been lazy. I never asked."

"Understandable." Her fingers danced across the tablet's surface as she looked down, and the machine beeped softly. "If you decide someday that you'd like to be rid of them, I know someone who is quite deft at scar tissue revision."

"I imagine you do." Her skin was flawless—brutally, calculatedly so. "But I'm not scared of a few scars."

"Everyone has to choose their own way of dealing with the memories." She pursed her lips and tapped the tablet again. "I can't detect your implant."

"I know." At her questioning look, he shrugged. "Luna suppressed the signals on our implants to guard against broadcast scans."

"Really?" Both of Ava's eyebrows shot up. "The software I'm using can find hidden and passive signals. That girl is inordinately clever." She swiped her fingers over the tablet and it gave a final beep. "Well, I don't detect any trackers, which is good. No radioactive isotopes, either. If he's tracking you, he invented a new method."

"I know that, too. We already checked for everything, including isotope tags. Twice."

She stared at him for a moment, unblinking. Then her expression blanked. Her movements were precise as she unclipped her scanner, but there was temper in the way she snapped her tablet shut. "If that's the case, then why did you agree to let me do this?"

"Well, you didn't exactly ask, did you? You just *informed* me, and I didn't argue. Figured I'd just be wasting my time." He smiled again. "You know, you're kinda cute when you're pissed off."

Ava's blank stare hardened. "I am not, nor have I ever in my life been, *cute*."

"*So* damn cute." He braced his hands on the side of the exam table and paused before hopping down. "Can I get dressed now?"

"You know, I still haven't ruled out stabbing you."

He'd be tempted to let her. True, he was mostly calling her cute to irritate her, but that didn't make it untrue.

In fact, Mace was surprised by just how *not* untrue it was.

"So what's your story, anyway?" he asked as he dragged his shirt back over his head.

"My story?" She huffed as she slipped her equipment back into her bag. "I thought you had it all figured out. I show up here to be creepy all over my sister's idyllic life and then leave again."

"You don't always, apparently. Leave, I mean."

"I occasionally do irrational things to make my sister happy. Like sleep on a cot instead of in my penthouse." She eyed him warily as she rose from the stool. "And not stab dangerous strangers who are lurking on her roof."

She was as evasive as she was prickly. "Fine, don't tell me. It's more fun to make it up, anyway. Like . . . you trained as a knife-thrower in a traveling circus. That's why you're obsessed with stabbing people."

"Don't be ridiculous," she retorted. "A knife-thrower in a traveling circus couldn't afford these boots."

"Hey, it could have been a very posh circus."

"You're closer than you think." She swung the strap of her bag over her head. "Do your best to remain sane, James Mason. Surprisingly, I'd rather not have to kill you."

He actually almost believed her.

RICHTER

The beating heart of the TechCorps was 1,027 meters of concrete, steel, and glass thrusting high into the clouds to dominate the Atlanta skyline. There were fifty-two elevators, forty-seven doors with access to street- and sublevels, thirty penthouse AirLift pads, and nineteen full-size landing pads, three of which could accommodate the Protectorate's largest transport helicopters. Twenty-four skyways connected the central headquarters to seven smaller buildings, with a combined 407 points of potential access.

It was Tobias Richter's job to control each and every one.

The sheer impossibility of such a task might have daunted a lesser man. Richter lacked the capacity to be daunted. In the wake of the Flares, he'd coolly evaluated the various opportunities presented by the ensuing chaos and recognized two realities:

Without federal oversight or local regulation, the ruthlessness of the Board would escalate without limits.

The only way to avoid being their eventual prey was to be their most dangerous predator.

From his office on the hundredth floor of TechCorps Headquarters, Richter held most of the Hill in his grasp. He controlled all elevators and doors of the main building. Through the mandatory RFID chips embedded in every TechCorps employee or subcontractor, Richter could track their locations and grant—or revoke—entry to all those points of access at his whim. His most trusted driver sat ready on his private landing pad, and his personal elevator ensured that his sprawling network of informants could come and go discreetly.

Today, that was an especially good thing. Lucas Taylor hadn't even bothered to dress appropriately for the Hill. His patched denim jeans and scuffed boots alone would have marked him as an outsider. The leather vest that bared his tattooed arms was positively barbaric. Long hours in the sun had tanned his pale skin and lightened his sandy hair. He slouched in a chair, looking large enough to collapse it, and stared at Richter with barely contained hostility.

That was the problem with deep-cover agents. Without a sufficient leash, you risked losing them as they sank into a comfortable life on the outside. The precarious state of their position could fade. Loyalties could shift.

The fact that Taylor was here at all was an indication that Richter hadn't lost him completely. Still, a tug on the leash couldn't hurt. "You'll be happy to know that your sister is doing very well. So are your nieces. Coralie is quite a bright little thing. She'll be taking the general aptitude test next year, I hear."

Taylor's jaw clenched. The anger intensified, and Richter didn't mind. You couldn't threaten a man's family and not expect hostility in return. The expensive genetic treatment that had saved his sister's life might have been the initial leverage that pushed Lucas Taylor into Richter's employ over a decade ago, but fear for his nieces' safety kept him in line now.

Richter allowed Taylor a moment to regain his self-control, then offered him a polite smile. "So. Whatever you've found must be important if you've come in person."

With visible effort, Taylor swallowed his anger. "That BOLO you sent out? For the rogue Protectorate squad?"

A thrill of excitement whispered up Richter's spine, though he let none of it show on his face. Or in his voice, which he kept deliberately casual. "The Silver Devils?"

"Yeah." Taylor dipped into his vest pocket and pulled out a data stick, which he tossed onto Richter's desk. "I found them."

"Intriguing." Hiding his eagerness, Richter plucked up the stick and rose. The firewalled computer he used for data from his various informants was set up on its own desk, connected to a massive monitor embedded into the wall. More than one traitor had left this office in a body bag after handing him a drive loaded with malware, thinking he'd be foolish enough to plug it into a networked computer.

No matter how tight the leash, Richter *never* trusted an outsider.

This stick held no viruses, just a video file that passed his security scan without red flags. Richter played it.

The monitor filled with an outdoor scene. A sea of tables spilled out from a warehouse's open doors, each heaped with various items for sale. It took him only a moment to recognize Jaden Montgomery's open-air market, though it was significantly larger than he'd realized. Allowing the rabble to the south a pressure valve to keep them from the simmering edge of outright rebellion was one thing, but Jaden Montgomery was clearly becoming something more dangerous.

Richter would have to consider that.

The market wasn't the immediate concern, however. As Richter watched, Rafael Morales strolled across the screen. A few moments later, Garrett Knox himself drifted into frame, his attention fixed on a tall brunette who strode confidently at his side.

Heady vindication snaked through him. For *months* he'd known the truth, even as the Board shut him down at every turn. The Silver Devils were dead, they insisted. Their bodies had been recovered, their DNA and implants confirmed. When Richter had pushed back against their conviction, he'd received his first ever reprimand. The Board did not want to spend its time chasing ghosts.

The Board did not want to spend its *money* chasing ghosts.

Of course, he'd done it anyway. What was the point of becoming the dominant predator if you couldn't secure the resources to do what was necessary, regardless of the foolish whims of the sheep?

Granted, he'd made an error of judgment with James Mason. He'd seemed like the perfect weapon—pure emotional devastation, delivered directly to Garrett Knox's door. Of course, that devastation had depended heavily on Richter's ability to break the fool. Who could have imagined that a *medic*, of all people, would prove stronger than the worst Richter's team could devise?

They'd wasted months trying to turn him into an obedient killer. Something in him resisted as strongly as if the refusal were coded into his damn DNA. And then that disaster with the transport convoy—Mason had been quick enough to kill the soldiers who were meant to bring him to a secure location. The competent brutality of it had irked Richter most of all. Not so much the loss of men, but the proof that at least *some* of the deadly lessons he'd attempted to impart to the medic had clearly stuck.

He'd made MD-701 stronger, deadlier, faster, and angrier, and then he'd lost him. Failure upon failure—just like everything involving Garrett Knox and his squad.

It was a good thing he'd kept the entire mission off the books. He would have been hard-pressed to rationalize the millions of credits that had evaporated when Mason had cut free of his trackers and vanished into the city. Richter was already on thin ice with the Board for losing control of the Silver Devils to begin with, not to mention his insistence that they weren't dead at all.

He shouldn't have tried to get fancy with James Mason, not when the real solution had been within his grasp the whole time. Not aggressive action, but patience and trust.

His carefully cultivated information network had never failed him.

The Silver Devils were alive, and now he had *proof*. He could rub the Board's collective nose in its error, make it clear that Tobias Richter had been the only one to see the truth. Their safety depended on believing in him.

Their lives depended on deferring to him.

"Listen, the chicks they're running with are good people, okay? There ain't a Protectorate soldier out there who isn't elbow deep in the blood of decent folks, so I don't give a shit what you do to them. But you gotta leave Nina and her girls . . ."

Taylor's blustering demands faded to a distant buzz. Matthew Gray had appeared on the screen, stopping in front of a table overflowing with tech. Oh, now there was a betrayal that *hurt*. The rest of them Richter had had little use for, and Garrett Knox had always been a particular thorn in his side . . . but 66-793 had been something special. Elite. Cool and unruffled. The best sniper in the history of the TechCorps and an unparalleled weapon.

How many times had Richter stepped in to protect him? That meddlesome bitch Birgitte Skovgaard would have tossed him aside on one of her idealistic crusades to purify the ranks more than once without Richter's intervention. He alone had recognized Sergeant Gray's value.

And the traitor had walked away without a backward glance.

On the screen, Gray smiled. An odd expression, one Richter had never seen on him before. He was looking down at a short, curvy woman whose face bore a smile that didn't look odd at all. In fact, the familiarity of it stole his breath.

With a tap of his fingers, Richter froze the screen. Was he imagining the resemblance because his anger at Birgitte felt so fresh?

Heart-shaped face. Warm-brown skin. Big, brown eyes framed by thick lashes. The elbow-length black braids were new and so was the makeup. Thick eyeliner, shimmering colors. Her face had lost the fullness of childhood, and the cosmetics expertly played up the difference. He doubted facial recognition would have flagged her, though he suspected the cleverly designed sunglasses propped on her head were one of the ways she'd thwarted the city's surveillance all this time.

Computers could be fooled, but Richter couldn't. This was not his imagination. It was a damn miracle.

"Where are they?" he demanded, cutting off whatever Taylor had been saying.

From the corner of his eye, he saw Taylor pull out a second data stick. "If you promise me you won't fuck with Nina or her girls, I'll give you this. It's the data on a corp they're chasing. I figure if you find them, the Devils will come to you."

Richter turned back to the screen. No, the frozen image wasn't a miracle. It was the simple result of his incredible foresight. He'd embedded his spies everywhere. He'd *earned* this. "I'm not interested in Nina," he said truthfully. "And, of course, I would never do anything to compromise your cover. Your position with Montgomery is extremely valuable to me."

"Fine." The second data stick landed on Richter's desk with a soft clatter. "Don't cross me on this. I mean it."

"Of course not," Richter lied. He would allow the man his bluster today. There was plenty of time later to give the leash another firm yank. The threat of his niece being swept up into a dangerous experimental program would be sufficient, even after Richter broke his promise.

Which he would.

The private elevator door whispered shut, carrying Taylor to the sublevel tunnel system, where he'd vanish back into the mass of foot traffic on the Hill. Richter couldn't care less. He stepped closer to the monitor and swiped his hands across the screen, blowing up the image.

Marjorie Chevalier stared back at him. Birgitte Skovgaard's intractable, rebellious data courier. The fact that someone had smuggled her out of the TechCorps under his nose was proof that Birgitte's rebellion still seethed through the halls of his empire like a poison. The names of every remaining traitor were locked behind those clever brown eyes.

And she was smiling up at Gray like he was the most beautiful thing she'd ever seen.

A touch just beneath his ear activated his comms. "Cara?"

His data courier's voice came immediately. "Sir?"

"You can finish cataloging security footage later. I need you up here."

"On my way."

He disengaged his comms and went back to staring at the gift in front of him.

Life was presenting Richter with a second chance. This time, he wouldn't move recklessly. He'd be *deliberate*. Once he had Marjorie Chevalier in his grasp again, he wouldn't stop until he'd peeled every last secret from her precocious brain.

Then the Board could cross him at their peril.

November 13th, 2078

Marjorie is a ghost.

Four months of dissociation training has changed her. She no longer laughs. She rarely smiles. She's stopped studying, stopped learning, stopped feeling. Her gaze barely focuses. She listens, remembers, and repeats. The perfect data courier.

I hate what they've done to her. I hate myself for allowing it.

Never again.

The Recovered Journal of Birgitte Skovgaard

TWENTY

Gray hovered outside Maya's bedroom door, turning the worn hardcover book over and over in his hands. He wasn't exactly invited—hell, Maya might not even be home—but he hadn't seen her since breakfast, and he'd made her a promise.

He'd spent the day being poked and prodded and scanned by Mace, who'd taken his vow to study Gray's condition as seriously as he took everything. It left Gray with a feeling that wasn't quite hope but was far more comfortable than the fear that had ridden him the past couple of days. Peace, maybe. An understanding of his fate, if not an acceptance of it.

For now, that was good enough.

Finally, he rapped on the door.

It opened after only a few seconds. Maya stood on the other side, in tiny cotton shorts and a tank top with one strap drooping down her shoulder. She blinked, clearly surprised to see him, but before he could speak, her gaze dropped to the book. A sudden, brilliant smile lit her face. "Did you come to read to me?"

"I figured a promise is a promise. *The Call of the Wild.*" He held up the battered book. "I found it in your library."

She stepped aside, pulling the door wider in silent invitation.

He'd been in her room before, but he'd never really looked at it. It had just seemed to fit her, possessing a sense of *rightness* that hadn't merited further consideration.

Bookshelves lined the walls, meticulously hung, arrow-straight and evenly spaced. But that was where the regimented order ended. Those shelves overflowed with items—books and little boxes, mementos and folded paper figurines. The rest of the wall space was covered with posters and other hangings, as brightly colored as the lamps with their stained-glass shades.

A large desk sat against the far wall, covered with tablets and components and other bits of tech. And beside it . . .

The bed, made but a little rumpled, as if she'd been lying on top of the covers. Gray gestured to it, stifling the urge to clear his throat. "Can I sit?"

"Sure." Maya slid onto the head, her legs crossed and her back resting against the wall. She dragged one of the colorful pillows into her lap and smiled shyly. "Sorry, it's kind of a mess."

"It's nice. I have a bunk, with all my stuff in a trunk at the foot of it."

"Really?" She hugged the pillow to her chest and studied him. "Because y'all are still working on stuff over there? Or is that how you like it?"

"Yes, and kind of?" He shrugged, suddenly feeling self-conscious. "Kids in the home would take anything that wasn't nailed down. You learned fast not to get too attached to *stuff*. And then there's the Protectorate—they're not exactly known for their luxurious accommodations." He shrugged again. "It's a habit, I guess."

Maya reached out to touch his hand, her fingers soft. "You've never really had a space of your own, have you?"

"Bouncing from an orphanage to basic training doesn't leave a lot of room for it."

"No, I guess not."

Her pity hurt—not because he couldn't take it, but because he hadn't come here to drag her down.

So he lifted the book. "Shall we?"

They stretched out on her bed, Gray with his back propped against the headboard and Maya curled up by his side.

"Is this okay?" she asked softly.

"Yeah." But words weren't enough, not for this, so he pulled her closer, until she was nestled against him, her body flush against his side. "Better?"

Her eyes gleamed with an affection that tightened his chest and the rest of him, all at the same time. "Better."

He cleared his throat, opened the book to the first page, and began to read. "'Buck did not read the newspapers, or he would have known that trouble was brewing, not alone for himself, but for every tide-water dog, strong of muscle and with warm, long hair, from Puget Sound to San Diego. Because men, groping in the Arctic darkness, had found a yellow metal . . .'"

Maya made a soft noise of contentment and practically melted into him. He smiled through the next few paragraphs and shook his head a little. He knew she liked his voice, but he hadn't realized how *affected* she was by it.

He'd have to read to her more often.

By the time he finished the first chapter and prepared to move on to the next, Maya had practically molded herself to him, her heat warming him even through their clothes. His voice grew huskier, then flat-out hoarse, and he had to keep clearing his throat.

All the while, Maya's face tilted more toward his, up and up until her parted lips presented an unmistakable invitation.

"Maya," he groaned.

She lifted her hands to frame his face. "Gray."

He covered her hands with his, intending to pull them away from his face, but somehow, they just sat there like that. "Maya, we need to talk."

Her gaze didn't waver. "I know."

"Do you?"

She wet her lips. "I know people, Gray. People who owe me favors. I can reach out . . ."

His stomach twisted. "No. If that's what you're telling yourself, we can't do this. I need to know that you get it, Maya. That you understand my situation."

Her brown eyes seemed huge, her expression on the knife-edge between hope and hurt. "You've been spending a lot of time with Mace. Does he . . . What does he think?"

He wished he had better words to give her, but this was the truth. His truth. Theirs. "I'm dying. He can give me more time, but that's it. I'm sorry, but . . . he can't fix me."

She was silent for a long time, her hands still beneath his. Her gaze roamed his face, before her eyes locked with his again. "What do you want for the time you have left?"

He wanted her—and if he said as much, she would fall recklessly into his arms. And it didn't seem right to want anything, *anyone,* not when he'd be gone so soon. He felt like a thief, snatching at things that weren't destined for his grasp.

And the fact that it was Maya only made it worse. She wouldn't take the pain along with the sweetness, knowing that, one day, the pain would fade and leave behind some beautiful memories. She'd remember *all* of it, every whispered word. He'd be gone, but he'd be haunting her just the same.

He pulled her hand to his mouth, kissed her palm. "I need you to say it. Say that you understand."

"You're dying." Her voice wavered. "It doesn't matter. If you told me tonight was all we could ever have, I'd still want it. You don't have to promise me forever to be worth it. You're worth it because you're you."

Because you're you. The words made a giddy warmth bloom in his chest. Maybe he didn't have to promise her the future, a life he didn't have in his power to give. But this—one stolen moment followed by another, perfect snapshots of peace where they hadn't expected to find any. This could be enough.

He could be enough.

It was the most natural thing in the world, pulling her closer. Stroking her cheek. Pressing his lips to hers.

Falling into her.

Maya thought she was prepared for Gray's kiss.

It wasn't as if it was the first time. She'd kissed him before, up on the roof. She should have been prepared for the rush of sensation, the giddy overwhelming *intensity* of it.

But it wasn't less intense with repetition. It was *more.*

Her mind latched on to every individual detail, savoring it. Exploring it. Wallowing in it. The way he threaded his fingers through her braids to cup the back of her skull, the firm heat of his mouth, how hard her heart pounded when he tilted his head and teased her lower lip with his tongue. And oh, the *sound* he made—all low and deep, a hum of satisfaction as she tangled her fingers in his hair and parted her lips for him.

"It feels like we've been waiting for this forever," he whispered.

Oh, that voice. Liquid gold with a smoky rasp she could feel to her toes. She let her head fall back and shivered as his lips grazed her jaw. "Your voice."

"You like it?" He spoke the words against her throat, chasing tingles through her whole body.

"It's the only thing I've ever heard that I'm glad I'll remember forever."

His hands settled on her hips, and he lifted his head. "Then I'll use it as much as I can."

He kissed her again, his tongue sliding between her lips as his hands moved up and beneath the hem of her tank top. The soft brush of his fingertips up her spine drove a moan from her, a helpless sound lost to his mouth.

Maya tightened her grip on his hair, unsure if she wanted to drag him away or pull him closer. If the barest touch felt this intense, she wasn't sure she'd survive actual fucking. She'd never tried before like this—all of her hard-won TechCorps training abandoned, her rigid grip on her other senses eased.

What a damn waste that had been.

When she dragged his head back, it was only so she could kiss his jaw. His cheek. His throat. She parted her lips and savored the salty taste of his skin. Inhaled and wrapped herself in his scent—aftershave this time, she thought, and that hint of pine from when he'd helped with the dishes after dinner.

His hand splayed wide between her shoulder blades, and she arched back into his touch, shuddering. "More."

He growled softly.

The sound of it rumbled through her. *Need* pulsed, bright and hot. Arousal made her ache, already so sharp she wanted to crawl into his lap and rock her way to bliss. She dragged his mouth to her throat, gasping as he pressed his teeth against her skin.

But only for a moment. Then pressure eased, only to be replaced by a sharp nip and a not-quite-apologetic hum as he soothed the ravaged spot with his tongue.

Oh God, she was going to fly apart. She'd explode into stardust, but nothing in the world could make her stop feeling every moment of this. She wanted the memory imprinted on her atoms.

She pulled at his hair again, gasping out her command. "More."

He tugged at her shirt, pausing long enough to rasp, "Can I?"

"Yes." Except she had to release him long enough to hold up her arms, but it was worth it when he tossed the fabric aside and touched her again.

His fingertips glided up her ribs, stopping just shy of her breasts. "What do you want, sweetheart? Something slow and endless? Or quick and hot?"

"Endless," she gasped, anticipation a buzz beneath her skin. "Endless and hot. I want to feel you everywhere."

"So hard to please," he teased as he released her again. He caught her gaze and held it as he dropped his hands to the buttons on his shirt and pulled them free, one by one.

She held her breath as he shrugged out of the shirt. She'd seen him in T-shirts that hugged him like a lover, and even shirtless once or twice, but nothing compared to the slow, deliberate baring of skin as he smiled at her in smug confidence.

He was perfect. Of course he was, he'd never had any other option. Nothing marred his skin, no lingering sign of the hundreds of battles he'd fought. The TechCorps would have put him back together again after any injury—not out of any particular concern for him, but because they always took good care of useful tools.

She finally found a single scar on his arm, pale with age, probably from before he'd joined up. She touched it, *shocked* at the heat of his skin, and let her fingers drift up his arm. "I'm not trying to control this," she told him, tracing a fingertip along his collarbone. "I trust you. Even if it gets intense, even if it gets overwhelming. I trust you."

"I'll take care of you," he promised, then gathered her to his chest, skin to skin, and kissed her again.

Her knees slid to either side of his thighs as her head spun. The rough fabric of his jeans rasped over her skin. Her pajama shorts were flimsy, and they might as well have not been there when she rocked her hips against his. She moaned into his mouth as pleasure unspooled low in her belly.

He took over the movement, one arm around her to hold her close and the other at her hip. Unbidden, the music from Convergence whispered through her head, the low bass throbbing through her. She matched the beat, moaning as the movement pressed her bare breasts to his chest. Her nipples were tight and aching; the abrasion from the hair on his chest soothed her and wound her tighter at the same time.

So fast. Too fast. She dragged her lips from his and panted against his cheek, her whole body shaking. "Is it supposed to feel this good?"

"Yes."

She shivered again. His fingers tightened on her hip, guiding her to grind down against his denim-encased erection. Another of those noises escaped him—low, rumbling, almost a growl—and this time she felt the vibrations against her chest.

Her nails pricked his shoulders. She clung to him, her head falling back, her body on fire. He licked a fiery path up her bared throat, then closed his teeth on her jaw and whispered her name.

Maya choked on a desperate noise. The need inside her twisted tight, and the rhythm of her hips faltered as her focus shattered. The moan of loss had barely escaped her when Gray's fingers splayed wide on the small of her back, guiding her against him so right, so *perfect—*

"Take it," he murmured.

She did. All of it. She chased pleasure until it broke over her, and she wallowed in it. Sweaty and messy and glorious, tingling all the way to her toes. It had never been like this before because *she'd* never been like this before—open to the world, hungry to feel, ready to imprint every second of this on her soul.

Release burned through her like wildfire as Gray rasped encouragement against her ear and stroked her skin. When it was over she slumped against him, lips parted against his shoulder, panting for breath. Her head swam and the world spun around her in lazy Technicolor, but nothing hurt. Nothing could.

The crash might be coming, but oh. She wanted to see how high she could go first.

Lifting her head, drunk on sensation, she met his oh-so-smug gaze. "More."

"Careful what you ask for." He laid her back on the bed and stripped away her cotton shorts and her underwear at the same time, leaving her completely naked before him. "You might get it. And then what?"

Distantly, she thought she should be self-conscious. It wasn't like she'd gotten naked in front of very many people. But she loved the way he looked at her, hungry and barely restrained, as if that formidable self-control was the only thing keeping him in check. He was breathing hard too, his gaze drifting down her curves before sliding back up to lock on hers.

"I'm done being careful." She reached out to him, an entreaty. A demand. *"Now."*

Gray stretched out beside her, catching both of her hands in his. He guided them to the bed above her head and held them there as his gaze met hers once again. "Okay?"

She curled her fingers around his hand, grounding herself in the steady touch. Maybe he could keep her from floating away on the fresh wave of anticipation sparked by the heat of his body all along hers. "I trust you."

"I know." He trailed his free hand from her jaw down between her breasts, his fingertips barely grazing her skin. "So open."

The approving whisper tickled her ear and sounded utterly filthy. She arched her body into his touch, eager for it, but his fingers stayed tauntingly gentle. Twisting didn't help, either; he just chuckled against her ear as his knuckles grazed the side of her breast, her collarbone, the soft, sensitive skin over her ribs—anywhere but where she needed him.

Now she knew why he'd pinned her hands down. If she'd had one free she would have tangled her fingers in his hair and dragged his mouth straight to her aching nipple. But she'd asked for endless, and that was what he gave her. Slow strokes, relentlessly patient, until her skin was so sensitized she wondered if she could come again, just like this, just from a low whisper against her ear and his finger tracing an idle path down the center of her chest.

His parted lips brushed her ear, her shoulder, then nothing. Just as she was about to open her eyes, his tongue flicked wet heat over her nipple.

The sudden shock of it drove a cry from her. "Gray!"

Her breath—and the rest of her cries—cut off as he closed his mouth around her nipple and sucked gently. It was exactly what she'd wanted, what she'd *needed*, but it only stoked the craving hollowing her out. She whimpered, lifting her hips in restless entreaty, but the warm hand on her hip pressed her back to the bed.

There was nothing to do but feel it. His lips, his tongue—then his teeth, gentle as they scraped sharp sensation over her skin. Her hips jerked again, but he was relentless as he murmured something she couldn't understand against her skin.

The tone of his voice was enough. Liquid smoke, shivering over her, and she'd barely regained control of her breathing when his mouth closed around the other nipple and started again.

"Please," she rasped, squirming in his grasp. Squeezing her thighs together offered scant relief from the throbbing need. *"Gray."*

He lifted his head. "Look at me."

She forced her eyes open, only to find him hovering above her. Those beautiful Gothic eyes, his always-serious face, the hair that had gotten a little too long and was now wild from her fingers.

That focus. The focus of a sniper who would spend an hour setting up the perfect shot—and all of it was currently centered on her. On her responses.

On her pleasure.

"Watch me." He held her gaze as his fingers slid down, over her stomach.

Oh God, oh God, oh—

"Fuck." His fingers brushed her clit, and pleasure so sharp and bright it almost hurt jolted through her. Her body jerked in response, and he froze, watching her face with that gentle, careful patience. The second graze of his fingers was softer, barely there. Sweeter warmth shuddered through her, and her eyelids drooped.

"Maya."

She forced her eyes back open as he stroked her again. She felt naked for the first time, utterly exposed as he slicked his fingers deeper and watched her every response like he was committing her to memory. It should have been a vulnerable feeling. The fingers locked around her hands were unmovable steel. He had the strength in him to bend metal and shatter stone.

All of that power . . . All of it focused on giving her anything she wanted.

Breathing unsteadily, she let her thighs fall apart. There was no shame left in her. No hesitation. Just want. She stared up into his intense blue eyes and did her best to shake that perfect control. "I want to feel you inside me."

"Getting there." His stare intensified, as if he was refocusing some bottomless well of attention on her. "Patience, sweetheart."

Patience was a distant memory. She was burning up from the inside and parted her lips to tell him so. But his fingers returned—and instead of stroking, they thrust deep. Her words vanished in a satisfied moan. Two thick fingers filled her completely, and the slick sound of him working them into her again was so illicit, she had the wild thought she'd never be able to see his hands again without blushing.

But relief was short-lived. Her body twisted in dizzy knots as he fucked those fingers into her, but it wasn't enough and he knew it. She could *see* it in his eyes, in the hot anticipation there.

He bent and nipped at her earlobe. Then the rasping sound of his voice filled her. "If you want more, tell me. Say the words, Maya."

Gladly. Eagerly. She turned her head and whispered them against his lips. "Make me come."

He kissed her hard, then scraped his teeth over her cheek in a rough caress. "It's going to be so good." His thumb began to circle her clit in slow, steady strokes. "When I finally take you, it's going to be *so good*."

It was already too good. By the second stroke she was trembling on a knife's edge. By the third she was gasping, straining, so close, so close—

"I'll never forget one single goddamn second."

The tension shattered. Orgasm ripped through her, the intensity of it stealing her breath. She couldn't make a sound as the first bright wave of bliss washed over her. Heat raced down her spine and out. Her toes curled. The second wave crashed down harder, and she gasped out his name as the undertow swept her away.

For an eternity, that was all there was. Pleasure, and the echoes of it, and she couldn't tell if she was still coming, or if the memory of it was so bright and real that the physical reaction shivered through her every time it replayed. She whimpered, clutching for something solid.

Gray's hand was there. Warm, strong. She clung to it, following that one contact with reality down her arms. She felt the quilt beneath her back, the heat of Gray's body along one side of her. His free hand was stroking gently over her hip, as soothing as the soft murmurs against her ear.

He peppered her brow with kisses. "You with me?"

"I think so." She couldn't help the lazy smile that curled her lips. "You broke my brain, but only a little."

He was tense, a fine tremor running through his body, but he returned her smile. "And I'm not finished yet."

He shifted to the edge of the bed and took off his boots. The moment they hit the floor, he stood and reached for his belt.

Maya rolled onto her side and watched him, languid satisfaction battling a fresh spark of anticipation at the soft sound of leather against metal. The rasp of a zipper followed, and she held her breath as he moved with his usual careful deliberateness—except this time he was stripping off his pants and everything underneath.

He stood there for a moment, naked, his rapid breathing the only break in his careful control.

Well, almost the only break.

Maya sat up and swung her legs over the bed. He was close enough to touch, and she did, dragging her fingers up the outsides of his thighs. His muscles tensed as she ghosted her fingers across his abdomen. She glanced up at him, meeting those blazing eyes, and smiled. "Can I?"

He caught her wrist. "Only if you want to blow all my careful plans. Literally."

She laughed, tracing the fingers of her free hand back down his hip. "What happened to all that patience and self-control?"

"I've been listening to you moan, that's what." He lifted her in his arms and dropped to the bed, holding her above him. "Feeling you come."

Maya's knees pressed against the quilt, her legs forced wide by the width of his hips. He lowered her slowly, and they both hissed when his erection brushed her clit. She braced both hands on his chest, resisting the urge to grind down against him. "I've never done it this way before," she whispered. "Help me."

He guided her, the taut muscles in his arms standing out in sharp relief, tilting her hips until the head of his cock was perfectly aligned to slide into her.

Then his fingers tightened, digging into her skin. "It's whatever you want," he panted hoarsely. "You're in control."

She wanted to go slow. To torment him the way he'd teased her. To watch pleasure break over him as she made it last forever. But he was so hard, and she was so *empty*, and the first downward rock of her hips drove a helpless groan from him that shattered her self-control.

Digging her nails into his chest, she took him deep. The stretch of it was dizzying, but nothing compared to the thrill she got from watching his face. His lips parted around a silent moan as he drove his head back against the bed, his expression as unguarded as she'd ever seen it.

She shuddered and gave an experimental rock. Gray's jaw clenched, his fingers flexing on her hips, and she reveled in the tiny fractures of his control.

"Maya."

Oh, she was drunk on the feeling of him, already floating as she rocked again. The memory of recent pleasure teased at her, tingles shivering down her spine every time she took him deep.

"Maya."

He growled her name this time, his eyes wild, and she let her hands slide up to curl in the quilt on either side of his head. The angle was sharper this way, the friction exquisite. She nipped at his jaw, then moaned as his hips jerked up in response. Bright lights sparked on the edge of her vision like fireflies, a warning that the high couldn't last forever. Every touch, every sound, the scent of him and the *taste* of him—she pressed her parted lips to his throat and licked his skin, salt and sweat and lightning.

Maya pressed her forehead to his. Her braids cascaded over her shoulders to form a curtain around her, even the brush of her own hair over her skin a liquid heat.

Too much. It was too much. And she didn't care. She grabbed on to the quilt as if for dear life and told Gray what she wanted. What she *needed*. "Fuck me, Gray."

His fingers tightened on her hips. He lifted her effortlessly and thrust up into her, the first stroke powerful enough to make her limbs feel boneless. It didn't matter. Gray held her in place as if it were effortless, all of his strength and grace focused on one obscene and glorious goal.

The first orgasm might have been a memory. She couldn't tell the difference anymore—she could feel his thumb circling her clit like it was happening now, could feel his lips against her ear, his teeth on her throat, his tongue on her nipple. Pleasure was a kaleidoscope, every hard thrust turning over a new pattern made of memories overlapping reality.

Then he shifted the angle somehow, and his next thrust ground the base of his shaft against her clit, and *that* was new. She slammed back into the moment, pressing her open mouth to his shoulder as if she could muffle the scream building inside her. But everything was bright and hot and beautiful, and her whole body shook as the pressure inside her unraveled without warning.

She moaned at the beauty of it, especially when Gray groaned her name and his final thrust carried them both into bliss.

Maya floated there. For hours. For centuries. It was better and worse than the last high. Tiny aftershocks trembled through her. She couldn't see the stars and didn't know if she remembered their names. But her cheek was pressed to warm skin, and beneath she heard a steady thud.

She focused on it as it slowed, blocking out everything but that steady thump. Her shaky breaths slowed in time . . . in for five beats, out for five beats. When she didn't have to think about breathing anymore, she let herself feel. A strong hand rested on her back, the thumb gently stroking her spine.

"Whoa," she whispered.

"Uh-huh."

"That . . ."

"Yeah."

Maya hid her face against his chest as irrepressible laughter bubbled up. "Oh God, I'm never going to be able to look at you in public again."

Gray chuckled. "Let's be real—you could barely do that before we had sex."

She growled and bit his chest lightly. "Yeah, but now you're gonna give me one of those filthy-hot little stares and I'm going to remember—" She faltered as even the *thought* of it threatened to summon a full sensory replay of Gray staring down at her, his fingers and thumb shattering her apart. "Oh *God*," she groaned. "I'm so doomed."

He drew her closer with another rumbling chuckle. "Somehow, I think you'll manage."

"Never," she declared. "Everyone will know."

"Everyone *already* knows."

Maya's cheeks heated. "*No.*"

"But I'm sure they find it excessively adorable," Gray offered teasingly.

It felt so *good* to lie here with him, basking in this warm glow, prolonging it with gentle teasing and slow, soft caresses. She could have cuddled there in the warmth of his arms forever, but a sharp rap shattered the peace of the night.

"Up and at 'em," Dani called through the door. "The intel came in on Emerge BioCore. We're rolling out." She paused. "This means you, too, Gray."

Maya groaned again, and this time there was no amusement in it. Dani was going to give her *so* much shit, and she definitely needed to soundproof her bedroom. But she shakily separated herself from Gray and swung her feet over the edge of the bed. "We're coming," she called. "Give us ten."

Gray sat up as well. "Are you ready for this?"

"I think so. My brain's a little mushy, but I know how to lock it down. I may pay for it later . . ." She smiled at him. "But some things are worth it."

He took her hand and raised it to his lips. The kiss he brushed across her knuckles left the sweetest tingles in its wake. "Be safe."

"I'll just be in the van," she countered, turning his hand over to press her lips to the center of his palm. "Keeping you safe. Now go, before Dani decides to poke her head in here to see what's keeping us and gets an eyeful."

"Frankly, she'd deserve it." But he slipped away to gather up his clothes anyway.

Maya closed her eyes and curled her fingers around her rumpled quilt. Her thoughts were enthusiastic puppies again, tumbling over one another in glee. Hopefully, the drive would be long enough for her to wrangle them into obedience.

She had a feeling she'd need *all* of her wits on the other side.

August 13th, 2066

The only reason the entire mess with 66–221 wasn't black-holed is that he hurt the wrong person. A TechCorps VP has the power to demand consequences. Vice President Anderson was impressed by my foresight regarding her grandson's murderer.

Now I have a powerful ally. And a goal.

The Recovered Journal of Birgitte Skovgaard

TWENTY-ONE

Emerge BioCore had come down in the world.

The abandoned office building in which they'd taken up residence had seen far better days. Half of their security seemed like plausible deniability—from the outside, no casual observer would guess the place was even occupied. The flexible solar arrays unrolled across the roof and the wide satellite dish were the only tells, and they were only visible from the air.

A useful deception, unless the people hunting you had access to satellites.

The place was a dump. Rainbow probably could have broken in. Dani could have infiltrated it sleepwalking. Even so, Maya's heart pounded as Nina maneuvered their van toward their target. The familiar sounds of last-minute mission prep filled the tiny space. The rasp of Velcro, the whisper of knives going into sheaths, the rhythmic click of people checking their firearms. Conall's fingers were already flying over his keyboard.

Knox's calm, authoritative voice rose above it all, repeating the plan in all its blunt, brutal glory one last time. "The back door is our point of entry. Nina and I go first—"

"With me," Ava interrupted.

"With Ava," he continued smoothly. "We'll clear a path. The rest of you cover us. Conall and Maya . . ."

"We find the kids," Maya supplied, "and lead you to them. As fast as we can."

"As fast as you can." Knox's gaze took in every one of his soldiers in turn. "This isn't about stealth. This is about destroying everyone between us and those kids and anyone who tries to stop us on the way back out."

"A real fucking pleasure," Rafe growled, flexing his hands inside his tactical gloves.

"Understood." Dani fastened a sheath around her right thigh, a twin to the one she already wore on her left. The only difference was that one was for pistols, the other for knives. "This is a take-no-prisoners operation."

Ava sat across from Maya with her legs crossed, watching them all with faintly amused superiority. Even her armor was bespoke and fashionable, from her knee-high heeled boots to her tailored tactical vest. Rows of delicate, shiny throwing knives lined the front like accessories, and her usual tightly braided bun was adorned with silver spikes she'd no doubt rammed through many an enemy's neck. The silver bracers buckled around her forearms were so polished Maya could see her reflection in them.

"I still question the tactical wisdom of bringing compromised men into a firefight," Ava said, her gaze taking in Mace and Gray in turn. Gray stiffened next to Maya, and she briefly contemplated snatching one of those pretty hair ornaments up and poking Ava somewhere nonlethal with it.

"The last time we rolled out with you in our vicinity, you were the asshole zip-tying our hands together and shooting at us." Dani grinned, baring her teeth. "If I didn't get to peel your face off for that, you don't get to question shit."

"I have a perfect grasp of their skills and limitations," Knox said in a tone that allowed no argument. "A far more thorough understanding than I have of yours, quite frankly. You trust my judgment and obey orders, or you stay in the van."

Ava studied him for a moment before inclining her head. "Fair enough."

Knox seemed to accept that as agreement. "Is everyone clear on the plan?"

Mace tapped a full magazine on the frame of the van, then slid it into a pistol bigger than a person's head. For the first time Maya could remember, his hands weren't shaking. "Crystal."

"Good to go, boss," Conall agreed.

As the van coasted to a stop and Knox ran a final comms check, Maya snuck her hand down to Gray's and curled her fingers around his. The warmth of his skin kindled memories that she couldn't allow to drift into glorious focus, but they brought with them both peace and a purpose.

"Have faith," he murmured.

She usually did. Nina had infected her with it, with boundless hope and a belief in miracles. Some part of her still thought she might find a way to pull Gray back from the edge. To steal back the months and years that could have been theirs.

All it would take to snuff out her dreams was a stray bullet.

Maya swallowed back the fear. Trying to stop Gray from doing what good he could in the time he had left would be a betrayal. She rallied a bit of her usual sardonic humor and gave him her best no-bullshit stare. "Don't get dead," she told him tartly. "Or I'll kick your ass."

"Deal."

Nina caught Maya's gaze, then glanced at Conall. "Keep your comms open. We're not being sneaky, but we still need to be quick. The second you get into their systems and find those kids, let us know."

"We got this," Maya promised.

"We know."

Knox gestured with two fingers, pointing toward the back of the van, and everyone exploded into movement. Gray's fingers tightened on hers for a brief moment before he followed Rafe out the open door. Mace and Ava followed, with Dani behind them, keeping an eye on both.

In a matter of moments, it was just Maya and Conall. She slid next to him at the mobile workstation and powered up the monitors as his fingers flew over the keyboard. "How bad is security?"

"Negligible," he muttered, which for Conall meant *actually pretty good.*

Conall cut through most systems like a blade honed to a killing edge, but there was a furrow between his brows now that Maya didn't like.

"They got an upgrade since last time?" she asked.

"Probably fired the last asshole. Whoever set them up this time is not a complete idi—" He whooped suddenly. "Got you, fuckers. I'm in."

Over the comms, Maya could hear the team advancing on the point of entry Knox had identified. The crunch of boots over gravel, the soft scratch of fabric against armor. The single external guard announced his presence with a startled intake of breath followed by a soft crack and a heavy thud. Nina and Knox's whispered voices followed.

"Is the lock biometric?"

"Key code."

"Can you crack it?"

"Fuck that. *I'm* cracking it." That was Rafe, his voice a low rumble. Metal protested with a shriek, and Maya tried to conjure what was happening in her imagination. Rafe, literally weaponizing all those muscles this time, as he gave in to the rage at what had been done to Rainbow and tore the front door off the place.

"Got cameras," Conall announced a second before video appeared on Maya's screen. Conall slid the tablet he'd used to crack the system toward her, and Maya started to flip through the camera angles, comparing them to the shape of the building from above.

Gunfire erupted over comms as she tried to unfocus her eyes just enough to ignore the details and just absorb the shapes of hallways and the size of rooms, the angle of light falling through the rare windows and the intersections and gaps in coverage.

It was like assembling a giant puzzle of overlapping pieces, but her brain thrilled at the challenge. She felt that same giddy rush, and this time she didn't fight it. She'd pay whatever price required when the crash came. When she flipped to a camera that showed seven kids with shaved heads staring into space with the glazed eyes of the heavily drugged, she knew she'd pay it a dozen times over.

As long as they could get the damn kids out.

"Got them," she said, throwing the entire array of camera angles up onto the monitor with a flick of her fingers. Another flick gave her a blank screen and she started to sketch the layout she'd visualized, labeling each camera on her rough blueprint. "East side of the building, fourth floor. They're all together in one room. You're going to have to fight your way through."

Another spatter of gunfire was followed by Ava's crisp, "That won't be an issue."

"We're on our way," Knox confirmed, moments before Maya watched a guard back onto one camera, firing repeatedly at something off-screen. Ava stalked into view, swatting a bullet aside with one of her bracers like she was flicking away an annoying fly. A second later she'd turned the guard's gun on him without even stripping it from his hand, blowing off the top of his head and letting the body fall aside without slowing her stride.

Conall snorted. "Guess this was a good mission to bring the murder clone on."

The gunfire cut off abruptly. No cutting reply came from Ava. Maya frowned and tapped her comm, but everything had gone silent on the other end. "Conall?"

"I hear it," he muttered, spinning to a second display. "Or rather I *don't* hear it. Probably just interference . . ."

Dread slithered over Maya, an intense feeling that something was wrong. She skimmed the cameras again, looking for any external view, but every angle just showed the inside of the building.

That was weird.

"Con—"

"Fuck," he hissed. "Someone's jamming us."

Dread coalesced into certainty. She compared the cameras to her sketched blueprints again, her eyes finding the blank spots—too many blank spots. So many places where all the people who weren't showing up on those conveniently sporadic cameras could be hiding.

The van door creaked. Conall spun toward her, his eyes widening in shock. "Maya!"

Three bullets slammed into him before he could move. With her mind fully open, the sound of it sank into her bones. The thunder of each shot rolled forever before the terrible liquid thud of the bullet tearing through his clothing and slamming into his flesh. Conall exhaled in shock and rocked back, the velocity tipping him out of his flimsy makeshift seat.

Shock held her paralyzed for the eternity between heartbeats. Training kicked in, dragging her in two directions. Self-preservation lost to her terror for Conall. She dove for him, fingers scrambling to staunch the flow of blood.

She barely found the wounds before a fist closed around her braids and dragged her backward. She flailed instinctively, fingers closing around the handle of her stun stick.

Too late. It was all too late. Pain flared in her neck along with the familiar sound of a pressure injector. Another jerk to her hair toppled her over, and the sight of Tobias Richter's pleased smile chased her down into terrifying oblivion.

TECHCORPS PROPRIETARY DATA, COMPANY-WIDE ANNOUNCEMENT

On the anniversary of her 25th year of service, please join us in congratulating Birgitte Skovgaard on her promotion to executive vice president of Behavior and Analysis.

January 3rd, 2067

TWENTY-TWO

Gray missed his rifle.

He missed the hurry-up-and-sit-on-your-ass quiet, the adrenaline-soaked solitude of setting up position as quickly as possible, followed by the pounding of his own pulse in his ears as he waited for his mark to show.

Being in the middle of an infiltration was different. When he was on his own, he could be still. It was tense, sure, listening to the other members of his team do their thing as he ran through the scenarios and contingencies in his head. But here, the tension pressed in on you from all sides, an external thing that had claws and teeth.

And when the firefights erupted . . . Those were messy. Raw chaos distilled into something so primal it almost wrapped around into looking like art. A dance. Nina pirouetting around Mace to squeeze off a succession of shots. Ava following through on a knife throw with an arabesque that dropped into a deep lunge.

Wait, where the hell had he even picked up all this dance terminology?

A laugh caught in his throat, and he narrowly avoided taking a bullet point-blank to the face. He whirled on his attacker, using his momentum to strike the butt of his pistol across the man's face. He dropped like a rock sinking into an oily puddle, just in time for Dani to hop over him as she rushed past.

"Rafe, boost!" she yelled.

"Ready!" He held out both hands, catching her booted foot in midair. She launched herself up and grabbed hold of a light fixture. It swayed wildly with her forward momentum, and she knocked down three more men who had just run into the lobby.

The longer they stayed there, the more time the rest of these fuckers would have to fully entrench. They could be setting up ambushes already—hell, maybe even getting ready to blow the place. They had to advance, and Gray led the charge.

In the past, when he was in the thick of combat instead of set up in a sniper's nest, he hadn't minded taking point. There was a certain mindless inevitability in it. The only way to get past the paralyzing fear of death was to disregard it. He'd often thought that if he had to go out, all in all, it wasn't a bad way for it to happen. It would be quick, maybe even over so fast he wouldn't even have time to realize it, and it would be *useful*. A good death.

He didn't feel that way now. His thoughts refused to be pushed down, locked away in the numb haze of adrenaline. And they kept drifting back to Maya.

If he went down here, now, it wouldn't be good. It would hurt her like all hell on fire.

He had to risk it anyway.

He hurtled down the darkened hallway with the rest of the team hard on his heels. They cleared each recessed doorway as they passed, with guns at the ready and little more than monosyllabic communication passing between them. More often, it was silent, a look or gesture that was immediately, exquisitely understood.

A door near the end of the hall slammed open, and a man stepped out only feet from Gray, his stance planted wide as he began to swing his rifle up. The narrow hallway effectively functioned as one long choke point, and all he would have to do to mow them all down was close his eyes and fire.

Gray kicked the rifle's muzzle aside then followed it with a hard blow to the man's sternum. His breath left him in a cracking *whoosh*, and he stumbled back, bouncing off the wall and flailing back toward the door he'd just exited. Gray caught the edge of it and swung it around hard, banging it into his opponent's helmet hard enough to rattle his brains.

And that was it. End of the line.

"Where to now?" Mace muttered.

"Up." Nina nodded toward a door indicating a stairwell.

"Stairwells are bad," Dani protested, even as she was moving to haul open the door. "Easy for them to keep the high ground, and they can hear you coming a mile away."

"Watch my back," Ava ordered, striding past Dani. But Dani just stood there, dumbfounded, as she disappeared up the stairs, her boots silent.

Ten seconds later, a thud echoed down, followed by a hoarse scream. A body plummeted to the cement floor, the limbs splayed and eyes staring up, unseeing. Five seconds later a second followed, his screams echoing all the way down.

Dani sighed, a long-suffering, entirely put-upon sound. "At least she's effective."

"And not trying to kill us." *This time.* Gray kept that last part to himself as he took the stairs two and three at a time.

The doors on the second and third landings weren't just locked or chained, they were fully boarded up. Something about that rankled at Gray, like a sore spot on the roof of his mouth he couldn't stop worrying with his tongue. Why go this far, this deep, into a derelict building if you didn't have to? With abandoned buildings, lower wasn't just quicker and more convenient, it was safer.

Then he reached the fourth-floor landing and didn't have time to think about it anymore, because another security squad had already converged on their location. Ava fought viciously, holding one flailing man in front of her as a human shield as she fired on his comrades.

Nina's favorite trick. He remembered that one well.

Dani broadsided one of the soldiers—*that's what they are, soldiers*—and his submachine gun fired an arc of bullets in Nina's general direction as he went down. She hit the floor, and Knox dove after her before catching her hand signal that she was fine.

As he straightened, he never saw the pistol aimed at the back of his head.

"Knox, down!" Gray shouted.

Knox dropped, and Gray fired, a dead shot to the heart. The man who'd drawn a bead on Knox went down, but he must have been armored, because he still struggled to roll to his knees.

Mace was on him, knife in hand, before he managed it.

Ava's human shield went over the balcony with a weak scream that ended in a dull crash far below, and she stood in the doorway with a confiscated pistol pointed at the floor and her brow furrowed as she stared down at the sprawl of bodies.

"Something is off," she said, rolling a body over with the toe of her boot. "You said the guards they had before were mediocre and poorly equipped. This is quality armor, custom fitted."

"They were." Gray slid a hand roughly through his hair. "Something is worse than off. They should have shut us down in the lobby, but instead they let us get all the way up here. *Drew* us up here, like—"

"Like rats in a maze." Dani frowned.

Ava crouched next to the body, frowning at his wrist. She yanked the knife from the dead soldier's boot and used it to slice the sleeve on his jacket, revealing a tattoo.

It had a distinctly military feel, reminding Gray vaguely of some of the unit and squad insignia he'd seen during his tenure with the Protectorate—a bleeding shield inscribed with what looked like Latin. But he didn't recognize it.

Nina brushed Knox's sleeve. "I think we have a problem."

"No shit, we have a problem." Dani shoved past Gray, yanked the dead man's arm up, and waved it at them. "He's Ex-Sec."

"Are you sure?" Mace asked.

"Yeah, I'm sure. It's not an official insignia, and they're not supposed to mark themselves like this, but some of the real dedicated company fuckers get the ink anyway."

Knox looked at Gray, who stared back at him in horror. He wanted nothing more than to blot out Knox's words. "Executive Security deployed off the Hill means Tobias Richter is here."

Then Nina made it worse. A thousand times worse. "I can't raise Conall and Maya on comms."

Richter. A couple of Ex-Sec squads. Blocked communications. Gray could see the vague outline of the trap now . . . but not *who* it was meant to ensnare. Only a few short days ago, he would have assumed Richter was after the Silver Devils, that he'd finally found the perfect bait to flush them out. But now there was Mace to consider, even Ava, for Christ's sake.

And Maya.

He tried to calculate how long it would take them to get from here back to the van. Even at a dead run, with a clear path and no resistance, it was too long. Too fucking long.

"I'm going to the van," he said flatly. "If Richter's here . . ."

"Maya's a target," Knox finished. "Rafe, back him up."

"Got it." Rafe dropped the empty magazine from his pistol, loaded a full one, and shot Dani a look. "Watch his back."

Dani regarded him mildly. "Nina might get jealous."

He winked at her and swept up another discarded weapon from a fallen soldier on his way to Gray's side. "Let's do this."

He and Rafe hurried down the stairs, the thump of their boots echoing loudly in the stairwell. It seemed to mimic the blood pounding in Gray's ears, each thud spiking through him with painful possibility.

So many reasons Richter would come for them. And only one that could close his throat with sheer panic.

"We should have killed him before we left, Rafe. Even if it meant we wouldn't all make it out."

"Maybe." Rafe shook his head. "And maybe this is the best chance anyone will ever have. He's outside of his base of power. And he won't see Nina and Dani coming. We sure as hell didn't."

"Maybe. But that's—" Gray stopped short as he entered the long hallway they'd fought their way through before. It was deserted, exactly the way they'd left it . . . except for the heavy blast door closing off the far end. "Fuck."

Gears ground behind them. Rafe spun, bolting back the way they'd come. He caught the blast door with six inches of clearance, the muscles in his arms straining as he fought the machinery with everything in him.

Running footsteps filled the narrow space as soldiers started to file out of the rooms, and Gray finally saw the whole trap.

Isolate. Divide.

Conquer.

He turned. The six inches of clearance had shrunk to four, the tendons standing out under Rafe's skin in harsh relief. He wouldn't be able to hold it for much longer, but that was okay.

This part of the trap was for Gray.

"Go," he whispered. "Hurry. Find Conall."

"Gray—"

"I got this, man." It wasn't even a lie.

Rafe roared his frustration and heaved a final time, driving the door open for the few precious seconds it took to dive through it. The soldiers fired after him, but he vanished as the blast doors slammed home.

Gray raised his hands and locked his fingers behind his head. It was the only way to still their shaking as he stared at the closed blast door.

Maybe he was wrong. Maybe fear had driven him to the wrong conclusion.

Richter was after most of them, after all. He might not have realized what—*who*—he really had within his grasp.

But Gray hadn't lived this long by lying to himself, and brutal honesty said otherwise. *Expect the worst,* it crooned, *and you'll never be wrong.*

"On your knees!" someone bellowed.

He dropped, fingers still interlaced behind his head. "I won't fight you. Richter and I have business."

He had to get to Maya. And the only way to do that now was to go through Richter.

June 3rd, 2079

I suspect the relationship developing between Marjorie and Simon is inappropriate, at the very least. I should discourage it, for both of their sakes.

But he does seem to have distracted her from that troublesome friendship with DC-025.

The Recovered Journal of Birgitte Skovgaard

TWENTY-THREE

Maya couldn't tell if she was awake.

So many of her nightmares started this way. The darkness, the disorientation. The zip ties digging into her wrists. The hard back of a chair digging into her shoulders every time she tried to move. If she struggled too much, the plastic binding her wrists to the chair would cut off circulation.

She'd done that, last time. Twisted until numbness claimed her hands, then focused on the painful prickling as they came back to life. Discomfort was a distraction. It was an escape, the only one she'd had. They couldn't deliver her real physical pain—her brain would short out and shut down long before they broke her will. Though that reality never seemed to matter in her nightmares. In her nightmares, they hurt her.

Please let this be a nightmare. Please.

Her head swam. Groggy, like she'd been given drugs. Her breath came faster, stale and warm against her face with every exhale. This wasn't a natural darkness—there was something covering her eyes. Not a blindfold, something large enough to cover her whole face.

Panic jacked her heart rate higher. She twisted her wrists again, hard enough for the plastic to cut into her skin. Her other senses clamored for her attention, a dizzying press of chaos battering her fragile self-control. Memories—nightmares?—surfaced in overlapping sensory flashes.

The crash of the door to the van flying open.

The crack of gunfire.

The metallic scent of Conall's blood. The *sound* of his flesh tearing.

Oh God, oh fuck—*no*—

A sting in her neck. Tobias Richter's smug face.

Darkness.

She dragged in a frantic breath, then another. It was the smell that convinced her she wasn't dreaming. Subtle, but undeniable as she hauled in another shaky breath. Lilac. Vanilla. A subtle musk. Expensive perfume, achingly familiar.

But not from her nightmares.

Maya stopped struggling. She flexed each finger, working stiffness out of them, and forced herself to *listen*. An industrial air conditioner rumbled in the distance. The quiet hiss of cool air through the vent came from somewhere to her left. After a moment, she heard a soft whisper. Not a voice. Fabric. Silk, brushing against silk as someone moved. Then a barely audible metallic creak. A near-silent exhale.

Gray had been right. She knew what so *many* things sounded like. Now that she knew how it felt to make the connection between memory and her senses, it was effortless.

She straightened and turned her head three inches to the left. She envisioned what she knew was there. A pale woman with her long, red hair twisted into a tight bun atop her head. Brown eyes. Freckles across her nose. Professional makeup. Expertly tailored silk. Seated in a metal chair. Her legs crossed.

The perfect mental picture stripped away the fear of the unknown. Maya's voice didn't even tremble. "Hello, Cara."

The chair creaked again, then the fabric on her head vanished. Maya blinked at the sudden light, squinting at the woman who resumed her position, her soft, brown eyes gazing on Maya with such tender sadness you'd think *she* was the one tied to a chair.

Cara Kennedy. DC-025. Maya's first friend.

Tobias Richter's data courier.

"Maya." Cara leaned forward, that familiar floral perfume evoking such a violent sense memory that for a moment, time overlapped.

She was fourteen, sitting cross-legged and still on the end of her bed as a nineteen-year-old Cara held her chin in one hand. "Your skin is flawless," Cara murmured, using a steady hand to apply eyeliner to Maya's lash line. "You don't need makeup. But sometimes it can be fun. Just because we're silent doesn't mean we have to be invisible."

Maya squeezed her nails into her palm, grounding her in the present. Cara's makeup was still perfect. Effortless and elegant, as it should be when she could afford the best of literally everything. Her expensive perfume was a custom blend. Her silk blouse was unbuttoned to reveal a massive emerald on a chain at her throat. Emeralds studded with diamonds sparkled at her ears. Her pants were clearly tailored to her narrow hips and long legs, ending perfectly before the heels of her sensible but fashionable boots.

As a display of wealth, it was meant to awe. Maya mostly wondered how many people in Five Points she could feed by fencing those earrings.

"I grieved for you, you know." Cara's voice remained soft and sad. "When they found you dead, I wept for days. I'd begged Tobias to let me talk to you after Birgitte's treason was uncovered. I told him you couldn't be blamed. I know you, Maya. I know you better than anyone. You would never hurt people."

"I was hurting people," Maya countered, her voice scratchy. Her mouth tasted like cotton gone bad, thanks to the drugs. "Every day on the Hill, I was hurting people. You're hurting people. That's all the TechCorps *does*. You of all people know that. You know his secrets."

"Oh, Maya." Cara lifted a hand, and Maya jerked her head back before her fingers could make contact with her cheek. The wounded pain in Cara's eyes deepened as she let her hand hang there for a moment before settling back in her lap. "Birgitte damaged you so badly with her lies. I wish I'd seen how she was abusing you. I should have done something."

It was like falling backward into a mirror reality. The fervent conviction in Cara's eyes was so earnest. She was a true believer because she'd never been given a chance to be anything else. Tobias Richter had been manipulating her from the age of five, patting her on the head like a puppy when she performed, showering her in affection and then terrifying her with the threat of its removal to make her work even harder.

Cara probably thought it was love. Maya had, for all the years they'd been friends. Even knowing what she knew about Richter, even *knowing* he was evil, part of her had always thought, *At least he loves Cara.*

Tobias Richter didn't love anyone.

"Let me go." Maya leaned forward, locking gazes with Cara. "Do you know what he did to me? Did he tell you how he tied me to a chair for twenty-three days? How he cut pieces off of Simon and then healed him so he could do it again?"

That stung. Maya could see it in Cara's eyes. The brief hesitation, like a tiny crack had opened up. She was probably remembering how she'd been the one to point out that Simon had a crush on Maya. How she'd encouraged them. How she'd clapped her hands and laughed at Maya's blushing admission of her first kiss . . .

"You knew Simon," Maya whispered, trying to wedge the crack wider. "He was sweet and he was good and he didn't deserve to die like that. *No* one deserves to die like that."

Cara's serenity faltered. Maya could *see* her desperate need to believe in the world Richter had built for her battling the memories of their friendship. For one heartbeat, Maya thought she'd gotten through.

Twenty-five years of training rushed in to fill the cracks in the wall. Maya watched her oldest friend slip beyond reach. "Simon was a traitor." Cara's voice held a shivering intensity, as if making up for the momentary lapse. "He betrayed you as much as Birgitte did. If they'd cared about you at all, they wouldn't have dragged you into their treason."

"It's not treason if the people don't deserve your trust and loyalty to begin with. Look what they did to you. Ripped you from your parents. Fucked around with your brain. Gave you to a monster to raise—"

"He is *not* a monster," Cara snapped.

"You *know his secrets*. You know all the terrible things he's done."

"To protect everyone! Honestly, Maya, the world nearly *ended*. The entire Southeast was on the verge of starvation. Someone has to enforce order. Someone has to do the horrible things so the rest of us can live our lives." Cara leaned forward, her brown eyes burning with the fire of a true believer. "Birgitte always hated him. She was jealous of his power. But she couldn't have made the hard calls that keep us all safe."

Us. Maya clenched her jaw, knowing better than to argue. Cara had never come down from her sheltered tower and walked the streets of Southside. She didn't know that *safe* ended at the base of the Hill, and for most of Atlanta—hell, most of the Southeast—the only safety to be had was what you and your neighbors could scrape together. Not because of the TechCorps, but in spite of them.

Cara wouldn't believe it without seeing it. She might not even believe it if she saw it. There were a dozen excuses for people's poor circumstances, and the TechCorps had practically set the litany of blame-passing to music.

"Fine," Maya ground out. "It was nice catching up. Love that smoky eye, and your boots are killer. Now run along and get Daddy so we can start the torture."

Oh, it was like kicking a puppy. All shock and big wounded eyes, and Maya wondered for a moment if Cara was going to cry. But she just reached out again, her hand hovering by Maya's cheek. "Don't make us do this. We don't want to hurt you, Maya. We want you back with us, where you belong. You're our family. You're *my* family."

It was a tragedy because it was true. Cara loved Maya the only way she knew how, with conditional affection and unspoken threats of violence. For so many years, that had been enough. Maya hadn't known that love could come without ultimatums or threats until she met Nina and Dani.

And now she had Gray. Gray who would destroy himself before he hurt her.

With quiet sadness, Maya slammed the door on the past. "Thanks, but no thanks. I got a better offer."

And her family was coming for her this time. Maya just had to hold on.

TECHCORPS INTERNAL
EXECUTIVE COMMUNICATION

From: RICHTER, T
To: SKOVGAARD, B
Date: 2067–01–04

Congratulations, Birgitte. Now you can be an executive pain in my ass.

From: SKOVGAARD, B
To: RICHTER, T
Date: 2067–01–04

I certainly intend to be.

TWENTY-FOUR

They didn't drag Gray far, just to a mostly bare room near the far end of the locked-off hallway. The room was rectangular in shape, roughly three meters by six, with blank, gray walls. A table had been placed in the exact center of the room, flanked by two chairs and a rolling stool.

Gray was seated in one chair, his wrists bound behind him with a zip tie. A second one secured his bindings to a rung on the back of the chair's frame. The other chair was identical to his, precisely placed at the other end of the table.

Everything about the room was precise, surgical. From the furniture to the harsh, naked lighting overhead, it was all designed to evoke fear. To unsettle.

And the show hadn't even started yet.

With the basic layout of the room committed to memory, Gray began to look more closely. Finally, he spotted the tiny camera wedged between the pitted tiles of the drop ceiling. No doubt it had audio capabilities, and there were probably more microphones scattered about.

He took a moment to steel himself. At least they hadn't bashed him in the head on sheer principle. The blow alone could have killed him, and then Maya would have to go up against Richter alone.

Gray stretched his neck and locked away all the panic and dread someone in his precarious position was duty bound to feel. Then he spoke. Calmly, carelessly. "You can let me stew in here, sure. But it won't work, and you know it."

He silently counted off the seconds. After precisely sixty, the door opened, and Tobias Richter walked in, flanked by two guards. As the guards took up their blank-eyed posts on either side of the door, Gray studied Richter.

He looked so *normal*. He wore black slacks, a white dress shirt, and a silver-on-silver tie woven with a delicate paisley pattern. Somewhere outside this room, he'd already discarded his jacket. His auburn hair had been neatly trimmed into a conservative executive style, framing a nondescript but pleasant face and piercing blue eyes.

Average height. Medium build. You'd never guess that he could—and did—routinely murder people with his bare hands.

Those deadly hands now carried a titanium hardside case. Gray tried not to look at it as Richter spoke.

"That's what I always liked about you, Sergeant Gray. You're indomitable. Unflinching. Brave to the point of foolhardiness."

He even sounded pleasant, and a genial, *real* smile curved his lips. And why not? He had the upper hand and was well on his way to turning that advantage into his best day ever.

"However." He set the case on the table. "While I have historically admired those qualities, they are, at the moment, incredibly inconvenient for me."

"How tragic."

Richter's eyes tightened, and his smile vanished. "Do you know why I'm here, Sergeant—?"

"Gray."

"Pardon?"

"Just Gray. I'm not a sergeant anymore."

"An understandable misconception." Richter smiled again. This time, it completely lacked any warmth or sincerity. "But you are still a Protectorate sergeant. You will be one until you're promoted, demoted, or dead."

It wasn't a threat, merely a statement of fact. It brushed against that secret fear, the idea that Gray would never be rid of them. That the Protectorate was more than his past, present, and future; it was part of him, like his blood and his bones and the goddamn implant in his head.

"Now." Richter said it like, *that's settled, moving on.* He used his palm to release the biometric lock on the case, but he didn't open it. Instead, he sat down on the rolling stool close to Gray's position. "Do you know why I'm here?"

"No."

Richter chuckled, the sound devoid of mirth. "Yes, you do. But what if I'm bluffing? Of course." He nodded, satisfied. "It's a solid interrogation strategy, feigning ignorance."

Gray tracked the beats of Richter's performance. He had attempted to establish rapport, asserted his dominance, and asked his leading questions, the ones meant more to make his captive nervous than elicit answers.

Right on time, he unlatched the case. It held, as expected, an assortment of tools—blades and pliers alongside things Gray didn't even recognize. But he didn't need to. Everything lovingly packed into that case shared a single common purpose.

In Richter's hands, they were meant to cause pain.

"*Fuck,* you're good. Not a flinch." Richter's eyes gleamed as brightly as the instruments as he began to lay them out on the table. "I wish we had you on telemetry. I bet your pulse didn't even budge."

Gray lifted one shoulder. It gave him an excuse to test his range of motion—which turned out to be pitiful. "I've seen worse."

"You've *done* worse." Richter clucked his tongue. "But it's not a competition, is it?"

Bullshit. For an organization like the Protectorate of the TechCorps, for a man like Richter, everything always was. They called it a lot of things—survival of the fittest, the law of the corporate jungle—but it always boiled down to not giving a damn about anyone else. Getting ahead at any cost, and staying up no matter who you had to step on.

Gray shrugged again.

"Mmm." Richter turned his head and barked at the guards. "Leave us." As they silently obeyed, he lifted a scalpel from the case, held it up to the light, and rubbed at a spot with his thumb like he was polishing Grandma's silverware. "Marjorie Chevalier."

Good thing Gray wasn't on telemetry, after all. "Don't know her."

"Don't insult me. You two seem to be . . . quite close." Richter placed the scalpel precisely five centimeters away from a wickedly curved pair of pliers—probably meant for yanking teeth. "It's fascinating, really. The woman who raised her wanted you dead, you know. Probably would have put the bullet in your head herself. She thought you were a monster, a sociopath who tortures kittens for fun."

Gray remembered the endless evaluations. The fact that Birgitte had seen something lurking behind his carefully cultivated facade only proved that her instincts had been pretty damn good. It was hard to hold a grudge—especially considering the woman's fate. "Was she wrong?"

"Sadly, I think so." Richter stared at him *hard*, the sheer weight of it pressing Gray back in his chair. "I chose you for a reason, Matthew. Handpicked you out of that hellhole of an orphanage because I thought you'd be a team player."

His brain tripped over the words so abruptly he lost the script. "Wait, *what?*"

"Do you have any idea how many people I had to lean on? How many carefully worded warnings I had to hand out?"

The full import of what Richter was saying clicked into place in Gray's head smoothly, like a well-oiled bolt on a rifle. He hadn't been overlooked, passed over. People had *wanted him.*

Richter kept spitting out his angry words. "One guy was so persistent I had to pay him off *and* threaten to conscript his kid. All because I thought you had what it took to serve the TechCorps."

It was the answer to the biggest question that still lingered like a cloud over his life—*why wasn't I good enough?* He had been, the whole time. He'd just had the profound misfortune of catching Tobias Richter's eye. The man had seen the blank mask that Gray had worn like camouflage, that he had relied on for his continued survival, and he'd not only bought it, he'd *coveted* it.

Gray couldn't help it—he laughed. "I guess you made a mistake."

Richter stood and regarded him with cold fury, all pretense of charm and guile gone. "The rest of your squad is dead."

His helpless humor evaporated. For all Gray knew, it was true. Sorrow tried to sink its inky-black talons into his heart, but he brushed it away. If it *was* the truth, he'd either have time later to grieve or he'd be just as dead. Either option was better than giving in to the burgeoning triumph in Richter's eyes.

"If so, how come I'm not in a ditch somewhere with crows pecking out my eyeballs? You could be in a TechCorps boardroom by now, getting a shit ton of commendations along with your piles of credits."

Richter said nothing, but the tight muscle in his jaw ticked as he ran his fingers over a slim, silver rectangle. It looked like a generic rechargeable battery pack . . . except for the electrodes extending from one end.

But Gray understood. "Ah, right. You're not exactly in their good graces right now."

"Bring her in." Richter leaned closer to Gray—though not close enough to attack. "I'm going to find out everything Birgitte's data courier knows. And after I've cracked her head open like a melon, I'll drag her back there to get all those commendations. And you'll be far too dead to help her."

Gray's hands clenched in his bonds. "She'll never talk to you."

"When she sees what I have in store for you, Sergeant Gray? I believe she will."

The door swung open. A massive guard dragged Maya through, one rough hand locked so hard around her upper arm her boots left the floor when he swung her around to face Richter.

She had dirt on one cheek and her wrists secured behind her back, but she looked physically unharmed. Her gaze was wild as it skittered over him though, the depth of her panic a gut punch before she managed to lock it down.

"Oh boy," she drawled. "He's literally plagiarizing himself."

Gray offered her a reassuring smile. "You didn't expect him to be original, did you?"

"I guess not." The smile seemed to ground her. He could still see the panic in her eyes, but her voice dripped lazy disdain. "Someone should tell him that sequels never really capture the magic of the first time."

Gray tensed as the new guards shoved Maya down into the other chair. One flickering glance at Richter's face showed he'd caught the reaction.

He smiled slowly. "Enjoy your moments of levity, Miss Chevalier. They will be brief."

Maya held Gray's gaze as if clinging to a lifeline. Her lips moved in a silent whisper. *I'm sorry.*

That wouldn't do at all, so he shook his head firmly. "Remember what I said, Maya."

Richter reclaimed the stool and rolled it closer to the table—and his villainous collection of torture devices. "Shall we begin?"

Maya's breathing hitched. "Gray—"

"Remember what I said," he repeated. He knew she did, so he could only hope she understood.

I will never let myself be used as a weapon against you.

Then Richter lifted the scalpel, and Gray folded in on himself. It was the only way.

KNOX

Knox had successfully sprung his share of traps from the inside. The key, unfortunately, was being underestimated by your opponent.

No one was underestimating him today.

A bullet dug into the wall in front of him, shattering concrete in a tiny spray. Knox swore and swung around the corner, firing off three rapid shots that forced the approaching soldier to dive back under cover.

A spray of automatic fire forced him back. The assault was followed by the clink of a canister skittering down the cracked floor.

"Dani!" he roared, but she was already moving. A blur of black clothing and blond hair darted past him to scoop up the grenade. She'd tossed it back and whipped back around the corner in the space between heartbeats, and the building rattled as the explosion shook the hallway.

A fresh hail of bullets was the response, and Knox flinched as another spray of concrete pelted his face. He checked his magazine and swore. "I'm out."

Nina frowned. "Me, too."

"Here." Dani tossed two 9mm magazines their way, and Knox caught them.

"That's the last of it," Mace said flatly.

The slides had locked back on both of Ava's pistols, indicating the magazines were spent. She threw them aside, exchanged a silent look with Nina, and received a nod in return.

"Toss a smoke grenade, Captain," Ava said without looking away from Nina. "Give us three seconds, then follow."

Knox didn't argue that he wasn't a captain. He didn't ask questions. He jerked the pin from the grenade, waited until the last moment, and sent it skittering down the hallway, spewing heavy white smoke.

Ava dove after it, with Nina hard on her heels.

One.

Gunfire exploded. A man screamed.

Two.

Something thudded hard. A body skidded out of the smoke, eyes wide and blank, staring upward.

Three.

Knox dove into the hallway, holding his breath. A flash beside him marked Dani's passage, disappearing toward the sounds of combat ahead. Mace was a shadow behind him, covering his back.

Bodies littered the hallway. Knox leapt the final one and broke free of the smoke and into a room that looked like it had once been a cafeteria.

Right now, it was anarchy.

Half a dozen bodies already littered the ground. Two dozen more were battling for their lives against an absolute maelstrom of graceful destruction with Nina and Ava at its heart.

He'd never seen anything like the way they moved together. Calling it a dance felt inadequate. Knox had learned to move with Nina, but their connection paled in comparison to the instinctive, complete understanding between Ava and Nina. They flowed through the soldiers with perfect awareness of each other and everything happening around them.

While Knox scrambled to assess the situation, Nina slid beneath Ava's outstretched arm to hamstring a man as Ava slit a second's throat. Spinning with the momentum of her knife stroke, Ava hooked elbows with Nina and vaulted her back into the air, flying at an opponent.

Nina crashed into him and carried him down in a dizzying roll that snapped her opponent's neck before momentum carried her through a graceful leg sweep that tripped the man trying to close with Ava.

Deprived of her current target, Ava swung and swatted a bullet from midair with a negligent swipe of her shiny, silver arm bracer. The bullet ricocheted with terrifying precision into one opponent, but Ava had already turned to fling a knife in a deadly arc toward a soldier who'd made the mistake of targeting Nina.

Six men eliminated in a heartbeat. A seventh staggered by, screaming as he clawed at Dani's arms. She was riding his back, stabbing him repeatedly.

Two dozen men didn't have a chance.

Static wailed over their comms, followed by Rafe's panicked voice. "Fuck. Can anyone hear me?"

A man charged—whether at Knox or just trying to get to the exit, he didn't know. His gun rose, and Knox charged, knocking his arm up so it fired uselessly at the ceiling. Then he engaged his comms. "Rafe. Sit rep!"

"They have Gray. Maya's missing, and Conall's been shot. Three times, center mass. One round made it through his vest."

Mace ducked behind a column. "Where's he hit?"

The sound of Velcro ripped over the comms. "Right upper quadrant."

"Exit wound?"

"I don't see one."

"Vitals?"

"He's tachycardic at 115, with a weak, thready pulse. BP is low—90/55. Resps are shallow."

"He's hypovolemic. Got your IV access?"

"Working on it."

Mace stepped out of cover, took slow, careful aim, and used one of his last rounds to bring down one of the Ex-Sec soldiers. "Talk to me, Rafe."

"Got it!"

"Good. Run a green bag, wide open. And Rafe—" Mace exhaled. "You have to open him up."

"A laparotomy," Rafe said flatly. "In the back of a fucking van?"

"I know," Mace soothed. "But if you don't get a handle on the bleeding, he's going to die."

Rafe cursed. Then a flurry of sounds interspersed with his panicked breathing tickled Knox's ears—paper ripping, metal clinking, and one low, pained groan that froze Knox's heart in his chest.

Then Rafe sucked in a sharp, shocked breath. "His liver's shredded, Mace. Massive parenchymal disruption."

"Pack it with med-gel dressings."

"Will that even—"

"Just do it!" Mace barked. But his expression had melted into one of sick, resigned dread.

No. *No.*

The massive Ex-Sec soldier grappling with Knox dropped his gun and whipped a pressure injector from his vest. Knox jerked his arm out of the way, but the man jammed it into his own neck. His eyes glazed over as he let out a feral roar.

Before Knox could react, the man gripped him by the vest and slung him across the room.

Knox crashed into the cement wall hard enough to crack it. The window next to him exploded in a shower of glass he barely blocked from shredding his face.

A timely reminder. This wasn't just two dozen men—it was two dozen highly trained Ex-Sec soldiers with God knew what enhancements and unfettered access to top-of-the-line biochem stimulants.

Tobias Richter had Gray. Maya, too, most likely. A tactical catastrophe and a personal horror. The secrets in her head were priceless. Gray's pain would be the leverage Richter used to unlock them.

Every second Knox was delayed would cost them both too much.

"Fuck, Mace, I can't get control of it!"

And Conall was still bleeding.

A chill resolve swept over Knox. He dodged easily as a table crashed into the wall where he'd been and kicked the nearest fallen chair into the air. He caught it mid-flight and whipped it back toward his attacker's legs, turning his charge into a tripping stumble.

"Dani!" Knox roared. "Get Mace to Conall."

Dani brushed her hair out of her face and pulled a fresh knife from her boot. "You heard the man, Doc."

Mace hesitated, then nodded. "I'm on my way, Rafe. Just hold on."

Dani had been Ex-Sec, too. She'd get the medic to Conall's side in time. Knox let himself believe it for one vital moment.

Then he locked it away. Turned.

Ava and Nina were still dancing their path of elegant, glorious destruction through the Ex-Sec squads. Fast and brutal, there was no doubt they would persevere. Eventually. But every second they lingered here would be measured in Maya's and Gray's agony. Tobias Richter would *hurt* them.

Just like he had hurt Mace.

For the first time in eight terrible months, Knox eased his iron grip on his own anger. He let himself feel the pain, the loss, the bone-deep rage. He let himself feel *everything* he'd been holding back since Mace's reappearance in their lives.

It must have shown in his eyes. The soldier about to close with him took a stumbling step back. Knox lunged, grabbing him by the front of his armor with both hands and swinging. He released the man with a roar and watched him plow through two of his squadmates, knocking them all to the ground.

Knox didn't let them recover. His resolve absolute and his rage like fire in his blood, Knox threw himself into the dance.

TECHCORPS PROPRIETARY DATA,
L2 SECURITY CLEARANCE

Order a full psychological assessment on 66–793. He was recruited before I adjusted the sniper evaluation criteria. We will *not* have another 66–221.

Recruit Analysis, April 2068

TWENTY-FIVE

Gray hadn't made a sound.

The scent of blood had lodged in Maya's throat like glass. Not that there was so much blood, really. Richter had been precise with the application of pain. But a dozen shallow cuts in sensitive places meant to cause slow-burning agony had failed to provoke the desired response.

Gray didn't flinch. He didn't gasp or hiss. He didn't give any indication that he noticed Richter's attempts at all. The gentle warmth in his blue eyes never faltered as he held Maya's gaze, willing her to remember.

I will never let myself be used as a weapon against you.

The effort had to be costing him. He was burning through the months he should have had left, spending the strength of his body to protect her heart.

She had to move faster.

Her wrists were already rubbed raw from her slow attempts. Her arms ached with the effort of holding rigidly still and giving nothing away. But gentle flexing had allowed her to work the bracelet Dani had given her around until her thumb could just brush the catch.

Such a clever gift. Much more practical than trying to smuggle a fork everywhere. The guards hadn't even given it a second look when they roughly searched her for weapons. It was just a pretty little thing of hammered silver, a useless accessory.

Except nothing Dani chose was ever useless. Maya finally managed to trigger the catch, and the fastening parted with a silent click. A tiny blade no thicker than her thumbnail and twice the length slid from the clasp—not enough of a weapon to do much damage against trained soldiers.

But plenty of knife to saw through the zip ties holding her.

She exhaled and glanced at the guards. They stood on either side of the room now, dispassionate gazes fixed on Gray in tense anticipation of him exploding into violence. Neither showed the slightest concern for the literal torture playing out in front of them.

Just another day on the job at the TechCorps.

The scalpel flashed out of the corner of her eye. Maya had tried not to look, but now she couldn't help it. Richter slid it along Gray's upper arm, parallel to the bone, peeling up a thin layer of skin, and Maya couldn't choke back her whimper of protest.

"The mountains," Gray murmured. "Most people think of them in the winter or fall, but they're beautiful in the springtime, too."

"We'll go see them," she promised him, setting the blade against the plastic tie on her left wrist. The tip jabbed into her skin, and she ignored it and flexed slowly, grinding the sharp edge against the plastic. "After this. Another road trip."

"How offensive." Richter turned his icy-blue gaze on her. "Sergeant Gray isn't offering *you* false promises."

"They're not false," she snapped, hating the fact that her voice audibly shook. Not fear this time, but rage. Gray might be able to sit there, holding it all in, but hatred smoldered inside her. "The two of us are walking out of here over your fucking corpse."

"Classy." He held her gaze as he reached down and dug his fingernails into Gray's partially flayed arm.

Her fingers slipped. The tiny blade jabbed into her skin again. Maya took a shuddering breath and fought for the control Birgitte had taught her. But the metallic scent of blood scraped over her already raw nerves, dragging her back toward panic.

Panic would be worse than rage. She exhaled on a hiss and let the anger curl around her like fiery armor. "Dani won't need a knife to peel your face off. She'll do it with her bare hands."

"They're already dead." His voice was matter-of-fact, without a shred of victory. "There's only you two left. And you're making him suffer needlessly, Marjorie."

The lie was so cool, so confident. Maybe it wasn't even a lie, maybe it was just the reckless overconfidence of a bully who wasn't used to being told *no*. Maya didn't believe him either way.

But Gray *was* suffering. He was killing himself to hide it, but she knew his face too well now. The tightness around his eyes. The sweat at his brow. His breathing was off, hitching and a little raspy. How much of this could he take before his body gave up?

Buy time, whispered Nina's voice in her head. *Keep his focus on you. He won't physically harm you.*

"You haven't even asked me a question yet." She let her words tremble this time. Richter's arrogance would read it as fear. "What do you want to know? Maybe we can make a deal."

"Are you interested in a deal?" The scalpel hit the table with a clink, and Richter reached for a small box with a switch on one side and two metal probes jutting from one end. "If you were open to negotiation, perhaps you should have offered before I started peeling pieces off poor Sergeant Gray here."

"Isn't that the fucking point? To make me talk?"

"You still think you're in control of this. The point is to remind you that you are not." His thumb ran along the side of the box in a chilling caress. "I *will* break you this time."

Maya heaved in an unsteady breath. Not entirely an act—she wasn't sure she *could* have matched Gray's even, steady breathing—but her body shook with the force of it, and it hid her desperate attempt to saw through the rest of the zip tie. "So come break me," she snarled.

Richter made a disappointed noise. "You know better, Marjorie."

"Wait—"

He turned and jammed those cruel probes against Gray's body and flipped the switch.

Even Gray couldn't hide involuntary responses. His muscles seized and his body lurched as the electricity tore through him. He clenched his jaw tight, refusing to make a sound, but his agony raced over Maya. Her own body shuddered in response, sympathetic pain racing along her own nerves ahead of a growing wave of helplessness.

How could she take a risk when none of the consequences would hurt her? Anything she did would rebound on Gray. He'd pay for her bravado, her fury, her failure.

He'd pay and pay and pay, and the rest of her life would be a living nightmare, locked in the memory of this terrible, chilling silence. Gray, loving her too much to put more scars on her heart.

As if knowing she was the cause of this wasn't going to shred her heart to pieces.

"Stop," she whispered.

Richter kept going for another three more horrifying seconds that felt like an eternity, grinding in the conviction that nothing about this was within her control. Rubbing her face in her own helplessness. When he lifted the box, Gray's body slumped back into the chair.

"Maya," he rasped. "Look at me."

"Yes, Marjorie," Richter mocked, jamming the cruel little box and its torturous probes back against Gray's chest. "Look at what you're doing to him."

The switch flicked. Gray's body jerked. His muscles locked. Rage, panic—Maya couldn't tell them apart anymore. Nothing felt real and everything hurt. Her heart pounded in her ears so viciously she felt her own scream before she heard it, the pain of it shredding her throat as she jerked against her chair. "Stop it, *stop it.*"

Gray's lips pressed together, bloodless with the effort. Her voice was the only sound in the room, an echo of terror and grief that rattled her bones. When Richter pulled away this time, Gray sagged in the chair. The strain carved deep lines around his eyes. But when she met them—

Warm. Soft. The gentleness that he always saved just for her. "Trust me," he murmured, that honey voice a sweet balm over shredded nerves. "Trust yourself."

His eyes flicked down and to the side, just for a heartbeat. Toward where her arms disappeared behind the chair. He'd noticed, as the guards and Richter hadn't. He knew about Dani's gift. He'd seen the telltale movement.

Everyone else thought she was helpless, but Gray never had.

Gray was waiting for his moment. Maya had to give him one. She held Gray's gaze, even as Richter applied his nasty little torture box a third time. She let the faith in his blue eyes form a wall against panic. She used his words as a shield, conjuring them from too-perfect memory, imagining him whispering them against her ear as she focused on the blade and her bindings.

Trust me. Trust yourself. Trust me. Trust yourself. Trust me. Trust—

A silent snap was followed by sudden give. She stiffened her muscles to keep from revealing that her wrists were no longer bound together. A tiny movement clipped the bracelet back together, and she exhaled and checked the guards. One was watching the torture with a blank expression, the other seemed kinda into it.

Neither were paying Maya the slightest bit of attention.

She waited until Gray was sprawled in his chair again, breathing hard. She inclined her head in a tiny nod. The left corner of his mouth twitched up in silent encouragement.

Maya flexed her fingers. The pins and needles were already fading. She shifted her weight forward and relaxed her mental grip on her senses. Every detail of the room locked into place, a replica she could repaint across the backs of her eyelids. A chess board waiting for her opening move.

So she took it.

Her metal chair was solidly constructed but light enough that she could heft it easily in one hand as soon as she'd gained her feet. She didn't have super-speed or super-strength, but she had something more vital when it came to fighting overly trained soldiers—she was easily dismissed. A nonentity.

The guard on the left was the one who seemed to be enjoying Gray's agony. He didn't realize Maya had moved until the chair crashed into his stomach. She'd been aiming for his face—maybe she *would* have to start lifting weights again—but the stomach was good enough.

Time expanded. Maya got to enjoy every detail of the chair crashing into him. The thud, his sharp exhale. The shocked confusion twisting his face, swallowed by pain as he doubled over. The hilarious bafflement on the other guard's face as his gaze darted around the room, looking for a threat he could comprehend.

Richter spun to face her, his smug pleasure evaporating. In that single second that stretched for a lifetime, she could *see* his thoughts scrambling to make sense of all the things he couldn't have anticipated. Her resilience. Her inexplicable freedom. Her brazen defiance. Her Dani-given ability to turn literally anything into a weapon, including the chair he'd tied her to.

Underestimating her would be the last thing he did.

Gray was running out of time.

He didn't need a medic to tell him this. He knew it, the same way he knew his own name and designation, his reflection in the mirror, the trigger weights on his favorite rifles.

The way he knew the scent of Maya's hair.

All he could smell right now was blood. It dripped into his eyes, slid slickly over his skin. He was bleeding, but he couldn't tell how or why. The pain was far away, buried under . . .

No, not buried. Frozen. He'd watched a pond freeze over once, tiny crystals forming and then reaching for one another until they locked together in a thin shell that obscured the water beneath.

That's what this felt like. Something was under the ice. Waiting.

Waiting.

Then Maya sprang from her chair and launched it across the room, and Gray remembered what it was—purpose.

He had a mission, one that was as clear to him now, in his admittedly altered state, as it had been when he was lying naked in Maya's bed. Shield. Protect.

Love.

Gray moved.

The chair clattered loudly to the floor, the sound covering the snap of Gray's bindings as he surged up and toward Richter. With the element of surprise on his side, he managed to wrap one bloody arm around Richter's neck. He jerked him into a chokehold so vicious that his muscles strained and burned.

But Richter wasn't a fool. He still clutched that fucking silver box in his hand, and he jammed the prongs against Gray's arm. The burning spread over Gray's entire body, his muscles contracting as the current flowed through him—but it also kept his arm locked tight around Richter's throat.

The man quickly realized his mistake. The electric pain ceased as he tossed aside the stun gun, and Gray went down in a heap of quivering muscle, dragging Richter down with him.

Richter's face was turning red. Gray tried to count the seconds, but it seemed like it took an eternity for Richter to grope for the pistol in his shoulder holster. Gray caught his wrist in a punishing grip, grinding the bones together—

But the effort was costing him. Richter slammed his elbow into Gray's side and managed to dislodge the chokehold. He broke free, gasping, and reached again for his gun.

The guards were still standing there, stunned into inaction. They barely reacted when Maya shot past them, screaming an incoherent denial. She kicked at Richter's hand, and Gray heard some of the bones in the man's hand shatter—

thin ice on a pond

Richter snatched at Maya's boot, but she evaded him, dropped to her knees, and grabbed the gun from his shoulder rig. She lifted it and fired at the single naked bulb. It shattered, and darkness exploded through the room.

Glass rained down on him, and Gray laughed.

Richter had *no fucking idea* what he'd unleashed.

Gray grabbed at Richter, came up with a handful of shirt and leather gun holster, and used it to drag the man closer. Richter struck out at him, finding the wound on Gray's upper arm and digging his thumbs into it.

It didn't hurt. Gray felt it, a strange sort of pressure that made him tense in anticipation, but the waves of agony never came. He slammed Richter's head against the floor to dislodge his grip, then did it again as his opponent raked his nails viciously across his face.

Gray ignored it all, grappling with Richter until he managed to get his forearm across his neck again. Richter rained blows on him, but Gray shrugged off every one in his single-minded pursuit of his goal.

If this was what Dani felt like all the time, no wonder she thought she was bulletproof.

A gunshot followed by a heavy thud rang out in the tiny room, momentarily distracting Gray from Richter's struggles. If Maya took out the guards—

Two more shots, and the other guard went down, slumping to the floor to land on Gray's legs. He kicked free of the corpse and bore his weight down on Richter's neck. His struggles were weakening . . .

But so was Gray. The lack of pain didn't feel so magical now. It only felt like spiraling down into a numb void.

Maya called out to him. "Gray?"

"Go!" It was an order. "Get out of here, Maya. Now."

Shield.

"*No,*" she shot back. "I won't leave you."

Protect.

She didn't have to. *He* would be leaving *her*, and no amount of anger or struggling could change that.

Love.

End of the line. All he could do now was make sure he took Richter with him.

NINA

By the time the last Executive Security guard fell, Nina felt like she'd been fighting for days.

It had been a long time since she'd been in a battle this vicious, with waves and waves of indefatigable enemies that kept coming, no matter what. It reminded her too much of the failed mission years before that had taken Zoey's life and torn her and Ava apart.

She glanced at Ava. Their eyes locked, and she knew her sister felt it, too, that heavy drag of memory. Then Ava broke the contact, bending down to gather more ammunition from the fallen bodies.

Nina locked it down, too. There would be time later to process. First, they had to get everyone home alive.

She activated her comms. "Rafe? Did Mace and Dani make it?"

"We're here," Dani answered with a tiny but telltale hitch in her voice. "They're working on Conall."

Across the room, Knox swiped at one bloodstained cheek with his arm and only managed to leave even more blood behind.

He raised one eyebrow, and Nina nodded. "Did Rafe say where he and Gray were separated?"

"That long hallway on the first floor, but it's sealed off. You'll have to figure out a way in."

Nina started for the stairs, Knox and Ava hard on her heels. "Suggestions?"

"Windows would my first choice," Knox replied.

Ava frowned. "We could go through the floor on the second level."

Nina considered both options as they pounded down the stairs, but she knew they didn't have time for either. Going through the floor required tools they didn't have. And without knowing the layout of the building, it would take a tedious process of trial and error to find the correct set of windows to attempt entry.

The only people who had a chance in hell of quickly pulling up the blueprints were either missing or bleeding out.

Nina clenched her jaw as they hit the first-floor landing—and almost ran face-first into the heavy blast door. There was literally no way around it. She and Knox would have to physically force it, and they'd be sitting ducks for any potential firepower on the other side of it.

She pushed up her sleeves and gripped one handle near the edge anyway. "Ava?"

Her sister nodded and drew two pistols. "I'll cover you."

Knox grabbed on to the door as well, worry creasing his brow.

"We can do this," Nina reassured him. "We *will* do this. On three."

She counted it off, and they pushed at the door with a strength born more out of desperation than physical alteration. Two people they loved, two members of their *family*, were probably on the other side of this fucking door.

Failure was not an option.

At first, nothing. They pushed harder. Knox grunted with the effort, and Nina opened her mouth, ready to scream her frustration—

The door creaked, groaned, and began to move.

Once they got it going, it went fast. Neither of them had time to check their force, so they stumbled and landed in a heap on the floor. Ava planted her expensive boots in the newly opened doorway, raised her pistols, and fired down the hallway.

By the time Nina and Knox made it back to their feet, she'd killed the four guards waiting for them.

Nina didn't wait to clear the area. Nothing could have stopped her from dashing down the hallway, calling Maya's name, not even an ambush. If anyone tried to jump out at her, she'd bear them down by sheer force of will alone.

Instead of an answer, she heard weeping. She pushed open the door closest to where the guards had fallen, and light flooded into a dark room.

It illuminated Tobias Richter's dead-eyed corpse lying on the floor. Next to him, Maya wept bitterly, cradling Gray's motionless head in her lap.

"Help me," she sobbed, her fingers buried in Gray's hair. "He's dying."

Nina knelt at her side. "It's okay," she whispered, tugging at Maya's hands. "We're here. Everything's going to be okay."

She could only hope it wasn't a lie.

December 15th, 2079

I told myself I could never be her mother. I told myself she was a soldier in this war. I thought I understood the monster that I am. I accepted it. What I did was monstrous.

When she was eight years old, I made this terrible choice, knowing it might lead to both our deaths.

Now that she's seventeen, I find myself unable to tolerate the idea of sacrificing her.

I didn't anticipate this weakness. I suppose this terrible feeling is love.

It's very inconvenient.

The Recovered Journal of Birgitte Skovgaard

TWENTY-SIX

Maya couldn't remember how she got outside.

It was an odd feeling—not remembering. Her entire life was defined by *knowing*, knowing facts and statistics, languages and history, knowing precisely what had happened, and when, and how.

It wasn't really a natural state for humans. After Birgitte had warned her that her genetic modifications carried debilitating side effects, Maya had grown obsessed with researching the science of memory. Most people remembered the world through a constantly evolving filter, with everything they thought they knew growing increasingly blurry around the edges, shaped by their emotions and experience. The very act of recalling a memory could change it—and that was if they'd even remembered an event correctly to begin with. The human brain had an unfathomable ability to protect itself with gentle lies.

Maya had never had the comfort of self-protective deception. Her memories were crystal clear and sharp enough to cut, with every foolish mistake she'd ever made wrapped in perfectly preserved agony and humiliation. Sometimes she thought that was what really happened to data couriers. Who wouldn't eventually snap under the pressure of remembering a lifetime of mortifying fuckups and interpersonal conflicts and other people's dark, terrible secrets?

But Maya couldn't remember how she got outside.

She couldn't hear, either. She knelt at Gray's side and stared at Mace. His mouth moved as he checked Gray's vitals, but all Maya heard was a hollow ringing. She watched Mace's lips as they formed shapes she'd never learned to convert to meaning.

Why would she need to read lips? She'd always heard everything.

Pain twisted Mace's features. He rested a hand on Gray's forehead for a second, then shoved himself to his feet as if every movement hurt. Maya watched him move to Conall's side in slow motion as the ringing sound vibrated down an endless tunnel.

Tinnitus, identified a voice inside her head. *Brought upon by significant emotional shock.* And of course she could still hear that—the one thing she'd always wanted to escape. The endless ghosts echoing in her head.

Movement out of the corner of her eye drew her attention. It took forever to turn her head, and even that gentle adjustment made the world swim.

Rafe was striding out of the building, carrying a dazed child in each arm. Nina took one and carried her across the parking lot to where Dani was parking a windowless van she must have stolen from somewhere.

The children would be fine.

Gray wouldn't.

Maya looked back down. Gray was stretched out on a thin strip of dead grass, paler than death and just as still. She reached for his wrist, distantly terrified when she couldn't find a pulse at first. She adjusted her fingers until she felt it—weak, too quick, unsteady.

Mace couldn't do anything for him. That was why he'd left and gone back to Conall's side. It was simple triage. You didn't spend time on people you couldn't save. Instead, you moved on to the people you could.

Gray was dying. But he wasn't dead. Not yet.

Not yet.

We ran an op down near the Gulf once.

Maya squeezed her eyes shut as Gray's voice drifted up out of her memories. But closing her eyes only made it worse—her grip on reality was already so tenuous. She fell backward into the past.

A shitty bar outside a shittier town. A cage fight. The sound of flesh on flesh. The panic—*her* panic—

And then Gray had been there. A solid wall. Her protector. Cutting a path through the crowd, guiding her out into a night pulsing with the promise of a vicious storm.

His voice. Soft and warm, curling around her to speak of nothing more demanding than the weather. He'd soothed her panic with his words, and in doing so he'd slid beneath her defenses. It had taken her months to admit the truth, but she'd fallen a little in love with him that night.

While we were there, a hurricane hit, and we had to hunker down.

His pulse fluttered under her fingertips. So fast, so weak. The ringing in her ears felt like the roaring of violent winds.

A hurricane had slammed into Maya's life. Not so many hours ago, she'd been in bed with Gray, breaking apart under the bliss of letting herself *feel.* So vulnerable and yet still so safe—Gray had given her that.

In the middle of the storm, everything got quiet. The whole sky was the strangest green I've ever seen.

Gray had given her peace.

She had given him pain.

She'd given him torture at the hands of a monster, because that was the lot of anyone who got too close to her. Did it matter that Richter was dead now? There would always be another TechCorps executive who wanted the secrets in her head, because Birgitte had left so many. So *many.*

Maya's love was poison.

She'd be the death of Gray, just like she'd killed Simon. Just like she would no doubt kill Dani and Nina someday. Knox and Conall and Rafe, too. Probably even Mace.

Maybe Maya should have died with Birgitte and her revolution. Maybe she never should have crawled off the Hill, trailing peril and death in her wake.

I thought it was all over, but Mace said no, it was just the eye of the storm. The middle.

The world spun on around her.

The world spun on *without* her.

She felt a thousand years old, a million miles away. Nina drifted into her field of vision, her lips moving, her arms gesturing. Confident and strong, directing the rescue mission because that was what Nina did. She saved people.

She'd taught *Maya* to save people.

Instinctively, Maya rejected the thought, clinging to her broken numbness. But it drifted up again, nagging and insistent. Forcing her to remember.

She *had* saved people. Sometimes it was big and obvious—rescuing kids or shutting down bullies or arranging medical help in the nick of time. But the little stuff mattered just as much. The food she helped preserve. The knowledge she shared. Every heater or air conditioner she fixed, every generator or engine. The books and the music and the tools and the *hope*.

Nina could have done some of it without her but not all of it. Maybe not even *most* of it. Five Points would have been colder and darker and sadder if Maya had never been a part of it.

Maybe it was a good thing she'd crawled off the Hill, after all.

And Tobias Richter had been the worst the TechCorps could throw at her. He'd hurt her. He'd bruised her. Maybe he'd even broken her a little.

But he hadn't beaten her. He was the one lying dead on a floor, not her.

And not Gray. His heart was still beating. Too fast, too weak, but it was *beating.*

Sure enough, after that, it started right up again.

Tobias Richter was dead.

Tobias Richter was *dead.*

It was too big a thought to absorb all at once. Trying to process it *hurt*, like the pins and needles of a limb waking up, only everywhere. The numbness cracked as she let the full impact wash over her.

Tobias Richter had gathered power into his own two hands for decades. His lieutenants were nothing but glorified henchmen. He'd never trained a replacement because he hadn't trusted that replacement not to supplant him. It would take five people, minimum, to even attempt to do his job—five people working at cross-purposes, jockeying for position and power.

Maya had evaded discovery by Richter at the height of his influence. No one left at TechCorps HQ had a chance of outthinking her. Cara had escaped, and if she was smart, she'd keep running. But if she wasn't, Maya would be facing off against an enemy she knew all too well. A grim part of her savored the challenge. A more vicious part anticipated certain victory.

No one left at the TechCorps scared her the same way Richter had.

And she knew those bastards' secrets. Oh God, so many secrets. The vices of Board members. Their hidden vulnerabilities. Their second families. The sins they'd do anything to keep private. The people who were hungry to betray them.

Push a few buttons—the right buttons—and she could have half the Board at war with the other half.

Maya wasn't poison. She was *power.* That's why they wanted her so badly.

She could ruin their sweet little world.

Like it had never stopped.

The world snapped back into place, vivid and bright. Painful. Maya scanned the furious activity around her, her mind absorbing the chaos and sorting through it as if hungry for stimulation after its brief deprivation.

The ringing faded. Sound came back in patches. Her own breathing first, harsh and unsteady. Then Mace, calling out a command to Ava. "Keep him steady."

Gray was still silent. Someone had wrapped the worst of his wounds, but there was nothing else Mace could do for him. Conall had problems the medic knew how to solve, so he had prioritized.

Maya had to prioritize, too.

Gently, she released Gray's wrist and folded his hands over his chest. His too-long hair had fallen over his forehead again, so she tenderly stroked it back before leaning down to brush a kiss to his forehead. "You protected my heart," she whispered to him. "Now it's my turn."

She let go of the world again, but this time she wasn't in the eye of the hurricane.

This time, she *was* the hurricane.

Somewhere inside her vast and endless memories and her sprawling network of contacts was a chance for Gray. Maybe a remote one. Maybe a desperate one. But she'd scour the earth bare and sweep away anything in her path on her way to finding it.

And then she'd fight for him. Whatever the cost.

MACE

Mace had slipped back into the comforting detachment of running a trauma.

It wasn't fun for him—nothing about this situation was—but it was familiar. He knew how to pivot from one patient to the next, putting out fires. Emergency triage had *rules*, and there was never enough time to linger over decisions so long they became painful to make.

Being in the clinic helped. It wasn't finished yet, but he recognized it in his bones, the colors and smells, even the way the noises from the telemetry equipment echoed off the unfinished floors and bare walls.

This was what he knew. Where he did his best work.

The frantic drive back to the warehouse had passed in a blur of blood and desperation. He could have used Rafe's help, but Rafe was busy keeping a hot-wired truck full of cloned children calm. Mace had managed to stabilize Conall on his own, but keeping him that way had taken all his focus.

And then there was Gray.

He'd had another seizure. It had subsided, and he was awake, but Mace would never go as far as to call him alert. He could move, but would only do so when guided, and he didn't even blink at painful stimuli. His body was running on pure, adrenaline-fueled autopilot.

What Mace didn't know—what scared the absolute shit out of him—was how hard Gray would crash once the adrenaline faded.

But that was a problem for five minutes from now. Maybe an hour, if they were lucky.

With Conall finally on a monitor, Mace studied the display. "Keep an eye on his blood pressure," he instructed Luna. "If it starts to drop, it might mean he has another bleed. When Dr. Wells—"

Rafe ducked his head through the empty doorway, terror painted across his face. "Gray's not breathing."

Fuck. He immediately started for the door, but called back over his shoulder, "I want to know the second Wells gets here."

Gray was lying on a gurney in the main lobby area. Nina stood over him, rhythmically squeezing air into his lungs through a mask secured over his face. Rafe had already set out most of what he'd need to intubate—laryngoscopes, tubes, paralytic drugs.

Mace checked his pulse, half of his attention on the reedy thumps in Gray's wrist . . . and the other half on Knox. "It's time to make the call, Garrett."

"Which one?" Knox demanded.

"Do we put him on a vent," Mace clarified, quiet but firm, "or do we let him go?"

Knox closed his eyes, his face stricken. "Can you fix him? Is there *any* chance at all?"

"No." It was the only honest answer. "But intubation buys us time."

Dani was leaning against the far wall, but her whispered question carried easily in the tense silence. "Time for what?"

Mace eased Nina to Gray's left side, pulled the intubation tray closer, and started assembling the laryngoscope. "To figure out how to say goodbye."

"Do it." Maya stood in the doorway, her expression blank and her dark eyes unfathomable. She hadn't allowed anyone to touch the wounds at her wrists, or even wash Gray's blood from her hands and cheek. She looked fragile, dwarfed by Rafe's sweatshirt, but her eyes were pure steel. "Put him on the vent. We're going to try to replace his implant. He'd want to try."

Mace didn't wait for Knox to confirm her words. She had as much right to make the call as either of them; more, because she was the closest thing Gray had to a next of kin.

He nodded to Rafe. "All right, you heard the lady. Push the paralytic. We're gonna go down fighting."

The intubation was swift, smooth. Once Mace had confirmed the tube's placement and hooked up the ventilator, he turned back to Maya.

"What's next?" she asked.

"You and me? Later, we have a long, hard talk about Gray's odds. I don't lie, and I don't give false hope. Before we go one step further, I want you to understand what we're up against with this surgery."

She returned his gaze, unblinking. Unflinching. "I have half of the bad outcomes in TechCorps history shoved into my head. I know the odds are almost impossible. Tell me who could help you. A TechCorps neurosurgeon? An implant specialist? A bioengineer?"

"If you're offering, I'll take all three."

"How about Nikita Novak?"

The stress of the situation made his words sharper and shorter than he would have liked. "Yeah, sure. Bring me her, too. And maybe a unicorn while you're at it."

She gestured. "Dani—come with me?"

He moved on, already focused on the next thing on his mental checklist. It took him a moment, but he finally spotted Ava hovering just outside the room. "You. You're rich, right?"

She stepped closer. "By most people's reckoning, yes."

"I need to outfit an OR. Will you help me?"

She looked at Nina. They stood there, facing one another like mirror images locked in silent communication. Finally, Ava answered. "Give me a list."

All he could do now was wait. The tape securing Gray's endotracheal tube had peeled up on one edge, and Mace carefully smoothed it back into place.

Beside him, Knox sighed roughly. "Are you ready for Maya to come back dragging Nikita Novak behind her? Because she will, you know."

"Good." If she managed to pull that off, she just might get her miracle after all.

**TECHCORPS PROPRIETARY DATA,
L2 SECURITY CLEARANCE**

This is 66–793's tenth psychological workup in nine years. His results consistently place him among the Protectorate's most reliable and stable assets. But something about him continues to bother me.

I know he's lying to me. What I don't know is why.

Recruit Analysis, April 2075

TWENTY-SEVEN

The VIP ring worked like magic.

Dani flashed it at the guards, and they parted in silence. The party was still raging, even with dawn fast approaching. Maya barely noticed the tangle of bodies on the balcony this time. The music was a distant, annoying buzz. She was wrapped in a dozen layers of cotton, floating through a world that didn't feel real.

This time, Dani didn't wait to be acknowledged, and she wasn't laying on the charm. She stopped in front of the dais, folded her arms over her chest, and announced, "We need the room."

Savitri glanced at Adam, who stepped forward. "Come on," he rasped. "Out."

Dani ignored the command. "In my experience, it takes a while to break up an orgy, so you might want to get cracking."

Adam sighed. "I will remove you, if necessary."

Dani finally looked at him. "You can certainly *try*."

He reached for her. Instead of dodging his grasp, *she* grabbed *him*, her slender fingers locking around his wrist. The move seemed to stun him—not so much the speed of it, but the audacity.

Her words were quiet, a whispered warning. "Consider your next move very carefully, Ryan."

Savitri surged from her seat, but her expression was frozen. The abrupt movement drew attention from all over the room, a ripple that drifted through the crowd as heads turned and whispers started.

She clapped her hands together once. And people began to scatter.

Maya had to admire the swiftness of it. It turned out Dani was wrong—it *didn't* take long to break up an orgy. No doubt the tension on the dais urged anyone with sense to run for cover. Savitri stood like a statue carved from ice, her eyes promising chilly death to anyone who crossed her. Adam and Dani were frozen in a silent battle, both fairly vibrating with the promise of sudden violence.

When the door had shut behind the final partier, Savitri resumed her seat. She crossed her legs, leaned back, and murmured one word. "Adam."

It sounded like an instruction. "How?" he asked.

Dani released him slowly. "I recognized you."

The set of his shoulders relaxed the tiniest bit. "Executive Security?"

She nodded. "Databases can be manipulated. But people remember." She looked over at Savitri. "We always remember."

"People," Savitri said coldly, "can be made to forget."

As threats went, it was far from idle. But all of their cards were on the table now.

Almost all of their cards.

Maya stepped forward, and for the first time met Savitri's gaze head-on. She refused to be cowed by the power staring back at her. She had her own kind of power. "Do you remember Birgitte Skovgaard?"

Savitri's brow furrowed. "The TechCorps VP of Behavior? Vaguely. I heard she was promoted to lead her own facility a few years back."

"Yes, that's the story." Maya took a deep breath. Saying this out loud felt like handing Savitri a stick of live dynamite with a half-inch fuse. "Birgitte was the head of a reformist rebellion within the TechCorps. It spanned all seventeen departments and included everyone from VPs to janitorial staff. Tobias Richter found out about it and executed her. Personally."

Savitri's perfectly shaped eyebrow arched. Her gaze raked over Maya. "You're what, twenty years old, at most? How could you possibly know that?"

"I'm twenty-four. And I signed my first executive-level contract with the TechCorps sixteen years ago." Maya channeled the data courier Birgitte had raised. Ice cold, confident, fully aware of her precarious—but powerful—place in her world. How ironic that it was Cara who had taught her the true value of this haughty, fearless facade.

Maya didn't care. She'd use the tools she had. "I didn't introduce myself properly last time," she said, the easy rhythm of Southside's more casual speech gone. She made every word crisp and sharp enough for a boardroom on the Hill. "I am DC-031, former data courier to the vice president of Behavior and Analysis."

Theatrical, perhaps, but Savitri rewarded her with a sharply indrawn breath—the first *real* reaction Maya had ever seen her make. Savitri leaned forward, eyes alight with naked avarice. "A data courier," she whispered. "Out in the wild, and apparently no worse for the wear. Remarkable. I bet your brain is something to see."

"No doubt it is," Maya replied, refusing to back down. "And I'll let you scan it until you're thoroughly tired of looking at it. I'll give you dirt on any TechCorps exec you want. I'll owe you a dozen favors. But you have to come with me and try to save Gray. Now."

"Gray?" Savitri sat back, her game face settling back into place. "The quiet one who was with you last time? What's wrong with him?"

"Delayed implant rejection."

"Delayed for how long?"

"Almost twenty years."

"And his current status?"

"On life support."

Savitri frowned. "He didn't seem too far gone. What precipitated the abrupt decline?"

Maya dragged in a deep breath. It wouldn't be a secret for long. Even if the TechCorps covered it up, rumors of Richter's disappearance would tear through the criminal underworld. But speaking the words barely felt real.

"He was tortured," she said softly. "By Tobias Richter. Gray killed him before collapsing."

The words provoked the expected reaction. Savitri came out of her chair again, voice shivering with excitement. "Tobias Richter is dead?"

"Extremely." Savitri's bright-eyed anticipation only underscored the depth of Maya's distraction. Without a doubt, this was the most pivotal turning point in Atlanta since the Flares. It was the realization of one of Birgitte's most cherished goals. The monster from Maya's nightmares had been slain.

But she had a new nightmare now. A worse one. Darker and real and digging loss into her heart as she laced her trembling fingers together to hide their sudden shaking. "I'll tell you everything about it. Anything you want. Just *please.* Come help him."

Savitri exchanged a look with Adam. Some sort of silent communication seemed to pass between them. Maybe it was actual silent communication. Maya wouldn't put it past them to have subvocal comms or something even wilder. After a moment, Adam tilted his head. "Two percent."

"Two percent," Savitri said, turning back to Maya. "That's the probable chance of survival for that sort of procedure, even with my considerable skills and experience. Will you still offer me brain scans and secrets and favors and anything I want for two percent, DC-031?"

Her designation left Savitri's lips with a chilly precision that turned the query into a test. Savitri was probing for weakness, prodding to see how far she could push Maya. A political game endemic to the Hill and a sharp contrast to the blunt honesty of Southside, but Maya couldn't be intimidated.

Not this time. Numbness had some benefits.

She lifted her chin and answered without hesitation. "If there's even a fraction of a fraction of a percent, I'll offer you the damn world. Just come. *Now.*"

Maya waited. For seconds. For years. Time had lost meaning the moment Gray started seizing. She waited as Savitri turned toward Adam again, waited as the two of them assessed risk or odds or maybe just drew out the moment for the drama of it all.

Then Savitri stepped off the dais. "Take me to him."

TECHCORPS PROPRIETARY DATA,
L2 SECURITY CLEARANCE

Recruit 66–793 is our top sniper. His marksmanship is unmatched. We are aware of Behavior's continuing concerns about his emotional reticence, but we submit that if fourteen years of aggressive monitoring has uncovered neither troubling pathologies nor questions of loyalty, the issue should be considered resolved pending further developments.

He's an extremely useful tool, Birgitte. Stop trying to throw him away because he creeps you out.

Recruit Analysis, May 2075

TWENTY-EIGHT

"I'll take care of him," Savitri promised, squeezing Maya's shoulder briefly as Mace rolled Gray into the operating room. "You've given him the best chance possible."

The best chance possible. Two percent of a chance.

"Come on." It was Nina, warm and gentle at her side, coaxing her away. She followed because doing otherwise would require thinking, and she couldn't do that. She couldn't allow herself to think.

Unfortunately, it was the one thing she had never been able to avoid. Her brain, overwhelmed from the chaos of the past twenty-four hours, taunted her with endless worst-case scenarios. God knew she had enough of them shoved into her memory, an endless litany of the TechCorps' experiments gone horribly wrong. *Neurological experiments, physical augmentations, xenotransplants, tissue replacement—*

After the ninth hour of surgery, Maya fled for the roof.

Unlimited resources and access to a genius had done their work. By noon, Ava and Mace had constructed a cutting-edge operating room. Savitri took confident control, conscripting Rafe and Ava to assist. She and Mace disappeared into it with Gray, while Dr. Wells hovered over an unconscious Conall.

There'd been nothing left for Maya to do but wait. Wait, pacing anxiously, while Dani tried to convince her to eat and Nina tried to convince her to sleep and Knox channeled all of his obvious panic into fretting over Maya.

Their concern was well-meant and terrifying. The more they petted and hovered and tried to make her feel better, the more it felt like disaster was imminent. By hour five, her nerves were raw. By hour seven, she wanted to scream.

Nine hours in, she snapped.

But while her flight to the roof freed her from their solicitous concern, nothing let her outrun the anxiety.

Two percent. The number throbbed in her head, despite her best efforts to banish it. She settled cross-legged on the walkway and glared up at the TechCorps. Night had fallen at some point, and the bright glow on the Hill burned into her sleep-deprived eyes.

Little lights darted around the main building like nervous fireflies. Cars, carrying people to late-night meetings. Did they know Tobias Richter had gone rogue, yet? Did they know he was dead? The aftershocks of what had happened would rip through the TechCorps, eroding their foundation. They'd be vulnerable.

Two percent.

Maya squeezed her eyes shut.

Two percent wasn't that low. The chances of drawing three of a kind in poker was barely over 2 percent, and she'd done that a ton of times. Only 0.2 percent for a flush, and she'd taken Rafe's entire stash of fancy chocolates a few weeks ago after pulling one of those.

Four of a kind was 0.02 percent. Conall had won his way free of his bar tab at Clem's with four kings a month back and had almost gotten into a fight over cheating—which he had not been doing—and counting cards—which Maya definitely had. She'd ended the night with a straight flush of bleeding hearts and only defused the fraught situation by using her winnings to buy everyone drinks.

A straight flush wasn't even 0.002 percent.

There were so many numbers in her head. She worked her way through them, buying herself hope with blackjack, praying with poker, cataloging every long odd and lightning strike in TechCorps history.

Her eyes burned with the lack of sleep and her body coiled tighter and tighter, a spring that exploded into startled movement when the door opened at the far end of the walkway.

Maya lurched upright, so wobbly she had to grab at the railing to steady herself. Savitri stepped out onto the walkway in a pair of scrubs and strode to Maya, her lips moving.

Sound came slower, through an endless tunnel. Her blood was pounding in her ears so hard she couldn't make sense of the words. Didn't know if she wanted to make sense of them. If this was the moment she found out the worst—

Savitri touched Maya's shoulder. Her mouth moved again, and this time the words slammed into Maya and knocked the breath out of her. "He made it through surgery."

She struggled to inhale. To get enough air to ask the only question that mattered. "Did it work?"

"I replaced his implant, and I made some modifications to the interface, so rejection shouldn't be an issue." She held up a hand. "But complications can and do happen. We won't know much more until he wakes up."

Maya swallowed around sudden tears. "Will he wake up?"

Savitri smiled gently. "Obviously I can't say for sure. But I think so. The surgery went smoothly. Your medic is *very* skilled. I have a good feeling."

Maybe 2 percent was enough.

Relief surged through her body, sapping the last lingering strength adrenaline had given her. Maya gripped the railing until her fingers ached, and her words cracked. "Thank you. Thank you, Savitri."

"Here." Savitri gently pried her hand free and steadied her. "Sit. Before you pitch over the edge and crack your head open. I just operated for ten hours and I'm not young enough to enjoy back-to-back brain surgeries anymore."

Maya sank obediently to the catwalk, her knees feeling like rubber. "I should have taken a nap. I just . . ."

"Couldn't." Savitri leaned against the opposite railing. The city rose behind her, framing her with its shimmering glow like a halo. For a giddy moment, Maya thought she looked like an angel.

Her words, however, were far more pragmatic. "You must love the man a great deal, to hand a person like me a secret like yours."

No, definitely not an angel. Savitri might be dressed in scrubs with her hair in a plain ponytail, but her dangerous charisma hadn't been all manufactured by makeup and expensive clothing. Even like this she was lethally beautiful, her light-brown skin flawless, her cheekbones sharp enough to cut, those dark-brown eyes watching Maya with a scary kind of brilliance.

Savitri's full lips curled into a knowing smile. "Ah, yes. There's the look. You made a hasty promise in a moment of weakness, and now you're regretting the debt you incurred."

"No," Maya countered. "I'd do it again in a heartbeat, if it means Gray lives. But I'm not stupid. I know you could fuck up my life."

"I could," Savitri agreed. "And you could be a tremendously useful asset to me. Especially in a world without Tobias Richter. But here's the thing, Maya. I don't want your grudging acquiescence. I want your gleeful participation. Which is why I'm going to forgive this debt. I saved your man's life, and you don't owe me anything in return."

Oh, like *that* didn't sound too good to be true. "Sure."

"Really." Savitri tilted her head, a superior little smile curving her lips. "And since you trusted me with your secret, perhaps the quickest path to a mutually beneficial arrangement is to trust you with mine."

The smart move was silence. She could let Savitri play out her little game and not let her know that the condescension was getting under Maya's skin. She'd lived her entire life like that—pulling inward, making herself small. Pretending she wasn't as smart as anyone else in the room.

Pretending she wasn't smarter.

It was exhausting. Another thing she'd been holding in, and Maya couldn't see the point. Tobias Richter was dead. He'd done his worst, and she'd beaten him. With help from her family, admittedly, but wasn't that the damn point?

Maya wasn't alone. She didn't have to hide.

And she was tired of all the predators assuming she was easy prey. "Which secret is that?" she drawled. "We've already established that I know who you are. Nikita Novak, former lead researcher on the Guardian Project. And that Adam's name is actually Ryan Lemieux."

Savitri narrowed her eyes. Her patronizing smile slipped.

"We also know that Ryan Lemieux is supposed to be dead," Maya continued. "Though to be fair, who here isn't supposed to be dead? I assume you faked his death somehow."

"I didn't," Savitri replied. "Ryan Lemieux is quite dead." Her expression was still a pleasant mask, but her eyes . . . Oh hell, her *eyes.*

Pain. Rage. Loss.

Those could have been Maya's own eyes, during those first horrible days after she'd escaped the Hill and was still grieving Simon's loss. They might have been her eyes again if Savitri hadn't come to a warehouse in Southside and used her skill and talent to give Gray a second chance at life.

Maya had too many emotional bruises to take pleasure in poking someone else's. "You don't have to tell me," she said gently. "Your secrets aren't my business."

"No, I deserved it." Savitri's mouth quirked in a sad little smile. "I'm not used to sparring with people on my level."

"It's a pretty impressive level," Maya acknowledged. "Level One specialist at twenty-seven."

"Youngest in company history."

"And the Guardian Project?"

Savitri shifted her weight against the railing and stared past Maya. "Do you know what the Protectorate's problem is?"

Maya couldn't hold back a rude noise. "They only have one?"

"Depends on who you ask. But if you ask the people in charge, the main problem is that smart men are hard to control and the ones who aren't smart aren't very useful. Take your Captain Knox—undeniably one of the Protectorate's most talented recruits. They worked hard to keep him in a patriotic bubble in an attempt to secure his loyalties. Breaking him would stunt the skills they found so useful, but he did have that terrible habit of thinking for himself, didn't he?"

Confusion knotted Maya's brow. "How do you know so much about Knox?"

"Because my job was to fix the problem he represented." Savitri met Maya's gaze squarely. "I was designing the next iteration of the Protectorate. Soldiers who wouldn't suffer Knox's fatal flaw."

"Guardians," Maya whispered. It was so like the TechCorps. A shiny name wrapped around a brutal lie. "But how would they . . ."

Savitri's file flashed through her memory, the words dropping like stones in a pond.

Father, Dimitri Novak. L2 scientist, Bioengineering. Mother, Jaya Novak. L1 specialist, Neural Networks.

Her brain made one of its *leaps*. Endless rows of data, thousands of personnel files. All those TechCorps secrets that she could never escape. She knew almost every project undertaken involving neural networks. She knew most of the jobs that required a top-tier bioengineer.

She knew what sat at their intersection.

"You were making supersoldiers." Maya could barely get the words out around her horror. "Ones who couldn't disobey."

"There's no need to hide your disgust." Savitri gripped the railing on either side of her body, the only indication she wasn't as calm as her voice sounded. "Trust me. I've come to understand the full implications of what I was dabbling with."

Maya doubted she could have hidden her disgust. Not from her face, or from her eyes, or from her voice. "Some sort of control implant."

"Integrated Artificial Intelligence." Savitri's laugh held little mirth. "Of course, it wasn't supposed to be AI the way most people think of it. After all, the last thing the TechCorps wanted to grapple with was true artificial sentience. But with sufficient behavior training, the theory was that we could create the perfect soldiers without all those pesky human flaws."

They would have taken men like Gray. Like Knox and Rafe. Turned them into soldiers, only this time the TechCorps wouldn't have needed the constant threat of a kill switch to keep them in line. Just some fancy little program hardwired into their brain that stripped them of the will to think, to want, to *be*.

It was worse than what they'd done to the Devils. Worse than what they'd done to Dani or Maya. Maybe even worse than what they'd done to Mace, because at least he could still fight.

This was worse than death. Worse than anything.

And Savitri had tried to make it a reality.

For one horrible moment, Maya wished the railing behind Savitri would crumble and send her on a thirty-foot tumble. In the next, she reminded herself of the truth—Savitri clearly hadn't done it. And she was outside the TechCorps now, undermining them with gleeful regularity.

It still took effort to swallow down bile. "I don't understand how Adam fits into it."

"Most people don't." Savitri pushed off the railing and stared down at Maya. "Ryan took a bullet meant for me. They declared him brain-dead. But I know more about the human brain than anyone, so I decided to save him."

Maya wet her lips. "I thought you said Ryan Lemieux died."

"He did," Savitri said just as softly. "But I'd trained my AI using his insights and personality. Ryan was my protector. The most brilliant, courageous, and compassionate warrior I had ever met. A true guardian."

The impossibility of the implication was almost dizzying. Maya opened her mouth to ask the question, then closed it. Then opened it again. It was ridiculous. It was *insane*.

"Are you saying . . ." Maya hesitated. Tried again. "Is Adam . . . ?"

"Adam is everything I made him to be." Savitri smiled. "But more importantly, everything he chooses to be."

Holy *shit*.

Savitri tugged her ponytail down and ran her fingers through her hair as she started for the walkway door. She paused with one hand on the handle, looking back at Maya. "Now we're even. I'll keep your secrets. You keep mine."

Oh, sure. Maya was a runaway filing cabinet for corporate espionage, and Savitri had just admitted to *creating life*, but they were even. Totally even.

Except . . . that wasn't all Maya was. She was the anchor of her community. An invaluable resource, not just because of what she knew but how she'd learned to use it. She made people's lives better every day in big ways and small. She used the big, wild brain she'd been given to build a better world that undermined the dominance of the TechCorps at every turn.

And she was the heir to Birgitte's revolution. The secrets in her head could bring down the TechCorps, applied properly. Savitri was looking at her like someone eager to apply a few of those secrets in places that would make the TechCorps hurt.

Maya wanted to make them hurt.

Plus, now if Maya got trapped in a room with any bad guys, she could just shoot out the lights and take them all out. Because she was a fucking superhero. She didn't even need a renegade AI bodyguard.

But she'd have a protector. Her own guardian, who didn't have to be coerced into battle. Gray would fight for her because it was what he wanted to do. To keep her safe. To help her achieve her dreams.

To love her.

Maya's lips curled in a slow smile. "Yes. We're even. Thank you, Savitri."

"You're welcome, Maya."

Maya sat for a while after she was gone, watching the lights on the Hill as they flashed and sparkled and glowed in the night. She breathed in the scent of honeysuckle and kudzu, and it was peaceful and familiar, but it wasn't what she wanted. She wanted soap and coffee and sweat and sawdust and the sound of Gray's even breaths, each one a promise that there would be thousands more of them.

They would have time. Maya wasn't going to waste a second of it. So she climbed to her feet and went downstairs to wait for her future to wake up.

NINA

The kids were breaking Nina's heart.

She watched them as they sat around the table for dinner. Ivonne had prepared a thick, savory cazuela with chicken and butternut squash. Some of their guests were already halfway through devouring their meals, while others were still eyeing their bowls—and everything else—with suspicion.

At least they were properly clothed now. A quick canvass of the neighborhood had yielded enough secondhand garments to get them out of their identical, purely utilitarian jumpsuits. The clothes were a bit mismatched, but they were clean and warm.

When Ivonne joined her in the kitchen, Nina asked softly, "Are they all right?"

"Who would be?" Ivonne sighed. "They'll be fine, Nina."

Eventually—the word hung between them, unspoken but understood. "Thank you for taking point with them. I just . . ."

"You've been busy." Ivonne patted her arm. "How is Gray? Awake yet?"

"No, not yet. But he will be soon." Nina knew that much. Mace had been walking around since the surgery with a mildly stunned look on his face, as if he couldn't believe they'd actually pulled it off, and that had to count for something.

"And Conall?"

"Don't worry, Mace and Dr. Wells finished his regeneration therapy already. He's on his feet, and he'll probably be over here for a bowl or three of your cazuela soon."

Ivonne smiled, clearly pleased, though the expression quickly melted into a troubled frown. "The girl—Rainbow? I couldn't find her for dinner. Earlier, she seemed . . . sad."

There was no telling what she was going through. She'd definitely come out of her shell since her arrival, but seeing the other children, the ones she'd been imprisoned with . . .

It would be enough to send anyone spinning. "I'll look for her now. Thank you, Ivonne."

She didn't have to search for Knox. She found him exactly where she'd known he would be—hovering outside the tiny room that was serving as Gray's recovery suite.

Nina leaned against Knox's back, relishing his solid, steady warmth. "Any change?"

"Not yet." He slid his hand over hers, twining their fingers together. "Rafe found a cot for Maya, and I convinced her to eat and try to get some sleep. Maybe she will, if she doesn't have to leave him."

Nina peered past him. The narrow cot had been placed close to one side of Gray's bed, close enough that Maya could reach out and touch him if she needed to reassure herself he was still there. Whether that was purposeful or a side effect of the cramped quarters, Nina didn't know. But she suspected the former.

"Poor Maya." At least she was actually resting, if only for now. The last day—Jesus, had it only been a day?—had been rough for everyone, but for Maya most of all. If she'd brought Gray this far, through an absolutely impossible surgery, only for him not to make it now . . .

Nina closed her eyes, as if she could block out the thought. "Rainbow's around here somewhere. Can you help me look for her?"

"Have you checked the warehouse?" He turned and wrapped his arms around her, pressing his lips to her temple. "I know she's been curious about the books."

"No, I came here first. I wanted to check on Gray, Maya . . . and you."

His soft sigh tickled her ear. "I'll be better when he's awake."

She looked over to where Maya's hand lay, curled halfway into a fist, so close to Gray's. "I know."

They walked, hand in hand, around to the back entrance of the warehouse, where Knox's instincts once again proved accurate. Rainbow sat on a high stool, her thin shoulders hunched over the 3D scanner.

She looked so fragile that it made Nina's throat ache.

Knox squeezed her hand in silent understanding. "Hey, kiddo," he said gently. Rainbow's shoulders stiffened, but Knox continued, his voice soft and soothing. "You need any help?"

"I won't break it." Rainbow didn't turn, all of her focus on adjusting a book until it was perfectly lined up. "Maya showed me how."

"We're not worried about that," Nina hurried to assure her. "Are you hungry? The other kids are having dinner."

Rainbow shook her head and pressed the button. The scanner started, and she watched it intently. "I promised," she whispered. "I made a deal with Maya. To scan books in exchange for the clothes she bought me."

"Okay, but . . . you don't have to do it right this second." Except maybe this was her way of dealing with the tension and stress that was permeating everything. "Unless you just want to."

The girl finally looked at Nina. Only for a moment, her eyes huge and haunted, before her gaze jumped back to the scanner. "I won't be here much longer."

She said it so matter-of-factly, but her eyes held such startling pain that Nina reflexively shook her head. "Where are you going?"

It was Knox who answered. "Did you hear us talking, Rainbow?"

Rainbow hunched her shoulders again and said nothing.

Oh, *hell*. "Honey—" Nina turned the stool so that Rainbow was facing them and bent a little at the waist, putting her face level with the girl's. "We wanted to talk to you about why Syd's coming here and what's going to happen."

Her small feet swung above the floor. She was wearing the shoes Rafe had helped her pick out—sneakers with rainbow laces. Knox crouched down and tightened the loose laces on her left shoe. "How much did you hear?"

"Just that she's coming to take us." Rainbow bit her lip. "I wasn't trying to eavesdrop."

Nina smoothed an errant lock of hair behind the girl's ear. "Syd is coming to help, because that's what she does. She has a place for people like us, where we can be safe while we figure things out."

"I hear it's pretty nice." Knox smiled up at Rainbow. "There's a lake, and horses. Lots of space to run around. Ava has been there, so she could tell you more about it."

Rainbow's big, green eyes still looked sad. "And that's where we'd live?"

Knox nodded. "For a little while. Some people stay there, but most people . . . Syd helps them find families. People who are special, like you, who can help you learn how to live in the world."

"So the question," Nina said softly, "is whether you want to go there with the other kids or stay here. With us."

Rainbow's head jerked up. She looked back and forth between them, eyes widening. "I can stay?"

"Oh, honey. Of course you can. We don't have ponies, and it's not as nice as Syd's compound. You'll be the only kid. But we all want you here, if that's what you choose."

"Oh." It was a whisper of wonder. Her small brow furrowed. "What about the others?"

"Nina already talked to them," Knox told her. "They decided to go with Syd and see if they can find families of their own. But you already found one, if you want it."

Rainbow moved in a tiny blur, flinging herself off the stool and into Knox's swiftly opened arms. Her arms twined around his neck, and he held her, one hand gently patting her back, and smiled at Nina over Rainbow's shoulder.

Nina had no idea if this was the best decision for Rainbow or not, but Knox spoke the truth. In the short amount of time she'd spent with them, she'd become part of their little blended family. They could have let her go if that was what she wanted, but otherwise, it was unthinkable.

Tears pricked Nina's eyes, and she blinked them away with a smile of her own. "Come on. Ivonne made dinner—everything fresh, nothing freeze-dried. We can't miss that."

Knox rose to his feet and extended a hand to Rainbow. She accepted it, and offered Nina her other hand shyly.

Instead of grasping it, Nina hooked their little fingers together and raised their hands in a gesture she remembered so well from childhood. "Families are forever, especially the ones you make yourself. Remember that, Bo."

"I will," she promised solemnly.

"Good." Sometimes, that vow was all they had.

TECHCORPS PROPRIETARY DATA,
L2 SECURITY CLEARANCE

From: SKOVGAARD, B
To: RICHTER, T
Date: 2075–05–09

You may want to update your latest addition to 66–793's recruit file. It's unlikely you've been aggressively monitoring him for fourteen years, as he's only been a recruit for nine.

From: RICHTER, T
To: SKOVGAARD, B
Date: 2075–05–09

I monitor a lot of people, Birgitte. It's a fact you'd do well to remember.

TWENTY-NINE

The first thing Gray heard was Maya's voice.

"'. . . but that didn't matter. All the intimidation in the world didn't matter. She was Marjorie Starborn, and she had a job to do. Thankfully, she wouldn't have to do it alone.'"

He frowned—or, at least, he *tried* to. Her voice was so clear, lilting over consonants and vowels, rising and falling in a rhythm he knew now like the beating of his own heart.

Was it a dream? It felt like one, hazy darkness pierced by one single dazzling point of light. Or maybe—

Maybe—

He flexed his fingers, then tried to curl them into a fist. It didn't work perfectly, which was perversely what convinced him he was definitely alive. Imperfection was a realm reserved for the living.

He opened his eyes.

Maya was sitting cross-legged on a cot next to his bed, a paperback book open on her lap. Her fingers traced the edges of the page as she read, the touch reverent.

Maya. It came out garbled, more like a groan than her name.

Her head jerked up. The book fell from her lap as she scrambled to her feet, her fingers closing around his hand a moment later. "Gray? Can you hear me?"

It took a herculean effort, but he squeezed her fingers.

Tears filled her eyes. She lifted his hand, kissed it, and turned toward the door. "Mace! He's awake!"

Heavy, quick footsteps pounded through the building, such a flurry of them that Gray thought he could feel each impact jarring up through the bed. Mace hurried in, intent on listening and measuring and assessing.

Gray kept staring at Maya. She looked *okay*, tired and sad but unhurt. He ignored Mace's fussing and asked the first thing, the most important—for all their sakes, but especially hers. "Richter?"

"Dead." She twined her fingers with his and smiled shakily. "Do you remember choking him?"

When he tried, everything was fuzzy and far away, more like trying to picture something imaginary than anything real and remembered. "I don't think so."

"You were incredibly badass." She used her free hand to dash away tears. "And so was I. I shot out the lights and took out the guards, just like you taught me."

Pride made his chest swell—until Mace intruded, ruining the moment. "Your vitals look good. We'll keep monitoring your ICP, but I'm pleased. You'll need a full neurological workup—"

"Will it wait?"

"I'm afraid not," Mace said. "You made it through the surgery alive somehow. Now, we have to keep you this way."

Maya moved over to make room for Mace's exam, her eyes still wet with tears. Gray struggled to sit a little straighter but winced when surgical tape pulled at the skin of his neck and scalp.

He reached up and felt only bare skin punctuated by bandages. "What happened?"

"You started seizing after you killed Richter. You were crashing. I—" She hesitated, then plowed ahead. "I'm the one who made the call. I thought you'd want to go out fighting. So I told Mace to try to replace your implant."

"I don't understand. That wasn't . . ." He trailed off as he realized what she *wasn't* saying. What the look in her eyes meant. "Savitri?"

"It wasn't as bad as you think." Maya perched on the edge of his bed. "I mean, I would have made a deal with the devil himself, but . . . I don't think she's going to get pushy. I'm worth too much as an ally, now that Richter is gone."

But she had promised the woman *something*, and Maya had too much integrity to renege on a deal once it was struck. Gray stared at her, searching her face as well as his soul.

And he didn't know *what* he felt.

A handful of memories surfaced in his brain at once. A wickedly sharp blade slicing into his skin. Unimaginable agony. Silence. Maya, sobbing.

Then another recollection supplanted them all, just as painful in its own way as the others—the certainty of death.

He'd been ready to die.

The door flew open, and Knox rushed in, his face tight with tension. He stopped at the other side of Gray's bed, his assessing gaze sweeping over him in a familiar manner. Knox's expression finally eased. "You're alive?"

"I am," Gray answered, almost wincing at the wooden sound of his own voice.

Maya noticed. Beside the bed, she went rigid, doubt clouding her eyes. Gray wanted to say something, to comfort or reassure her—

But he'd been ready to die.

"Yeah, yeah, you're alive. Show-off." Conall shoved past Knox, looking a little paler than usual but grinning like he couldn't stop. "You know, I survived a gut shot and was planning to milk it for maximum sympathy, but you had to one-up me with impossible brain surgery."

That startled Gray out of his distraction. "You *what*?"

"Later," Dani said from the doorway. "Nina's going on about how you need ice cream. What flavor do you like?"

He had no clue. "I've never eaten ice cream before."

"What the fuck?" Dani seemed truly affronted. "Well, I guess that means we're getting all of them."

"Make sure there's peach," Maya told her. "And get some pie. I think we all deserve pie."

"I know *I* deserve pie," Conall said. "I had Rafe's hands in my guts."

"Lucky you." Rafe slipped past Conall and slugged Gray lightly on the shoulder. "Good to see you up, man."

"Not quite yet. Did we find the kids?"

"Ivonne's taking care of them for now. Ava has a contact who's coming to pick them up." Rafe's smile widened. "All except Rainbow."

Maya tilted her head up to meet Gray's eyes. "She's staying with us," she said softly. "That's what she wanted."

"Good." So many of them were orphaned in one way or another. Their families were dead, or had disowned them, or had to be kept at arm's length in order to protect them. Hell, a few of them were exactly like Rainbow—they'd never had families at all.

It was the one thing Richter had stolen from Gray before he ever even knew the man's name. Not his future, or his potential, or even his peace of mind. He'd struggled through and found all of those things, after a fashion.

But never a family. Not until he'd been assigned to the Silver Devils. They crowded around his bed, eager to reassure themselves that he was still here. And he was—there, alive, and going to be just fine.

Gray mostly hated himself for not knowing how he felt about that.

November 13th, 2080

I believe Richter knows. Worse, I believe he's gathering proof. Contingencies must be set in place.

He will *not* have Marjorie.

The Recovered Journal of Birgitte Skovgaard

THIRTY

Scanning books had lost some of its charm.

With Gray still oddly withdrawn and silent, Maya had retreated to her safe haven. Box after box sat stacked against the wall, waiting for her to lovingly digitize and catalog their contents. Thousands of books that had waited underground for decades, alone and forgotten, would finally flow out into the community again.

Usually the potential of it excited her. But she'd finished the cookbooks and moved on to gardening without feeling the spark. The 2030s rooftop gardening craze had provided ample how-to guides that would be in hot demand come spring, but Maya couldn't find her usual enthusiasm.

She'd saved Gray's life. And now she wasn't sure he had actually wanted her to.

So much for miracles.

The scanner beeped softly. She set aside *Upcycled Container Gardening* and replaced it with *24 Gardening Containers You Already Own*. She didn't even have to think to start the process all over again. Press the button. Check the entry. Confirm the metadata.

This had been more exciting when her algorithm was buggy as hell.

"I'm glad you're finding my gift useful."

Maya didn't even jump. Maybe she was just too tired to be startled. Which was probably a good thing—if she'd pulled a gun on Ava, she would have lost a few fingers. "It's very nice," she said without turning around. "If I tell you how nice it is, will you promise not to buy me a citrus juicer?"

Ava appeared in her peripheral vision, dressed in her usual chic business-casual black—a blouse with a neckline cut deep enough to show off her necklace that matched Nina's, wide-legged black trousers, heeled boots, a sleek leather belt, and a statement buckle so large Maya was pretty sure the prong doubled as a throwing knife.

Ava leaned one hip against the counter and picked up *Upcycled Container Gardening*. "You shouldn't be so hasty to reject the juicer, you know. I saw one last week that recycles the rinds in order to 3D print biodegradable cups."

"I don't need biodegradable cups," Maya said patiently. "I have normal glass cups. You wash and then reuse them. Multiple times."

"If you insist." She paged through the book, speaking her next words without looking up. "You seem sad."

Great. Her distress had reached levels so perilous even *Ava* had noticed. Maya's eyes burned, and she bit the inside of her cheek hard. She would *not* cry in front of this woman. "In case you didn't notice, I've been through some shit."

"I know." A brief pause. "Did Nina tell you much about our sister?"

"About Zoey?" Her curiosity finally piqued, Maya turned on her stool to fully face Ava. "Some. You were all designed to be good at different things. Nina was the fighter, you were strategy, and Zoey was . . ."

"Our heart." The corner of Ava's mouth barely ticked upward. "You all think Nina is warm and loving, but even she could seem harsh and pragmatic compared to Zoey. Zoey was light. Zoey was everything good in the world."

"I never really understood that," Maya admitted. "Why make someone like that and give them superpowers? Seems like it'd be impossible to get them to go out and do bad shit for you."

"You of all people know better than that, Maya." Ava finally closed the book and set it aside, turning the full force of her gaze on Maya. "How many of the people in the TechCorps are completely convinced that every day they are working to advance the greatest good?"

Too many. Of course, the *greatest good* for them somehow never took into account collateral damage. "Are you trying to make me *even sadder*?"

"No. I'm trying to . . ." Her brow furrowed and she made a frustrated noise. "I'm *not* Zoey. Or Nina. I can't soothe you with hugs and soft, comforting words."

"Uh, no shit," Maya retorted. "Trust me, Ava. Last thing I expected from you."

"But I *can* tell you the truth."

Oh, God help her. Maya wasn't sure she wanted whatever truths Ava had to offer. But the quickest way to get rid of her was probably to just let her say her piece. She could curl up in a ball and cry once Ava tired of trying to connect. "Sure, let's hear it."

Ava met her gaze squarely. "What's happening with Gray isn't your fault."

It hit her straight in the chest, and tears filled her eyes. Maya wasn't sure why she hadn't expected it—Ava always knew exactly where to hit to cause the most pain. Except she wasn't looking at Maya like she wanted to cause pain. If anything, Maya's tears seemed to agitate her.

"It's not your fault," Ava repeated, her voice soft. "You didn't do the wrong thing by saving him."

To her horror, a sob welled up in Maya's chest. She tried to choke it back, but the question tearing through her came out in a broken whisper. "Then why is he pushing me away?"

"Because it hurts," Ava whispered. "It's so hard to give up a dream. You have to kill it every time it tries to take root. You have to tell yourself over and over again that you don't get the future you want more than anything. You have to salt the earth in your own heart."

Maya had never done that. She'd accepted the risk, she'd promised Gray she was okay with it. But she'd never torn out hope by the roots. She'd held on, daring reality to take him from her.

Gray hadn't had that luxury. He'd had to face his own mortality.

"And then," Ava continued, "one day someone hands the dream back to you.

This tiny, fragile seedling. And you have to find a way to plant it in barren soil and keep it from dying. And that hurts, too."

An ache totally unrelated to Gray settled in Maya's chest. For a moment, with her expression unguarded and her eyes soft with remembered pain, the resemblance between Ava and Nina was uncanny.

And that was the dream Ava was talking about. The dream of finding her sister alive. Ava was clearly still struggling to find fertile earth to shelter the awkward, feeble seedling of that dream. The fact that she was here, making an obviously difficult effort to comfort Maya, said it all.

Weirdly, it *did* make Maya feel better. If Ava, in all her dysfunctional glory, could come back from the edge, Gray would find his feet. She just had to hold on.

She had to trust him, the same way he'd trusted her.

Maya dragged in a shuddering breath and scrubbed tears from her cheeks. "You did pretty good with the truth."

"I don't usually," Ava admitted. Then, surprisingly, she smiled wryly. "If you'd like to hear something soothing . . . So far Gray has handled this better than I did. He hasn't kidnapped anyone that I know of. Perhaps that's a good sign."

She wasn't sure if the sound she made was another sob or hysterical laughter. "I don't know how soothing that is considering he just underwent brain surgery. Maybe you should stick to hard truths."

"Probably." Ava picked up Maya's tablet and idly scrolled through the recently scanned book. "I think it will be all right, Maya. I may not have Zoey's emotional intelligence, but I have an extremely developed awareness of the tactical implications of interpersonal relationships."

Maya sorted through the tangle of words. "Is that *he cares about you* in Ava?"

"*Cares* is an insufficient descriptor." Ava eyed her over the edge of the tablet. "Matthew Gray loves you. You are his weakness, and he's yours."

And that was why the tactical assessment of interpersonal relationships would never be the same as emotional intelligence. Ava saw the ways their relationship made them vulnerable. Maya imagined she knew how Zoey would have responded.

Gray was her strength. And she could be his.

If only he would let her.

December 12th, 2080

I'm starting to doubt my own instincts. I was so sure about Matthew Gray. But is he truly a danger or simply an echo? I've been so deep in this for so long, I see shadows everywhere.

I see my failure in him. What have I missed while chasing a ghost? Probably too much. Possibly everything.

The Recovered Journal of Birgitte Skovgaard

THIRTY-ONE

Mace found him in the training room.

"I'm not doing anything not doctor-approved," Gray assured him, never halting his steady strides on the treadmill. "Just a nice, leisurely jog. See?"

"I could not give less of a shit about that." Mace shut off the treadmill and pointed at him. "Get down from there. We're going to have a chat."

Gray snagged a towel and his water bottle. "What's going on?"

"You're fucking up."

"My exercise?" Gray asked.

Mace slapped the water bottle out of his hand, startling Gray. "It's not funny, smart-ass. You're going to lose her."

An aching bolt of pain gripped Gray's chest, and he turned away. "Shut up. You don't know what you're talking about."

"Oh, you haven't spent the last week pushing Maya away? My mistake."

Sudden, fierce anger gripped Gray. He didn't have to stand there and get lectured like this. It wasn't like Mace had all his shit together, either. He was still running around, stabbing people by accident. "We're not doing this right now."

"Yes," Mace said firmly, "we are. Knox and Rafe and Conall can't do it, because they're still scared they're going to lose you. So it's my job—as your friend—to say this and make damn sure you hear it."

The rage bubbled over. "Oh, like when you told me I was going to die? That I had to accept it, really stare it in the face, and give up on *everything*? Like that? Because news flash, Mason—you were fucking wrong."

Mace frowned at him, his affronted expression almost comical. "No, I wasn't."

Gray choked on a laugh. "Then what the *fuck* am I doing still standing here?"

"From what I can tell? Shoving your head as far up your own ass as it'll go."

Gray took a swing at him, but he still wasn't quite steady on his feet. The punch went wide as Mace sidestepped it, and the momentum carried Gray to the mat beneath their feet.

Mace held his hands up by his sides and sighed. "Fuck. Here—" He reached down to help Gray up.

Instead, Gray jerked him off his feet. "Asshole."

Mace hit the mat with a thud and a disgusted groan. "Adolescent."

By unspoken agreement, they both lay there, staring up at the ceiling.

Finally, Gray whispered, "I was ready to die."

"I know," Mace murmured. "But you didn't. Your girlfriend pulled a miracle out of her back pocket, and now you get to live. But you have to *live*, goddammit. You can't keep punishing the world for thwarting your expectations."

"I don't know if I know how."

Mace rolled to a sitting position. "To start, you can stop making Maya feel like you hate her for saving you."

"I don't," Gray protested. And it was true—he couldn't blame her. If their positions had been switched, he would have pledged anything, given anything. No price would have been too high to pay for a chance to save her.

Oh, but it hurt. It hurt so much, the back and forth. Wanting and needing and having and losing, until he could stand anything, even sheer desolation, over another dashed hope.

"Prove it," Mace challenged. "You're running out of time. *Again.*"

And wasn't that what had scared him before? What had held him back? The fear that Maya would fall in love with him, and he would have to leave her. Now, he was doing it anyway, and she didn't even have the luxury of telling herself he had no choice.

He *was* fucking up.

He sat up and nudged Mace. "Where's Rafe?"

"I don't know. Why?"

"I need to find some forks."

It had taken a lot of practice, but Maya was starting to find the balance.

The darkness behind her mask didn't bother her. The basement room was as vivid behind her eyelids as the moment she'd tied the cloth over her eyes. There was a trick to focus, it turned out—an entire spectrum of nuance in between *on* and *off.* The brutal discipline she'd learned to exert over her mind could be . . . softened. Heightened.

Controlled.

It was like learning to flex individual muscles independently of one another. Messy at first, and frustrating. But as the targets Rafe had set up for her in their basement chimed one after another, Maya flowed through the room with perfect confidence, the laser pistol an extension of her body, each shot precise and effortless.

Ten bull's-eyes. She didn't need to look to be sure. She'd learned the room in minutes, internalizing the way the walls and furniture impacted echoes, parsing the pitch and timbre, the duration and intensity. It had always been instinctive, but now she savored the active experience of it, the almost synesthetic euphoria. She could feel the sharpness of sounds as they swept past. She could taste the sizzle of them on her tongue. They had colors and weight, they told stories.

Like the footsteps on the stairs. Steady and measured, but heavy with a lingering bone-deep exhaustion, like the effort to lift each foot was only surpassed by the struggle to put it down so precisely it looked effortless.

It took extra energy to project an aura of strength when you were barely recovered from brain surgery.

Maya didn't remove the blindfold. She used the control clipped to her belt to reset the targets, setting aside a tiny slice of her attention to track Gray's progress down the stairs. Nervousness at facing him after all the awkward silence tried to sizzle under her skin, but it couldn't compete with adrenaline as the first target beeped its challenge.

Counting constellations was nice, but she was learning to embrace the soothing potential of perfect bull's-eyes, too.

The targets beeped. *One. Two.*

Gray hesitated on the bottom step.

Three. Four. Five. Six.

His boots touched the cement floor, still well outside her ring of targets.

Seven.

Softer steps. He'd hit the threadbare throw rug. Ava had threatened to replace it two days ago, claiming it neither offered protection from the hard floor nor retained color sufficiently vibrant to qualify as decorative. Maya hadn't fought her. Maybe if Ava was buying area rugs she wouldn't buy a juicer.

Eight. Nine.

Ten.

She hit the final target and stopped, her back to Gray. He stood just outside the ring of targets. She could hear his breathing. Steady and even. Not even winded. Whatever Savitri had done to his implant to prioritize rapid healing had been astoundingly effective. Anyone else would have been flat on their back still, struggling for the energy to sit upright.

Not Gray.

She blew out a breath without turning. "I'm getting pretty good at this."

"Wasn't much room for improvement to begin with," he rasped.

His voice stroked over her skin, all the more intense because she'd narrowed her focus to sound. Swallowing hard around a sudden lump in her throat, she dragged off her blindfold and tossed it onto one of the cots next to her laser pistol.

Then she turned, and the sight of him punched her in the gut.

He was fully dressed, including his boots and ever-present jacket. His hair, which had just started to grow back, stood out in tiny blond prickles that caught the light. His face still bore bruises, though they'd faded to a sickly green yellow.

He was alive, and whole. He was a goddamned miracle.

He was *beautiful.*

Maya wrapped her arms around herself to keep from reaching out to touch him just to make sure he was real. "You seem good."

"Better," he confirmed. "I got the all-clear from Mace and Savitri. No more monitoring."

A tiny bit of tension she hadn't realized lingered unraveled so abruptly, the world wobbled. She took a half step toward him, then stopped again, remembering Ava's words. He'd come looking for her, but that didn't mean he was ready.

She couldn't push. So she settled for a shaky smile. "I'm so glad."

He shoved his hands nervously into his jacket pockets, but his gaze remained fixed on her. "I'm sorry, Maya."

"No, Gray—"

"Yes," he said firmly. "You need to let me be sorry, as long as it's for the right reasons."

The hurt she'd fought to extinguish trembled inside her. If she didn't acknowledge it, anything they tried to build would rest on a bed of dangerous embers. "Okay," she whispered. "Tell me the reasons."

It took him a moment to speak. "I was ready to die. I'd faced it, made my peace with it. It wasn't what I wanted, but it was what I had. My reality." He exhaled sharply. "Then I woke up alive, and I didn't know what to do with that."

"Because I made the choice for you." She bit her lower lip, then forced herself to ask the question that haunted her at night. "Are you mad at me for that?"

"No. *No.* It's not—" He drove his hands through his hair, just like he'd done a hundred times before—except this time his palms slid over his nearly bare scalp. "I'm not upset that I'm alive, and I'm damn sure not angry with you. But it's so hard to *explain*, Maya. You finally come to grips with the finality of it, and then it's all over, and everything's fine. It feels . . . like trying to turn a freight train."

"It's okay to not be okay." She took another step, closing the space between them to a scant meter. "You don't have to apologize for that. You got *tortured*, for fuck's sake. And then almost died. And then . . . everything else. You don't have to be okay. Not for me, not for anyone."

"That's not what I'm sorry about." His chest heaved. "I should have talked to you. I should have told you what I was going through instead of pushing you away. It wasn't fair, and it wasn't right, and I'm sorry I hurt you."

Tears stung her eyes. "You should have," she told him shakily. "I was so sad that Ava tried to give me a pep talk."

"Jesus Christ."

"Yeah." Maya rubbed her hand against her chest, but the ache there was easing. "You're so good at hiding what you're feeling from the world. But you don't need to hide from me, okay? I don't need you to be happy and fine all the time. I just . . . need you."

He held out his hand.

Trust me. Trust yourself.

She trusted him. She had since before she should have. She'd trusted him because her instincts had told her that Gray would destroy himself before he hurt her.

Her instincts had been so right. Too right.

She trusted him *because* she trusted herself. So she reached out and rested her hand on his.

"I need you, too," he said simply, as if it was a foregone conclusion. A known fact of the universe. "I'm not good at talking, but I'm good at doing things. So I made you something. If you want it."

"Of course." She smiled at him. "I want anything you made for me."

He shoved his hand into his jacket pocket again and pulled out a ring.

Her heart skipped a beat. It skipped a bunch of them, she was pretty sure, and that was definitely why her fingers trembled as he gently slipped the burnished silver onto her finger.

Not just any ring. A ring that could only be hers.

Because he'd made it out of a damn fork.

The craftsmanship stole her breath. The neck had been pounded flat and shaped to curve around her finger. The tines were twisted in delicate interlocking loops, framing a sparkling blue crystal that perfectly matched her favorite necklace.

"You made this?" she demanded, her voice trembling. "Like, with your hands?"

"And some tools." He smiled down at her. "Rafe helped me find the materials. Pretty sure he thought I'd finally lost it when I told him what I needed was the perfect fork."

The ring blurred as her tears overflowed. She made a protective fist around it—then thumped it lightly against Gray's shoulder. "Why are we wasting you as a damn sniper? We should be running a jewelry empire."

"No." He rubbed his thumb over her cheek, brushing away the tears. "This is only for you. No one else."

And he claimed he wasn't good at words.

Maya went up on her toes and twined her arms around his neck. His lips were right there, warm and gentle, welcoming her with a kiss that proved some things were beyond her burgeoning powers of mental control.

When he kissed her, she felt it everywhere. The tingles along her scalp, the sweet warmth sliding down her spine, the heat kindling lower—straight down to her toes, which were trying to curl in her boots again.

Kissing him might always sweep her away. But that was okay. Gray would always catch her.

"Do you forgive me?" he murmured against her mouth.

"Yes." She kissed the corner of his mouth. His chin. The tip of his nose. Laughter bubbled up in her. "Gray, you're going to live."

"I'm going to live," he agreed. "But, more importantly, I'm going to *try*. I'll be everything you deserve, I swear. I'll find a way."

"Just be you." She reached up, ghosting her fingers over the soft stubble above his brow. "That's enough."

"Deal."

CONALL

For a week, Conall had watched Tobias Richter's disappearance ripple through the TechCorps.

His absence was like a black hole at the heart of their world—visible at first only through inference. Messages piled up in his many inboxes. Pressing questions were left unanswered, security concerns ignored. Follow-ups started to drift in, cautious at first and then increasingly terse.

I would appreciate a response.

This is time sensitive.

Per my last three messages . . .

Conall had assumed at that point that *someone* would connect the dots and send up an alarm. Maya had been the one to point out the ironic reality: no one involved in day-to-day operations at the TechCorps had the authority to question Tobias Richter's whereabouts. He might have chipped every employee on the Hill, but he didn't have a convenient tracker embedded under his skin.

Tobias Richter came and went as he damn well pleased.

Conall had started to think they'd been delivered a miracle. If Cara Kennedy had a scrap of sense left in her, she'd be across the Mississippi by now. Conall sure the fuck would have been, in her shoes. And with no idea what had happened to Richter, the TechCorps could spin themselves in increasingly dizzy circles for weeks as his status slowly morphed from *not here* to *actively missing* to *presumed dead*.

Then again, they *had* been delivered a miracle. Gray was on his feet and walking around, apparently no worse for the wear. Savitri was over there now, assessing his progress and adjusting his healing protocols. If Conall had to choose one miracle, that would be the one: Gray, alive and healing.

And it looked like that was the only miracle they were going to get.

Maya was seated next to him in the warehouse, idly scrolling through her catalog. They were ostensibly in charge of the kids while Nina and Knox scoped out Ava's contacts, but the kids didn't exactly need babysitters. They were tiny, overserious adults in a way that depressed Conall—and that was saying something, considering how young he'd been when the TechCorps had swept him into their program.

At least these kids would get a chance to *be* kids. That was worth a gut shot or two.

It was an idyllic scene. And Conall was about to ruin it. Sighing, he nudged Maya. "Something just happened."

"Hmm?"

She had a distracted, dreamy look on her face. Conall wanted more than anything to let her stay in whatever blissful daydream about Gray she was currently having. Maya deserved happiness. Hell, given the past week, Maya deserved to take Gray into a locked room and stay there with him for a year, if she wanted.

But Maya was the only one who could tell him how much shit they were in.

"There's been some weird chatter this morning," he told her, trying to ease her in gently. But there was no gentle way to say this. No way to soften the blow. "Cara Kennedy is DC-025, right?"

"Yes."

"She just turned herself in."

Maya's head turned slowly. By the time she was facing him, her expression was blank and her eyes dangerously hard. "Show me."

The message was short. A company-wide memo, restricted to Level One security, it consisted of two concise lines.

DC-025 remanded to acting VP of Security for comprehensive debriefing.

Impose radio silence.

"I don't know what the fuck it means," Conall said as Maya stared at the tablet. "Radio silence? Do they mean internal comms?"

"They mean everything." Maya was still looking at the tablet, but her gaze was unfocused. "It's code. It means the topic of conversation is too sensitive for anything but in-person communication. But this is a multi-department L1 memo." Maya finally lifted her gaze to Conall's. "Make sure there's no trace of you in the system. Because they suspect they've been compromised."

"Fuck." Not that there was much risk of leaving a trace behind—Conall had too much respect for his former classmates at the TechCorps to get sloppy. But of all the times to lose their eyes on the inside . . .

"Yeah." Maya rubbed a hand over her face. "Okay. Well, it's not great. But it's not necessarily as bad as it seems, either. If they think Cara just showed up to be a good little girl and hand over all Richter's secrets so they can decommission her . . ." Maya smiled grimly. "God help whatever sucker they promoted to Richter's place."

Conall barely heard her. Nina had pushed open the door and was holding it for Ava's mystery contacts. The tall woman at the front had to be Syd. She looked like she was in her mid-forties, which probably meant she was closing in on sixty. Tall, tough, and sporting a leather jacket and beat-up jeans, she was exactly what Conall had always imagined Nina would age into in twenty years.

But she wasn't the reason his brain had stuttered to a halt.

The man who prowled in behind her was a metric ton of broody in just under two meters of man. Salt-and-pepper hair cut brutally short, an equally trimmed beard dusted with silver, tanned skin, and a scowl that challenged the world to fight him clashed with the brightest blue eyes Conall had ever seen. He moved with liquid grace, assessed the room with a wariness Knox would envy, and looked like he could kill you in fifteen ways with his pinky finger.

"Conall," Maya whispered. "You're staring."

"How are you not?" Conall retorted. Fuck, the bastard made Gray look warm and cuddly. Though, to be fair, Gray *was* kind of warm and cuddly now. At least around Maya.

This bastard sure the fuck wasn't. He looked positively grumpy. Conall was half in love already.

Maya shot him a sympathetic look before raising her voice. "You must be Syd. I'm Maya."

"Good to meet you." Syd strolled over, and she had that same easy grace. Like a panther on the prowl, her predatory gaze assessing him and Maya in turn to decide whether they were potential prey. Her lips quirked a little as she eyed the tablet in Conall's hands. "You're the tech? I heard you're pretty good."

Conall cleared his throat and tried *not* to look at the guy, who was hovering behind Syd with all the brooding subtlety of a lion with a sore paw. "I'm not bad."

"Maybe you can talk to Max before we go." She jerked her head at her second. "We've been having some trouble with our satellite out on the farm. Even when we can connect to the GhostNet, our upload speed is shit."

"Sure, I know some tricks." He leaned sideways on the stool to peer around Syd, straight into the full supernova power of all that glowering sexy. "We can chat if you want."

Max made a noncommittal noise. Something between a growl and a grunt, all low and rumbly and hot.

Conall's brain glitched.

"*After* the meeting," Maya said firmly, planting one hand on Conall's shoulder. She pushed him gently upright. "Someone should watch the kids . . ."

"Max has got it," Syd said confidently. As if obeying a silent command, Max pivoted and stalked toward the opposite side of the warehouse, and the tiny children in their little protective circle.

Maya cleared her throat. "No offense, but are you sure . . ."

"Trust me," Syd told her with a feral smile.

Max stopped a few feet away from the children. In an instant, the dour expression melted away, replaced by a brilliant smile as he clapped his hands together. "Okay, who wants to learn about something fun, like quantum physics?"

Oh, fuck. Conall was *screwed*.

TECHCORPS PROPRIETARY DATA, L1 SECURITY CLEARANCE

When apprehending the Silver Devils, take special care not to permanently damage 66–793. I've invested too much time and money into him to let an idealistic fool like 66–615 ruin his future potential.

Internal Memo, January 2086

THIRTY-TWO

Conall fled two seconds into Max's lecture on quantum theory, and Maya pressed her lips together into a firm line to keep from laughing. Conall lost his heart regularly and swiftly—and predictably. Max would likely last as long as all the others did.

Then again, Syd had returned to her earnest conversation with Nina, and the two of them seemed to be hitting it off. Even Knox looked relaxed, which was rare around a stranger and damn near miraculous around a stranger vetted by Ava. If Max and Syd became a regular part of their lives, Conall's crush might not get an opportunity to subside.

Resolving not to tease him about it—unless he started teasing *her*—Maya swept up her tablet. And dropped it again just as swiftly when the familiar silk of Gray's voice curled around her.

"Need some help?"

Maya spun on her stool, opening her arms. "You're done already?"

"Yep. Savitri gave me a clean bill of health." He was standing on his own, his arms steady as they folded around her. He felt amazing. Strong and solid and *alive*. "Still a few patchy holes in my memory, but she said that's to be expected."

Maya leaned into his chest and savored the warmth of his embrace. "Where is she?"

"She headed out already." His lips brushed the top of her head. "Had shit to do, I guess. As any criminal, nightclub-owning genius neurosurgeon likely does."

She tilted her head back and smiled up at him. "Does that mean we get to sleep in my bed tonight?"

"Absolutely," he replied in a low voice full of promise.

It would have been easy to tilt back into the giddy memory of how *good* it felt to kiss him right there, but Nina lifted her voice. "Okay, grown-up talk inside."

"Later," she whispered. "When we're alone, you can grown-up talk *me*."

Gray's laughter carried them into the kitchen, where they found Savitri sitting at the head of their table, as regal as if she had her ass planted on her throne at Convergence.

Dani stood there, watching her as she nursed a steaming cup of coffee. "I found her here. We might need to beef up our security system."

Gray just shook his head. "I thought you left."

"It didn't seem prudent." She waved her hand at Syd. "You have such interesting guests. I don't want to miss whatever comes next."

Maya was sure she didn't. Information was gold for Savitri, and God knew there was plenty of that sitting around the table. "Is this you calling in your favor?"

"Maya, don't be crass." Savitri tapped her fingers on the table. "I just thought I'd raise a few pertinent questions you might be able to answer. Like how Richter found you, and who's in charge of security now that he's gone."

Maya focused on the easy question first. "Who's in charge? It's honestly hard to say. Richter was jealous about his power. He didn't trust his subordinates with it. The only person he trusted . . ." The ache of betrayal had faded, but she still had to force the words out. "We just found out that his data courier turned herself in. Normally, she'd be decommissioned—"

"Murdered," Conall clarified darkly.

"Yes," Maya agreed. "But Cara's probably the only person left at the TechCorps who knows all of Richter's plans. They definitely need her. They might be stupid enough to think they can use her."

The buzzer for the front door went off, and Dani abandoned her mug on the counter. "I'll get it."

"That covers the second question," Rafe said. "But not the first. How the hell did Richter know to set that damn trap?"

"It wasn't by something as simple as tracking Mace," Knox confirmed. "It had been carefully planned. Hours in advance."

"More likely days in advance."

The deep voice came from the direction of the door. Jaden Montgomery stood there, and even for him, his glower was fierce. He stopped at the head of the table, and his gaze found Nina's. "We were the leak. Lucas was working for Richter. He confessed to me after he heard what happened. He gave Richter all of the information you passed to us. He claims Richter promised him that you three ladies wouldn't be harmed, but . . ." His jaw tightened. "A promise from Richter means nothing and he knew it."

Dani cursed softly, but Nina just stared at him. "What are you going to do with him?"

Jaden's expression didn't change. "I dealt with it."

"Uhh . . ." Conall raised an eyebrow. "Care to elaborate?"

"No."

"Not even a *hint*?"

Jaden's silent stare made Conall sink back in his chair, both hands raised in silent apology.

"I guess that's that, then." Gray crossed his arms over his chest. "Unless it isn't. Nothing in the rule book that says there can only be one leak."

Nina shook her head. "Wondering won't help, and it doesn't matter, anyway. We're not just going to sit here and wait for the TechCorps to come after us again."

"And they will," Knox said. "We have to assume that, if nothing else, Cara Kennedy has already told them we're still alive."

"What about the server access I procured for you?" Ava asked from where she leaned against the wall, carefully situated to be able to see all of them and both exits. "That should give you some insight."

"I think that's been burned," Maya admitted. "Conall just intercepted a memo. They're shifting all communications about Richter and Cara to in-person only. We have to assume that anything relevant we come across going forward was planted there for us to find."

"Assuming they don't shut me down entirely," Conall grumbled.

Savitri's gaze found Maya's, and her lips curved in a tiny smile that whispered of shared secrets. "I may able to do something about that," she murmured, and Maya remembered her confession on the roof.

Adam is everything I made him to be.

No wonder Adam had trounced Conall's attempts at hacking so handily. And no wonder the TechCorps couldn't touch Savitri. She had a miraculously sentient AI trained in combat and strategy running her security.

She was probably the safest out of all of them.

"Information will be good in the long run," Knox agreed. "But we already know what's going on inside right now. They're in turmoil. Richter was the scary monster who kept order on the Hill. Right now, everyone with power is going to be scrambling to solidify their base, and everyone who wants power is plotting to step on someone else to get ahead."

Syd's grin was utterly predatory. "Sounds like a fun time to fuck with them."

Yes.

It had always been an impossible dream before. The hellfire she wished upon them while she took her tiny victories, her petty crime and her rebellious but invisible middle fingers. The TechCorps had always been so massive, and she was *so small . . .*

Maya let her gaze drift around the table, taking in everyone. Dani and Nina—her first family. Conall and Knox and Rafe, the brothers she'd never known she needed. Gray, the man she loved.

The man who loved her.

Maya didn't feel small anymore.

But there were allies around this table, too. Dangerous allies. Mace, whose commitment to saving lives went so bone deep, even Tobias Richter hadn't been able to torture it out of him. Savitri and her terrifying genius, and Adam, who was the terrifying result of her genius. Mysterious Syd, who had already confused and concerned the TechCorps with her single-minded mission. Jaden, who had built a smuggling empire under the TechCorps' nose and used it to constantly undermine their grasp on power.

Ava, who would set the whole damn world on fire if it made Nina happy.

For the first time, her dreams of righteous hellfire didn't seem so implausible. Maya found herself smiling, too. "Honestly? Fucking up the TechCorps sounds pretty damn good."

"That's a dangerous game," Savitri noted with an utterly predatory smile. "I love dangerous games."

"Are there any other kinds worth playing?" Syd retorted. "Besides, I'm already fighting them and a dozen other bastards besides. Been doing it most of my damn life."

"So have I," Jaden said quietly. "But I don't think any of us can afford to keep fighting them alone. You know what they'll do if they feel threatened by the loss of Richter."

"They'll crack down," Knox said quietly. "It's probably already starting. Winter is a good time for it. People are cold and hungry. Can't worry about revolution if people are just trying to stay alive."

"Technically this wouldn't be a revolution," Ava noted. "A revolution generally involves the overthrow of an existing government. The TechCorps never officially established one."

Conall groaned. "Does her pedantic dictionary setting come with an off switch?"

But Rafe leaned forward, bracing his weight on his elbows. "I hate giving Ava any credit at all, ever, but she has a point. The revolution already happened back in '42, when the government collapsed and the TechCorps took over. These are just neglectful dictators with profit sharing."

"Oligarchs," Ava supplied.

Conall leaned forward and thumped his head against the table.

"We can settle on the correct terminology later." Knox's voice was firm. "In the short term, we have to consider the cold reality of this. All of our faces could be spread across the vid network tomorrow. They could declare a city-wide bounty on us. Or they could just decide to squeeze every neighborhood so hard everyone's too tired to think about fighting back."

"They're doing that already," Jaden said. "Like you said. Winter's coming. Most everyone just cares about staying alive."

Maya braced her hands on the table. "So that's how we fight. On two fronts. We use my contacts to weaken them from the inside. And we use everyone else's to help people stay alive."

"A noble goal."

They all whirled toward the kitchen at the sound of the new voice. John stood in the hallway leading from the back door, calm and collected, heedless of the fresh round of curses Dani ground out.

"I swear to fucking Christ, I will shoot the next person who does that," she spat.

He just blinked at her, then turned his attention to Knox and Nina. "If you're going up against the TechCorps, you'll need someone on the inside."

Rafe leaned across the table, eyes narrowed. "And how, exactly, do we know we can trust you, *Professor*?"

"You don't," he replied. "But you're talking about a full-scale uprising. Can you afford to turn away allies?"

Maya waited for someone to answer him, but silence hung heavy in the kitchen. Knox was looking at her. So was Gray, and Conall. Rafe and Dani and even Nina. Realization swept over her like a cold wind. For all her agonizing over when and how to use her power, for all her eagerness to see what she could do—somehow she had forgotten the stark reality of the situation.

This wasn't like a mission, where Nina and Knox would make the battle plans and she'd get to simply fall in line. She was the one who'd been raised for this. Trained for it. She'd grown up inside the beating heart of the monster. She knew the secret pressure points and the points of leverage. She knew where to find allies, who to trust, who to avoid. How to fight them. How to *destroy* them.

If she took this step, she wouldn't just be the heir to Birgitte's fight. She'd be the leader of her own.

For a chilling moment, the sheer responsibility of it terrified her. A sheltered girl from the Hill had no right to make decisions that might impact the lives of millions. If she chose wrong, life could get worse. And people would die if she did this. Maybe people she knew. People she loved.

Panic tightened her chest. She almost opened her mouth to shove the whole mess of it back into Nina's lap. Nina would never fault her for it. She'd shoulder the burden and do her best.

Gray's hand closed around hers. She looked to the side and found him staring back at her, his blue eyes warm, his smile just for her. "Trust yourself," he whispered.

Maybe he'd finally remembered that moment in Richter's torture chamber. Maybe he didn't and this was just what came automatically to his lips. His faith in her was unshakeable. Gray would make himself into a human shield or a weapon or a revolutionary. Whatever she wanted.

She just had to trust herself as much as he trusted her.

Maya blew out a breath. She squeezed Gray's hand in gratitude and turned back to the table. This time she barely felt the weight of all those gazes. She could do this. She could do *anything.*

"Okay, y'all," she drawled. "Let's get to work."

March 19th, 2081

I've done my best to prepare for every eventuality. I'd like to think that it will be enough, that someday I'll laugh at myself for my paranoia. Perhaps Marjorie and I will laugh together.

Diana is leaving at dawn with this journal and my instructions for Marjorie's inheritance. I suppose I have one last letter to write. The hardest.

There will be no absolution for me.

The Recovered Journal of Birgitte Skovgaard

EPILOGUE

Revolution or not, books still needed to be scanned. Tools needed to be checked out. The neighborhood needed movies, and music, and freeze-dried food, and Maya had files to organize.

She'd propped the warehouse door open to let in the cool autumn breeze. The oppressive heat had finally broken, and the wind whipped dead leaves past the door. Rain was coming tonight, maybe even a thunderstorm—the kind that shook the whole warehouse.

Maya would be snuggled up with Gray, cozy and warm in the bed he shared with her more nights than not. She turned her brand-new ring around on her finger as she considered that, a slow smile tilting her lips.

Later.

She finished uploading Rowan's remastered files to their shared server and pulled up her new digital to-do list. Savitri had been the one to suggest it, pointing out that just because her brain *could* do something didn't mean she should waste precious mental resources on it. Maya hated to admit it, but dumping her task list onto a tablet *had* helped clear her head.

Plus, crossing things off was extremely satisfying.

"Marjorie?"

The name felt so out of place here, it took a moment for Maya to understand the once-familiar sound. She glanced up and found the speaker hovering just inside the open warehouse door.

She was tall and thin, with a cascade of curly hair dyed electric blue braided back from her face and tumbling down her back. Dark lipstick and thick winged eyeliner stood out dramatically against her pale skin, and her clothes were the height of punk-chic fashion up on the hill.

But her arm was the show-stealer—her asymmetrical top was cut to show off the full prosthetic, composed of shiny chrome at the shoulder and wrist. The space in between glowed softly—a moving, full-length LED tattoo sleeve. An ethereal mermaid framed by a sunset, her dark hair floating on an invisible wind. Beneath her, the waves broke against her rock, the surf churning in ever-changing teals and greens and midnight blue.

The skill involved with creating such a thing was breathtaking. Not just science but *art*, and it took hearing her name—her *old* name—a second time to drag her attention back to the woman's unfamiliar face. "I'm sorry, I don't . . ."

Her memory caught up a moment later. The face had thrown her, but she knew that voice. "Diana?"

A gentle smile curved the woman's lips, and even if the face had changed, that smile hadn't. Neither had the mischievous spark in her eyes. "Hey, Starborn."

Shock held Maya in place as the stranger with Diana's voice approached the wide counter. If Maya had been the brains of Birgitte's rebellion, Diana Cameron had been its gleefully dirty hands. Birgitte would have denied having a fixer, but that was exactly what Diana had been. She dabbled in forgery, dipped her toe into larceny, navigated the black market with ease, and cheerfully laundered TechCorps cash into clean credits.

She'd vanished in the month before Birgitte's death. Maya had always assumed Richter had gotten to her, too.

Diana stopped on the other side of the counter, both hands resting lightly on the surface as she studied Maya. "God, you're all grown up now, aren't you?"

"Time does that." Maya tilted her head, taking in the green eyes—probably contacts—pointed chin, and more prominent cheekbones. "So . . . I got older, and you got a new face."

That won her another cheerful grin that was pure Diana. "It seemed prudent, all things considered."

No doubt it had. Tobias Richter would have done damn near anything to get his hands on the woman who had helped Birgitte fake deaths, embezzle funds, and pay for sedition. And unlike with Maya, Richter wouldn't have been forced to avoid carving pieces off Diana until he got what he wanted. "I looked for you after I got free."

"I was long gone. That was my deal with Birgitte." Diana dipped a hand into the bag slung across her shoulder and withdrew a bulky envelope. "To leave Atlanta and not come back until Tobias Richter was dead."

Maya glanced down at the envelope. It was ragged around the edges but had clearly once been one of the standard white envelopes meant for internal printouts, one of the thousands available in every storage closet in HQ but rarely used in a mostly digital world. This one had her name written across the front in Birgitte's crisp penmanship, the ink faded but still sharp.

A chill claimed her. "What is it?"

Diana pushed the envelope across the counter. "There were things Birgitte wanted you to know if she didn't survive to tell you herself. But she made me promise not to bring this to you unless there was absolutely no chance Richter could find it."

Hesitantly, Maya touched the package. It was thick across the middle, like someone had placed a small book inside. A diary, maybe? She'd never known Birgitte to write in one—but Birgitte had been far too paranoid to put her private thoughts down in a digital format. Maya had been the receptacle of her secrets.

Maybe this was where she'd kept her secrets about Maya.

Diana cleared her throat. "Anyway, Starborn, I can't stay long, even with my new face. I still have enemies in this town. But here." She slid over a scrap of paper with an IP address scrawled across it. "If you need me."

"Thank you, Diana." Maya folded her fingers around the paper. "And I'm glad you're okay."

"You, too, kiddo." Diana gave the envelope one last tap, an odd glint in her eye. "You'd best look at it soon. Birgitte left you more than you realize."

"I will."

Diana gave a two-fingered salute and pivoted toward the exit. Maya watched her go before she dropped her gaze to the envelope.

Birgitte's handwriting was a punch to the gut. Even now, with the demons of her past dead and buried and her focus turned toward finishing the revolution Birgitte had started . . .

Maya had been a child drafted into a war she didn't understand by a woman who had no doubt hated herself for it but had done it anyway.

Did she *want* to know whatever secrets this envelope contained? Secrets so terrible, Birgitte had been willing to let them vanish forever rather than fall into Tobias Richter's hands?

Put that way, could Maya afford *not* to know them?

Taking a deep breath, she ripped open the envelope. A thin leather journal spilled out onto the counter, along with a dozen credit sticks and another envelope marked *Last Will and Testament of Birgitte Skovgaard.*

Ignoring the second envelope, Maya carefully unbuckled the journal and opened to the page marked by a thin, black ribbon. Birgitte's clean, sure strokes marked the date at the top—June 1st of 2069.

I met my data courier today. If hell exists, I've surely secured my spot there for agreeing to this.

The girl is all of seven years old and already fluent in six languages. She's studying astronomy and just started integral calculus. The scientists are excited. Few of their subjects have adapted to the procedure as well as DC-031 . . .

Gray came in, rubbing the top of his head. He did it almost habitually now, running his hand over the short but growing stubble on his scalp. "Ready for a break, sweetheart?"

"Yes." She slapped the journal shut and shoved it away. "Way past ready."

He wrapped his arms around her and peered down at the package's scattered contents. "What's all this?"

"Birgitte's last gift to me." She started to sweep the credit chips back into a little pile. "A journal and her will. Apparently she left it with someone who was only supposed to bring it to me if Richter turned up dead. So . . . congratulations to me, I guess."

He picked up a chip and idly turned it over in his hands. "Are you going to read it?"

"I think I have to," she admitted reluctantly. "There might be something in there that can teach me about myself. Or help us take down the TechCorps."

"I can do it—if you're not up to it, I mean." He held up the chip. "How much?"

"No idea." She shoved the envelope with the will toward him. "It probably says in here. Will you look? I don't know if I can."

He released her, took the envelope, and eased open the flap. It was so old that the adhesive cracked open, yielding several folded papers. Gray straightened them and started skimming the first page. After a moment, he froze, his eyes wide. "Uhh, Maya? Scan one of those chips, would you?"

She slid her stool to the side and jerked open one of the drawers set under the table. A jumble of tech and solar batteries cluttered it, but the chip reader was right on top. She grabbed it and rolled her stool back.

It only took a second. The reader *beeped*, and she waited for the amount to pop up.

1,021,008.

Maya dropped the scanner.

Gray looked up at her. "Birgitte left you just over ten million credits. Clean and untraceable, according to this."

The number stared up at her, stark and undeniable. Not quite believing her eyes *or* Gray's words, she snatched up the scanner and tried again.

1,021,008.

She dropped the credit chip and grabbed another one.

978,213.

"Holy shit," she whispered. "Holy *shit*."

"I think you can afford to finish and heat the basement this winter."

A hysterical giggle bubbled up. Maya slapped her hand over her mouth, but it escaped anyway. "Oh my God, am I rich?"

He chuckled. "You are very, *very* rich. Rich enough to do whatever the hell you want."

Her mind spun with the possibilities. They could heat the basement. They could provide free meals for people struggling through the winter. Hell, they could buy a whole new building and heat *that*, too, and fill it with food and warmth and hope.

She could fund her revolution.

She bounced off the stool and threw her arms around his neck, laughing as he lifted her off the ground and spun her. His mouth found hers, and the kiss wove heat through her. She wrapped her legs around his hips and clung to him as the pleasure of touching him—of having him alive to touch—swept her away.

The money would be useful. But she already had her miracle, and she was never letting him go.

March 19th, 2081

Marjorie,

If you're reading this, you survived and Richter did not.

I know because I've arranged for it to be delivered to you only after confirmation of his death. I couldn't risk this journal falling into his hands, you see. In the back, I've recorded the truth of you. Your true aptitude test results, which are astounding. Your undoctored neurological benchmark tests, which are unprecedented. If the TechCorps saw these, they would take you apart to try and replicate you.

You are something special. I think you would have been, even without our genetic tampering. Your mind is a gift. You shouldn't hesitate to use it to its fullest potential.

There will likely be consequences. There always are. Those you'll have to figure out on your own, because we have no road map for this. I believe in you, though. There's nothing you can't do if you set your formidable mind to the task.

I shouldn't have smothered your potential. I have done so many terrible things in my life, but there's nothing I regret more than making you fear yourself.

You are a miracle, Marjorie. Learn everything you can. Be anything you want to be. Do it in spite of us. Do it to spite us.

Do it for yourself.

Birgitte

TESSA

Tessa Morales was growing to hate Monet.

Perhaps it was an uncharitable thought. After all, the canvas propped on her easel was going to score her twenty thousand in clean credits. She'd run herself ragged as a delivery girl in her teens and had been lucky to bring home a hundred credits a week. This? This was easy. She could paint water lilies in her sleep by now.

Which was why she hated them.

She'd never understand the fixation of the rich people on the Hill. It wasn't as if the water lilies were even Monet's most interesting works. He'd painted pieces that would have been a challenge and a wonder to recreate. And there were *so many works* that had gone missing in the chaos after the Flares. Hell, huge chunks of the Eastern Seaboard were underwater. The opportunities for miraculous "discovery" were endless.

But the boring rich people wanted Monet. They wanted water lilies.

Tessa wanted their money, so she painted her expert forgeries and tried not to resent the utter banality of their collective taste.

At least the technical aspect still held her attention. There was a science to creating the perfect forgery, and Tessa had refined it to high art. She mixed her own pigments, stretched and aged her own canvas. She'd learned to rescue antique frames and fit them seamlessly to her perfect creations. She knew how a painting recovered from the end of the world should look and feel and even smell. She made it all happen.

And then she sold it to the highest bidder.

Well, *she* didn't. Tessa lived a painfully circumspect life almost entirely off the grid. She delivered her forgeries to a middleman, who passed them off to a fence, who supplied an art dealer, who sold them for millions, probably. The fact that only a fraction of the score trickled down to Tessa in return for doing the hardest part sometimes rankled, but she didn't have the luxury of taking risks.

Rafael had given up everything to buy them their snug little life on the outskirts of Atlanta. She had no right to endanger that.

He'd be horrified to know Tessa felt the weight of that sacrifice, but how could she not? Her softhearted big brother had turned himself into a weapon, mortgaging larger bits of his soul every year. Rafael lied about it, of course. He came home with gifts for the babies and painting supplies for her and endless stacks of untraceable credits for their mother, who always hid her heartbroken tears until he was gone, because Rafael wanted them to be happy.

So they were. Or at least they pretended when he was around.

They pretended they couldn't see the pain in his eyes, too. The shock, that they'd grown so much. The hurt that he'd missed it. The sharp sting of realization that he had at best a few hours before he had to leave them again. Every family reunion was forced cheer wrapped around grief and impending loss.

And now they couldn't see him at all, because he was supposed to be dead.

The small fortune in credits that had come with *that* announcement had been enough to keep the family comfortable until even Rosa was fully grown. She was thirteen already, with a green thumb and a love of gardening that had turned their backyard into a wonderland of living things. Fifteen-year-old Antonio had finally won their mother's permission to apprentice with the mechanic two doors down and was showing a real flair for it.

And Tessa, at twenty-one, was a master forger. Wouldn't her big brother love *that.*

Maybe these water lilies would be her last one. The challenge was losing its appeal, and she didn't need to supplement the money Rafael could send anymore. Not with his final windfall resting in her mother's stash in the floorboards under her bed.

Maybe she could take this money and do something for *herself* with it.

Shame at that bit of selfishness surged, and she welcomed the pounding on her cramped studio door. "Just a second!"

She draped her current work and put up her brushes before opening the door. Rosa stood on the other side, in the middle of a growth spurt that put her eyes almost level with Tessa's. She'd have their father's height, no doubt . . . but the wariness in her eyes was their mother's. "There's a stranger at the door, and Mama's still down at the baker."

Tessa's heart thumped. Strangers rarely came to this boring little community, and they never came to the Morales's front door. But Tessa held her calm expression and put a hand lightly on her baby sister's shoulder. "Go out into your greenhouse. Stay until I come and get you or until Mama comes back."

"But Tessa—"

"*Now,* Rosa."

Rule number one in the Morales household was obedience. Rosa hurried down the hallway to the back door. Once Tessa heard it shut, she opened a drawer, pulled out her stun gun, and thumbed the biometrics. She walked to the front and canted her body so that her hand would be out of sight before cracking the door.

And immediately knew she was busted.

The stranger was from the Hill. She had to be. Her shiny, red hair was twisted up in an elegant knot that revealed diamonds sparkling at her ears and emeralds circling her throat. Her expensive suit was the height of fashion and tailored perfectly to her long legs and lanky frame. Tessa had seen the advertisement for the woman's boots on the vid network—this year's exclusive from the hottest designer on the Hill. There were only a hundred pairs in existence.

The idea that those boots would have found their way to her doorstep if she weren't about to go down for felony forgery was unimaginable.

"Tessa Morales?" Perfectly outlined lips curved into a smile in her perfectly made-up face, but those eyes sparkled as hard as the diamonds she wore.

Tessa fought a shiver and tightened her grip on her stun gun. But there was a massive bodyguard lurking a few paces back and another next to the silent car with tinted windows idling in the street.

Fight? Or go quietly? Going quietly might be the only thing that saved the rest of her family. "I'm Tessa," she said hoarsely.

"Wonderful." That smile was utterly predatory. "My name is Cara Kennedy. I'm here to make all your dreams come true."

ACKNOWLEDGMENTS

I imagine the acknowledgments for any book written during 2020 will either be incredibly long and detailed . . . or just broken laughter punctuated by emoji sobs. We don't have to tell y'all why. You were there.

But for posterity: Hi. Welcome to our pandemic book.

This book was hard. We came into 2020 thinking we'd finally put a string of health and personal crises behind us. February was *our month* for writing this book. We were going to dig in, get it done, be amazing.

Yes, this is where you say, *Oh, you sweet summer children.*

We turned in this book Late. We were late *before* 2020 dawned, and surviving political horror and pandemic devastation as we struggled to keep ourselves and our families going did not help. On top of that, the release for *Deal with the Devil* had been pushed back, and we launched our first traditionally published book into a chaotic world where bookstores couldn't open and everyone was having to learn how to Zoom.

Without our team at Tor, this would have all been unlivable. The Mercenary Librarians rode out into the world thanks to the tireless work of publicity badasses Caroline Perny and Laura Etzkorn, as well as marketing geniuses Renata Sweeney and Rachel Taylor. Our incredibly encouraging editor, Claire Eddy, held our hands the whole way, and her editorial assistant, Sanaa Ali-Virani, has never met a question she can't find the answer to. And we ask a lot of questions!

Our agent, Sarah Younger, coaxed us through this book one paragraph, one page, one chapter at a time. It would not exist without her. We would have given up sometime shortly after The Age of Sourdough Starters. We love you, fierce mama shark.

For years, Lillie Applegarth has kept the ever-growing series bible of our world in tip-top shape. The fact that anyone has consistent eye color is a tribute to her. Sharon Muha has been the final proofreading pass on all of our books for just as long. Any mistakes that slip by them are our own (and very determined). Also big shout-out to our copy editor, NaNá Stoelzle, who was a dream to work with. We're sorry that Bree can't decide how she feels about typing out numbers.

Thank you to our readers, whose patience through our Rough Years has been unflagging and whose encouragement has been uplifting. Thank you to our families, who rode this rocky ride with us. Thank you to our friends, who hauled us through this pandemic one step at a time.

Thank you to every essential worker who faced peril to pull us through a terrifying year, and to the teachers and healthcare workers and librarians who went back into perilous situations to ease the burden on others—often, and regrettably, without due recognition.

Thank you especially to Alyssa Cole and Courtney Milan, who put their lives on pause in November to help us and an amazing group of volunteers accidentally raise $475,000 to save democracy. If the legacy of this book being late is knowing we had some small part in flipping those Senate seats in Georgia blue, then I cannot imagine anything more in keeping with the spirit of the Mercenary Librarians.

And if you take anything away from this book, the rocky and perilous path it took to the finish line, and our detour into political organizing via Romancing the Runoff, we hope it is this: even in the face of literal apocalyptic events and the imminent collapse of democracy, book nerds GET SHIT DONE.

We are forever grateful to be part of this glorious tradition.